## THE

**THE ENGINEER,**
beaten to death with his hands cut off. Obviously,
say police, the work of cannibals.

**THE MATHEMATICIAN,**
bound and bitten to death by giant forest spiders. The
killers were still spinning webs around the victim's body
when it was discovered.

**THE SCIENTIST,**
impaled by spears identified as originating from a
nearby tribe.

**THE PROJECT DIRECTOR,**
found tied up in a kneeling position with his
heart hacked out.

**THE HERO:**

**JOHN LOCKE,**
the man who must find the murderers, the guy with the
boat on his back, the civilian soldier for hire with a
hunger to keep moving!

# STEEL TIGER

**He packs every moment
with the excitement of a lifetime!**

# STEEL TIGER

## Stirling Silliphant

BALLANTINE BOOKS • NEW YORK

Library of Congress Catalog Card Number: 82–91079

ISBN 0–345–30428–4

Manufactured in the United States of America

First Edition: June 1983

FOR TIANA

# CHAPTER

## 1

**"S**tand off or I'll commence firing!"

I listen to my words resonate through the hand-held bullhorn across the thousand yards still separating us. The word "commence" waffles pretentiously. It is not a word you'd anticipate using in the Coral Sea, forty-six minutes shy of midnight in time zone minus-eleven.

They do not respond, except to bend more ardently to their paddles. In the guttering blossom of my parachute flare, they are pinned for one astonishing second in the glare from the lighthouse on Amédée, a perspective of dusky figures slotted behind each other within the confining shoulders of their approaching war canoe.

Pure luck I spotted them. Ordinarily I'd have been sacked out below in the beamy aft cabin. Or asleep on deck.

An hour ago I hove to, setting jib to wind, backing the wheel, standing well off Grand Récif Abore, planning to run in through Passe de Dumbéa tomorrow morning when sunshafts would help me skirt the peacock shallows inside New Caledonia's fringing reef.

But the night was too tonic for sleep, the scent of the island too heavy on the senses. I stretched out in the cockpit to stare up at Canopus, then southeast, above New Zealand, found Achernar sinking ruddy as a miner caked with iron dust. The heavens of the Southern Hemisphere always make me feel as though I'm standing on a new planet, drinking in uncharted skies.

I looked back at the sea to rest my eyes from so much

splendor. Then I saw the intruders breaching Amédée's warning beacon—blocking the three short cautionary blinks, the one lingering flash, and intersecting for a split second the white path lying on the sea. I saw—or maybe I imagined—masks and clubs crowned by bird-beaks, warriors hunched into a proa, bow toward me, outrigger to windward, six men, paddles chunking. Then once more the fleeting ribbon of Amédée's light on the inky sea, and no sign of the apparition.

These are international waters out here, forty-three kilometers from Nouméa.

Six men in a war canoe, so far from shore at midnight? With ritual masks and weapons?

I have timed such moments before, so I know it took me less than five seconds to go below and return to the cockpit with some useful equipment.

First the flare.

A twenty-five-second float splatters the night, hanging three hundred feet above the intruders like the glowing tentacles of a hovering jellyfish. As the flare drifts down I count six men, all wearing masks of woven sago fiber, some with collages of palm leaves and feathers, others of hardwood. I have seen masks like that at a museum in Auckland, representing water spirits or honorable ancestors brained in battle. These oarsmen wear black cloaks so voluminous the wind easily ruffles the patches of human hair and the clusters of feathers on them. The yawning mouth of the mask worn by the front oarsman grins wider than if some maniac had slashed the face with a razor. Red beads give the mouth a hydrophobic frenzy.

It occurs to me I'd better not overlook a possible communications zilch.

For half a century New Caledonia has been more French than Melanesian. These six will certainly respond to the conqueror's tongue, if not to my California American.

"Arretez-vous! Ou je vous tue!"—"Stop, or I'll kill you!"

2

I deliver this ultimatum with combat coldness, yet it comes out of the bullhorn sounding even more pretentious than my earlier warning in English. No visible effect.

I waft up another chute, this one red, a symbol of what must certainly follow unless the intruders change course. But they persist.

We seem drawn to each other.

I accept what must be. We exist for each other, it seems, purely as a physical force, as lines of magnetism exist, our humanity neither seen nor felt.

Other times before, when I've been on point for long-range patrols, I've experienced the same thing—felt the killing zone as a magnetic field, attracting me and the enemy to each other, linking us like those charged lines of force so neatly diagrammed in physics books.

Having failed with my French, knowing little Melanesian, I conclude it is time to call upon that universal language devised by those sly masters of survival, the Chinese—the language of gunpowder.

I offer one final conciliatory gesture.

I lay my opening round alongside their canoe.

They're unimpressed. Everywhere the wind ripples the sea into helter-skelter rifts of indigo and silver. But even in daylight, the bullet's obscure splash would have failed to persuade. I had hoped the clap of the gunshot might sober the canoemen, but they chose to ignore it.

I steady the HK-91 on its bipod, snugging its barrel alongside an aft cockpit winch. I read the apparent windspeed on my Brookes and Gatehouse—twelve knots out of the southeast. Range off: four hundred meters. I rotate the rear sight to the appropriate setting. Then, with my ever-handy Phillips-head screwdriver, I loosen the clamping screw clockwise for windage, allowing myself a deviation of twenty-six point seven inches and turn it counterclockwise one full turn to raise my elevation five point sixteen inches.

Now I devote myself to the first masked man, bringing

my front sight into the diopter hole and forming that mag-ical perfect circle, front sight centered precisely as I squeeze off.

The round whispers away, gulping distance.

Through the Starlight scope I watch the birth of the 7.62 in dead center of the ritual mask. The mask flips up, a toy disc struck by a child's forefinger.

With a flood of nostalgia I welcome back that surge of primitive fulfillment which comes with a well-placed shot. I study with the same dispassion the always-bizarre fling of dying arms snapping up in rubbery surprise and angry re-linquishment. Even in the dark I can see crimson splash black feathers. The one who has been foremost sprawls into the bow.

Yet even so exemplary a death appears not to dishearten the survivors. Closing still. Silently. Too silently. No aveng-ing cry, no chorused bravado of war chants. I hear only their paddles, tolling my time. I breathe deeply, twice, let-ting myself drain, letting security rush in, seeking bedrock. I ease lower behind the Kevlar-lined combing of the cock-pit. Any second now, cross-fire may lace the night. I hope that their ordnance is small-caliber, that they don't carry rocket-grenades, as many of the South Sea pirates do. But whatever they throw at me, I'll still kick ass, I tell myself, for I've got a full banana clip in the HK-91 and a second clip reversed and taped onto the first so I can flip the mags and keep right on firing with less than a tenth of a second's interruption.

At three hundred yards I take out the second warrior in line.

As he buckles, I think about all those people back home who at this very moment are worrying about the Dow-Jones average or the forward price of oats for January delivery. I admit to myself, Locke, there's that good, de-pendable high again, that sudden rush, the same indefin-able current you felt outside Dak To, east of Attopeu in Laos, when you and Archie ambushed fourteen NVA, reading them their last rites with AP rounds from sawed-off M-79s. What *is* that reaching love for those you out-shoot, that empty pity, that joy and ache of sadness all at once within so fleeting an eternity? Can I ever admit that in killing my enemy I am killing a part of myself?

Or *am* I? The true primitives, our ancestors, believed otherwise. After a kill they became positively lyrical. Their senses soared with the knowledge that they had achieved something of value—they had removed an enemy who had been equally lyrical about trying to remove them. On the lone criterion of self-preservation, you have to admire them for the singular honesty of that reaction. But the splendid surge did not end there. By taking the life of their enemy, they believed they had transformed an evil spirit into a benevolent one, which now would serve them for-ever. Now they could speak to the souls of those dead de-parted they loved, those still lost among the fires in the skies. They could tell them now to cease their empty wandering, for a warrior spirit had been sent to guide and watch over them for all eternity.

Two hundred yards now, still closing.

Abruptly the one furthest astern stands. A gesture unac-companied by any scream of defiance. Colorful but absurd —a statue without a horse. An exaltation of pure savagery. This warrior is covered by an enormous war mask, coconut palm for visage, furrowed brows and eyes fiercely carved but without actual openings. The man's black, glittering appraisal darts out at me through the enormous hungering mouth in the pale wood, a war demon who sees through his teeth. Matted human hair meshes down from the chin to his knees.

My flare is dying.

I pop a third star-burst upstairs.

He is so close I count the seashells surrounding the blind eyes of his mask. They appear to be radular sheaths of the lethal tulip cone.

The warrior crouches in a waist-bending stomp. I have seen it in Melanesian rituals patiently danced for bored tourists, but out here on the midnight water his posture signals a deadly consecration. I know that he has already linked an index finger into the raffia throwing sling and that the long black lance he holds is poised in my direction and that his lips beseech the help of his wind god.

My marksmanship to this moment has apparently lacked the necessary flamboyance.

I gut-shoot Throwing Lance.

The 7.62 round has been designed by better minds than mine to shatter its way through a brick wall. This round has no interfering wall.

The statue, for a final moment at least, erupts into loudness, his inner music bursting free in a glissando cry, "Gouné! Gouné!" Then he founders from his pedestal and plunges over the gunwale of the war canoe, spewing up phosphorescence from the violated surface. Still screaming, he vanishes, mask and all, down a tube of enveloping green. In the exaggerated stillness that follows I hear the soft thumping of sea against the hull of my own boat.

The warriors stay their paddles, dipping them as brakes. The proa glides to a stop, no further away now than half the length of a football field.

I fire my fourth flare.

I count the seconds.

Nobody moves. They seem graven in a stop-motion photograph already browning at the edges—happy Caledonians in a fading illustration from an issue of *National Geographic* circa nineteen-oh-eight. But through my nightscope, I watch the trade wind teasing the fleecy feathers on the robe of the nearest oarsman.

Then in the penumbra of the dying flare I see the warriors pivot in their places, still keeping their outboard sled to windward. Now they face away, their backs to me.

Almost majestically, they begin to paddle the double-ender north, off toward wherever it is they've come from.

I adjust my scope to 9X. I watch them blend with the horizon.

I flip on the safety catch, rest the butt of the HK-91 on the seat of the cockpit and slide below.

Continuous Distress Frequency for Nouméa is the standard 2182 kHz.

I put my transmitter on the air.

"Nouméa Marine Operator, this is *Steel Tiger*, Bravo Victor six three zero six. Over."

I listen for a reply. I punch in the time on my Memosail wristwatch.

Four minutes since I warned the intruders to stand off. No response from Nouméa.

I wait ninety seconds more.

I repeat my call.

A voice touches my elbow. In English, French accent, so close I feel its sibilance on my naked forearm.

I tell Nouméa that in defense of my life and my ketch I have had to terminate three unknown indigs some forty-three clicks offshore. Two have been borne away by those who brought them. One has been given to the Coral Sea. I will institute a search for his body in the morning, but finding it ahead of the reef sharks I estimate is a thousand-to-one shot.

Nouméa requests me to proceed into Baie de l'Orphelinat at first daylight. I will be met by appropriate authority.

I thank them, close down the transmitter, log the call.

I return topside, the HK-91 an impersonal reminder that it did indeed happen. I will disarm the weapon and clean it after a moment.

But first I light up, making a mental note to deep-six the last of a fine Maui lid before sailing into the arms of the gendarmerie in the morning. I return my attention upward to Canopus and Achernar.

In the interval neither has moved.

Or so it seems.

# ═══CHAPTER═══

## 2

**E**ven in sleep I must have turned to face the light in the starboard port of my cabin. Now that July has come to the South Pacific, I was dreaming of winter sun. It rises low this time of year and scurries across the horizon like a furtive flying fish, so I must force my eyes open, must rush with the sun into Nouméa before the world sets and other war canoes envelop me.

But as I rise on one elbow in my bunk and blink up at the light in the port, as I peer at its wheeling radiance, I know it's not daylight. The searchlight of a boat larger than mine probes my deck.

I am awake at once, the HK-91 within reach, but before I make any move toward it I hear the booming of a voice heavy with authority. The language is French, the intent clear. I am to stand by to be boarded.

I clutch the grab-rails as I go forward into the salon and to the companionway ladder, for *Steel Tiger* is rocking in the surge of whatever it is out there that has slid alongside me.

When I emerge onto the deck, I am blinded by the searchlight. At first I can sense only the massive shape abeam, then as my eyes adjust I make out the high forward section, the deck cut away at the single stack and sweeping low all the way to the stern, the gray hull—a French patrol boat with a gigantic *P-653* painted on its bow. I am surprised to find a Marine Nationale boat this far west. What limited naval force the French maintain in the Pacific they keep in Papeete, forty-eight hundred kilometers to the east. *P-653* lies alongside me to leeward, engines idling, the bridge continuing to pin me in its light. I hear the fluttering of the ensign on its staff. I look back and concentrate until I can at last distinguish the tricolor standing out of the dawn light.

"M. Locke!" This is not the voice I first heard.

This is a voice which by its tone suggests an almost ingrained impatience.

"May I come aboard?"

"Of course."

I release the pelican hooks securing the lifelines between two starboard stanchions and stand by as uniformed sailors on the patrol boat quickly lower a rubber dinghy. The man they help down into the tender wears a business suit. The dawn wind which strums *Steel Tiger*'s rigging also ruffles his sparse strands of hair. He stands facing me, his feet planted on the floorboard of the oncoming dinghy in a stance as resolute as that I remember from schoolbook drawings of George Washington crossing the Delaware, and as the sailors row him across the few yards of sea between us his eyes never leave mine. He has the face of a punished child and I see, as he draws ever closer to my toerail, that his fingers are stained from cigarette smoke. He is smoking now, even as he lets me assist him aboard, holding a short, dark cigarette between his thumb and forefinger, his other fingers cupped over the burning end like a small chapel in which sacred smoke is preserved.

"Gauloise?" I ask him.

He makes a quick, delicate gesture with the cigarette hand and his intelligent eyes dart from the cigarette to me.

"I have smoked Gauloises and nothing but Gauloises since I was nine years old," he says with an edge that signifies he has not come forty-three kilometers onto the sea at zero four hundred hours to discuss such trivia.

"How do you know my name?" I ask him. "When I called Nouméa, I identified myself by boat, not by name."

His eyes half-close, as though he must preserve what little patience he has. Suddenly he is holding up a wallet.

He flips it open with style, deftly using his left hand, since the right is still husbanding the cigarette. The French police schools must give a special course to train their officers to flash their badges with such finesse.

"An inspector," I comment evenly. "Inspector Bazin. Correct?"

"I suggest we go below," he replies.

He does not wait for me, but descends into the salon.

I find him already at the navigation station. He continues to smoke with his cupped right hand while his left hand, fingers seeming to probe, slowly explores the hydrographic chart I had laid out before I fell into my bunk in a restless sleep.

"You were planning to come in?"

"What else?" I tell him. "That's the way Nouméa Radio and I left it. At daybreak. After I tried to find the one who fell overboard."

He looks up at me and I see in his eyes what I know must often appear in my own—the look of a man who has embraced death.

"What course did you set? To go in?"

Without consulting the chart, I tell him. "Zero-five-one for le Mont lo on Île Nou until I hold Îlot Te-Ndu on my port beam and Île Nge to starboard, then to zero-seven-six, straight toward the Croix de Lorraine."

"Have you an ashtray?"

"I never smoke belowdecks."

He crosses past me to the ladder, takes two quick steps up, flips the stub of the Gauloise into the sea. He comes back down the ladder more deliberately and I observe him flexing his shoulders as though he has been spending too much time at a desk.

He lifts back the cuff of his jacket to expose a thin and surprisingly elegant gold wristwatch.

"At one o'clock this morning," he tells me, "I made two calls, the first to the U.S. Coast Guard in Washington to check the documentation of this vessel. It was eight o'clock in the morning there, yesterday's time. Then I called your father in San Diego. Five in the morning, his time, still yesterday. From both I obtained all the information I need about you for now. I trust that answers your question about how I know your name. So, having indulged you that, please indulge me. *I* am the police officer. Not you. *I* will ask the questions. I begin by asking you if we understand each other on this point."

"We do," I say. "Do you drink coffee?"

"Only Turkish," he tells me with no visible sense of humor, simply as one more transient fact in a universe of facts. "Turkish coffee and Turkish tobacco. Certainly nothing else from that fly-ridden country."

"Their soldiers are among the boldest in the world," I say.

He appears uninterested.

He settles on one end of the salon couch and I see that his eyes are directed aft, into my cabin, at the HK-91 on my bunk.

"Is that the weapon?"

"Shall I go get it?"

"I think not," he says. I will give him this. He does not loosen his jacket with precautionary emphasis and expose a holstered pistol. I doubt that I could handle such theatrics before daybreak.

"Tell me about the masks they wore."

"I didn't say they wore masks."

He considers this. Finally, he brings from an inside pocket—worn and soiled, I assume, from countless times of reaching inside for documents to be produced for the scrutiny of suspects or victims—a folded message on teletype paper. "This is an exact copy of the transmission between you and Nouméa radio in which you reported the incident. Would you care to examine it?"

"I don't need to," I tell him. "For you it's Turkish tobacco and coffee. For me it's my eyesight and my memory. Both are remarkable. I know exactly what I told Nouméa

—and I did not say I was attacked by men wearing masks. I would like to ask you why you asked me if they were— wearing masks, that is—but you've made it pretty clear you don't want me asking questions. Frankly, we're not going to get very far unless there's more give-and-take."

"Monsieur," he says, after a grave silence during which I have conservatively bet myself ten dollars he would light up another cigarette, then lost the bet, "there are things here which involve the security of the state. You are an outsider. I have the responsibility. You must let me proceed in my own way."

"Okay," I agree. The man can be appealing if he chooses to.

"The masks," he reminds me.

I tell him every detail.

"The mask with the red beads around the mouth originates in the region of Ponérihouen," he says when I have finished. "The others come from Hienghène and from Oundjo. That there should be three separate tribes involved —most alarming!"

"I know this is a question," I say, "but it's been bugging me for hours. Why *me*? And why way out here, so far offshore?"

"You come to Nouméa on some special business, possibly?"

"I'm not free to discuss that." I mean that. It's built into my contract. He will get nothing from me on this.

He half-closes his eyes again. For a moment I believe he may have fallen asleep.

"I will see the gun now," he says in a whisper.

I go get it and bring it to him, keeping the muzzle well away from his eyes, wide open now, watching me.

He observes, I think with silent approval, how I have used tape to bind two magazines together, thus compounding the killing capability.

"What other firearms do you have aboard?"

"A Browning 9mm."

"Bring it to me, please."

12

I'm gone about six seconds, then I'm back with the pistol. I drop the clip and clear the round in the chamber, check the weapon once more and hand it to him, butt first, safety on.

He seems to be savoring its Belgian steel. He pushes the safety off, activates the gun, and snaps the trigger on the empty chamber. An expression of tranquillity appears around his lips. "You've eased the trigger pull," he announces.

"Down to five pounds," I tell him.

"You've removed the adjustable sights," he continues.

"Took the rear sight off," I point out, "painted the front end with Day-Glo. Strictly a defensive weapon. All the distances are going to be inside fifty to sixty feet. This front sight lets me put them all on target in a matter of seconds, fourteen rounds—thirteen in the mag, one in the chamber—a dependable one-inch pattern at twenty yards."

He is nodding approvingly as he asks me, "Where do you keep your High-Standard .22 with its silencer?"

Curious how trigger words or phrases fire off your recall. "High-Standard .22"—and I see myself again as Captain John Locke, leader of an OPS-35 SOG group over the fence and above the seventeenth parallel, a spring-muscled younger man wearing a cotton-poplin jungle fatigue with long sleeves, my blood type embroidered over my right pocket and OKAY PEN over my left, canvas leggings laced midway up the calves, shoelaces on the side and leggings covering soft-soled jungle boots. STABO rings with ordinary pistol belt, the snap links sturdy enough for chopper lift-out, freeing the arms for firing during dustup. First-aid gear carried forward. Small gas mask worn over the left chest and a sheathed Randall fighting knife worn upside down, cutting edge outward, on the chest strap near the neck. A can of albumin blood-expander, a rubber IV tube in the shirt pocket, along with your standard piano wire for garroting and three one-quart canteens carried behind. Army-issue Seiko watch. Radio URC-68. The Browning in my shoulder holster, the High-Standard .22 with silencer in a canvas pocket at the back of my rucksack. In one hand a Swedish K-gun, plus the sawed-off M-79 grenade launcher with snap-link through the trigger guard and an antipersonnel round in the chamber.

I see him looking at me from across a clearing. He lingers in green twilight and I reach for him with my thoughts, but he is gone again, lost back somewhere I've never been able to leave.

I smile at Inspector Bazin. What else can I do? Inspector Bazin, baby, you are good. But are you good enough?

"There's a lot of sentiment attached to that little gun," I tell him. "I'd hate for anything to happen to it. You know?"

"A question, monsieur, or a statement?"

For an instant I assume he is smiling at me, but I see that I have misjudged him again. In front of his now implacable face I observe the outstretched hand, so I go in and dig out the .22 and lay it in his palm, complete with silencer and memories.

He is not entirely insensitive. "If it could only talk," he murmurs at last, and I know I can trust him with it.

However, you've got to ask. "I do get a receipt for these, don't I?"

"But of course. Later. Meanwhile, I will also need your passport, your health record, and your boat's documents."

"If I give them to you, what will I have left to show Customs?"

"You may dispense with the Q-flag and formalities. I will see that pratique is granted. Also zarpe when you are ready to leave. How long do you plan to stay with us?"

"That depends on you, Inspector."

His shrug is refined indifference. "I have no reason to arrest or otherwise detain you, monsieur."

"I shot three Caledonians."

"Where are their bodies?"

"They might still turn up. At least those two in the outrigger might."

"I have no evidence anyone was shot."

"Isn't it standard procedure to have some kind of hearing?"

"Do you enjoy such inquiries?"

"Less than anybody."

"Then why do you press?"

"I need to know the ground rules."

"Our laws are the laws of France." He suspends his breath, extending the word "France." "Made applicable as the occasion demands. *I* determine both the application and the occasion." He gives the "I" a full second of emphasis.

Instantly I place the name of Bazin at the top of my list of local names. He is not to be underestimated. Not if I hope to leave New Caledonia alive—and with the money I've been promised.

I assume my most casual manner. "In that case," I assure him, "I shouldn't be here more than two weeks."

"As a tourist?"

"I said I was not free to discuss the purpose of my coming here. A corporate confidentiality is involved."

"Ah, yes, I believe I remember your saying something like that. Well, then, two weeks will offer no one any problem. We permit thirty days to all visitors. After that, one does require a visa. However, monsieur, in your case I would personally discourage you from applying. Now, if you please, the documents. Also, four photographs and two dollars forty-five cents."

"Two forty-five? U.S.? Not Pacific francs?"

"A local surcharge. Every visiting yachtsman pays it, usually in dollars, but we accept CFP at the current exchange rate, of course. It is simply a contribution toward the harbor maintenance, similar to an airport departure tax. Which we do not charge."

I cross to the navigation station, unlock the drawer in which I keep *Steel Tiger*'s documentation papers. I give them, my passport, and yellow health card to the inspector, along with four snaps of myself in living color when I was passing through my full-beard transfiguration period—and three single American dollar bills from a diminishing stash.

"Sorry," I say, "no small change. Give the whole bundle to harbor maintenance. Is the water potable?"

He frowns slightly. "In the harbor?"

"The tapwater."

"But of course."

He gets up, somehow managing to carry the HK-91, the Browning and its ammo, the .22, and all my papers without losing any measure of grace. He goes up the ladder and onto deck.

I follow him. He lights up another Gauloise.

"I will put two sailors aboard with you," he tells me, watching the smoke from his lungs waft away with the wind. "Meanwhile, we will comb the area for a man foolish enough to topple from a canoe when warning shots are fired."

He looks off to the east. The sun is already brightening the far lip of the sea. I watch Bazin reading the surface. Like me he is a man who searches for signs and portents on every quarter. Like me he is even now feeling the fair breeze from Australia ripple the hair on the nape of his neck. Like me his eyes are tracking the long fetch of polar waves up from the Tasman Sea as they flatten here and tame themselves in the benign Melanesian waters.

"When we have concluded our search," he says, "you will follow us in. And as you sail in, think of this: Because New Caledonia is a thousand miles from nowhere, it would appear an ideal place for troublemakers. That, unfortunately, seems to be its unhappy history."

He leaves it flapping there for me like morning wash as he climbs down into the rubber dinghy and as the sailors—except for the two wearing sidearms he has ordered aboard *Steel Tiger*—row him back to the patrol boat, his cupped hand with the cigarette close to his lips.

I notice one thing. He is no longer looking at me or at the sunrise.

He is looking north.

Toward Hienghène. And Ponérihouen. And Oundjo.

To where I know now I shall have to go.

# CHAPTER

## 3

While we wait for *P-653* to stitch back and forth, making a show of searching the immediate quadrant, I prepare coffee and share it with the two sailors.

One is still young enough to be embarrassed by the pimples on his chin, afraid to smile for fear he may invite even more attention to his face. As he drinks his coffee, he holds up one hand, consciously shielding his chin from scrutiny. He reminds me of some of the Saigon bargirls who covered their mouths when they tittered—long, painted fingernails up over their lips in scarlet deception to conceal inferior dentistry or no dentistry at all. The other sailor displays an almost arrogant confidence in his use of English. He tells me he learned it in a single summer on Australia's Gold Coast, where he took third place in an open-class windsurfing competition. He exists only, he tells me, for the hours he can spend on his board. He prefers the German boards to the American. In his opinion they are faster and stronger. I mention our windsurfers at Hookipa Beach on Maui's north shore. Using the standard American board, they climb the faces of breakers, soar into the sky, land with perfect balance, and sizzle away toward the next oncoming crest. He develops a faraway look in his eyes and lapses into silence. Thereafter, he is careful to speak only in prudent French. The first sailor asks where they can put their empty coffee cups. I tell him to deposit the cups in the deep galley sink. They do, then retreat to the forepeak of *Steel Tiger*, where they remain isolated.

*P-653* slides in on my bow. She runs a two-letter alphabet group up her masthead—the red-and-white checkerboard Uniform and the white-crossed red Foxtrot: UF, "Follow me." In response I hoist Charlie flag for affirm, lifting it only halfway to the spreader so it flies at the dip in clear acknowledgment.

Between November and May in this segment of the Western Pacific the trades flow dependably out of the east or southeast, but on this July morning I have twenty knots out of the south to play with. I check everything below for stowage, including the coffee pot and the unwashed cups, run up the French courtesy flag, then hoist the unreefed main. The two sailors offer their help, but the offer is halfhearted, more from fear I shall find them inexperienced than from laziness. I smile at them and single-handed get the working jib and mizzen up and trimmed, and in a matter of minutes *Steel Tiger* is at hull speed, slightly above eight knots, creaming along credibly in the wake of the patrol boat.

As we proceed through Passe de Dumbéa and into the protected waters lying between the outer barrier reef and New Caledonia, the sea flattens, yet I am able to find even more wind inside and now the boat drives forward with such unabashed power I can sense in the young French sailor who windsurfs astonishment that one can also surf a forty-four-foot ketch, providing it has been designed and built as lovingly as this one has.

Ahead to windward, I try to imagine New Caledonia as a pristine landfall. It is something I do, a private little game, whenever I make a sighting, to put myself back in time, aboard whatever ship first found each island on each sea. It is not possible to do this now, for I already know too much about this place in preparation for what I must do here. I know this to be the fourth largest island in the Pacific, exceeded in size only by New Guinea and the North and South Islands of New Zealand. I know this Grande Terre to be four hundred kilometers long by fifty kilometers wide with a mountainous spine running up its center and a barrier reef offshore, the longest insular reef on the planet, stretching almost a thousand kilometers from Île des Pins in the southeast to Îles Bélep in the northwest and extending beyond sight into the Coral Sea in the distant northwest.

The first European to guess that land existed in this part of the watery world never sighted New Caledonia—the French voyager Bougainville circling the world with the frigate *La Boudeuse*. In 1768, passing across the Coral Sea, he observed vegetation floating on the surface and conjectured that an island must lie nearby. Two centuries later the French postal authorities thought to add his portrait to a colonial stamp and I certainly bear no disrespect for the gentleman, but simply assessing the proximity of land from observing floating vegetation has never impressed me as being that spectacular an achievement. I would have preferred that the French postal authorities commemorate the unknown navigator who brought the first settlers all the way here from Southeast Asia twenty thousand years ago.

Six years after Bougainville's near pass-by, the English explorer Captain Cook, following notes from Bougainville's log, brought his vessel the *Resolution* within sight of New Caledonia. A lookout, high in the rigging of the *Resolution*, beheld mountains rising to the west. I see him in my mind, rubbing salty knuckles into his eyes, hardly daring to shout his discovery down to the deck below. When you're accustomed to sighting white foam of breakers on Pacific atolls not more than two miles distant, seeing five-thousand-foot mountains poking out of the sea can be a staggering experience. But this man—his name was Colnett, I have read—shouted "Land ahoy!" and Captain Cook sounded along the outer reef seeking a passage until finally he was able to anchor north of what is now called Balade. If you look on your charts you will see that to this day the cape below the foot of those first-sighted mountains is still called Cape Colnett, after Cook's lookout man, something to my way of thinking more significant in one's honor than a postage stamp.

But I am unable to view New Caledonia through Colnett's eyes, for Cook approached on the windward side of the island and at its far north end, while I am sailing *Steel Tiger* in on the opposite coast and to the south, where the French later established the island's main city Nouméa.

I pass a reef on which a Japanese freighter sulks abandoned, rusting in the dove-gray morning, her bottom gouged out where she struck, her hull awash and inhabited by pencil sea-urchins, blue starfish, and cowrie shells. She is no ancient relic of World War II, a skeleton left by TBFs, but a more recent casualty. She died in behalf of Japanese international commerce. Her remorseful captain, I overhear the two French sailors saying, committed harakiri in atonement for his faulty navigation. They consider him a fool—not for losing his ship, but for taking his own life. When I question this, they insist that the Asian has no regard for existence. I ask them if they have ever heard that the French architect who designed and erected the obelisk in the Place de la Concorde in Paris had summarily shot himself when he calculated that his obelisk was not properly aligned within the distant Arch de Triomphe, as he had intended. We must not dishonor the perfectionists, I tell them, and once more they retire and leave me alone to look off at Grande Terre coming up now in purple knife-ridges spilling down into the coastal plain, Grande Terre where the dawa fish still swim below thunder clouds and where the sacred yam is still carried as though it were an infant.

I am close enough now so that even without the binoculars I can see the savanna and niaouli trees along the shoulders of Mt. Koghis. Nouméa itself is perched about a hill-flanked peninsula, looking more like Nice than a South Pacific maritime city, a French gemstone placed incongruously in a Coral Sea setting. One hundred and twenty-eight years, one month, and sixteen minutes before this very second, Tardy de Montravel, sailing in and marveling at the first sight of so spacious and sheltering a harbor, decided to found the capital here and to name it Port-de-

France. The name persisted for eleven years, until it was changed to Nouméa because of postal confusion with Fort-de-France in Martinique. *Nouméa*, the prep work for my mission here has informed me, is a native word meaning peninsula.

As the patrol boat leads me in, I note three vast skirts of smoke overhanging the smelters of the Doniambo refinery of the Société le Nickel to the north of the city, one column a poisonous blue, another a scruffy white, the third a biting orange. Cargo boats lie along its wharf, gigantic cranes crouched over them as though feeding. Above me an Air France 747 whistles lower on its approach to the international airport at la Tontouta, certainly not the sight that greeted Montravel. Yet I find it easy to dismiss the knowledge that little more than a hundred years ago where office buildings and factories now stand, Melanesian tayos —definitely on a losing roll, black faces smeared with warstripes—were still vainly staging massacres of the colonials, cooking and eating the French invaders at victory kai-kais, reserving for the chiefs human eyes that had moistened at the sight of Versailles and breasts of nubile white girls which had never risen to the tight clasp of Gallic lovers. The master machinist who created the human machine built in all kinds of magnificent compensatory gears. If the machine commits a barbarity, it has a device which first justifies the barbarity, then another device to erase even its memory.

We enter the Baie de Pêcheurs. I observe the Citroëns and the Renaults whisking along Rue Jules Garnier at harbor's edge. I even hear the nearby clang of traffic signals and the waspish progress of motorbikes, nothing even remotely comparable to the racket of Saigon's traffic a decade ago, but when I tell this to the young French sailors, they stoutly refute it, claiming I have imagined such a thing, that Nouméa has no traffic noise and that Saigon's stridence was an American export, not French. I do not pursue this with the two of them. Besides, we are pointing in now toward a narrow channel and a labyrinth of masts, private yachts tied up at the Club Nautique de Calédonie inside the marina.

Bazin appears at the rail of the patrol boat. He holds a loudhailer.

"The end tie," he calls to me, pointing. "Astern of that power yacht."

I look past his imperious arm toward the transom of a hundred-and-fifty-foot Benetti tied up inside the marina. With her Italian styling, her rakish bow, and streamlined superstructure, she appears to be planing, even though she's tied—bow, stern, and quarter—to the dockside. She flies the American flag on her backstay, above the flag of the Cayman Islands on her stern flagstaff. I read the name *Reckless Living* above her port of hail, Grand Cayman, and I know that because she goes for five million dollars in the showroom, her American owner must have made it running mountain snow from Colombia to Nassau. A five-million-dollar boat named *Reckless Living* doesn't belong to a *Town and Country* family that sells cereal.

I'd already doused the mizzen. Now I hand the jib down, then sail *Steel Tiger* straight in with main alone on a beam reach, turn bow up at the last possible millisecond, straight into the wind and up to the dock and the looming transom of the Benetti, swinging the boom around to spill air and luffing to a stop so precise the two young sailors, braced for collision, stare at me with slack jaws.

I'm a big advocate of the use of spring lines in preference to bow or stern lines, so while the midshipmen are still gaping, I snug up and secure.

The patrol boat is idling alongside me, Bazin gazing down at me from their higher deck.

"I shall be along within a few minutes," he says through cigarette smoke. "Some other matters have come up."

Of course they have. They always do. I watch him steam away, off to the military docks of the Maritime Nationale.

I begin to tidy up *Steel Tiger*. I am bored with the two straphanger sailors. I gesture them to wait on the dock so I don't have to hose the deck around their feet. They climb off awkwardly, trying to get their landlegs back. I wonder how good the windsurfer can really be to stand there so spastically.

Suddenly through the thunderhead of ten million fantasies obstructing my thinking, I am hearing the Rolling Stones' "I Can't Get No Satisfaction."

I glance up and on the helicopter pad of *Reckless Living* discover a girl leaning over and smiling down from some fifteen feet above me. She is naked from the waist down, the hair around her labia impeccably manicured into a heart-shaped patch. She wears a T-shirt over her breasts and I read HAPPINESS IS A CONFIRMED FUCK emblazoned on its front. She is holding the biggest portable cassette module I have ever seen, speakers big as platters, to let me enjoy good concert sound.

"I'm Kim," she announces.

"That's a nice little boat you have up there," I say. "Too bad you don't have a chopper to go with it."

"They flew off to Yaté for the day," she says. "It makes a bitchin' sundeck. Wanta come aboard? I'll show you the gold pipes in our crappers."

"I haven't exactly been cleared into the country yet."

"How about I come down to you?"

"Negative."

"Rather look than touch?"

"I can't stand asshole numbers," I tell her, somewhat surprised at the sharpness in my voice.

"You think *this* is an asshole number?"

"It'll do till a better one comes along."

"Hey, bubbie, I'm boy crazy. I watched you sailing in. With these . . ." She holds up in her free hand a pair of binos. "I saw a churlish mouth, cruel blue eyes, and a high, beautifully rounded forehead. Somebody told me Alexander the Great had a forehead like yours. And I've always had the hots for Alex baby, God knows why."

"Alexander the Great died in Persia," I tell her. "Persia's not there anymore. Neither is Alex."

"Does that make *me* the asshole—or *you*?"

23

Even from fifteen feet I can see past her diverting crotch to the wide-set, vulnerable eyes in a hard-boned though delicate face. She is clearly a girl in need of rescue from herself, but I'm no longer in the salvation business. Once you've learned that it ain't nothin' but a life, that there are no lessons to be learned, no meaning to be derived, and that every new day is the one you may not be getting out of anyway, you can't worry too much about the dispossessed. We're all dispossessed, only most people refuse to accept it, refusing to see that today may always and forever be the last day, the very last day.

"You're not going to believe this," I say, knowing it's the terminal shot yet not regretting it, "but I'm just not impressed."

"Go shovel squirrel shit!" she shouts at me and disappears, manicure and all. Her backside, with its young firmness, has a decided bounce to it. Definitely a matched pair.

I have no doubt which part of this young lady a New Caledonian chief would have eaten, but were I to have told her this she would have leaped straight down onto my upturned face, definitely injuring one or both of us.

I am struck suddenly in the chest by a shaft of one-hundred-and-fifteen-grain alarm. It's the old reliable early alert, warning me that once more I'm back in the AO and that there's a real skate out there somewhere. I have visitors. I feel primitive eyes, primitive hatreds scabbing over me. From what point of the compass? I peer everywhere about the marina. A Chinese-checkers-board of hulls. Halyards snapping at masts, an ear-lulling symphony preventing me from using my ears to isolate the origin of the scrutiny I'm under. They know I'm here. Obviously they knew it last night too, out on the water. But here I have no moat around me, no shark patrol. Here I can be ambushed without the means to protect myself. I remember the morning we were operating north of Vancouver I in a real hairy TA and I felt that same bullet-strike of warning as I knelt in the area and whirling, without bothering to aim, scythed the grass beyond me with the sweet little Swedish grease gun I used to carry in those days. Then I saw the young NVA captain still sighting me down the barrel of his SMG, but he was already dead, unseamed from the belly down by my instinctive burst, bloodied rice tumbling in clots from the bullet-severed food tube slung diagonally across his slender body.

Something, God knows what, compelled me to slide through the grass to him. For all I knew he could have had a company of men with him. But drawn to him, needing the standdown, I went. His dead eyes, open, stared up at me. I stared back into them for a long time, looking at myself in his place, reversing our roles, until finally I noticed the tattoo on his chest. I unbuttoned his tunic with a tenderness that surprised me and I read the words tattooed in Vietnamese: "Born in the north to die in the south." What irony, I thought. They had probably honored him with a funeral ceremony before he left his village, mother, father, wife maybe, kids even, and here he was on the way back to the noble war in the south—but because one particular enemy had come north into the denied zone to harass and interdict he had ended up born in the north and dead in the north. Some craziness possessed me then and I radioed for a medivac and I lay there for minutes guarding the body of my enemy until they were above me and I had him dusted up, despite their cries of Jesus Christ, Captain, and ordered them to fly him south and bury him somewhere outside Saigon, facing the city, and for all I know they did it.

I see Inspector Bazin hurrying along the dock toward me in the company of another man, this one taller than Bazin, who tends to be chunky, I decide. This one is somehow storklike, yet his suit with its obviously elegant European tailoring succeeds in partly concealing his gaunt frame.

I step off the boat and onto the dock to meet the two.

"M. Locke." The tall man extends his hand, which I take. "Marcel Gallante."

I had told myself, as he approached, that it could be no one else but the man who had hired me, a man I'd never seen until this minute. But I had heard his voice, on my boat's radio in the westernmost track of the Coral Sea, and it had persuaded me to postpone the sentimental search that had brought me and *Steel Tiger* to this part of the world in the first place.

"I have told Inspector Bazin everything we discussed, you and I," Gallante says, fixing the inspector with an accusatory look. "At first he demurred. There was even some talk of his taking the matter up with his immediate superior, our mayor. In turn this required my pointing out to him that I had already discussed the situation with the High Commissioner for French Affairs in the Pacific and that approval had been handed down before I engaged your services."

Bazin makes a little gesture of surrender, but he doesn't fool me for a second. I have seen a tiger shark hanging on a dock hook at high noon, apparently dead, until somebody foolishly cut him down and got his leg bitten off.

"I am leaving a car and a driver at your disposal," Gallante continues, in the manner of someone already late to a board meeting. "I suggest a mode of operation, if you find it reasonable. Accompany the inspector to his office. He will turn over to you the necessary police records. He will also make available whatever other assistance you may wish to call upon. Then—" He checks his wristwatch—a Piaget, I note in passing, with two gold time zones, one for local time, the other for Paris time. "—the driver will bring you to me for lunch at one-thirty. I am grateful you have come, monsieur."

As swiftly as he has appeared, he leaves, Bazin watching the departure with measured respect.

"Went over your head?" I ask.

He lectures me without even looking my way. "We French understand that power gives a man the right to do certain things. You Anglo-Saxons do not have the same ethic about the true nature of power—neither what it is nor how it operates."

"We Anglos do bristle with all kinds of guilt buttons," I admit.

"If Marcel Gallante sent for you, whether or not I approve has no significance. I accept this. It is the way matters are. No rearrangement is possible."

"None, at least, you can think of at this particular moment," I say.

He closes his eyes against the freshening wind. But the deception no longer works on me. He had better spruce up his repertoire if he wants to stay in the game.

"I'll just button up the boat," I tell him. "Then I'll be right with you. Where do I find this car and driver?"

"I will take you to it. He will follow my car."

I step aboard, go below to be sure everything is turned off that needs to be off and that everything is on that needs to be on. I discover, lying in the middle of my navigation table, a small vial filled with bluish water, and floating in it a piece of paper. Through the glass I can read the writing on the paper. It reads JOHN LOCKE, something strangely obscene about it, as though I were to come around the corner of a ghetto in a strange American city and discover my name sprayed in paint on a tenement wall.

I examine the vial carefully without picking it up. They don't graduate you out of Special Forces without a comprehensive course in booby-traps. Okay, no wires. I examine the surface of the glass, then touch it with the corner of a piece of notepaper. No acid outside. I sniff the vial. If that's nitro inside, it doesn't smell like any nitro I've ever sniffed.

While I'm still analyzing the object Bazin appears behind me.

He has come down into the salon without my hearing him. Not good. Now he reaches past me and picks up the vial. I find myself turning away, for I have taken grenade bursts on the back of flak jackets; they're not too horrendous if you properly calculate the upward route of the fragmentation.

"A t'kata has been aboard," Bazin comments thoughtfully.

I have recently read the word as part of my self-briefing.

"They think *sorcery* will do it?" I ask.

"They *know* it will," he replies. "They've put your name in the bottle, corked it up. Now you are 'under control.' "

"You've seen this stuff work?"

"Sometimes," he answers. "No one can explain it. We have even had a few cases of homicide brought about by native sorcery, but we cannot prosecute. Besides, for a man like you, who believes in nothing, what is the harm of your name floating in blue liquid?"

"No harm at all," I reply.

"As a matter of fact, we on the police encourage the local sorcerers. Their work serves as a cathartic for people with deep-lying hatreds toward us. By allowing the natives to destroy us in their imaginations, we avert the real acts of violence that could cause blood to run from one end of this island to the other."

He hands the vial to me.

"Dispose of it as you will," he tells me.

I put it away, next to my sextant, another piece of witchcraft, and I move toward the companionway.

"Monsieur," he says quietly.

I turn. I see he is holding out to me my Browning pistol and its magazine, together with the box of ammo he had taken from me earlier.

"Higher authority has requested I return this to you."

"What about the HK-91 and the .22?"

"Do not push too hard."

I accept the gift. Already I am feeling less naked.

"I caution you," he says, and now I see the core of hardness in him, "if you should happen to shoot the wrong people, not even the High Commissioner can protect you. We French may appreciate power and its uses, but we are not above the law, not one of us. And you are in my country now, subject to my laws."

"I could have lived without that," I tell him, just as hard toward him as he has been with me.

And we go out—into his country.

# CHAPTER

# 4

I settle into the back seat of the Citroën limousine Marcel Gallante has put at my disposal. I evaluate my driver as he swings us onto the harbor boulevard to follow the inspector's blue-striped police car topped by cobalt-blue light domes smaller than cold-cream jars.

When Bazin had walked me to the car waiting near the Club Nautique's modest tin-roofed clubhouse and turned me over officially to Gallante's driver, I noted at once the man was no ordinary chauffeur. In a rack under the dash he had snugged an Uzi sub-machine gun with its fire selector in the forward position and two twenty-five-round magazines in a special "L" clip configuration slotted in for business.

His traveling eyes take in everything around us, including my own lurking scrutiny, our glances intersecting for a split-second in his rear-view mirror. I decide I could be tight with this gungi. There were days I could have used him on either flank.

"Where you from?" I ask him in French.

He answers me over his shoulder in an accent I cannot place.

"La Flotte."

"Sorry, I don't know where that is."

"The oyster capital of France," he says proudly, "the principal fishing village on the Île de Ré in the Bay of Biscay, north of Bordeaux—the only place a man can eat oysters in the non-R months, glorious oysters all twelve months of the year."

29

It registers with me once more that even were I to live forever I could no more set foot on all the islands in our world than I can visit the stars.

"Where did you take your antiterrorist training?" I ask him. "In West Germany or outside Milan?"

He's bright enough not to shift his eyes to mine waiting in his mirror. He merely shrugs.

"I do not understand the question, monsieur."

I leave it there. At least I know that while I'm in Gallante's Citroën I am not entirely alone in the world.

I'm certain Marcel Gallante travels nowhere without this young man from Île de Ré. Gallante, I had found out in the nine days and nights it took me to beat south to New Caledonia from Kira Kira on San Cristóbal, is one of the richest, most influential men in France. He is vice-chairman of the Société Financière pour Coopération Pacifique, better known in financial circles as SFPCP, a Paris investment bank with major holdings in all of France's Pacific Overseas Territories. SFPCP retains interests in rubber, coffee and palm-oil plantations in Africa and owns the controlling shares in the nickel mines of New Caledonia, husbanding the world's largest known nickel deposits.

The inspector's car turns into a courtyard at the intersection of what I read to be Avenue Maréchal Foch and Avenue de la Victoire. All police headquarters in the tropics tend to look and smell like crocodile pits, but Bazin's domain is an exception. A block-long modern white stucco building sits backed up to a bone-clean Bureau de Poste. Headquarters is interfaced by green horizontal iron bars over a façade of red looping tiles, giving the building the semblance of a giant wine-storage rack.

As we leave the cars, Gallante's driver staying with the Citroën, Bazin leads me past parked white police vans with their characteristic blue stripes. Smart-looking officers, not a fat belly among them, patrol the entrances. They wear visored hats, blue shirts, dark-blue creased military trousers, holstered pistols carried too high on the hip for my taste, and in their belts what once were called clubs, now euphemistically called batons. I think, as I enter the dark interior with Bazin, that the whole story of our time is told by these finely turned twentieth-century batons, totally neutered, slicked-up, all symbolism lost, nothing like the clubs my visitors of last night had been carrying, with warheads formed after predatory birds, the *bec d'oiseau*, or even more fear-impelling, the *casse-tête phallique*, clubs shaped like the male organ, the killing part the swollen glans penis, death at full erection. It occurs to me, just as we enter the inspector's office, this has got to be the original giving of head. I begin to laugh. It has been awhile since I've had any reason to. Bazin glances back at me, disapproving, yet curious. I doubt that he will wish to share this sudden insight, so I keep it to myself.

We enter his office, pleasant enough for someone who spends his time in the scruffy business of pacification. I sit down and wait for Bazin to do what Gallante has ordered him to do, give me the police reports I need in order to get on with fulfilling my contract.

A young French policewoman in a blue skirt sweeps in efficiently. She carries a serving tray with its carafe of coffee and two surprisingly delicate demitasse cups and saucers. She wears chic high-heeled shoes straight from Paris, setting off a thoroughbred's ankles. She goes out without looking at me—until she's out in the corridor, beyond Bazin's supervisory eye-range, when she fires a parting smile my way, the more warming because it's human, not sexual. For the first time since I've landed in New Caledonia I feel less a stranger.

Bazin is pouring coffee. He offers it to me.

"Turkish?" I ask.

"I see you remember."

"I told you," I remind him, "my eyesight and my memory—my two treasures. Both are positively spooky."

"After your war service," he says, sipping his coffee with what he must surely think is deceptive sociability, "you returned to San Francisco. You became a police officer. You spent almost three years in homicide and narcotics. Why did you resign?"

"I didn't want to be just another dancing bear."

"I do not understand the term 'dancing bear.' "

"Just another big bastard stomping bullshit," I say, but I can see that for this moment at least he is really trying to comprehend me and I'll get more out of him if he regards me less as an alien.

"Okay," I say, giving him a small slice from the truth pie, "I like to try to beat the odds. I found out that when you're a cop you can't gamble, not even your own life. Nobody's about to let you. Too many internal politics. Too much control."

"More than the army?"

"More than the army I was in. I had a free hand in the war I fought. We had only one rule in my particular outfit —don't fuck up."

"And you never did?"

"I wouldn't be here if I had."

"I think there was another reason you didn't remain in law enforcement," he says, leaning back and tamping one of his Turkish cigarettes before lighting it. "There is little public respect for policemen. And you needed that, didn't you? After Vietnam?"

He has me there, the sonofabitch. He somehow knows that however you did your time in Indochina, whether you were one of the "it-was-him-or-me" peons or a redneck who wanted to carve his initials on some dink's ass, or were genuinely repulsed to realize that the only way you could live through it was to cross the bounds of reason, as I did, and make up your own morality minute by minute— whichever you were, you wanted the people at home to tell you they understood that you had done something of value. Yes, by God, you wanted respect! And expiation! And a lot of other things beyond naming. Maybe, even, revenge.

"No," I lie. "I didn't quit because I wasn't getting my share of public respect. You said it yourself, Inspector. I don't believe in anything. Hell, if seeing my name floating around in blue water doesn't bother me, why should I be bugged by a shortage of public respect? The coffee's been fine. The rap session's over, okay? May I please see what I need to see?"

He's already opening the top drawer of his desk.

He places the file in front of me.

Then he rises.

"Take all the time you want. When you're finished, I'll be back."

He goes out.

I open the file.

Four homicides.

All have occurred within the past two months—since Marcel Gallante arrived from Paris with a hand-picked staff of engineers and project officers to supervise the installation of a high-technology communications system, which when finished will give New Caledonia the most powerful TV-microwave capability in the entire Pacific, owned and operated solely by SFPCP.

First, a thirty-two-year-old engineer from Burgundy, Jean-Paul Saurès, had been brained to death by assailant or assailants unknown while surveying the site for the new tower on Mont-Dore. Both hands cut off. Obviously for the cooking pot, the police investigation concludes, since splinters from an obsidian Kanaka war club from the area around Hienghène were found in the brain of the victim.

Second, a forty-year-old mathematician, on a morning jog away from the project dormitory, was found tied with fiber bindings in the bush, his body fatally bitten by huge red-spotted forest spiders, two of them still spinning their gigantic webs around him when he was discovered.

Third, the project's youngest scientist, a brilliant twenty-nine-year-old from Paris, was found impaled by spears positively identified as originating from the Oundjo district.

Fourth, Gallante's close associate and right-hand man, the project director, was discovered less than two kilometers from the worksite, his body bound in a kneeling position, his heart hacked out.

The four killings have several obvious elements in common. First, each would appear to be the work of native tribes. Second, each victim had been alone at the time of death, no witnesses anywhere at the scene. Third, no leads of any kind had been found in terms of footprints, fingerprints, or other tangible twentieth-century-type forensic clues. Obsidian fragments from Hienghène war clubs or the shafts of Oundjo spears, while suggesting that the homicides were the work of tribesmen, could just as easily been used by whites covering their identities by trying to divert the investigation elsewhere. Fourth, each victim had been in the employ of SFPCP and specifically working on the microwave project.

And finally, each had received a vial of blue water containing his bottled name.

It appears, I note with more than passing interest, that each victim had been given the warning vial only some six or seven hours before he was killed. This conclusion Bazin has reserved for the last paragraph on the closing page of the police report.

As I finish reading the final words I sense him watching me. He has come in on those panther feet of his and has been waiting for my reaction even as I read the end of it.

He is somewhat surprised to discover I am smiling as I hand him back his report.

"No alarm, monsieur?" he asks.

"Child's play," I tell him.

He closes his eyes, this time longer than I have seen him do it before.

"You still with me?" I ask impatiently.

"I suggest that a little fear is not entirely uncalled for," he says, opening his eyes at last. "Whoever—or whatever —is behind this terror is highly organized. Personally, I suspect a major conspiracy with political motivation. I believe that so far we have seen only the tip of the iceberg. I would urge you, monsieur, if you hope to survive much past your lunch with Marcel Gallante, to be less the hero."

"His lunch that bad?"

He shakes his head at the affront of humor at a moment such as this.

"I am not afraid," I tell him, "because by coming after me they're setting themselves up."

This baffles him. I see I will have to explain.

"It's standard ops once you're into the target area to make your enemy hunt for *you*. If you move around hunting *him*, you risk being dinged. Once he attacks, you let his point go by, hit his middle, then go in and clean up the ends."

He remains unconvinced.

"There is one last thing," he says, "before I let you go out there. When I spoke to your father earlier this morning, he said a curious thing. He didn't ask me how you were—or what trouble you were in that would prompt a call from New Caledonia. He simply said to remind you— and I now use his exact words—'It ain't nothin' but a life.' What did he mean?"

"Just what he said," I reply. "It ain't nothin' but a life. Nothing more. It has no other meaning."

I leave him there in his office, fumbling for a Gauloise.

Outside, crossing the courtyard toward the waiting Citroën and the stout driver with the stashed Uzi, I think of my father and the times we spent together and how he taught me as a child to swim through the kelp beds out beyond Point Loma in the wake of incoming aircraft carriers, and I feel better than I've felt in hours.

I look up at the mares' tails splashing an otherwise faultless morning sky. They are dissipating, signifying continued fair weather.

I slip into the back seat.

"Run me over to the offices of *L'Indépendance*," I tell the driver.

We pass around the perimeter of the Place des Cocotiers, the long, rectangular grounds dominating the center of Nouméa. At one end a botanical garden surrounds the statue of Governor d'Olry, the statue in honor of his pacification of the natives after their 1878 revolt. Within this garden I see old men with black skins and bushy graying hair, possibly descendants—if your mind runs this way— of the very Melanesians d'Olry had executed. They are cutting grass with practiced strokes of their long blades. These caretakers appear solemnly intent upon their work, unmindful even of the touring squadrons of young Japanese girls passing them, secretaries and bank tellers on package vacations from crowded Tokyo, vibrant youngsters in daring white shorts, exposing their sturdy legs to the warm winter sun, stopping everywhere, like interrupted ants, to photograph each other—with native caretaker, with statue of unknown French governor, with taxi stand of Peugeots.

We turn onto Rue de la République, and on the whitewashed stucco wall of the Treasury building I see VOTEZ COMMUNISTE sprayed in red paint, a political mural badly in need of an artist, for the accompanying hammer-and-sickle lacks authority. Lenin in paradise, I think, as we stop in front of a hardware store displaying in its show window the latest in bidets.

Up a dangerously worn stairway, I find next to a padlocked red door—a porn shop closed on Tuesdays—a small, noisy office that serves as the city room for one of Nouméa's three daily newspapers, of all three the most struggling, or so I have been told in the occasional lamenting letters I've had from its editor-publisher Maurice Aragon.

I observe him now at his typewriter, and although it is years since I saw him last I am more fascinated by the fact he's typing furiously on a brand new Olympia electronic machine than that he has aged so markedly that I might have passed him on the street without recognizing him. New Olympias do not go hand-in-hand with corporate poverty. His usually melancholy features brighten as, at the soft urging of a woman at a desk near me, he looks up from his work, discovers me waiting on his threshold. He pushes back his chair, rushes to me. We embrace in the way of two who have old sharings and years behind them —I even more than he, though he's turned fifty and I won't be thirty-four until this fall, a Scorpio rising, I'm told.

He introduces me to the three others on his staff.

They compliment me on my French, ask me where I learned it.

I tell them my mother is French. And that I have spent a little time in Indochina.

"I've saved lunch," Maurice announces when these formalities are done. "Wait until you taste our mangrove crab!"

"I have a previous commitment," I tell him. "But not til one-thirty. How about coffee somewhere?"

He takes my arm, hurries me down to the sidewalk. He appears elated to see me and I wonder why so high on such a minor event.

He starts to lead me up the Rue de la République.

"I have a car," I tell him.

He looks at the big Citroën rolling silently toward us along the curbside. He gives me a conspiratorial wink, jumps in. The driver, I notice, takes him in with a one-hundredth-of-a-second appraisal.

He gives the driver an address. We settle back and smile at each other, covering a lot of ground without words.

"Of course you have no intention of telling me what brings you to New Caledonia," he says at last.

"Not for print. But as an old friend, for personal knowledge only. Okay?"

He looks disappointed. "I was hoping there would be a big story in your being here. We need a diverting story. Our readers are shocked by the horrible murders of the past two months."

"When it's over," I tell him, "you'll be the first to know —whatever the story turns out to be. If I'm still around."

He's happy again, then he frowns. "Are you in some personal danger?" In answer to his own question he glances from me to the strong neck of my driver, the ears without lobes, the head as clean and forthright as the barrel of an elephant gun.

"Forgive me, John, for being so insensitive. I shall ask no more questions. At least for now."

The coffee bar occupies the veranda of a hotel on a

corner across from the Place des Cocotiers. On the one wall lacquered turtle shells hang as lampshades. Two young men in black cotton drill trousers and white Lacoste T-shirts are busily streaming multicolored paper and tinsel from the turtle shells to the pipes supporting the veranda awning.

"For Bastille Day," Maurice tells me. "Will you still be here?"

"If I can make it through lunch. Private joke."

From our table alongside the wrought-iron railing enclosing the veranda I look out at the weathered yellow bandstand in the park. Just as the police have overdone the use of blue, here someone in charge has run amok with yellow—fluted park benches in yellow, tulip-shaped refuse containers in yellow.

"You should come in December," Maurice says, reading my mind. "Then it is not only yellow and green in the Place des Cocotiers. Then the flamboyant is in blossom. The whole park is aflame with its crimson."

Suddenly I'm watching the spill of clerks and shopkeepers from stores and boutiques fronting the Place de Cocotiers. Even banks and offices appear to be undergoing a swift evacuation.

"Everything closes at eleven in the morning," Maurice says, "except, of course, for the bars and restaurants. At two o'clock—to the very stroke—everything opens again. The tide, she goes out. The tide, she comes back in."

Two French girls rush out of a dress shop directly below us. One locks the door while the other wheels a motorbike off the sidewalk. Both girls put on helmets. They mount the motorbike in tandem, their skirts up around their thighs, and throttle away with a rasp of power.

The waiter brings us coffee and cognac and for the next hour or more we toast the dead men whose names we still remember and damn the whining pussies who survived in their places. We ruminate together about how incredible it is that you could go fight a war in a distant country where your enemy was everywhere and everything—not only the NVA, but worse, yourself, and the land and swamp leeches, the ticks, mites, bedbugs, deer-flies, mosquitoes, lice, scorpions, spiders, jungle rot, sunburn, heat and thirst and diarrhea—that's when things were going great—when you were managing to keep your viscera inside your abdominal wall and your arms and legs attached to your trunk . . . All this and more, yet you found when it was done that something in the country, something in its earth and among its durable people, something in its dawns and sunsets, had worked a quiet spell, so that it became, in retrospect, not the fault of the country or of its people, but the fault of those who were blind or willful, and you remember Vietnam with inexplicable nostalgia as a place, sometime in better days if they ever come, you hunger to return to. Was it the country or what you left there of yourself? I don't know. Maurice—he doesn't know. He had fought with the French at Dien Bien Phu, a young paratrooper, defeated, captured, finally released. But he stayed on. For a while he was a planter, then a war correspondent when I met him there in the late sixties, an expatriate who had chosen never to leave the Far East.

"Why New Caledonia?" I ask him.

"I've been everywhere else," he says, with a shrug.

Then he asks me what I know he's long been waiting to ask, what I've deliberately never touched on in our occasional correspondence. "There are rumors you became a soldier of fortune after you left San Francisco."

"Negative," I tell him truthfully. "Somebody already said it—there's no fortune to be made soldiering. Anyway, a merc's nothing more than a hired gun, no matter how he tries to hype himself."

"So what *do* you consider yourself?"

"I sail."

"One needs money to sail. Especially a boat like yours."

"Okay, then. I'm a guy with a boat on his back."

He signals the waiter for more cognac. I signal no more for me. You never know when you'll have to drive.

"You are aware, are you not, John, that your reputation is spreading throughout the Pacific basin?"

"Fascinating," I say. "What do you hear?"

"That whenever the local police come to an impasse, those above them see if they can bring in the man with the boat on his back."

"True," I admit. "To earn my passage, I've been accepting a job here and there. But if you want to know how I really see myself—I'm a civilian soldier, a contract military technician with a hunger to keep moving."

"I'll tell you what you really are," he says, and I observe the genuine friendship in his eyes. "You're obsessed with why things *aren't*—and can't ever be again—the way they once were."

I don't find it easy to counter this. But I do ask him. "The way they were *when*, Maurice?"

He doesn't know—and of course I don't either.

"You cabled me you'd be wanting information," he says at last, seeing that he's touched the part of me I don't even touch. "What may I tell you?"

"What's the political situation here right now?"

"Precarious."

"In what sense?"

"The FI has just made an alliance with the FNSC—the FI being an umbrella of black independence parties—the FNSC a centrist group of whites. Between them they've gained a majority of the thirty-six seats in the Assembly."

"That's precarious? Why?"

"It gave the right-wing anti-independence groups an excuse to invade the assembly and to start fighting with the pro-independence groups. Fist-fighting and brawls! It is not to be believed!"

"Which of these political parties do you consider the most extreme?"

"That depends, does it not, on whether one is *for* or *against* separation from France."

"More, please, about these particular groups."

"Well, the most extreme is the Fédération Calédonienne. It demands total independence from France. It also demands the immediate return of land held by European settlers."

"Is this an all-Melanesian group?"

"On the contrary. It is uniquely all-French—French communists, many of them Stalinists. One suspects they believe that if the native population can regain their island, these enlightened communist benefactors could bring true paradise here with the Soviet navy. They have always been a radical group, but the past six months they have become almost frenzied, ever since the murder of their secretary-general."

"Tell me about that."

"There is little to tell. He was shot by two masked men at point-blank range early one morning last September when he stepped outside his apartment to leave for work. His killers have never been arrested."

"But you have your own idea who was behind it?"

"Of course."

"Well?"

"There is a secret organization here, so secret it has no name. We of the press call it our God-to-the-Right group. It is said to have originated back in Gaullist days when New Caledonia threw out the Vichy traitors and went with the Free French and the Allies. But in those simplistic times the issues were less ambiguous."

"How popular is this demand for independence? Among the people, not the politicians."

"By the people, do you mean the Melanesian people or the Europeans?"

"What *is* the balance?"

"There are sixty thousand Melanesians remaining in New Caledonia, most of them disadvantaged, both socially and economically. And there are almost that many French and Europeans, together with another thirty thousand Polynesians and Asians, who favor continuing links with Paris. If you were to put the issue of separation to a vote, there's no doubt of the outcome. The majority clearly prefers to stay part of France."

"So there's no chance of achieving autonomy by any democratic process? Not by popular vote?"

41

"Would you expect our wealthy Caldoches to give up land their grandfathers claimed and developed? Paris has finally set up a tribunal for the transfer of land back to the original Kanak owners, but this recent decree has only stiffened the resistance of the white owners. Would you Americans give Manhattan back to *your* Indians?"

"They can have my share of it."

"And you must also bear in mind that we're sitting on the world's largest deposit of nickel. This isn't just another exotic Pacific isle. It's God's own stash of minerals. Paris and London and Tokyo will all keep digging here until we're below sea level. Until then they'll never relinquish control of this place. Anyway, if they did, if they left us on our own, we'd be bankrupt in no time. Without economic assistance from home, our position here is untenable."

The waiter brings Maurice's cognac, then leaves. A bitch dog wanders through nosing for table scraps. Her underbelly sags with weighted teats, her eyes are desolate. At the bar two girls wearing sequined slacks are drinking beer and singing raucously off-key to a young man they share on the stool between them. They could be German or Danish. At an adjoining stool an older man, clearly a local who hasn't shaved in a week, huddles, trying to sip his aperitif, his back to them indignantly, his eyes appealing to the rest of us, can you imagine such indignity in the morning? For a moment I wonder where I have seen eyes like his before, then I glance again at the bitch dog as she passes and I see that her eyes are less desolate than his.

"What's the prevailing mood of the native population?" I ask Maurice. "Not the black politicians—the people?"

"The true natives, those still living in some semblance of their traditional past, are on the west coast, mostly up north," he tells me, "or in the outlying islands, particularly on the Loyalty group. The ones here in town live our lives. They are black Frenchmen."

"Could any of the tribes actually have come in here and pulled off those murders?"

"Why not? We had a full-scale rebellion here as recently as 1917, considerably later than the last time your Indians rose against you. And just this year a group of Melanesians virtually blockaded the roads into Nouméa as a show of power. But I find it hard to believe that any Kanaka would do these killings. Essentially, they're a gentle and loving people. And we've left them their yams, haven't we?"

Maurice, I remember now, has a tendency to get arch at times.

"Could they be stirred up by some agent provocateur?"

"One clever enough can stir up anybody, even the whites in Nouméa. Only a few years ago we had a general strike for greater local control of the mines. Until then it had been unthinkable that any local group would dare oppose the mining or farming consortiums. Now, aside from the separatists, it's the environmentalists who are kicking up sand. They claim that the mining and smelting operations are contaminating the shoreline. They want these operations closed down."

"You don't consider *them* extremists, do you?" I ask him.

"Dreamers," he says. "What good does it do to demonstrate or to strike in Nouméa, ten thousand miles away from where the decisions are made? Does it pinch any bellies in Paris? Not at all!"

I can see that he has no solution. The twentieth century has clearly arrived in New Caledonia.

"I need to be duked in," I tell him.

I'm expecting puzzlement and he doesn't disappoint me. "*Duked* in?"

"Out of my police vocabulary," I tell him. "It means getting somebody to slip you into the gang, undercover. To vouch for you."

"Into what group do you wish to be introduced?"

"The Hienghène tribe up north."

He laughs at this.

"You're the wrong color, for one thing. But even if you weren't, there's no bridge between us and them you could cross, not even if you spent fifty years here learning their language and their ways. Their culture is so radically different from ours, you could never make the crossover, even if they encouraged you."

"I didn't say I wanted to marry the chief's daughter. I simply need to satisfy some basic questions in my mind."

"I'll think about it," he says finally. "It is a matter of some delicacy—and danger. But I may know someone who could act as a go-between."

"Thanks, Maurice. Oh, and one other thing. Can you work me up a list of those political parties and their leaders? Right away?"

"Of course. I'll get it to you. Where will you be staying? On the boat?"

"I think not," I tell him. "But I'll be in touch."

I rise to leave. He drops a hand on my arm.

"Tell me, John, what *was* the logic of it?"

"Of what?"

"Of Vietnam."

"Counting the dead," I tell him. "There was no other logic."

He stays behind to finish his cognac.

In the Citroën the driver takes me past colonial houses with corrugated tin roofs rusted a flamingo pink.

We are on Route Territoriale No. 13.

The driver and I see it at exactly the same second—the truck stalled in front of us, blocking the highway.

I don't have to tell him his business.

He throws the limousine into reverse, smashing backward with the strong rear bumper into the car which has suddenly turned out of nowhere to close in behind us. Water spouts from its useless radiator as he spins the undamaged Citroën around and pounds for the shoulder of the road.

He almost gets us out, but a burst of automatic gunfire shatters the windshield and disintegrates his clean head.

Now, reaching for me, incoming rounds chew into the

car from both sides of the road and from the truck dead ahead.

I don't dare expose myself even long enough to reach over the front seat for the Uzi. It's me and the Browning now, and a big surprise for the bad guys outside. I roll out the back door, firing at the nearest ambush point, the embankment to my left.

The last thing ambushers ever expect is to be attacked. Their defense positions usually tend to be sloppy poor, since their fire lanes are set up primarily to rake the victims, who are supposed to attempt either to flee or to stay pinned down within the initial target area and be obliterated.

My unexpected counterattack and the Browning's fusillade as I run, low and weaving, to the left flank carry me over the embankment and into a ditch, where I find the bodies of two dark-skinned men I have shot while taking their position from them.

I've emptied the Browning in the process, but no sweat. The dead men have obligingly left me their two AK-47s, the Soviets' blessing upon the world. I take up the first of the two rifles and direct a full clip of closely interspersed fire at the truck down the road. It tries to run off, but the rounds probe its fuel tank. The truck explodes in a searing puff of black and red heat that I can feel even at this distance.

I pick up the other AK-47. It's time to tidy up the opposite side of the road.

I run low, crouching below the embankment's profile, and when I've gone fifty yards I wheel onto the highway into the billowing cover of the smoke from the burning truck. Quickly I gain the opposite side of Route 13.

From shelter, I sight down the embankment, back to where we'd been ambushed.

Three men are scampering away.

I stitch all three across the backs of their knees.

I need information, not corpses.

The three go down as though roped.

I ease toward them, keeping myself out of the line of return fire from their grounded position. They shoot back at me, wild and random.

I hold my fire. They're not going anywhere, any more than tobacco cans on a fence. I have all the time in the world. I hunch back, under cover, to wait. I hear an explosion.

One of them has used a grenade to kill himself and his two companions, holding it close to their temples as they crawl in close together sacrificially.

"Dumb bastards!" I scream.

I run forward recklessly, hoping a breath of life can be found somewhere in the bloody stew.

They were young.

They are Melanesian.

They are all dead.

From here and there, from traffic stopped yards away to either direction, stunned people are beginning to cluster.

I put the Browning in its holster, sling the AK-47 over my right shoulder, and walk to a gas station not more than a hundred yards away.

The attendant keeps wiping his face with an oily rag and staring at me and mumbling mon Dieu.

I ask him where his telephone is.

He points inside, his hand unhinged.

I go in and dial the number I had jotted down before I left police headquarters.

Bazin is at his desk when I call. Good man.

I suggest he come over, somewhere along Route 13 about six minutes out of downtown Nouméa, a spot where in less than three minutes a group of us has managed to trash the neighborhood. I ask him if he'll be kind enough before he leaves to call Marcel Gallante and tell him I may be late for lunch.

# CHAPTER

# 5

**W**hile I wait for Bazin, I sense thirst. I decide to get an orange Fanta from the gas-station vending machine. I remember I haven't had time to exchange my Aussie dollars for CFPs.

The man with the oily rag hastily obliges me. He finds the correct change in the pocket of his coveralls, delivers the bottle to me. He is anxious to please anybody with an AK-47. I thank him, let the lukewarm liquid sting my throat as I empty half the bottle. I advance to the pyramid of bodies the grenade has built. I settle down beside it to finish the Fanta.

I gaze at the havoc on the highway. The spectators are properly hushed and solemn, mothers cloaking their fascinated little boys from the grisliness. It's certainly not your run-of-the-afternoon fender-bender.

I let myself come back up in stages, making intuitive decompression stops on the way to the surface.

Once I'm steadied off, pulse normal, when the pure silence suddenly pops, clearing my ears for normal reception and I can hear the voices of the gathering crowd, hear a dog barking somewhere nearby, know I am back again among the living, I walk to the Citroën and look in at the man whose name I never knew—who would, given the choice, have died for me and who did, without the choice, do just that.

No need to verify. He is thoroughly terminal, has been since that opening fusillade took out the windshield and his face—one more reason I never ride in the back of a vehicle directly behind the driver. Those initial rounds are almost always funneled into that lane of fire.

I hear the strident two-note siren of the French police vans coming. Their sirens have always sounded more civilized to me than our American sirens yapping bloody murder, I suppose because I remember Vietnamese children pointing at fire engines and calling after them in a laughing chorus, "Cháy dâu? Cháy dâu?" "Fire where? Fire where?"

The inspector's car arrives first, a second police sedan directly behind it, then a van.

Bazin climbs out with immense energy, and I realize he probably works twenty hours a day, has no wife, no family, no life aside from this, if he can give so much of himself simply to getting out of a car. He is surrounded by other officers, but these are no shake-and-bake provincial clowns. They give off a no-nonsense professionalism as they fan out and go to work. I see crowd control put into effect. I see two officers beginning to interrogate possible witnesses. I see a couple of crime-lab types starting to collect spent casings and one officer taking photographs as though he knows what he's doing.

Of course Bazin saves me for himself.

"It would be ridiculous to ask what happened," he says as he hurries in, his eyes sweeping over the body of the dead driver.

"No," I say, "I don't think it would be ridiculous at all. Did you reach Gallante?"

"He is on the way."

"Well, Inspector, what happened is that that truck, the one still burning down there, pulled out in front of us. He"—I nod at the dead man behind the wheel—"made all the right moves. He backed into another car which came out of that side road over there to block our retreat, smashed its radiator, started to get us the hell out of here when the rest of them opened up from the point and both flanks—there and there . . ."

He stares over at the three heaped together, his photographer covering them from every angle.

"The driver was killed instantly," I continue.

"How many were there? Is it possible to estimate?"

"Nine," I tell him. "Two in the car behind us. They split, early on. Two over that embankment to the left. You'll find them where I left them. Two in the truck. Afraid they're too charred to be of much use. Then the three over there. They killed themselves with a grenade. Otherwise we would have had ourselves some live lobsters."

"Killed *themselves*?" he asks. "I find that difficult to understand. You are quite sure *you* didn't kill them?"

He is looking accusingly at the AK-47, as if the gun itself had exceeded all reason and on its own had deprived him of valuable witnesses. I have seen Ivy League interrogation officers equally vexed when Charley preferred death to interrogation.

"I shot them behind the kneecaps," I tell him. "When you examine the bodies, the sequence of events will become self-evident."

"An ambush by nine men! Seven dead, only two escape —and you untouched?"

"Congratulations, Inspector, or regrets?"

"Simply impressed. Extremely impressed. Counting the three from last night—that brings your total to ten in less than twenty-four hours. If I leave you unchecked for a week, it is quite possible you may personally eliminate our entire criminal population. The gun, please!"

For a moment I don't believe I have heard him. "The gun? *What* gun?"

"The AK-47!"

"No!" I cry, one hand going to the sling protectively. "I'm goddamned if you can have it! I put my butt on the line for this gun and it saved my life and I'm by God *not* going to give it to you!"

"You are overvaluing your cachet, monsieur!" he says coldly. Finally we are eyeball-to-eyeball, with no compromise in view. We are saved by the bell.

Marcel Gallante arrives in another Citroën limo. He has tough company, three young paratroopers carrying submachine guns.

Gallante looks at me for only a second, mutters Thank God you're alive, then he's at the front seat of the ambushed car and staring in with disbelief at the dead driver.

"What was his name?" I ask.

"André."

"Sorry about this," I say. I've said it a hundred times before and meant it just as passionately every time. "I feel we both could have gotten out if they hadn't caught him with their opening rounds."

"He was like a son," Gallante says. "I offered him any number of positions in the company, but he was a simple man. He liked to drive, he liked to fish. He was saving his earnings. To buy a fishing boat."

He turns to face me.

"I wish to renegotiate your contract."

"I wouldn't recommend that," I say. "Not after *this* little tea party. I have to tell you, my first day in this tiny corner of paradise is causing me to have second thoughts about the degree of congeniality I can expect around here."

"When we reached our agreement," he continues, as though not having heard me, "you told me you work only one way—either for nothing, or for double the original offer. Is that not correct?"

"That's right. Unless I score, no payment. *If* I score, the fee doubles. That's the way I like it."

"I propose an amended arrangement. Bring me the man behind this, I will double what we agreed upon."

"Double the double? Four-hundred percent over scale?"

He nods.

"Why?"

"I feel a personal responsibility for André's death."

"I accept—on one condition. Buy him his fishing boat."

"I'd buy him a fleet if it would bring him back to life."

"Buy it out of the increase in my fee. Deduct it from what you pay me if I deliver."

"You are quite serious, aren't you?"

"About this, yes. Give it to his brother, if he has a brother. To his son, if he has one. Or to his wife or mother or father or uncle—or the village—*some*one who will name it after him and tend to its engine and wash its decks and give it honest work at sea."

"Consider it done," he says.

Bazin, who has left us alone for reasons of his own, reappears.

"There are no deceased behind the embankment," he accuses.

"Then they've taken their dead," I suggest. "Standard guerrilla ops. But you'll still find some more shell casings. And probably blood samples in the soil. As I recall, they were both head shots."

"The gun, please."

So he's back on that again, his hand outstretched, demanding, all the presumption of Napoleonic law behind it.

I grip the sling. Two can play the relentless game.

"Monsieur, I do not wish to place you under arrest!"

Gallante has been listening only peripherally. Now he intervenes.

"What is this?" he demands of Bazin. "Do you expect him to survive with a pistol in a climate of automatic weapons? A climate, I remind you, that neither you nor your men appear able to predict or control."

"It remains a felony," Bazin points out, maintaining a judicious balance between respect and warning, "for a private citizen to possess a fully automatic firearm in New Caledonia. Aside from that inescapable fact, this particular weapon is needed as evidence."

"Evidence of what?" Gallante cries. "Look around you! Have you not evidence enough?"

Bazin arches a rueful eyebrow. "It would appear so, sir."

"Let me ask you," Gallante says curtly, "may French military personnel carry automatic weapons on duty?"

"But of course!"

"Do you wish to put me through the trouble of having this gentleman appointed an officer in the French Territorial Forces, on temporary duty advising the troops the Governor-General has already assigned to our installations?"

Bazin is the only man I have met who can sigh through his pores, the unheard yet seen exhalation of a suffering saint. He stoops his shoulders slightly, as though under the lash, bows his head in mute acceptance, the very picture of the unjustly oppressed. "I would find that a lamentable invasion of your valuable time," he murmurs. And then I see him looking archly my way. "However, if I may pursue the issue for one final moment, I would like to ask M. Locke why he insists on keeping *this* particular gun, especially in view of the fact it is not easy to obtain additional rounds for it. Would he not—this is merely a suggestion—take more comfort, say, in that Uzi there in the front seat, a weapon which, unhappily, was never used, yet which was in fact properly issued to your unfortunate driver with all the necessary permits? Unlimited supplies of ammunition are available for *it*—and since M. Locke is a weapons expert I am certain he holds the Uzi in high regard, knowing it to be the ultimate tool for urban use."

"You asking *me*—or Mr. Gallante?"

"Either, or both. As you wish."

"Then *I'll* tell you why I intend to keep this gun. Whoever planned this ambush is obviously escalating the balance of terror. He *wants* us to know that what's coming down is a lot more significant than four tribal killings among Mr. Gallante's project engineers. Take my case. Last night it was clubs and spears in the dark, a long way from shore. This afternoon it's automatic weapons in broad daylight right outside the center of town. It's illogical to use this much force to try and eliminate me. The whole regatta has to be only a diversion."

Bazin assumes the face of a man contemplating a dinosaur abruptly poking a toothy snout out of a downtown manhole.

"A diversion for *what*?"

"If we knew, we wouldn't be standing around rapping, would we? You told me we'd only seen the tip of the iceberg, right? That you suspect a broad conspiracy, politically motivated? Okay, I agree."

"We are discussing that AK-47," he says quietly. "I fail to see the connection between my feelings about a political conspiracy and your felonious possession of a forbidden firearm."

"I *need* an enemy gun," I tell him, "because they weren't using either French or American ordnance!"

"You tend to lose me at times, monsieur. How can you know they were not using French or American guns?"

"From the sound of their gunfire."

He appears to be nodding out again, but by now I know better. His mind, with its geared catalogue of infinite reference, is already confirming what a lot of us have reason to know—that nations, in some kind of bizarre mythologizing of their own, seem to produce weapons that reflect, either in performance, sound, or appearance, certain unique national traits. I remember times when, hearing the familiar argumentativeness of nearby Kalashnikovs, I'd find myself invariably matching up the sounds of their firing with Russian words I know.

"If they get me in the pocket again," I tell him, "and I use the AK-47, I'll blend. They have to *see* me to hit me. At least they won't be able to target me on the basis of gunfire sound."

"Is Monsieur Locke free to leave now, or have you additional questions?" Gallante demands. I expect steam to spout from his nostrils at any second.

"No others at this moment, sir."

Gallante, indicating I should follow, stalks off with the pace of an indignant heron.

I need a moment alone with Bazin.

"Couple of things you'd better know," I tell him. "I'm not a smartass. I don't enjoy having to watch your deferential performance whenever you're outranked. You're too good at your job to have to pull your forelock and do a tapdance. But we're all outranked at one time or another, so no hard feelings on that score, okay?"

He doesn't answer. I perceive myself as the butterfly, net

descending. Clearly, Bazin wants me in his personal collection. Preferably mounted. In a locked and sealed case, labeled in Latin.

I give him a retrieving opportunity.

"I also want you to know I don't do power trips."

"I do not understand this phrase, 'power trip.' "

"Ego-massage, self-stroking."

Once more he looks as though he's about to doze off, but he finally acknowledges understanding by the flutter of his eyelids.

"Okay," I say, trying to wrap it up for him, a lifetime of living in a quick laundry bag of words, "I've told you what I'm *not*. Now I'll tell you what I *am*. I'm in the dragon-stomping business. You understand what I'm saying? The bread I earn, enough to keep me moving on—and moving on is what I'm committed to—I earn by dealing one-on-one with the shitheads who breathe fire. In that company you never turn the other cheek. But in your case I'm willing to make all kinds of concessions because I have this gut feeling we can work together and make it fly. So that's how I'm going to play it. I'm expecting you to reciprocate. But please stop with the goddamned games! You have this annoying mannerism—opening and closing your eyes in the middle of a sentence, then letting the clock run. It's sending me up the wall. It wastes a lot of time and it's monotonous. Anybody ever told you that?"

"My wife mentions it constantly."

I suddenly bog down and don't try to hide it.

"You didn't picture me with a wife, did you?"

"No," I confess. "I had you listed with the loners."

I hold out my hand. "Can we start from here?"

He accepts my hand. And by God deliberately closes his eyes and laughs.

Bazin, laughing?

"You *are* baroque!" I tell him.

My last day as a cop I did a drug bust in Pacific Heights, a spacey girl with hair like an airedale caught in the rain. She listened with astonishment to the tiny click of the cuff closing around her bony wrist, just below the tracks running up her arm as far east as Kansas City. She peered at me from some empty cosmos and whispered, "Cuffs? On *me*? Do *I* look threatening?" Standard operating procedure, I'd said, one of those snap-ass goodies you toss off without thinking in jobs like that. And then she hit me with, "You poor miserable lost bastard. Are you ever baroque!" It occurred on the pinnacle of a hill, on upper Union Street, where I observed, at my moment of indictment, over the suspect's accusatory shoulders, a respectable-looking family backing out of a narrow-gauge garage in a nineteen-seventy-three maroon Olds, the family on the way to a horse show and an afternoon of togetherness. The wind was out of the west at the moment, as it usually is on that hill, but despite watching the Olds back out and noticing the boats on the Bay, I even had time to note the wind wrapping the tattered hems of surplus-store layered skirts around the scabby ankles of the girl in handcuffs. It was another of those classic stretched-out moments and I found myself repeating out loud—Baroque? Baroque? Nobody had ever called me *that* before! I started to laugh, out of some cosmos of my own. I laughed just as Bazin had a moment ago when he wanted to show me he is still essentially intact as a human, not entirely gone to stone as a symbol. I unlocked the cuffs, horseshoed them into Union Street and told her to scat, go do your thing, play out your dumb little scenario. Why should the good people of San Francisco, particularly those en route to horse shows or those jibing furiously to avoid piling up on the rocks outside the barroom window of the St. Francis Yacht Club, stand in the way of your death wish?

There are all kinds of rushes. Mine was the rush of discovery that right about then I had uncuffed myself too, made still one more crossover. A certain reservoir of humor is needed to survive as a cop in San Francisco—or in New Caledonia for that matter—but when you start patting them good-bye and throwing the key away just because they call you baroque, you are definitely no longer police material.

Bazin, I am reassured to see, does not have the same

hilarious response I had back there in San Francisco that freighted afternoon I packed it in as an officer of the law.

Without further valedictory, our bond apparently sealed in laughter, he permits me to buzz off toward Gallante, fretting at his limousine, with his three troopers, sub-machine guns at ready, triangulated around him.

Gallante gestures me into the back. Two paratroopers get in after us, hunch into the jumpseats and face out-ward, one to either side. The third trooper stations himself up front with the driver. Among us we have more fire-power than the English longbowmen at Agincourt.

Before the driver can mesh gears and slide us away, I discover a boy of five outside, one of the spectators at our little roadside puppet show. Fascinated by our bristling guns, he stares in and zealously picks a stubby, upturned nose. Suddenly he digs out the Hope Diamond, or so his expression conveys. Innocently, he flips the monstrous bugger. It strikes the outside of the glass directly before my gaze and clings like primordial ooze. Plunked straight be-tween the eyes, I acknowledge, in spite of so many compe-tent bodyguards, and I smile, baffling Gallante, who, since my surviving the ambush, has come to believe I can walk on water. I look at the snot on the window. I look at the dead men being humped toward an ambulance. I look at Gallante checking his Piaget in two time zones and I won-der again why the really good moments are always so incongruous. Can it be that irrelevance in the midst of crisis is the only thing we can count on?

We drive into country, away from the creep of laundro-mats, supermarkets, and gas stations, the silence among us forged stronger with each kilometer, until twenty somber minutes later we turn off the highway onto a secondary road. It tunnels through bordering columns of pin colon-naire, the stately New Caledonia pines.

We stop at a barrier pole of rusty iron thrust out from a roadside guardhouse, a three-man detachment deployed behind it, all three soldiers armed with automatic weapons. At the sight of Gallante inside the accredited limousine, they briskly elevate the pole and let the car pass through and up toward a settlement of colonial structures I can just now see leaning above us like some ancient walled monastery tumbling along a hill in Tuscany. Brahmin cattle nibble the pasture at the base of the rise and I note how the early afternoon sunlight bounces off their vanilla-colored hides and leaks away in subtle, shimmering rays to be caught and absorbed by emerald grass high as their hocks. Or so my mother would paint this landscape were she here within this exact fragment of time.

The dirt road feeds into a cobblestone lane passing through a square fronted by a Norman church. The cross on the steeple leans thirty perilous degrees to one side, Christ's symbol on this heathen mountainside in jeopardy of tumbling down at any moment, it would appear.

Gallante has been watching to see if I might notice.

"A typhoon did that," he says, curious foreboding in his voice. "Sixty-seven years ago this fourteenth of July— the night my brother André was born . . . in the chapel . . . on the altar. Our family had taken refuge from the storm . . ."

Although we have driven past the church, Gallante has pivoted in his seat to stare out the back window at the cross on its beam high above us. I detect apprehension in his eyes. Strange, after sixty-seven years. And his telling me has a hollow, ritualized cadence, as though he's said it many times before. Possibly only to himself?

"I guess fixing something like that takes time," I say— certainly not the best I can do, but Gallante's overkill attitude about the church and its dangling cross needs amplification. I hope my offhand response will challenge him to keep talking.

But he turns in his seat, his eyes avoiding mine, and nods toward the colonial chateau directly ahead.

I follow his gaze. The chateau dominates its hill, no woodline encroaching within a thousand yards at any point. High stone wings, moss-covered, with gun slits, extend from either flank, designed to protect the central block from direct assault. Give me a company of good men and I could hold this position against a division.

The limousine stops at a wooden gate, crumbly as old cheese, its black porous planks strapped with stout iron. Paratroopers on duty inside heave the gates open and we roll into a courtyard spacious enough to accommodate a regiment's dress parade. Both military and civilian vehicles have been parked in precise rows, except for a red BB-512 Ferrari loitering insouciantly to one side as though not deigning to be associated with such ham-fisted machines as half-tracks and personnel carriers.

Gallante lets our paratroopers out first.

I'm next, then Gallante.

He watches my eyes snapping all of it in, not least the proud tricolor streaming from the pole atop the central turret of the chateau.

"Bienvenue, monsieur," he says, "to la Ferme de St. Paul. In an earlier century it was a fort. Then a peaceful farm. Now a fort again."

I count at least twenty more paratroopers at various duty positions throughout the area, then I concentrate on the incongruity of the sensuous little five-liter Boxer Ferrari trapped within the austere motor pool.

"My niece's car," Gallante says. This is one of the obligations victimizing Gallante—his need to supply the explanation for whatever it is one questions with a mere look. I wonder, does he do this with everyone or only with me? "She had it flown in from la Côte d'Azur."

He leads me toward regimental steps rising higher than my head to a massive stone entrance.

"Her name is Rosine. She is considered one of the most beautiful girls in France," he tells me as we approach the steps.

"We're not in France," I say, with no idea what it is that prompts me to say anything so graceless at this moment, but I feel he's driving at something and I wish he would simply say it. I wish everyone would simply come right out and say it, every time, if only to save time, because that's what we're all running out of, mostly. Time.

"She has no idea why you're here," he continues.

"Any reason why not?" I ask.

"We never discuss business with her," he says. "Anyway, she will seek to distract you. One of the things I've found out about you is that you are not easily distracted, even by beautiful women. Am I correct?"

"I am not easily distracted by anything," I tell him. "I don't consider that a virtue, but it happens to be the way I am."

"Nevertheless," he says, "I must warn you—Rosine is a haunted child. Her husband was killed only three months ago in a roadside accident. Driving his Ferrari on the upper Corniche just outside Èze."

"Matched set?" I ask. "His-and-her Ferraris?"

"Yes," he says. "My wedding gift to them. Rosine is only nineteen. We still overindulge her."

He detains us at the foot of the stairs.

"M. Locke," he pleads, "if she should ask you to go driving—don't."

"Why not?"

"She is suicidal. She hungers to die. But not alone. Do you understand?"

"No," I say.

His eyes stay on mine until he can find the calm water, the sure center, and is no longer concerned that I may let the Lady of the Lake carry me off before I can do the work I came to do for him.

"You must be famished," he says. "I apologize for the inordinate delay."

We hurry up the stairs.

I discover a girl waiting above us.

Because she is further back on the threshold and the rise is so steep, I see her face first—the vision hanging there—and instantly I know I'll remember this first glimpse of her for whatever time may remain to me. Then as I continue up the stairs, I see her in segments even while I comprehend her as a complete person, standing there waiting for me, as if she's always known I've been on my way to her, a tall, supple girl with a gold cross around her neck, but breasts open to the world under a silk blouse tied at her tiny waist, her skirt slit fashionably to the top of her thigh, but teased closed here and there with buckles of pure gold.

"Permit me," Gallante says with incredible formality, since he must certainly sense the instantaneous current between the girl and me. "My niece, Rosine de Lacouture. M. John Locke."

Her hand and mine meet. We recognize simultaneously that this first touch is merely the beginning. We smile acknowledgment to each other.

But I feel a cold stab between my ribs. Beyond the excitement in her eyes, I see another, truer frontier, a dark wasteland of despair, a silent countryside of death, and this is where she is heading, this is where her heart searches, out where there is no road back. I see it in her eyes, the way I could inevitably see it in the eyes of the troopers in my unit who would be killed by the enemy that day, the first shadow of the owl that calls for all of us, calling to Rosine now, and she answering, even while she's smiling at me.

"M. Gallante!"

A soldier from far left on the long porchway trots toward Gallante, waving urgently.

Gallante leaves Rosine alone with me.

She speaks to me in French. "You do not have the look of a man who has just been shot at."

They must have already told her I have her language. What else have they told her? Gallante has said they do not talk business in front of her.

"Have you seen many men who have just been shot at?" I ask in French.

"None," she says. "Possibly this explains the heightened feeling I experienced when I first saw you."

"I am desolated it is merely that," I smile, but saying it in French makes it come out not only palatably, but convincingly.

Gallante returns, his shoulders contracted as if he had been sledged on the spine, his haggard face more drawn than ever.

"The Treasury in Nouméa has just been bombed," he announces gravely. "Nineteen people are known to be dead, sixty injured, children among them."

*"Bombed?"* I ask.

"Plastique," he says. "Timed to detonate as everyone returned for business and the avenue outside was crowded with afternoon shoppers. You were right, of course. Their ambush of you and André was simply the diversion for this attack."

"Can you loan me a car?" I ask. "Not a driver, no troopers. Just a car."

Rosine's eyes dance. "I'll drive you."

"No need to go rushing back," Gallante says firmly, his look rebuking Rosine and rejecting her offer on my behalf. "Bazin will provide us with the police report later this afternoon. Meanwhile, we have other matters to discuss. And a long-delayed lunch to be enjoyed, in spite of this tragic event."

"I knew you weren't just another engineer," Rosine says to me.

"Is that what I was supposed to be?" I ask Gallante.

He shrugs. "Very well," he admits to the girl. "This gentleman is an outside investigator. But your father and I prefer it not be generally known."

"Except to those who shoot at him?"

He dismisses this. "Would you please tell Georges we are ready?"

She goes inside.

I feel as though someone has just switched off the lights, left me in darkness. I shake my head at the pure pity of my condition. Locke, I tell myself, call down God's simple mercy upon your foolish head. You have not come all this way to New Caledonia to let the sight, sound, touch, and smell of a new woman turn you away from the central certainty that only the guiding scent of cordite and scorched iron are worthy of man's pursuit in this shitstorm world.

I clear my thoughts of Rosine.

"Something's bothering me," I say to Gallante.

"What is that?"

"The season for storms in this part of the world, in the Southwest Pacific hurricane belt, is December to March. You said it happened in July—the tropical cyclone that bent the cross on your church. You absolutely sure about that?"

"July fourteen, at ten o'clock that night, in the year 1916. It is a matter of record."

"Why does it frighten you?"

His eyes shift away from me, as though tracking a circling wasp.

"I should not have mentioned it," he says finally, trying to close the book. "It concerns our family only. It has no bearing on the work you have to do. Believe me, monsieur."

"Why haven't you had the cross straightened and reinforced?"

"I would have—ten thousand times before now," he cries, unable to restrain whatever it is that frightens him, "but my mother would permit no one to touch it—and my brother has perpetuated the nonsense."

"What nonsense?"

"The boucan."

"That's a word I don't know."

"Spell . . . curse. It's a New Caledonian term."

"A curse against the cross?"

"Against us—against the family, the Gallante clan. Come," he urges, "my brother is impatient about only one thing—not eating food when it is ready to be served."

But he sees I am not going to let go of it.

"Very well, monsieur, if you insist. The night my brother was born—in that church, at the height of the storm—our mother was dying in childbirth. Georges's father had not yet been able to fight his way with the doctor through the winds up from Nouméa to this place—in those days the road was little more than a wagon trail. A Kanaka seer, interceding between my mother and his pagan gods, saved her life. Melanesian midwives, chanting in the ancient tongue of the people, delivered my brother. He was born with incantations and to the burning of secret leaves and sacred yams and bits of bone on the altar. Our father broke into the church at a critical moment in the ceremony and screamed blasphemy for what he assumed was the desecration of a Catholic altar—that church has been the family chapel for more than a century—and he pitched the seer out into the night. Those who were there have said that lightning blazed on all sides of the old Kanaka, but he stood untouched and pointed his finger at the cross, and immediately the wind struck it, bending it as you now see it. And he cried out his curse: that if anyone touched it a Gallante would suffer . . . and that the child born that night would die when the cross fell of its own accord in time to come . . . and that with his death the Gallante clan—all of us—would end forever."

Somehow he seems relieved to have told me the story. Yet there is still a puzzling part.

"If your father was so unsympathetic to the native ceremony—and to the fact that the seer had actually saved your mother and brother—why didn't he have the cross straightened, reinforced, just to prove the curse was empty?"

Gallante drops his eyes. He appears to be studying his feet. I observe that they are unusually large for a Frenchman.

"He did. The very next morning. He ordered a ladder secured to the steeple. He insisted on doing the work himself. But he never completed it. He fell the moment he reached for the cross."

Fell? To his death? Then who fathered this man, this man I've assumed is Georges's brother?

As though reading my undisguised thoughts, Gallante replies, "He did not die from the fall. Not just then. He lived another two years and three months, confined to a wheelchair and in terrible pain. He died the day after I was born."

In the telling, Gallante has managed, whether deliberately or not I can't be sure, to create an aura of necromancy about his father's death, if not, in fact, about his own birth.

I file the story under To Be Accounted For and let my

thoughts rush elsewhere—to the bottle with my name float-ing inside. In my mind I see it sitting in the nav station next to the sextant aboard *Steel Tiger*. And then, for some inexplicable reason, I no longer see it. Somehow I know it has been removed. Somebody has come aboard and taken it away. Must be to release me from its spell—or to replace the bottle, so far ineffectual, with a more lethal curse. Must be, yeah.

"You think I am foolish to be concerned?" Gallante's voice sounds as though it's coming from the bottom of an abandoned well. I realize I have traveled away from him in the past few seconds. I haul myself back in time and place to the chateau.

"No," I tell him. "I do not think you are foolish. And yes, I am famished. Starved!"

We enter for lunch.

# CHAPTER

# 6

**T**hree of us wait at a table long enough to service a company of Crusaders, Gallante at one end, Rosine across from me, a fourth, still unoccupied place at the far end. The dining table occupies the center of a vaulted stone room hung with museum-quality tapestries.

A man enters almost joyously behind a serving cart pushed by a fat elderly Melanesian woman shimmering within a red and yellow mission dress, a scarlet band spanning her imperturbable forehead, her eyes taking no notice of me, or of anyone else for that matter.

The man is wearing a chef's hat and a spotless white apron. He bears only the faintest resemblance to his younger brother, Marcel Gallante, my storklike employer. Georges does not look more than fifty, although I know he will be sixty-eight this fourteenth of July. He is wearing a pin-striped suit. Ben Franklin glasses perch on the bridge of his nose, gold chains dangling from either frame and looped around his neck, the chains swaying with every movement of his animated, youthful face. Above the lenses his incredibly blue eyes blaze with good humor, as though he's the author of a thousand private jokes. I like him at once, since I can see past this outer conviviality layers of living and sensing and feeling within the man, like a reef descending for a hundred fathoms, life at every stratum.

He extracts a bottle of wine from a silver ice bucket shaped like a flying fish. Coming to me he pours a thimble-ful of white wine—a Bordeaux, I see, of a year I had been told could no longer be had—into my glass. I smell it with

65

the delicacy such vintage merits and then taste it and smile up at the man awaiting my approval. He half-fills all four glasses, returns the wine to the ice bucket, seats himself at the head of the table, satisfies himself that we all have our first course in front of us.

He raises his glass to me.

"I feel our troubles will soon be over," he says, toasting me. "Welcome!"

"Before we drink," I say, "I'd like to be sure I know with whom I'm drinking. You *are* Georges Gallante?"

He laughs, wagging a naughty-boy finger at his brother Marcel at the far end of the table. "You neglected to tell our friend I am also the chef around here?"

"Forgive me," Marcel apologizes. "I'm afraid I had other things on my mind. But, of course, this is my brother Georges."

I raise my glass to the chef—and we drink. I feel Rosine's eyes on me, but I avoid looking at her. I suspect I could not mask my feelings.

"This first course," Georges announces, "together with the entrée, I prepared in your honor. They are from Indochina, this one being salade de pamplemousse à la vietnamienne. Tell me if it pleases you."

I taste the salad. It is exquisite. It brings back memories of a week in Dalat.

"The secret," Georges confides, "is the sesame seed."

"It's marvelous," I say.

"We must talk about your war sometime," Georges says.

"If you wish," I reply, politely. "After *this* one is settled."

Both brothers glance at Rosine, who has quickly finished her wine. She appears not to have heard my remark.

"Cooking has become my passion since I retired," Georges says.

"I wasn't aware you had retired," I say. "The information I was given is that you're still chairman of the board of SFPCP."

"In an advisory capacity only. But in fact Marcel now runs the company. I left Paris last year—permanently. To spend the rest of my days here where I was born. As one reaches his final years, he seeks ways to extend his time. Nobody knows how to do that more effectively than our native Caledonians. Their time is symbolic time—time outside time. So I have come to live here, where the people refuse to let clocks devour them. In any event, I've taken great pleasure in cooking. Is the salad really to your taste?"

I hold up my bone-clean plate.

Georges smiles at me, claps his hands.

The Melanesian woman wearing the scarlet headband appears with the entrée.

"Des crabes à la vietnamienne," Georges announces. "Here the secret is to flame the dish with cognac and to add a sauce of nuoc-mam, which I get directly from Ho-Chi-Minh-Ville."

"Saigon," I correct. I have not yet been able to accept Hanoi's arrogant renaming of a city that lingers so painfully in my memory.

"Alas, no longer," Georges says, pleasantly enough. But I decide not to let it go so casually.

"Then let us call it by its historical name," I say. "Let us call it Gia Dinh, as the Vietnamese themselves called it before your country invaded Indochina and renamed the conquered city Saigon."

Georges appears enchanted that I have challenged him and thrown down the gauntlet to the Empire.

"Bravo!" he applauds. He gestures to his younger brother. "More wine, please, Marcel."

Marcel quickly circles the table with the wine as Georges continues to regard me with benign approval.

"Modern colonialism," he says, "was devised when the West discovered it was more practical to conquer people's things than their minds. Of course, the communists have notched that up a degree or two by conquering minds first, then taking people's things. But it's still colonialism, isn't it, whether it's yours, ours, or theirs?"

Rosine tosses down her wine, pushes back her chair.

"Excuse me," she says to her father.

"For dessert," he tells her, "I have made a charming little gâteau de riz au caramel. Actually, it's Indonesian, not Vietnamese, but I can recommend it without reservation."

Rosine runs from the room.

Georges's smile hangs dying on his face. His glasses slip from his nose, dangle around his neck by the twin gold chains. He appears to have aged. He stares at the doorway through which his daughter has vanished.

"She expects you to go after her," he says to me.

"Should I?"

"No."

We finish the crab in silence. Then the dessert is wheeled in.

Dessert with more silence.

Georges leads Marcel and me onto a terrace overlooking the distant pastures and the immobile blots of Brahmin cattle.

I accept coffee, decline the cognac.

"Now," Georges announces crisply, revealing the man capable of running a billion-dollar conglomerate, "we may talk. I have always found it helpful to ask anyone working in my behalf the simplest, most direct of all questions. How do *you* perceive your job? What do you think we expect of you? And what do you expect of yourself?"

"My job here is clear enough," I say. "I'm hunting Running Dog."

"Running Dog?"

"The honcho. The jefe. There's always a jefe. I intend to track him down, then to neutralize him."

"You mean, assassinate him?"

"If he comes quietly, I'll deliver him to Bazin. If he has other ideas, I'll leave him where I drop him."

Georges studies me through his snifter of cognac.

"How many men have you killed?"

"I count only the friends I lose."

He nods approvingly.

"All right, so you're in New Caledonia to find Running Dog. What else?"

"There is nothing else. When I find him, these little demos of violence and terror which are currently showcasing around town will come to an immediate end. The curtain will fall. Fini."

"Then you don't think this is a broad-based native rebellion?"

"No, I do not. I did tell Bazin I agree with him there's conspiracy here, probably politically motivated, but this definitely isn't a people's war. Just a band of sorry-assed terrorists, not very well trained, piss-poor fire control, not at all a cohesive unit. However, they are being supplied with heavy-duty firepower, so they've got good connections —and good connections always involve politics, either of the left or right. In this case their weapons are Soviet. Still, in my considered opinion this is not a neorevolutionary guerrilla activity. If it were, the leaders would be seeking to exploit contradictions in the imperialist camp. They'd be employing the national salvation theme, using a united-front concept—and most important of all setting up cadres in rural bases. I have no information that any of these typical prerequisites are being met."

"This is truly your field, isn't it?" Georges says, a note of admiration in his voice.

"These days," I tell him, "it should be everybody's field."

"Without doubt," he says, "you have the correct concept of your job. Has Marcel told you what this means to us?"

"He has," I say.

"I would like to hear it from you, if I may."

"Okay. There's something like fifty-five million dollars of risk capital at stake in the installation of the high-tech satellite system your company is installing here. If there are any further killings of your staff, the installation will come to an abrupt stop. Your demoralized engineers will fly home to Paris and no replacements will be volunteering. You'll miss your contract deadlines, and blow fifty-five million. That's point one. Point two: If social unrest escalates in New Caledonia it will quickly spread to your nickel mines and refineries. This will affect the country's main export, even the national balance of payments. Point three: If the country goes into economic depression, labor unrest will turn into national strikes, then to civil disobedience, riots, and massive property destruction, finally to racial war between the white population and the natives."

"Dominoes," he says solemnly. "It starts with an old friend being bitten to death by red-specked spiders and it ends in revolution. Yes, M. Locke, I would say you have a precise grasp of our situation. Marcel, I congratulate you on enlisting this gentleman."

"It was not easy," Marcel says. "He insisted that he had a personal obligation which took priority, something that couldn't wait."

"But it did wait?" Georges asks me.

"It's waited all these years," I say. "It can wait a little longer."

Of course, out of courtesy, neither man asks me what it is I was doing in the Coral Sea in the first place when Marcel Gallante reached me on my SSB radio. I am not sure if they had asked me at this moment whether I would have told them. But then I might have, for it is something I've dreamed of doing ever since I was a boy, and I have no reason not to discuss it, even though it is a quest many people might not understand—sailing *Steel Tiger* to the exact coordinates on the chart where my grandfather crashed his Wildcat Navy fighter and sank, hard by the spot where the *Lexington* went down in twenty-four hundred fathoms of water. That was a morning in early May, forty years ago. As a child, whenever they told me the story, I always pictured the triumphant Zeke with its symbolic orange meatballs buzzing my grandfather's final splash-in—an example of sheer technological superiority, for my grandfather was a natural flier, a real birdman, yet no matter how good you are you can't outclimb pursuing machine guns when your kite will only give you eleven hundred feet a minute at full bore to the enemy's easy three thousand. For years I have thought of sailing a boat of my own to this smoothed-over, no-trace cemetery and heaving to there for a few days, feeling the shifting depths between me and my turned-to-coral grandfather fourteen thousand feet below, and saying a few appropriate words of thanks to the man who brought my father into existence and through my father give me to life. It is the very least I can do and something I want with all my heart. And I shall do it, I shall sail out to where they fought the first great carrier battle of any war, the Battle of the Coral Sea, out toward Point Buttercup, latitude 16 degrees south, longitude 161 degrees and 45 minutes east, out to where Cincpac ordered Rear Admiral Fitch to rendezvous with Admiral Fletcher commanding the *Yorktown* task force then operating out of Nouméa.

I shall do it after I find Running Dog.

Unless Running Dog finds me first.

A trooper, this one an officer, appears. He's bearing documents from Inspector Bazin—the police report of the Treasury bombing this afternoon.

Georges and Marcel share the pages, then hand them to me. I scan them swiftly. I have seen scores of such reports. They tell little.

"Why," I ask, "has nobody taken credit for this? Doesn't that strike you as peculiar?"

"Not at all," Marcel replies. "The instant we know what group is behind this, they know we shall be upon them. This may be a large island, this Grande Terre, but it still remains an island. Where could they hide?"

I have already studied topographical maps of New Caledonia, preparing myself. "I could hide an army on this island," I tell him. "And I'll make a prediction. The next time they strike, they will make their declaration. I'm beginning to be able to sense the timetable in their operations."

"Timetable?" Georges asks, his interest peaking.

"That's what is coming through to me," I tell him. "There's something planned about all this. It seems to be advancing according to some schedule. It feels . . . orchestrated. And that's why I know it's not being led by Mela-

71

nesian tribesmen. I doubt that their minds run that way. I'm not saying that local warriors haven't been recruited—those unfriendlies who braced me offshore were definitely Melanesian, and the gunmen today—same bunch. But Running Dog is either European or Asian. This thing is programmed to go somewhere, somewhere big. I feel it, the way I can feel weather forming over the horizon."

"Remarkable," Georges comments.

"Assuming M. Locke right in his assumption," Marcel adds, "we should contact Paris at once. There is still time to have a major ship of the line sent to Nouméa for the celebration on July 14. The *Rochemont* is presently at Papeete. She could be here before the fourteenth."

"Yes," Georges agrees. "By all means. Do that, Marcel. Do it today!"

Georges looks at me. "To help us celebrate Bastille Day on the fourteenth, the Navy is sending us a frigate. The harbor fireworks are scheduled to be launched from her decks. But I agree with Marcel. Under the circumstances, it might be prudent to have a lot more firepower available in the harbor than a frigate can provide. A cruiser would serve us better. Particularly the *Rochemont*. She is the latest guided-missile battle cruiser in the French Navy. She has enough range and firepower to reach any inland command post."

He strides away from Marcel and me, stands looking out across the green domain at his feet, his property as far as the eye can reach.

"We tamed this land once before," he says without bothering to look back at me. "We tamed it with conscienceless companies of riflemen who went out among the tribes and taught the tayos they might occasionally eat Englishmen and Protestants, but never French Catholics. Possibly the time has come when this lesson must be taught again."

It is the last thing I am to hear him say that afternoon. He stands planted there, transporting himself into the past, when New Caledonia was still a cannibal island and the French hold upon its native population precarious, sustained only by muskets and artillery and occasional punitive gunboats.

I look at his proud back and even though I have a French mother I am tempted to dislike him for what he represents, his inherent conviction that the French enjoy a cultural superiority to the rest of the world. He may be right, but it's poor taste for him to insist upon open acknowledgment of this possibility.

For a moment I feel I must tell him that in Vietnam the French conquerors rewrote the schoolbooks for their Vietnamese vassals, so that Indochinese students of tender ages were given only the French version of the history of the rest of the world. I must tell him that I have seen schoolbooks in Saigon which, in describing the growth of the American West and our Gold Rush, dwelt not on our emerging democratic society, but rather on the mistreatment by the miners of the first Chinese in California. This is the way the American treats the Asian, the books taught the Vietnamese children. Is it any wonder that generations grew up to distrust the big-noses when we came with our tanks and warplanes? As Georges has just said, it was acceptable for New Caledonian cannibals to eat Englishmen, but never Frenchmen.

Marcel signals to me that the interview is over.

I walk out with him, without thanking Georges for the tailored lunch, but Marcel assures me his brother needs no thanks nor compliments. He himself is the judge of whether his cuisine has been up to his personal standards. I stop only long enough to retrieve the AK-47 I have leaned into a corner in the hallway.

"Stay here a few days," Marcel urges as I resume walking toward the entrance. "Formulate your plans. Then make your moves. Here you will be safe."

"Here I will accomplish nothing," I tell him.

We come out into the courtyard.

The red Ferrari glides up, brakes with a scattering of pebbles alongside the bottom step.

Rosine is at the wheel, a silk scarf looped over her tawny

hair. She pulls on driving gloves, smiles up at me challengingly, body styling by Pininfarina, selfish, self-indulgent car, girl to match, God bless.

I stroll around to the passenger door, place the AK-47 between Rosine and me, then fall in next to her, into a seat of whipped-cream leather.

Marcel appears depressed by my foolish bravado.

"I beg you," he begins.

But the rest of his plea is swallowed by the surging of the Boxer's 360 brake horsepower. Rosine unleashes the car with a smooth, authoritative burst of output. The troopers scarcely manage to swing the gates open as we rocket through.

I study the driver. Below her surface beauty I can see the hurt and the anguish and below that an almost maniacal silhouette, as though I'm seeing the negative of some old, familiar photograph. I have seen that negative many times before. A skull with empty sockets. I find it so amusing that I'll probably not be living past the next curve in the road, some quarter of a mile away, some matter of split-seconds from now, that I feel the widening smile pulling at my lips. Betcha she can't make the turn. For how much? For your ass, baby! I focus on her incredible lips. I decide to hell with the onrushing curve, to hell with being splattered across the countryside. Just look at those lips, imagine them fastened to yours in that final instant of life. What difference how you die? Why not this way? I start to reach for her, to kiss her, to time it precisely, but she cries out, turns her mouth away from what she must imagine is stark insanity and manages to make the curve with a skill that delights me. She accelerates out of it, whipping the back axle into line, then lets the car drift as she screams at me.

"Are you trying to get us killed?"

At least I think that's what she's cried out, but I'm not sure because the wind is still slashing around the sides of the car and buffeting in at us.

She requires another few hundred yards to stop the Ferrari.

She stares at me in total bewilderment.

"Did you?"

"Did I *what*?"

"Did you *want* to die?"

"I'm not sure," I tell her. "I'm never sure till afterward. Then I'm very sure I did *not* want to! But at the time, it usually doesn't seem like such a bad idea. Why? You disappointed?"

"You were actually trying to *kiss* me—when I was negotiating that curve?"

"Right," I say.

"Did my uncle or my father tell you I was suicidal?"

"Your uncle."

"Not true! I don't want to die. I just don't feel too much like living right now."

"Did you love him that much?"

"Who?"

"Your husband. Marcel told me he was killed in the other Ferrari only recently."

"Oh, my God! And you thought . . ."

"Look, Rosine, the days of suttee are over," I interrupt. "You don't have to throw yourself on the funeral pyre."

She starts to laugh.

I sit there in a puddle of foolishness. It isn't often you can use a word like suttee with a pretty girl, and when you do and it gets you the horselaugh you have to think seriously about taking your whole act back to the drawing board.

"That isn't the reason at all!" she says. "My husband was cheating on me. He died with some little tramp he was keeping in Nice. She was practicing her inept fellatio upon him while he was driving our wedding present at one hundred and fifty kilometers an hour, so stupidly preoccupied he drove the two of them off a cliff. In plain sight of Monte Carlo! Humiliating! I lost so much respect among my friends I simply had to leave France for a while. I came here, to be with my father, until the disgrace is forgotten— or until I can get my self-esteem back. But good Lord, not to die! Especially the same way *he* did!"

I sit grinning back at the essence of my stupidity reflected in her windshield. No wonder she reacted as she did. I'd almost killed both of us when I leaned over to kiss her, deceiving myself that she wanted to end it all and being the perfect gentleman who was willing, at considerable cost to himself, to oblige so lovely a damsel in distress.

"You're as crazy as my husband! He didn't have any fear either."

"Crazier," I confess. "Because I scare quite often."

"But you weren't frightened back there! Were you?"

"Not really," I answer. "I was impressed by your driving. And fascinated by your beauty. It was a gamble, but I thought we'd come out okay."

I discover her considering the assault rifle between us.

"Why did you put that there?"

"Where should I have put it?"

"On the outside, next to your door. Not between us."

I move the AK-47, placing it between my right foot and the inside of the door.

"Okay," I say, smiling. "What did you have in mind?"

"You sound like a different man when you speak English."

"You prefer me in French?"

"I prefer you in American. You're harder. Even—dangerous. I think in your American persona you say things more honestly. For example, right now, if you felt that you wanted me, you'd come right out and tell me you wished to take me to bed. True?"

"Not entirely," I correct. "I do want to make love to you, but I don't want to wait till we can pull up a convenient bed."

"One can manage quite nicely in the passenger seat," she challenges.

Do the taunting chevrons of her lips stand for cruelty or for passion? Such intricate clockwork in one so young.

"Too limiting," I counter. "I like to box the compass—you need the freedom of a full three hundred and sixty degrees for that."

She laughs, savoring the words as part of the foreplay. "Have you a better idea?"

"Do you know the Twenty-third Psalm?" I ask her.

She fingers the gold cross between her breasts. "What do you think?" she replies.

I get out, taking the AK-47 with me, come around to her door, open it.

"The part," I ask, "that goes: 'He maketh me to lie down in green pastures'?"

She rises from her seat like a cobra from a Madras basket until she is almost against me, not quite touching, letting me vibrate to the space still dancing between us, mongoose and cobra. Or could this be a ballet of two cobras?

"The Lord is my shepherd," she says so quietly I'm not sure I've heard her. "I shall not want."

I detect the needful glow behind her agate eyes. No, not cruelty. Not passion either. It seems that each of us has urgent absolutions to tend to. So be it.

We go out, hand in hand, into the pasture, out among the grazing Brahmin—a boy, a girl, and your standard AK-47.

# =CHAPTER=

## 7

I lie, still naked, on my back and follow flights of hurricane-birds washing above us along hard currents in the late afternoon sky. Intent surfers, they splash toward the shoaling mountains, then turn off, soaring.

"What *do* you think about?" Rosine asks, breaking the silence.

I turn to her, naked beside me on the carpeting we have woven over grass stubble with our shed clothing. All the fortifications of her body have softened and collapsed. Even her marbled eyes have turned lambent and now flicker at me pleasurably. We have not spared either ourselves or each other in this initial storming.

"What do I think about *when?*"

"Now. Right now."

"Oh, lots of things, actually. At the very minimum I'm your eight-track thinker, on average sixteen, sometimes even twenty-four—never only one track at a time."

"I don't understand."

"Like recording a song, you know? The people who do such things go into a studio and lay the guitars in on one track, the drums on another, the backup singers on another, and so on—until they mix them all together into one song. They're all separate, but still they're all together. Got it?"

"I like your imagery, monsieur. Share with me just one —just one of your thought tracks."

"You don't think you'd like to start calling me John?"

She brushes a fly from her forehead.

"I don't know you that well yet," she says.

"True," I acknowledge. "Okay. Well, on track three I was thinking about the time I learned how to give artificial respiration to personnel wearing gas masks."

She laughs, frightening away a calf boldly nosing closer.

"Is it possible?"

"Is what possible?"

"To give artificial respiration to someone wearing a gas mask?"

"Not only possible. Essential. There are two recommended procedures. Shall I demonstrate?"

"Will it excite us? Inasmuch as I'm not wearing a gas mask and there must be certain mouth-to-mouth contact, no?"

"It didn't do anything for me at the time I learned the procedures, but, yes, I think under the present circumstances it might excite us."

"Some other time then," she laughs, making a little pushing-away gesture with her hands. "I'm so gloriously *numb*! . . . On track one, what are you thinking?"

"You don't want to hear about track one," I tell her, trying not to sound too grim, but not succeeding, not in the least.

She's up on both elbows now, her breath so close to mine I can smell the pungent scent of our love-making still on her lips.

"Yes, I do," she insists. "You *must* tell me!"

"I never talk about track one," I say. "Not to anybody!"

I am appalled that I have acknowledged to another living human being that track one even exists, that there is in actuality one besieging memory that preoccupies me above all others.

"You're thinking of another girl—comparing me with her!"

She sits up, pouting, her shamelessly tanned breasts part of an amusing tableau of petulance.

"Will you settle for track two?" I ask.

She shakes her head.

"Track two," I tell her anyway, "is reserved to play back the memories of all my old buddies, most of them shipped home hermetically sealed, but on track two they're still every bit as alive as I am—maybe more so—because they've already cashed it. The terrible problem with track two is to play them back as they were before they got killed, to think of the incredible way Digby could sink a basketball, not to think of him as a terminal throat wound, or of Harrison only as a really messy abdominal, or of Marcus as only a spinal . . ."

"You'll never die in a bathtub," she says quietly. I have no way, of course, this early in our relationship and in the middle of all the pressures of what I have to do, to know how meaningful a comment this is for her to make, nor how revealing. But I do see her eyes turn wintry and in their cold reflection I deliberately defy her and picture myself sitting up dead in a tub of lukewarm water in a motel outside Peoria.

"Your post-coital conversation is truly remarkable," she says. "Remarkable—*and* unpredictable."

"You sound like a shrink!" I laugh. "Post-coital! What kind of rubbish is that for a nineteen-year-old to talk?"

Startled, she stares at me like a molested bird.

"Do I bring up *your* age?"

"Sorry," I apologize.

"At least," she says, "you didn't ask me if it was good for me or whether I had achieved orgasm."

"Hey, come on!" I say. "Guys don't really lay shit like that on you, do they?"

"I haven't had many lovers," she says. "Actually, only my first, an older man, our family doctor. And then my husband. Both of them inevitably asked me if I had climaxed and how I liked it."

"Well, be grateful," I say to her, "*I* don't have to ask! Like Satchmo said, if you gotta ask, you'll never get to know."

She touches my hand in acknowledgment. Then, perceptively, she adds, "You must be late for something, no?"

She's caught me stealing a look at the digital march of time on the Memosail around my wrist.

"Bad form," I confess, "not to have taken it off. But there's a plane coming in this evening from Australia."

"Someone you have to meet?"

"Let's just say it's part of my job."

Rosine gets up, stands above me, a superb vault of legs, a proud parapet of breasts. Perishable bliss, I tell myself, and watch her slip into her clothes, a matter of swirling seconds, since she wasn't wearing much to begin with—hardly your Maidenform woman, no soft cup, underwire, or light fiberfill. As I watch her, I punch in images of her on track eighteen, blank and available at the moment, and I play back her shivering under me in the grass, play back the furious beating of her heart against mine, the color mounting along her cheeks like parasols snapping open in Kyoto, play back my wonder at the tiny chittering of her teeth on her gold cross as she nibbled it and arched powerfully upward to meet me.

Then track one cuts in, overriding, dominating, almost erasing this brand-new track eighteen.

At least, this time your mind didn't whisper my name, I hear Doan Thi saying. At least this time you didn't close your eyes and pretend it was I.

Isn't that a beginning? I ask her. Isn't that what you insisted I *had* to do? But she doesn't answer. Had I really heard her?

You must know how urgently I've been keeping you alive in my mind, I tell her, guarding and nurturing you, in spite of the anguish. I'm afraid of nothing else, Doan Thi, except that I might someday forget even the smallest detail of our time together. How can I ever love again without diminishing my consciousness of you? A price I'm not prepared to pay.

You and the young captain I once was, my two visions on track one, both out there in the Ether Zone in the middle of nowhere, and why can't I have you both back? Why was *I* left behind?

In answer, Doan Thi conjures herself back to me from

beyond the sun, stepping down to earth and crossing to me through the mothering grass.

I see her now in Rosine's place, her body statistically older than Rosine's, yet somehow still younger, more delicate, more graceful, her obsidian Asian eyes ripe with light as she looks at me across these aching years. I see her lips moving, know she is speaking to me, but I can no longer hear her.

Now look, there he too is, just out there! Can it be he doesn't notice me? I begin to creep up on him, bidding Doan Thi not to leave. He doesn't move, nor does he appear to be aware of me. That isn't like him. I see his reddened eyes as some ancient intaglio. He's wearing cammies, face mud-smeared, no betraying highlights from those cheekbones of his, no, sir. He sits in the military squat firing position—rice-paddy prone, both elbows braced on his knees, supporting hand under the forestock completely relaxed, exerting no pressure on the assault rifle. He sits in the dying murk of an Iron Triangle afternoon just outside a VC redoubt in Bencat, a private figure on a monstrous landscape, a Category 1, an Expectant—expected to die and so much for glory and other minor indecencies.

Then why didn't he die? And if he didn't, where did he go? And what would I say to him even now if I could capture him? Am I really he? Did I really manage to bring him back and put him into policeman's blue in the city by the bay and bring him now to a cow pasture outside Nouméa where he has lain with a stranger?

I pounce on him. But he vanishes. I whirl to see if Doan Thi has fled with him. But she remains. Take me with you, I plead. I see she has not heard me. She is too busy trying to teach me. Love me, Doan Thi, don't teach me! But then she was fifteen years older than I was, two thousand years older culturally, acknowledged by everyone, even by Hanoi, to be Vietnam's most peerless poetess. And she had loved me. She had loved an American Category 1—an act of daring, an act of insanity.

"Someday you'll tell me? About this girl?"

Rosine's voice. I am deserted once more, this time in New Caledonia, in a pasture with cattle, naked on the grass, my trousers suspended at my face, Rosine holding them and looking down at me with a seraphic little smile that deceives me not.

I see that already she has become a different girl than the one I met three hours ago on the steps of la Ferme de St. Paul, not different in the usual sense that all women are perceived differently after sexual knowledge of them, even the ones you'd normally avoid sitting next to on a bus becoming creatures of grace and beatitude after that first coupling, after the electric, brain-jolting gratitude of the fornicator toward his fornicatrix. But not any of that in this instance. This girl has made a decision about me. She has decided to appoint me custodian of her immediate future.

I dress quickly.

Rosine holds out the keys to the Boxer.

"I'd like you to drive."

"Why?"

"For one thing, you know where you must go. I don't."

"True. That's one thing. What's the other?"

"I wish to see whether you can still control the car at one hundred and fifty kilometers an hour while I perform fellatio upon you."

"I'm not your husband!" I tell her reprovingly. "I'd appreciate your getting a clear and constant fix on that, okay? And please don't use those ridiculous clinical terms when you talk sex. It was that damned family doctor, wasn't it, who taught you those blank-out words? Probably put his index finger on your clit, cleared his throat, adjusted his stethoscope and announced, 'My dear, this particular protuberance we call the clitoris. It is a kind of erectile tissue, as I shall shortly demonstrate. Now, we stroke it just so and—voilà!' "

Rosine begins laughing. "Yes, yes, yes! That's exactly what he did!"

I accept the keys. "Okay, I'll drive. But you stay on your side, I'll stay on mine."

Her hand slips into mine, putting me in mind of a child eagerly gripping the chains on a swing. I pick up the AK-47 with my free hand. I do a three-sixty eye-sweep. If there be hostiles, there's no apprehension of them in the immediate area. But from the Gallante fortress on the hill I catch the twin flickers of reflected twilight off the lenses of a sentry's binos focusing down at me from an eastern barbican. So Georges and Marcel will know soon enough their boy Locke *can* be distracted, despite his earnest disclaimer to the contrary. I give that small note of self-reproach the tick of one second. It's not worth much more, for something other than perfunctory sex has been working on me this afternoon, something at the root of my task in New Caledonia. An instinct I have not yet been able to isolate has made me to lie down in green pastures with the niece of Marcel, the daughter of Georges, something far more impelling than simple lust. But what? I look around at the love nest Rosine and I have sculpted into the field and wonder how long it will take the grass to regain its natural contour. Then I lead this child-woman toward her fifty-five-thousand-dollar wheeled toy and direct my mind ahead to the particular things I must accomplish before I permit myself to sleep tonight, the first night ashore in weeks, if I can ever get to it.

We retrace the route I had come earlier in Gallante's limousine, back toward Nouméa. The Boxer suffers from an excessively heavy clutch, a typical Ferrari eccentricity I find tiresome in so civilized a machine. I test the fifth gear for high-speed fluctuation of pace, then try out her fast overtaking on a Citroën sedan far ahead down the highway. I slide in between the Citroën and an oncoming beer truck, to the consternation of all players except Rosine and me.

"Are you as covered with bites as I am?" she asks, lifting her skirt and scratching ferociously as I jam through ahead of the outraged Citroën, honking in shock.

"Nothing bites me anymore."

"Why is that?" she asks, twisting in the seat to get at an itch on her back cheek.

"If you'd taken all the pills I've taken and eaten all the C-rats I've eaten, you'd be immune too. That stuff changes your blood into sulfuric acid. Critters know better than to tap into that."

"What's C-rats?"

"C-rations. In Nam they were perfected by trained nutritionists to the ultimate inedibility. Example: one little number we called Ham and Motherfuckers."

"You Americans *are* colorful! What were *they*?"

"What were *what*?"

"Those things you just mentioned you ate with the ham."

"Motherfuckers?"

"Yes. What *were* they?"

"Say it!"

"Why should I?"

"I'm trying to get you to break a bad habit—your using Latin instead of Anglo-Saxon."

"I'm French! Why must I use Anglo-Saxon?"

"Suit yourself," I smile. "But if you don't give, I don't give."

"What are ham and motherfuckers, John?" she asks, with an almost perfect American accent. She's smiling like a porcelain doll in a shop window. For a moment I'm tempted to let myself care for her—motherfucker and John all in one breath!

*"Lima beans,"* I inform her. "Pop a pack of ham and motherfuckers, every insect inside the perimeter will evacuate on the double."

From the corner of my eye I sense the quiet hum of intelligent calculation and appraisal. Rosine is giving me a thorough screening, awarding and subtracting points for each feature. I wonder if my streamlined earlobes earn her plus or minus.

"I want to learn everything about you," she announces finally, just as we start to pick up Nouméa's heavy evening traffic. "Does that distress you?"

"It could, if I let it."

"Everything you do—the way you make love, the way you drive, the way you talk, the way you deal with my father and my uncle, your awareness of everything around you . . . I've never known a man like you."

I decide this dangerous artlessness needs defusing.

"Let's not betray the memory of the architect of your downfall," I remind her, "good ole Doc Horny-Hands. He must have been something else to be able to seduce you. How old were you?"

"Sixteen."

"No wonder the bastard made house calls."

"You're jealous!" she laughs.

"Jealous?" I repeat. "Do people still get jealous?"

"My husband did. Whenever I looked at another man."

"Do you do a lot of looking?"

"I did. Until now."

A little obligatory silence might serve at this point, I tell myself.

So we sit through a red light at an intersection on Route de l'Anse Vata without my responding to her tribute. On the green for go she says, "It does bother you, doesn't it, this kind of forthright talk from a woman? You can accept it from a man, but not from a woman."

"Wrong. I've always found women to be more outspoken than men—if you want to generalize."

"You're thinking because you made love to me I've become your slave."

"No big thing, okay?"

But she pursues it. "I liked making love to you. Not because you were so spectacular or because you made me feel anything I haven't felt before but because you kept your eyes open—you kept looking into *my* eyes. It wasn't simply you entering me, but you inviting me to enter you! How can I forget that? The doctor just kept staring at me. To him I was an object. What he never knew was that *I* was watching him—*he* was *my* object. My poor husband— he could only make love in the dark. Whenever I saw him draw the draperies, it made me laugh. He couldn't make love if I laughed, and he couldn't make love unless the draperies were closed—such problems!"

I admit to myself that so far I've been consistently wrong in trying to evaluate or categorize this girl. She is scarcely artless. What she seems to be is painfully honest. Her particularity blows illusion and pretense to smoke. It takes years to advance from the oh-wow school of behavior to her present level of sophistication, and the indisputable fact that her uncle and father must have spoiled her rotten since birth wouldn't have made the ascent any easier. Incidentally, why hasn't there been talk of a mother? No photographs of what must certainly have been an exquisite woman to produce this Rosine were anywhere to be seen when I had lunch today with the Gallantes. I recall seeing photos everywhere about the place, photos of Rosine and Georges together, but no third person, no other woman, no mother.

At nineteen, Rosine's age, I was just another leg in Ranger School trying to develop muscle memories and the tactical mind so my ass wouldn't be five miles out the window when I jumped into a hot LZ. In those days I could never have spoken to a woman about a sexual encounter as openly as Rosine has just spoken to me about our romp in the hay. She keeps startling me, coming up with transcendent moments, like the time I was trying to counterambush a VC ambush and some straphanger on my recon team pushed the play button on his tape deck instead of the safety on his M-16 and all of us, my team and the equally astonished Charlies, got blasted by Pink Floyd.

"Well?" I hear her asking.

"Well, what?"

"Is there time in your schedule for me?"

I park in front of a dive shop on the street called Engins de Plage. I'd notched the place in my mind this morning when André drove me past it on the way to police headquarters. Was that only this morning?

"I'll be over the horizon in ten days," I tell her. "Sooner if things work out. Or I could be gone the second I leave this seat."

I point to the nearby roofline, just now darkening as the day winds down.

"Man with the gong could be up there right now, waiting for a clear shot. You don't want to get into that."

Suddenly she is laughing.

"That funny?" I ask.

"Oh, it tickles, it tickles!"

"What tickles?"

"You," she says, "running down the inside of my thigh. So *much* of you!"

I get out, go into the dive shop. Aluminum air tanks, brighter than sunflowers, bloom in racks along one wall, gauges and respirators dangle on another, and inside gleaming glass cases stainless-steel survival knives are displayed. The swim fins range in color from basic black to crystalline. Everything in here but the Great White Himself. I cross to a display of gear bags, select what appears to be the top of the line, a long, deep-bellied waterproof stowage bag sporting a leather dolphin insignia. With this bag in hand I hope to give the impression to anybody troubling to glance my way that I'm just another bloke on holiday with my snorkeling gear, not a lobo packing an AK-47 in the bag and a Browning pistol in a shoulder holster.

I bring the merchandise to the counter. A wimp of a young clerk with a receding chin has been watching me with a whammy eye from the moment I entered his shop. He must have tuned into my negative reaction toward him. It isn't so much that I dislike him on first sight as it is that he reminds me of Polly Esther, a pet rat I shared a bunker with during three days of my first tour in Nam. I never really disliked Polly Esther. I simply resented the fact that she survived most of the rest of us—no training, no Ranger School, no courses in terrain comparison, route selection, or land-nav, but whenever we were getting down and getting some, and the smoke cleared and the dustup medics had removed the human debris, Polly Esther would come poking out from whatever sanctuary she'd found and begin to nibble, with her ceaseless vibration of chin whiskers, at the leftovers visible only to her. Once I had her in my front sight and could have puckered her ass for good—but what the hell, who appointed me keeper of her destiny? You can't blow everyone and everything away, right? I know a lot of things, maybe too many, but I don't know tatshit about the longevity of Indochinese rodents, so it could well be that Polly Esther is still somewhere in country, eating better than the people. But of course rats are not political creatures, which may partially account for their high survival rate.

"Cash or charge?" the young man, the very image of Polly Esther, asks me in Oxfordian English. I see now that he is half-Indian, I'd guess from the Punjab.

"I haven't had a chance yet to exchange currency," I smile. "It's been one of those days. Do you take Amex?"

"Of course," he snaps.

I fish out my plastic, hand it to him. He steps over to a catalog next to his cash register and starts running his brown index finger like a divining rod down the fine-print detailing the cards gone bad in the tropical sun.

Gleefully he isolates mine. I'd been afraid of that. When you're at sea for long periods, you can't always sock those payments back to the computer center on time. I had sent the computer a letter with my last check and explained about the twin typhoons in the Tasman Sea that had put me behind schedule and very nearly at the bottom of the drink, but apparently the letter fell on deaf receptors.

The young man clearly enjoys his opportunity to bully me. He holds up my iniquitous card, but well back of him, as though to ensure I'm not encouraged to vault the counter and snatch my card back.

"I'll have to keep this!" he announces. "Those are the rules!"

With his other hand he grabs the stowage bag from the counter and harbors it at his feet.

"Be right back," I tell him.

I feel his eyes branding my back as he watches me hurry out to the Ferrari and to the golden girl lolling within it. No wonder he can afford a car and a girl like that, I can imagine him thinking. Rich scum like him never pay their bills!

"You have any money?" I ask Rosine.

She hands me her purse.

I go back into the shop.

I open Rosine's bag while the young man smirks at me. I pull out a sheath of CFPs thick enough to stagger even a Singapore banker, all the notes of five-thousand-franc denomination.

I virtually fling the wad onto the counter. Why is it you can fling somebody else's money but always carefully count out your own?

"Would you like it wrapped?" he asks acidulously after he's deducted the cost of the bag from one note and carefully handed me back the rest of the bundle.

"I think not," I smile. "But it's nice of you to ask."

Reluctantly he hands me my purchase. He looks defiantly from me to the Amex card he's still holding with a death-grip.

"It's all right," I say, revealing myself to be a forgiving, even charismatic fellow. "You must do your duty. That's what it's all about, isn't it—all of us doing our duty? Have a socko evening."

A little more of life's nonsense.

I go out to where Rosine waits.

Just short of the Ferrari I stop.

She sits in a coffin of darkness. Even the lights flicking on in the apartment complexes ridging Mont Venus don't relieve the dark pall along this seashore avenue. At my feet the Baie de l'Orphelinat steals off in silent flotillas toward the distant fringing reef, already luminous with boiling foam silvered by the moon.

Yet the daughter of Georges Gallante waits in her red Ferrari, all alone, an easy kill for any lurking terr.

Never mind I'm with her.

I'm an unscheduled starter.

Let's not overlook the fact she'd driven away from la Ferme de St. Paul this afternoon on her own—once more keeping me out of this reckoning—with no escort of paratroopers, no watchful MAGS covering her flanks.

Strange!

Marcel Gallante goes nowhere without troopers.

Georges dwells within the heart of an armed fortress.

Yet their nineteen-year-old sits out here alone on the fringe of a town where only a few hours ago people were killed or maimed by plastique explosives.

I pull her door open. "Why?" I demand.

"Why what?" she asks without surprise, already beginning to catch the cadence of the way I talk and not be thrown by the conversational leaps I tend to make.

I run it by for her, just as I've run it by for myself, the illogic of it.

"No Melanesian would ever hurt me," she says. "I am safer here in New Caledonia than I would be at home in France."

"Do you have that in writing?" I ask her. "Speaking for myself, I find that I have to stay on my toes not to be clubbed, speared, or shot at. What gives *you* immunity?"

"It's something I *know*," she says. There is a conviction in her tone that puzzles me.

"*How* do you know it?" I insist.

"Because the true people love my father. He was brought into existence by one of their own t'katas."

"I've heard that story," I say. "But the way I heard it, he and all the Gallantes were cursed."

"He's never believed that story," she replies, "and neither have I. It's a story my uncle tells. I do not say Marcel made it up. The story does in fact exist as a part of our family's legend. But my father and I do not believe it. And we know from our own experiences that the native people of this island share our souls. They know that we, like they, are descended from the blood of the stone. Their ancestors read our dreams and we in turn hear their words without listening, the way you hear a waterfall cascade from rock to rock without asking yourself what it is you're hearing. You simply *know!*"

There she goes again, surprising me. Such animistic lyricism does not flow from your run-of-the-mill nineteen-year-old. She has told me all this in the same way a child tells you he's just seen something you somehow failed to see. The aspect of truth is present in the telling, but the vital details are hopelessly, irretrievably missing.

But it forces me to ask myself what else Marcel Gallante has told me that might not be gospel, what other false—if they are false—interpretations and shadings has he been feeding me—and why. Or is it the girl who is misled?

He insisted that Rosine was suicidal, warned me away from her. I have seen no evidence of a death-wish. Quite the contrary—she's ebullient enough to try to hitchhike for a while on my life. You could, of course—bearing in mind the nature of my work—consider that suicidal, but she knows little of me or what I do.

Here is a puzzle within a puzzle. My instincts about Marcel Gallante have all been positive until this moment. I dislike having to lose confidence in the man who is paying me.

"Marcel also told me," I say, "that your grandfather fell when he tried to straighten the cross. Is that part true, at least?"

"That he fell? Yes. That it was the result of a t'kata's curse? Ridiculous."

"Well, he does tell the story with great flair. As though there's a lot more to it than he's willing to divulge."

"But, of course," she says. "It affected his entire life. It even accounts for his bleak personality. You see, John, my grandpapa should have died from the fall. But he willed himself to live. He lived for more than two years after the accident until he succeeded in making my grandmama pregnant with Marcel. He was obsessed with having her bear him another son before he died—a son other than my father, a son untainted by any contact with a native sorcerer. I've heard stories that on his deathbed he made my grandmama swear to take this second, unblemished son away from New Caledonia, straight to Paris."

"Did she?"

Rosine laughs. "You should have known my grandmama! She had a mind of her own. She buried my grandpapa and stayed right here, running the business and spoiling my father, giving him all her love and shamefully neglecting poor Marcel. I suspect she always considered Marcel the fruit of her being raped by a madman in a wheelchair."

Suddenly I wish it were done and that I were well at sea again, far out of the shipping lanes, on a broad reach leading nowhere.

But my plane is due in less than an hour.

And Tontouta International Airport is almost that far away.

I slip inside, behind the wheel, close the door.

"The airport?" Rosine asks as I place the AK-47 into the dive bag and zip it closed.

"The airport," I confirm.

As I guide the Boxer onto Engins de Plage I detect the Renault parked ahead. Ever since I stepped into the scuba shop, this particular car has been previewing on my radar in sharp blips of warning prescience.

The Renault's headlights glow as I pass, then predictably fall in behind us with that citronella pallor that characterizes French nighttime traffic. The driver immediately establishes a measured distance between us, hanging far enough behind to prevent me from determining whether he has two passengers or three.

# CHAPTER

## 8

We're soon enough outside the city on Route Territoriale and crossing mountainous countryside dour as a Scottish moor, no lights to be seen anywhere except for those lemony headlamps fixed in silent civility behind us and the moon's gleaming off shards of bark dangling like melted tallow from niaouli trees on both sides of the highway.

"We're being followed?" Rosine asks.

"Discreetly. But doggedly."

"Why do you tolerate it?" she asks with an edge of annoyance. "This is a Ferrari!"

"I want him exactly where he is for every one of the next forty kilometers. I want him to see me arrive at Tontouta. I want him to see me leave the car and go into the terminal. I even expect him to follow me inside. Matter of fact, I'm counting on it."

"So you can shoot up the airport?" she asks accusingly.

"I sincerely hope that is not on the evening's agenda."

"I'll be terribly disappointed in you," she says with that capricious outthrust of lips which I have already learned to find so engaging, "if I discover you're so unthinking of innocent people you'd choose an airport for a battleground!"

"I'll even leave the rifle with you, how's that? Now is that not a beau geste? Could you ask for anything more?"

"What about the other gun—the little one under your arm?"

"Yes, you *could* ask for something more. Sorry, Rosine. That little gun comes along with me. Consider it as inseparable as my heartbeat."

"Very well! I *want* to believe in you, so I won't let myself think about it. Actually, I'm surprised you're leaving the rifle with me. Did you know your hand was never more than a few inches from its trigger while we were making love?"

I smile over at her. "My ladies either shape up or ship out."

She leans her head affectionately on my shoulder, a neat trick in a Boxer with a stout gearbox between you.

"Anyway," I say, turning my focus back to the Renault, "as long as the Shadow hangs in there a quarter of a mile behind us, it's an absolutely beautiful night in New Caledonia. But if he comes charging in, I'm going to have to leave him. Can't risk an exchange of fireworks with you along."

"Mon cher, I told you not to worry about me."

"From *monsieur* to *mon cher* in one afternoon? You trying to boost my ego?"

"I've only started."

There couldn't be a better time to tell her. So I tell her.

"Once we get to the airport, I'm going to take you up on something you said earlier."

"What did I say?"

"That I shouldn't worry about you going around unguarded. I'm going to count on that."

"Shall I repeat it for you?"

"Not necessary. I believe you. So I'm going to leave you on your own. I'm going to disappear in full sight of whoever's tracking me. That's the whole point of this little hocus-pocus. It all comes down at the airport—but no shooting! On the contrary. Now you're absolutely *sure* you'll be okay?"

"Positive! Anyway, it's my life, not yours."

"I hope that later I won't regret taking you at your word."

"I really don't want to talk about it anymore!" she says almost sharply, then immediately softening, asks, "How long will you be?"

"However long it takes."

"I certainly hope it won't take more than five or six minutes. I'm terribly impatient. You'll find it's one of my worst faults. I'm almost powerless in its grip. Besides, I want us to hurry back to town. I want to start spending the night with you as soon as possible—so we can make it last even longer."

"I don't think you heard what I said. I'm going to disappear. Drop out of sight! Vanish! I can hardly do that, then reappear to sleep with you."

"You have to sleep somewhere! Why *not* with me?"

"For one thing, our visibility is too high."

"It needn't be. I have a house in the city. On the heights of Ouen Toro. There's a wall around the property and we have a wonderful old dog. Monstro has no teeth anymore, but he still has an alarming bark. And the staff has been with my father since long before I was born. You'll be safe there."

"I'm not looking for that particular kind of sanctuary, Rosine," I tell her in my gentlest tone, which on the Scale of Gentle is virtually a kitten's purr. "I'm on a recon mission to target a very heavy dude. One of the only ways I can flush him out is to keep interdicting his troops. And I'm here to tell you that interdiction and intercourse do not walk hand in hand. I quote directly from Chairman Mao."

Both of us discover the control tower of Tontouta at almost the same moment. It's less than four kilometers away.

"When will I see you again?" she asks.

"Give me that address in town. It won't be for a couple of nights at the earliest, but if I can make it, it'll be after midnight. I'll lob some pebbles at your window. Incidentally, which *is* your window?"

"Six of them—around the corner facing the sea—the south end of the first floor."

"You mean the first floor *up*? *My* second floor?"

"I keep forgetting," she says. "To Americans the first floor is the ground floor, not one level up. Mon cher, I'm glad we discussed this, otherwise your pebbles would have awakened Koué."

"Is that bad?"

"Koué is a grandmother. And very fat."

"Fat grandmothers aren't entitled to midnight trysts?"

"*She* would be grateful, of course, but *I* would be consumed with jealousy. What if you prefer her to me?"

She writes an address on the less-decorated side of a five-thousand-franc note and hands it to me.

"Right near the peak of Ouen Toro, one of the first colonial mansions built in Nouméa. We have iron balconies on all four sides of the house, and a row of palms leads directly to the front door. And the gate is always unlocked."

"Let's not overlook the problem of Monstro," I say.

"Oh, he will attack you fiercely. But you have only to remember he has no teeth. His food has to be mixed with coconut milk. And here! You'll need money."

She gives me half her supply of five-thousand-franc notes.

"Thank you," I say. "I'll repay you as soon as I have time to get to a bank."

I turn the Ferrari into the air terminal, slowing in hopes of luring the Renault closer.

"There *is* something else," I say as I drive toward the arrival area, already cluttering with waiting taxis and buses. "The minute I get out of the car, you must do something for me. Your doing it exactly the way I tell you might be the difference between my living or dying at some point in the next week or so. You understand?"

"Whatever you tell me, I will do exactly!"

"The moment I stop I want you to take the wheel and drive away. I should say, give the people in the Renault the *impression* you're driving away. Then go park the car. Then take the bag with the rifle, check it into a baggage locker, give the key to the information desk, and tell the person at the desk that your husband—give them the name Ronnie James—will be picking it up in a few minutes.

Once you've done that, I want you to leave. Don't hang around and try to watch what I do or see where I go. Do you have all that? Especially the name Ronnie James?"

"You lied to me, Ronnie James! You *are* keeping the rifle!"

"I told you I was leaving it with you—I didn't say for how long. Believe me, Rosine, using it is the last thing I want to do tonight. I only want to shake these clowns, that's all there is to it—keeping the gun is for later, not for tonight. Okay, we're coming in—I'm counting on you."

I stop the Ferrari within as clear a line of sight as I can provide for the Renault. It's closer now, close enough so that I can count in the car three Melanesian men wearing sport shirts patterned with cagou birds, the symbol of New Caledonia.

I give myself the luxury of ten more seconds of Rosine's enchantress eyes, then abruptly leave her without another word, hurry toward the glass doors of the terminal, and try to shake off the distraction of thinking about her. For the good and definite reason that my mother fed me at an early age on imagery and the teeming phenomena in the world about me, I suddenly picture myself as a duck leaving water, shaking itself as it wades onto solid ground.

The moment I move toward the terminal doors and wave good-bye to the Ferrari thundering away, the Renault parks. All three men slip out, but take their time, doing nothing precipitous. It's apparent they've been warned that this alecron stings to kill and they are only to keep the creature under surveillance, not to gunfight, at least not at this moment.

As I had timed out things back there on *Steel Tiger* while I was still at sea, planning my moves for New Caledonia, using my Skanti SSB and its interfaced telex teleprinter to make certain arrangements and to call in old markers, I find the air terminal as I now need it to be, clamorous with arriving passengers, their waiting friends and relatives. On this particular night that I had selected, UTA, Qantas, and Air New Zealand all bring flights to Nouméa within half an hour of each other—a convenience for the officials in khaki Customs uniforms, but elbow-to-elbow for the arriving tourists.

In the year I've been taking on these occasional missions, I've learned that two factors are essential to my survival: information and camouflage. These have proven to be the keys to my getting through any given day. First, I have to know everything there is to know about any island where I'm to operate—its traditions, its customs, its languages, its frustrations, fears, ambitions, politics, joys, sufferings. I have to know who's got the power and who's out to take it away from them. Once I've accumulated as much information as I can get off-site, then I go in and gather more, even as I begin the operation. Now comes the camouflage. A lot of unfriendlies lurk out there in the alleys and in the bushes. They know me, but I don't know them—and that always gives them first shot.

To penetrate denied areas and to do damage, you have to move as lightly as a water spider until you're in a position to strike. Every spider has its hiding place. So the first thing I try to do is to set up a central base where I can hide out, a base only I know about, from where I can forage into the target areas until I'm finally set to bring smoke in.

Tonight's diversion at the air terminal is designed solely to take me out of circulation and to deliver me to such a hiding place. Ever since I approached New Caledonia, my enemies have had me under observation and attack. Attack is acceptable. Actually I need that contact in order to evaluate. But observation beyond my awareness can be the end of me. Within an hour, if everything works out, I shall be lost to them until I choose to have them see me again. Not even Marcel Gallante will know where I am.

I mingle with the crowds, but make no attempt yet to go into my disappearing act. The game of the moment is to cause these tails to believe I'm meeting an incoming passenger, possibly a backup gun, so that their attention is divided between watching me and watching out for whoever might be joining me.

The announcement of the Qantas flight I've been waiting

for comes through first in French, then in English, a flight from Sydney touching down now, docking at Gate 4.

I recheck my time. The first Qantas passengers off will be delayed for at least another seven minutes, until their bags roll out on the long conveyer system at Tontouta and before they're able to load them onto the self-service carts and begin to clear Immigration and Customs.

I go upstairs to the restaurant, find a table overlooking the main floor of the terminal. The waitress is a young French girl with an ugly brown mole on her chin which she's apparently learned to live with, because her eyes twinkle and she appears to enjoy her job.

"Coffee," I tell her as I hand her one of the five-thousand-franc notes Rosine has given me. "And keep the change."

"The American is an idiot," she says to herself in French, then adds in English, "Only coffee, monsieur?"

"Now that you mention it, there is a small favor you can do for me. Three men," I say to her in French, smiling all through it, "are following me. *Those* three, but don't look now. They're just now sitting down at the table near the stairway. They have the foolish ambition to kill me."

"You wish me to call the police?" she responds in French, her voice as low as mine, her face just as smiling. She is the perfect spontaneous fellow conspirator, the right girl at the right moment, something that seldom happens.

"No," I say. "These men are so desperate they would shoot the police on sight. What I want you to do is to bring me my coffee, then tell your friends in the kitchen I shall be coming through exactly five minutes from now and leaving out the back. When these three follow, I want your friends to point the way I went, but send them off on a different direction. Is that possible?"

She bubbles with the excitement of the plot. "There is a hallway that leads from the kitchen up to the observatory. My friends will insist you have gone that way, when in fact you must take the door to the far right of the kitchen. That will take you out at the back of the terminal, near the baggage loading, while your pursuers are milling around on the roof."

"Thank you," I say to her. "Four minutes from now. Precisely. But meanwhile, the coffee."

"May God keep you, monsieur," she whispers and rushes off to get my coffee and to alert the kitchen staff.

The three from the Renault get a different waitress. Through the screen of one hand against my face I watch them ordering, their eyes never leaving me.

My girl is back with the coffee, bending close to my ear as she serves it. "Everything is ready," she whispers.

She goes about her work, for not a table in the restaurant remains unoccupied.

I drink my coffee and think about Harry Carnes, who owns and operates a wine garden in Perth, Australia. Harry ran a company of tough Aussie troopers in Nam and is one of those good men who taught me how to improve my work with sidearms. The secret of fine-tuning your handgun shooting is, as any pistolero knows, to aim for the largest center of mass and to stabilize the pistol as you're squeezing the trigger—the gun *must* be stabilized when the hammer falls. He observed me one day in Nam when I was on a firing range with my Browning and discreetly suggested I might have my forefinger wrapped too far around the trigger. You probably learned with a revolver, didn't you? he asked me. I was surprised and impressed. Yes, I told him, an S&W M-29 .44 Mag was my check-out weapon, and he said, Well, that's your problem with the automatic, you're still using revolver trigger technique. Ease your finger back, keep it short of the first joint, you'll find a world of difference. He was so right.

I think about Harry now because what happens in the next three minutes will depend to a great extent on how well he did his job after I radioed him in Perth that I needed his help.

I finish my coffee, get up, and walk toward the exit.

The three Melanesians bristle into Alert One as I approach them.

Suddenly I duck into the kitchen, just ahead of a waitress with a shouldered tray of dishes.

My waitress is already inside the kitchen and waiting excitedly.

"That door," she cries. I'm through it a second later.

As she had told me I would, I come out on the ground floor near a baggage-loading ramp. I move swiftly, using the crowd now as a screen, keeping low yet trying to look inconspicuous. Suddenly I'm in front of the information desk.

A German tourist more demanding than an old man's parrot is quarreling loudly with the information clerk, an elderly man who for reasons beyond my present level of interest in trying to placate her. I ask him in French, "Why do you waste time with pigs who tried to burn Paris?" I am only a little ashamed of myself for using such a cheap jingoistic shot, but I'm on a tight schedule. He deliberately spurns the sputtering woman and smiles at me, asking what he can do to assist me. I tell him my French wife, very young, very lovely, will have recently left a key for me, Ronnie James is the name, and that I would thank him to give it to me. While the German lady pounds on his counter with a riding crop she produces from her shopping bag, he locates the key and gives it to me, asking that I sign for the record, which I do. All this takes less than forty-five seconds.

Another thirty-two seconds delivers me to the bank of lockers. I insert the key, open the lock, reach in, bring out the dive bag and its comforting weight.

I move toward the Customs exit. At seven minutes of elapsed time since my fixing an ETA, the first passengers from the Qantas flight come flooding out.

Harry had radioed me his courier would be a ruddy-faced twenty-five-year-old from Lightening Ridge who likes an occasional adventure, nothing much with firearms but good with his hands in a barfight, if it came to that. Ken Hilary would be his name. He'd be carrying two suitcases

—one his, one mine—and my paid-in-full voucher for five glorious days at the Club Med.

Ken is among the first out of Customs, a bag in each hand, arms hinged like iron bars.

"There you are, Ronnie, you old cattle duffer!" he calls to me heartily, as though we go back together to the Boer War.

He slaps an Aussie campaign hat on my head and helps me shoulder into a sheepskin jacket. No way they'll recognize me now. We honkies all look alike, but this change of costume will ensure confusion.

We edge outside, Ken and I, flowing along with the tour group from the Qantas flight.

Three buses from Club Med wait at curbside, drivers checking off names from master lists.

Ken and I get into line for the first bus. I look out from under the Aussie hat, see the three Melanesians pushing through crowds inside the terminal, searching desperately for their missing American.

"Ronnie James," I say to the driver and show him my voucher for free transfer to the club. I board the bus ahead of Ken, but have him occupy the window seat. Around me I hear robust laughter and the clipped accents of the Australian tour group, mostly married couples, some with children in tow.

The door closes. The bus grinds away.

Past Ken I look out the window. No sign of the Melanesians. Only their deserted Renault parked in passenger loading.

I conjure up this heartwarming vision of them shagging through the men's rooms, all three of them down on their knees and peering under the doors of water closets at the hairy thighs of startled tourists.

"Forgive me," I smile at Ken. "I may just caulk off—been a bitchin' day."

My eyelids drop like guillotine blades.

I remember nothing of that bus ride back to Nouméa.

I remember only the rude cessation of motion, the hiss of the bus door opening, and the excited screaming of people eager for holiday, one child crying on being awakened—I envy his honest protest. And then we're all filing out of the bus toward the entrance to the hotel.

We're herded into a lobby proliferating with bulletin boards and chalked agendas of scheduled activities. We're shaped into a reasonably cohesive unit by a bubbly ringmaster in a clown's outfit, then buffeted by a welcome-to-the-Club-Med chorale delivered by a company of gentils organisateurs—literally "amiable organizers," the famed GO's of the Club Med system—fifteen young men and women of assorted nationalities standing face to face with us and appearing almost as exhausted as we are. I wonder how many such groups as ours they've either welcomed and sung farewell to today.

Marvelous, I congratulate myself, as my brain stem begins to wither from lack of sleep. Who would ever look for John Locke among an Australian tour group at a Club Med on the beach at Anse Vata? Go Club Med—the "antidote to civilization." So the billboards say. Why not?

Ken and I take the elevator to the room we'll be sharing.

I find that the latch on the sliding-glass panel opening onto the balcony is rusted resolutely open. I place the Browning under my pillow, strip off my clothes, fall like a shadow from a tombstone onto the bed.

I don't recall saying good night to Ken.

# CHAPTER

## 9

**I** dream of Doan Thi.

We are walking hand in hand along Tu Do Street in Saigon.

She is telling me about a time when as a child she came with her parents from their home in Hanoi to visit Saigon. The trees along the broad street were so towering, so full, they actually reached across the avenues to each other. They captured the rain, then let it sift delicately down through their intertwined fingers. Saigon was a calm city then, languid even, not sputtering to death with traffic. The portent of the end came, Doan Thi says wistfully, with the arrival of American air-conditioning. That marked the phasing out of a gracious time when ceiling fans could be adjusted to "vite" or "moins vite," so that cooling was a gentle process, a simple rearrangement of the air, not the polar blasts that spear out of the efficient American machines.

I am not listening. I am watching a street drug transaction come down, a tiny backwash of the war as it was fought in Saigon. A Vietnamese girl of twelve, certainly not much older, is haggling with two young American Spec 4s. The intensity of their argument over price can scarcely be motivated by their desire to purchase anything off the miserable tray of sunglasses and cheap wristwatches the girl holds up as a cover should any MPs pass by. Obviously, agreement is reached. The men pay over their crumpled piastres, the girl lifting her dress and tucking the money into her cotton panties. Then she crosses to a five-year-old boy squatting patiently on the curb and opens the rucksack he wears so incongruously on his back. From this she extracts a packet of bach phien, "white opium," the name the Vietnamese gave to heroin. She delivers it to the troopers. They pocket it, hurry off.

"Does it bother you?" Doan Thi asks me.

"Fucking A it does!" I tell her.

She begins then to talk philosophy to me, softly, patiently, trying to set my moral indignation against a framework of reality. My reaction, I have to agree, is absurd. When you can blow a man's head into pulp and not even remember on what brain-burning afternoon you got that round off before he tried to do ditto to you, why should a simple drug transaction between an enterprising child and two needful, homesick young men so much as flag your attention?

I do not think it was only because Doan Thi loved me that she always tried to inspire in me a broader outlook on existence, but because she was by nature a teacher, a teacher especially of the young. And when I met her I was not yet twenty-one, she already thirty-six.

She tried to teach me what she truly believed, that everything—and she meant *everything*—in existence counted, particularly since the living time alloted to each species is so finite. The person striving to create any meaning out of his sojourn on this earth must accept all of it, she believed, whether it pleased or repulsed him—*that* judgment level didn't matter. All that mattered was that he not allow himself aversion toward anything that happened. The very fact of its happening made it a truth, and truth had to be accepted, not turned away from. Even one rejection, one avoidance, one recoiling from the face of anything, no matter how hideous, would constitute a failure, a fall from grace. To Doan Thi only one virtue stood above all others. That was endurance. She hated nothing and nobody, not even her enemies. Our enemies are there, she once said to me, to provide alternative images for us. All things surround us for that reason, so that we can enlarge ourselves by including them and so expand ourselves one experience at a time, like rungs on a ladder, to the furthest reaches of the universe.

You can imagine the trouble I had with virtually all of this. If you believe, as I do, that it's only a life, an accident, an incidental event in passing, and that there are absolutely, positively no meanings whatsoever to be shaken out of the prevailing shitstorms, then you're going to be a leading contender for the deafening-silence awards when your lover lays her contrary beliefs on you and struggles to show you the light.

Yet here and there she and I had contiguous membranes of belief—Doan Thi's phrase, not mine—endurance, for one thing, although we each endured for different purposes, she for total acceptance of whatever was, I for total rejection of everything except on my terms. Then why, she once asked me, do you insist you believe in nothing, yet try to change everything? If things have no meaning, why bother to stamp a meaning of your own upon them? Why not let them remain the way they are?

A real snapper, that one. I'm still working on it.

Another life-choice we shared was our mutual ambition to enlarge our own capacities to experience. Doan Thi tried to show me the only way you can swing that one is to externalize yourself, which brings you right back to square one: that is, you must accept—accept and absorb, even if the process destroys you. One of my difficulties, she told me, was that I constantly strove to internalize myself, bringing everything into me, into the filter of myself, rather than going out to it and becoming part of it. How else, John, she asked, can you ever hope to experience new births or partake of new existences, unless you move outward?

Then I would come up with an aphorism from Philosophy One, such as the tree is true to its roots, and she'd ask me with exasperating innocence what that actually meant. Did it mean a tree cannot walk because it is imprisoned by its roots? Did it mean a tree is only as strong as its roots?

Was I suggesting there is some relevant commonality between the rooted tree and the free, searching human spirit? And if so what is it, please, John, I would dearly like to know. What *are* you trying to tell me?

My lost love, I was only trying to tell you that ultimately they would kill you. That you can't externalize a Politburo, that greed for power is as uncontrollable as lightning—and as impersonal. Come away with me while there's still time.

But, of course, she wouldn't and didn't.

I dream of another time, in Dalat, in the rain, kissing Doan Thi, seeing her eyes searching into mine, the look between us fire on silk, my lips crushing hers, but not able to steal the ancient knowledge from her face, and in that instant my passion for her, for what in her I could never hope to possess, broke all restraint and I took her under a tamarind tree, half in the grass, half in the mud, like a rutting amphibian consuming its mate, and she matched me, passion for passion. I thought then that now certainly she can no longer do without me, now she'll listen, now she'll leave before their tanks break south down Highway 1. But, no, she believed she could go out even to tanks, make them a part of a larger experience.

I have the poem she wrote to me a week after that night under the tamarind tree. It is written in Vietnamese, as were all the poems she wrote to me, some forty-three over a period of five years. Even translated into English or French, the one from Dalat is the ultimate love poem. I have it and all the others locked in a safety-deposit box in the main branch of Wells-Fargo in San Francisco. Publishers in New York, Paris, and Tokyo have offered me a small fortune for the collection. Only Sky Six knows how they know I have them, although Doan Thi's open affair with me was one of the sensitive issues of the early seventies both in Saigon and Hanoi, an embarrassment to the Vietnamese of both governments, that an American captain in Special Operations, a man earmarked in Hanoi for assassination, would dare love Vietnam's leading literary figure, a woman as much an idol to the people of the north as of the south, her writing rising above political contention, deeply affecting both proletarian and mandarin alike.

I'd open my veins before I'd let another human being share with me a word of what she wrote to me. It is all I have left from the infected yesterdays.

Am I dreaming? *Is* that not rain in Dalat I'm hearing?

I open my eyes. The draperies in the small sparse hotel room are open, revealing a weathered white balcony and beyond its broken plaster the quaking pallor of palms against an indifferent morning sky.

No, not rain. It's Ken Hilary in the shower. Singing Rodgers and Hart with a New South Wales accent. I've heard other men singing in that same accent at Diggers Rest in the outback five hundred miles northwest of Sydney.

I get out of bed, slide the Browning from under my pillow and back into its holster, make sure the night chain is still in place on the hallway door, then I find a bathrobe in the suitcase Ken has brought me all the way from Perth.

Ken comes out, toweling himself.

"Harry wasn't sure you still wore that size," he says, "but knowing you he figured you hadn't let yourself go to fat."

"Not yet," I say, slipping into the robe.

"Be finished here in no time," he says cheerfully. "They stop serving breakfast at nine bloody thirty ayem. Can't miss that. I came for the food and the birds, mostly. I'll get crackin'!"

I check out the contents of the suitcase. Everything I'd radioed Harry to pack he'd packed.

"I'll have breakfast with you, then I'll be taking off," I call to Ken in the bathroom. "I may not be back till late afternoon. If then."

"Anything I can do?"

"Just hang in with the food and the birds. Enjoy."

"You sure now? I don't mind lending a hand. Harry said you probably wouldn't be needing it, but all the same it's here if you do."

"Thank you, Ken. One other thing, while we're at it."

"What's that?"

"I like your stroke. You haven't asked me any questions. Just wanted you to know."

"Harry tells me you're a heavy bloke. I admire heavy blokes. Not my business to ask what they're into."

"We're going to be fine together, Ken."

I shower quickly, something you get used to doing aboard a boat where water can be more precious than a following wind. Then Ken and I take the elevator down to breakfast.

A dining room the length of a football field fills the ground floor overlooking the swimming pool and the beach. Outside on the pool terrace a morning exercise group bounces up and down, resolutely trying to keep up with the vigorous movements of the muscled young instructor who looks about to lose his low-slung jockey trunks. Just ahead of us, Melanesian girls in short, starched white uniforms mop the tile floor as we enter. The ammonia in the wet mops pinches my nostrils. Bon appétit! I imagine myself a curling stone, sliding toward the target circle as the players energetically sweep the ice ahead. But Ken is as wary on his feet as I am. We manage to make it without falling to where a sleepy-eyed hostess awaits us. She indicates a nearby table set for eight, at the moment only half-occupied, all the other tables in this section of the room ringed by Australian and Japanese guests.

"It's buffet," she announces in amiable rote, "breads, pastries, croissants on that table, fruits, cheeses, marmalades on that one, cold cereals on that one. If you'd like bacon and eggs, omelettes, or French toast or pancakes or hot cereal, please fall into queue over there at the grill counter. Coffee and tea are already on table."

I pick out an apple and a wedge of cheese, cross to our designated feeding zone, while Ken, whistling through his teeth, takes inventory, a plate in each hand, at all the buffet boards.

I sit, saying nothing, but smiling impersonally at the six Australians already seated. One couple appear to be honeymooners, another couple are obviously long and grimly married, and there are two single girls, one of whom brightens at the sight of an unattended male joining her table.

"Weren't you on our bus last night?" the older married man asks me.

"You were wearing a blue turtle-neck sweater with the label hanging out the back," I say, pouring myself coffee from the community pot.

"American, are you?" he asks.

"From Perth," I say. "I've made it my home away from home while I'm on this side of the world."

"Perth? Emily, you hear that? *Perth!*"

"And what the bloody hell's so hysterical about Perth?" Ken challenges as he comes in, both plates laden, and sits next to me. But I notice that in spite of his abusive tone, Ken is smiling warmly at the older man.

"I'll tell you what's hysterical," the man grins back, but with undiminished zeal. "In the whole bloody world Perth's the most isolated outpost a bloke could ever get to. *Any-*thing's closer, and that's a fact!"

"Hi," one of the two single girls says to me.

"Hi," I say back to her.

"You staying for five days or ten?" she asks.

"I bought the five-day package," I say.

"So did we," she says. "This is Marla. I'm Queenie."

"I'm Ronnie. This is Ken."

"Have you signed up yet for the lighthouse excursion?" Queenie asks me.

"Not yet."

"They say it's really super. They take you out to Amédée lighthouse in a glass-bottomed boat. You get to see all the sea life and they serve a barbecued fish lunch and there's snorkeling in a lagoon."

"It sounds really super," I say. "Doesn't it sound super to you, Ken?"

"It sounds super to me," Ken says. "When are you two going?" he asks Queenie.

"We thought we might go this morning."

"Okay," Ken agrees. "I'll sign up. How about it, Ronnie?"

"Good deal, Ken," I say. "Sign up."

"Excuse us," the honeymooners say. They leave.

"How do you like Australia?" the older man asks me.

"I like it," I say.

"I'd damn well think so," he replies, "to go way the bloody hell west to Perth."

"Where you from?" Ken asks him.

"Canberra," he replies, somewhat guardedly.

Ken laughs out loud, leans over to me, his mouth full of food. "You know what we say about Canberra, don't you, Ronnie?"

"I've heard a lot of things said about Canberra," I reply. "None of them too favorable."

"One of my favorites," Ken says, "is what this one newspaper bloke wrote. He said the best view you can ever get of Canberra is in your rear-vision mirror when you're driving away from the place."

"It's a lot better now," the older man's wife volunteers. "Things to do there now."

"*What* things?" Ken laughs.

"You know how you can tell the difference between an Aussie and New Zealander?" the older man asks with a swift change of subject. I notice that his three upper front teeth are badly discolored.

"I'd like to know."

"It's the accent," he says.

"I know," I say. "If you hold up your fingers like this"— I hold up five fingers on one hand, only one on the other— "and ask an Australian how many fingers does he see, he'll tell you straight out, '*Six*, matey.' Now you do the same with a New Zealander, he'll say '*Sex!*' "

He nods, laughs approvingly until he almost chokes. I pour myself more coffee. His wife gets up. "Reggie," she says, "the bus leaves for town in ten minutes!"

He pushes his chair back, gets up. "We'll see you later," he says. "Duty-free shopping, you know."

I nod. He and Ken shake hands. The couple leave.

"Asshole!" Queenie mutters to his departing back.

"What do *you* say, Marla?" I ask the other girl. She has dark eyes, a thin, pinched little nose. She sips her tea with her pinkie tucked protectively into her palm.

"I hate Australian men," she says quietly.

"Thanks!" Ken says.

"You're welcome!" she says.

"Marla had a bad experience," Queenie hastens to add. "She doesn't really hate Australian men, Ken. I mean, you can't generalize that way. There have got to be *some* nice ones. I'm sure *you* are."

I feel returned to the real world, back where people don't carry AK-47s in dive bags, back where people don't ambush a fisherman driving a sailor to lunch, back where anguish over a piggish boyfriend is just as killing as a bullet through the heart.

For a moment I feel almost safe, sitting here at this kicky breakfast in a summer-camp atmosphere. But only for a moment.

"Excuse me, Ken," I say, rising. "Ladies."

I leave. I hear Queenie's surprised voice. "But isn't Ronnie going on the lighthouse excursion?"

"He's got business in town," I hear Ken telling them. "But I'll do m'best to look after *both* of you."

Upstairs again, I change into bathing trunks and the jacket of a wetsuit, place the Browning and some other items with the AK-47 in the waterproof dive bag, and go back down, this time out to the beach.

Sixteen-foot catamarans, Sunfish, and sailboards are colorfully arrayed on the sand, all at the disposal of Club Med guests, all part of the package fee.

The beachboy in charge is Australian.

These resort beachboys have an instinct about how much damage any given guest is about to do to the equipment, simply by looking the guest over. This laddie's instincts are good. He can tell I'm an old sun-and-sea dog.

"What'll it be this morning, sir? A nice dry sail, or do you feel like getting dunked?"

I've been reading the sky, judging the sea condition, estimating the backing offshore morning wind.

"Why don't I get dunked?" I say. "Make it a sailboard."

"Done much windsurfing?" he asks.

"Enough," I say.

"You want a stunt board?"

"Not especially. That one over there'll do fine. The one with the Hawaiian harness."

"That one's mainly for speed."

"Right," I say.

I give him my room number, bring the dive bag to the board, secure it to the mast-socket, lift the board.

"Need some help with that, sir?"

"Thank you, no."

I carry the board to the water, raise the mast, and hop aboard, sliding my feet into the straps.

At once the hard offshore breeze fills the small sail.

I lean back into the wind, bending into an inverted U, and instantly feel myself sizzling across the shallows.

I swing the rear of the boom toward me, sheeting the sail in closer, and the board accelerates even more.

I estimate I'm passing through twenty knots, something I can never remotely achieve with *Steel Tiger*, even on the proper side of a hurricane, if you're of the school that believes a hurricane has a proper side.

I straighten my body, slip into the bolerolike harness, which will make less tiring the distance I have to sail this morning. Now I lean back, allowing the harness to support my weight, and fine-tune my course, some six kilometers, across the waters of Anse Vata, across the Baie des Citrons, then out past the point and back inshore into the Baie des Pêcheurs, simply an anonymous windsurfer, one of hundreds already offshore this morning. Whoever's watching *Steel Tiger*, knowing that sooner or later I'll have to visit her and that they can once more pick up my trail, is in for a surprise when I come zinging in from sea, then back out the same way.

Seventeen minutes later I'm already tacking in on my

final approach to the Club Nautique. Ahead I can see the spars of *Steel Tiger* rising above those of smaller craft in the marina, yet still dwarfed by the big Benetti motor yacht behind which she is tied up.

I clear the marine entrance and savor the sight, as fresh for the thousandth time as it was when I launched her, of *Steel Tiger* with her black hull, her graceful, traditional lines, her clipper bow, curving counter, and raked rig. Yet I know instinctively that she has been boarded. From here I can feel her unspoken outrage.

I drop the boom of the sailboard exactly as I bear alongside the pontoon just astern of *Steel Tiger*, reach up and steady myself against a piling, untie the dive bag, place it on the planking above me, secure the sailboard, and climb up onto the pier.

I find myself looking into the austere eye of a police revolver and the impassive face of an officer who gives me the definitive feeling he'd like to fire off a test round.

"It's okay, it's okay. He's the owner!" I have heard that girl's raspy voice before.

I look up at the fantail of the Benetti. There's the same girl again. This time she's dressed.

What *was* her name? Kim! That's right, Kim. For a lady who just yesterday told me to go shovel squirrel shit, she seems to be pleasant enough this morning. Actually, quite helpful, for at her insistence the officer holsters his gun.

"We are maintaining a watch on your boat, monsieur. The inspector has made it clear he wants no one to go aboard. With your exception, of course."

"Well, thank you," I say. "I appreciate the security. To what do I owe this special attention?"

"Somebody broke into your boat," Kim interjects. She has come hurrying down from the high stern lounge-deck of the Benetti, and now I see her as something other than the crotch of Damocles. I would judge her to be somewhere in the midst of her exhausted thirties after an especially wracking twenties. Close up, she looks less a flake than I had thought her. In fact, on closer scrutiny she gives

115

me the feeling she's caught some mean kind of shit along the way and that if you push her too hard something vital might cave in. "They came up in broad daylight yesterday in a Zodiac, two men in wetsuits and scuba gear, like they were professional divers cleaning bottoms, and they started working on your boat. I was up on the sundeck of *Reckless Living* and I noticed one of them climb aboard and break into your companionway."

I step aboard, move to the cockpit. The teak companionway boards are undamaged. The intruder has used a cable-cutter to clip the padlock. It still lies to one side where he dropped it, half of its locking loop severed like butter.

"At that point," I say, "the boat alarm should have gone off."

"Oh, it did!" she says. "It blasted and blasted and blasted! And the strobe light on your masthead flashed like mad!"

"Who turned the alarm off?"

"Jerry, our skipper."

"I'll have to thank him."

"Thank me. I got him to do it."

"Kim, I thank you. You're a good neighbor."

"What did you think yesterday?" she laughs. "You think I'd really have balled you?"

"One can never be too sure," I tell her. "But there *were* indications."

"You were pretty fucking insulting, you know that?"

"I don't mind a lady coming on, but I don't want to be sacked in the pocket before I can throw the ball, okay?"

"Some slick frog in a three-piece suit stopped by just before you docked and offered me a thousand dollars U.S. if I'd try to divert you. I wouldn't want to take his money on false pretenses, would I?"

"He was merely testing me," I say, "to see if I'm taking something seriously enough."

"I'll bet you were really surprised to see me up there like that," she grins. "How'd I look?"

116

"Tailored," I smile. "Tailored—and tanned."

"You still look like Alexander the Great to me," she says. "I checked. We have a complete set of *Encyclopaedia Brittanicas* aboard. You were right. He did die in Persia. In Babylon, June thirteenth, 323 B.C. Malaria, they think. He asked them to float his body down the Euphrates, but instead they took it to Alexandria and buried him there."

"No respect," I say. "You conquer the world and they still won't listen to you. What did the intruder do when the alarm went off?" I address this question to the officer, but see he is no longer with us.

Kim answers for him. "The guy was really cool. He just cut the lock, took out the boards, and went below. He was carrying something with him. But when he came back up—maybe only five minutes later—he wasn't carrying it. Instead he had this little bottle in his hand."

"With my name in it," I say.

"It looked like blue water was in it," she says.

"That's the bottle."

"Right after that, the police came. But the two in the Zodiac had already split. This inspector—Bazoomb? Something like that anyway."

"Bazin," I say. "Closes his eyes a lot when he talks? Like this?"

I do my impression of Bazin. Kim laughs. "Yeah," she says. "Yeah, that's what he does all right. Do that again! It's wild!"

I do it again.

"Do I amuse you to that degree, monsieur?"

Jesus! Ol' panther-pads has slipped up on me again without giving me a clue. I'm not sure I'd want to be out in the bush with Bazin hunting me, no matter how good I like to think I am. He's uncanny, the way he can ease in on a man without a sound. He must be Dakota, not French.

"What can I say, Inspector?" I shrug. "You caught me red-handed and flat-footed."

"I told my wife you consider me an amusing fool," he says without rancor. "She asked me to tell you you're the first truly intelligent man to touch my life in months. Madame considers me not just an amusing fool, but a hopeless one. Despite that, I am happy to inform you, she holds me in the deepest affection."

"I do not consider you a fool," I assure him. "On the contrary. I believe you've got moves up your sleeve the rest of us haven't even dreamed of yet."

He smiles. "I have been told I'm full of feints."

He holds out a paper bag. "For you, monsieur. My wife baked them this morning."

I accept the bag. Inside I discover four flaky, fresh pains chocolats.

"She hoped you might enjoy them."

"Please tell Madame my Achilles heel is the chocolate croissant. My mother still makes them for me whenever I visit her. Would you thank her?"

"But of course."

I turn to Kim. "And thanks for your help."

"Why not? I'm a thousand dollars ahead. And speaking of money, can you use some?"

"What kind of money are we speaking of?"

"The kind that travels with hundred-and-fifty-foot Benetti motor yachts."

"Fascinating. But I happen to be currently employed. After that I'll be going west on an extended vacation cruise. But thanks anyway."

"Fifty thousand for one month's work!"

Bazin's left eyebrow elevates ever so slightly as he calculates the exchange rate.

"You did say fifty, not fifteen?" I ask.

She smiles. "Five-oh, comma, zero-zero-zero—exclamation point."

I smile back. "Is that a five- or a seven-day week?"

"You don't believe me! You think I'm just another souled-out chick?"

"I would never have thought of you as souled-out."

"The man who owns that Benetti, the man I work for, is

the one who wants to hire you—not me! He asked me if I saw you before he did to give you the message."

"Tell him his offer is so irresistible I'm going to force myself to resist it. An exercise in character-building."

"Don't kiss off fifty grand so fast, Alex, baby," she says. "You could buy a lot of gadgets for that little sailboat of yours. Frankly, you could do with a whole new stemhead and a lot beefier capstan forward than the one you're operating with. If you change your mind, we'll be at the casino tonight. And maybe I will just ball you. Anybody who insults me the way you do, and gets away with it, deserves to learn what he's been missing. Ciao!"

She saunters off. I see Bazin watching her gravely.

"A bad business," he mutters.

"And I didn't think she could even spell capstan," I grin.

"I mean that yacht, its owner, that girl, everything they stand for. The Immigration Office has asked us to assign an investigator. I am considering doing so—even with our other priorities."

"Narcotics?" I ask.

"I wish it were that simple," he replies. "Well, about your boat. I have allowed no one to go below since the break-in. I've been waiting for you to come back from wherever it was you'd disappeared to."

"Would you believe I found a secret hideaway?"

"You wouldn't care to confide in me? In the event I should need to be in touch with you?"

"Then it wouldn't be a secret anymore, would it? *Or* a hideaway."

He ignores this. "The Gallantes have been asking about you. Marcel, particularly. He insists I tell you he must be able to reach you at all times. Apparently, he considers reaching you an urgent matter."

"Tell him *you've* reached me. And that I work the way I work. If he's not happy, I can slip my lines and sail out."

"He thought you might still be with his niece. I drove up

119

to the town house on Ouen Toro last night. I spoke to her."

"What'd she say?"

"That she hadn't seen you since she dropped you off in front of police headquarters early yesterday afternoon—directly after lunch. Which, as *we* both know, she didn't do."

"Did you report that to Marcel?"

"No," he says. "I did not."

"May I ask why not?"

"One of my officers saw you and the lady at the airport last night. I ask myself, why should Rosine lie to me? I have known her since she was a little girl. True, she has been away in Paris for many years, but I have never known her to lie."

"What about that car André backed into yesterday at the ambush? Has that led anywhere?"

"It was stolen from a Hertz parking lot two hours before and the plates had been changed. We have magnificent fingerprints, but no suspects to match them to."

"The bombing yesterday? Nobody's claimed credit yet?"

"It still goes begging."

"Next time will be different," I tell him softly—and for no reason. It simply wells out. And in the middle of saying it I'm taken with a chill of precognition that almost causes me to shiver.

Bazin misses nothing. He is a man who would observe goosepimples forming on the back of a suspect's neck. "Whatever it was you were thinking just then," he says, "please share it with me."

"I had this image," I say. "God knows why—of your headquarters. In flames. A tape is then left at a radio station. In the Patyi language. The group names itself. Takes credit for the bombings."

Our eyes lock. I am seeing straight into his mind, a pure mind, open to anything and everything. He is a man who has lived among a people who still have visions and who follow the wisdom of dreams. He is not a scoffer.

"I shall see that the necessary precautions are taken," he says. "As soon as we have checked out matters aboard your boat."

"No!" I tell him. I hear the urgency in my voice. "Go tell your people now! Please," I add.

Carefully he cups his hand, lights a Gauloise. Only when he exhales the first lungful does he turn away and hurry down the dock to where his car waits with a police driver.

# ═CHAPTER═

# 10

**I** step down into *Steel Tiger's* salon, taking my dive bag with me.

This is my home, my world. I have walked every square inch of her teak-and-holly sole, even in stormy darkness when she's been laid almost abeam. There is nothing about or within her, nothing *of* her, which is not also part of me. I call now upon that shared intimacy.

I open the deep drawer under the nav station where I stow my boxed Weems and Plath sextant. The blue bottle has indeed been taken away.

What has been put in its place? What did the intruder bring with him that he has left behind?

I begin my search in the forepeak. Without moving or touching anything and using the palms of my hands as sensing saucers as I learned to do when I was on point trying to sense the enemy in the night, holding up one palm in front of me and moving it through a feeling arc, waiting for the warning impulse to trickle in, I work my way centimeter by centimeter toward the stern.

Bazin patters soundlessly down the companionway ladder, says nothing, simply watches me.

I finish in the salon. I ease open the door to the head.

The seat and lid of the water closet are down. I always keep them up when I'm docked or anchored, lowering them only when I go to sea.

Obviously, someone has lowered them since I left the boat.

I motion to Bazin. He joins me. I indicate that something is wrong in the head, wave him to stay clear.

I see his jaw set. He chooses to remain.

So be it.

I inspect every square inch of the toilet compartment, opening drawers only after probing inside them with a knife I bring from my cabin.

Soon I'm satisfied the compartment is secure except for the water closet itself. Inspection of both lid and seat convince me neither is booby-trapped.

Using the blade of the knife, I raise the lid.

In spite of what I consider steely nerves, my spine crawls. I step back precipitately.

The toilet bowl is a coiled mass made by two sea snakes, both yellow with black rings, slithering about the porcelain, half in, half out of the water. I recognize them as tricots rayes, their venom far deadlier than a cobra's. We called the Nam cobras Two Steps—that's as far as you went if one of them bit you. These two make the Vietnamese cobra seem as harmless as a garter snake.

I hear Bazin's tight exhalation behind me, smell his tobacco-breath on my shoulder.

"Somewhat more effective than a bottle of blue water," I say after a while. I have on a few occasions shared underwater patches with sea snakes, marveled at their graceful hemstitching through the coral heads. I have seldom found them aggressive, though certain species tend to be more inquisitive than others, especially the more common beige sea snake, one of the larger of these reptiles. I have had these swim directly to me, flick their tongues persistently against my mask. Once engaged in this questionable sport, they appear to enjoy it and make no effort to detach themselves from this playful contact. Since they can remain underwater for an hour and I can't, the only way I've found to make them lose interest in me is to remain as motionless as I can for as long as I can. Then, as though bored with it all, they stream off to hunt their prey in the sparkling lagoon waters. I have always reassured myself on the occasion of these few brief encounters that even if they had decided to bite me, their jaws are so petite they would have had trouble opening them wide enough to use their hook-shaped teeth and inject their venom. I calculate my only vulnerable areas to their tiny mouths are the lobes of my ears or the flesh between my fingers, both regions easy enough to deny to such a predator.

While I'm running these thoughts by, Bazin, still seized by disgust and instinctive dread, reaches past me to grasp the pump handle and to flush the snakes forever from his sight. I seize his wrist—just in time, for only now do I discover the cleverly concealed trip-wire.

My intruder has booby-trapped the flush-handle, counting on a shock reaction exactly like Bazin's.

I disarm the small plastique explosive. It is a primitive unit, lacking distinction or sophistication, but it would have accomplished the job.

So much for sorcery.

The t'katas have joined the rest of us in the twentieth century.

I feel comforted that they have decided to fight me with my own technology, but Bazin, in my opinion, is unduly shaken and angered. He takes the incident as dastardly beyond the call. He has not been bred on VC punji-stake traps or seen some trooper he'd let himself come to care for suddenly plunge out of sight, end up in a pit, stakes grotesquely through his chest. Sometimes a man could live for a few minutes in this situation. There is no expression you will ever see on any face, at any other time, quite like the expression of a man looking up at you from a pattern of punjis as he dies. I have never heard a single one of them scream or even call out, as those who have been shot will do. Their patient silence is unforgettable.

I close the toilet lids on the two sea snakes without flushing them into *Steel Tiger*'s macerating system.

"Possibly the aquarium would like them?" I ask.

"Possibly," Bazin says. "I shall inquire. And if not?"

"Then they might send an experienced person to remove them and return them to a happier environment."

"I shall attend to it."

We return to the salon.

"I can appreciate that you do not permit smoking below-decks," Bazin says. "But on this occasion would you consider an exception be made?"

"If I smoked, I'd even join you."

We sit across from each other at the salon table with its high, removable fiddles. He lights another Gauloise. Deliberately I look away as he holds the match to the end of the cigarette. I do not want him to see that I notice his shaking hand.

"Do you drink in the daytime, Inspector?" I ask.

"No, thank you," he replies. "I drink nothing but wine. And only one glass each night of an amiable red burgundy. This I enjoy while Madame and I discuss the events of the day."

"You'll tell her about this?" I ask.

"I tell her everything. We are as one person."

"How long have you been married?"

"Twenty-seven years."

"Children?"

"We were never blessed."

He seems calmer. The memory of those banded sea snakes is no longer as dominant in his mind.

"You are not married?" he asks me.

"No."

"It can be the truest happiness," he says. "But, of course, that is the exception. When one has a good marriage, he is superior to all other men. He is beyond their money, beyond their power, for he has what they have never achieved. Don't wait forever, monsieur. Those final years can be heavyhearted if you are alone."

"I hope I may meet Madame Bazin," I say.

He looks at me through cigarette smoke, his eyes sharp as the facets of diamonds.

"Why are they so intent on killing you?" he asks suddenly.

"I've been asking myself that."

"Can it be," he suggests, "that their killing you would be a symbolic act?"

"What do you mean?"

"Eliminating you might be a sign that nothing can stand in their way. That the final defensive effort of the Gallantes has failed. Somewhat like a trial by arms, in which the imported champion is vanquished."

"I hadn't thought of that."

He opens the briefcase he has brought aboard with him. He lays out five fully loaded AK-47 magazines on the salon table as a poker player might lay down a full house.

"These were recovered from yesterday's ambush. Since you are the only person on our side carrying an AK-47, I thought you might find some beneficial use for them."

"I can make some coffee," I volunteer. "It won't be Turkish, but it'll complement the pain chocolat."

"Thank you," he says, rising. "My wife insisted all four were for you only."

"There is one more favor."

"Certainly."

"A car. Something ordinary-looking, something that blends. Yet something I won't have to push uphill. Can that be arranged?"

"When and where?"

"Anytime from now on. In the Yacht Club parking lot. Tape the keys under the front axle. I don't know when I'll be coming for it."

"A Renault 5-TX," he says after a moment's thought. "It is very popular here. Yours will be green. Now, about your boat. I shall keep officers on rotating watch. Around the clock. Nobody will intrude again."

"Thank you," I say. "She's all I've got."

"I know," he says.

He smiles at me ever so faintly and I wonder why I read such loneliness in him. He goes up the companionway ladder and out. I listen to his soft footfall crossing the deck. Had it been anyone else wearing Bazin's hard-soled shoes, I'd have asked him to take them off. But not Bazin. He walks on air.

I sit, waiting until I know Bazin has gone and that one

of his officers has taken up patroling the pier alongside *Steel Tiger*, then I turn on my Skanti TRP 5000 radiotele-phone with its telex crystal filter and its interfaced SAIT teleprinter. I put the equipment in send condition and go to direct TX. I check that all teleprinter keys are correctly set and move the MAINS switch to ONZ. The green light-emit-ting diode brightens automatically as the unit becomes powered. From the MODE switch I select ARQ/BC position, then I depress the RESET push-button. On the control panel the standby indicator glows, while on the teleprinter the TERM READY key's indicator also glows. I continue proce-dure until my selcall number "*fow*-er six fife *nin*-er tree" is automatically sent and MASTER LED glows. I type in the code for the station I'm calling and wait for the answer-back signal. As I wait, I adjust the receiver tuning. I see that MARK and SPACE glow alternately, the meter needle stands at midscale, MASTER and SEND glow continuously, CS1 and CS2 glow alternately. I now perform a carriage-return/line-feed and begin sending my message directly from the keyboard, starting with identification codes.

Hello, Michael, you slick ol' boony bastard, how the hell does it really feel to make your first million bucks?

Of course, none of that or my other memories of Mi-chael Adams appear in the brief, businesslike request for information I tap out to him from across the China Lake. I'm asking him for anything and everything he can send me on the Gallantes. I want it all, personal and corporate, private and public, and I want a coded reply back to my selcall number at eleven hundred ayem New Caledonia time, exactly twenty-four hours from the sign-off second of this transmission, as to how soon and where this full packet can be handed to me in person by someone Michael trusts.

I first saw Michael Adams when I took a recon squad into the Laos Panhandle just ahead of Operation Dewey Canyon II. I never tolerated pogues coming in with me or my men, but this young lieutenant arrived behind papers I couldn't buck. He was some kind of special liaison between

127

the Tea and Biscuit company and General Abrams's staff at MACV, a spook in cammies, a preppy type who used verbs such as "actualize." I warned him we were going in on a survey a few days before some heavyweights from I Corps kicked off, into an area where the NVA were chien si—chien si means you could get lit up tangling with these fighters. I told him the first knee-jerk reaction I spotted from him I'd leave him behind in the boonies on his own. He assured me he'd be no burden to the team, that he could hold up his end. So in we went. And to my open amazement the Honorable Mister Adams more than humped his share. He was descended, it turned out, from some offshoot branch of the original Adams family of the American Revolution, and responsibility had been bred into him. He asked me some pretty stupid questions before we went in, such as how come I wore my dog tags around my boots, not around my neck, and I told him because I'm ticklish and if I got hit I didn't want some dumbass medic fucking with my neck and making me laugh while he was trying to fish out my tags. He really believed me and I remember thinking, God help the USA if this is the caliber of men the CIA is fielding these days. But we got into a firefight on the second day and Michael turned out to be quite a hand with an M-16. He admitted later he'd won a New England skeet-shooting championship or some such event, but I don't remember ever before seeing a man stand up right out there in the forest and exchange point-blank fire with an experienced enemy and pick off his quota as though they were clay targets on a fine spring day in Massachusetts.

So in the way of those things we got tight inside seventy-two hours, and when he left to go back to wherever spooks go I told him anytime, Michael, old man. I didn't see him again until I was on the San Francisco narco squad. He just sidled up to me one night when I was working the Mission District and asked me to have dinner with him the following evening at Ernie's. In that warm and resplendent establishment over a dinner I still remember he told me he had left the Agency and was trying to become a movie producer. He wanted me to know that the four days he spent with me and my team in Laos would always be the high point of his life, that he learned more about himself in those four days than he had in all the years before then and ever after. I know what he was talking about and it was good to hear somebody just come right out and say it for once. That was the next-to-last time I saw him. The last time was in San Diego, after my father had helped me launch *Steel Tiger*. I sat on the dock all that first night, just sat there looking at her getting used to the water and loving her, knowing we were destined to take care of each other, and suddenly I heard someone coming, trying to do it quietly, but not succeeding. Michael, joyously sneaking up on me. How about dinner tomorrow night? he asked. Can't offer you Ernie's, but there are a couple of fine restaurants in San Diego. Once more, over dinner, he brought me up to date on his life. It were as though he had this need to report in to me. I guess you've become my father-figure, he told me. The movie thing hadn't worked out. Too much bullshit even for him. He'd gone back into the Agency, but only on part-time assignments. He was about to concentrate on making his first million dollars. He was producing soft-core porno films for the growing home-use cassette market. He was convinced there was a fortune in it because Americans are still so uptight about sex they'll buy anything in a plain brown wrapper. He was right. He has a penthouse now in Hollywood with his own telex. He sent me a message early this year when I was in Tonga that he had just banked his first net million after taxes. I had telexed back inquiring whether his part-time employers in Washington felt there were any conflict of interest between his involvement in pornography and the occasional work they expected him to do for them—a naïve inquiry, but I was testing his sense of humor. He did not fail me. He messaged back: DR. ALBERT SZENT-GYORGYI, THE SEVENTY-SIX-YEAR-OLD NOBEL PRIZE WINNER FOR BIOLOGY, INSISTED WE ARE APPROACHING A FIFTY PERCENT CHANCE OF SUR-

VIVAL, ALL OF US ON THE WHOLE PLANET, BUT HE IS CON-
VINCED THAT BY THE END OF THE CENTURY THE ODDS WILL
BE CONSIDERABLY LOWER. HE TOLD THE NEW YORK TIMES
IN AN INTERVIEW THAT YOUTH WAS THE ONLY HOPE FOR THE
WORLD. WHEN ASKED BY THE TIMES WHAT HE WOULD DO
TODAY IF HE WERE TWENTY HE REPLIED AND I QUOTE I
WOULD SHARE WITH MY CLASSMATES REJECTION OF THE
WHOLE WORLD AS IT IS—ALL OF IT. IS THERE ANY POINT
IN STUDYING AND WORK? FORNICATION—AT LEAST THAT IS
SOMETHING GOOD. WHAT ELSE IS THERE TO DO? FORNICATE
AGAINST THIS TERRIBLE STRAIN OF IDIOTS WHO GOVERN THE
WORLD. UNQUOTE.

If anyone can get me the information I feel I need on
the Gallantes, Michael Adams is that man.

I shut down the SAIT system, check through the boat
once more to ensure everything is operational, take my dive
bag, the five magazines of ammo, and the four chocolate-
filled croissants, trigger the alarm system, and go topside. I
close the hatch and step onto the dock. I nod to the police
officer on duty, walk up the dock to a pay phone. Damn it,
I still don't have any coins, nothing but five-thousand-franc
notes! I wave to the officer. He hurries to me. I borrow
change, dial information, get the number of Maurice Aragon's newspaper, dial it, ask the voice at the other end if I
may speak to Maurice. He is out at a press conference.
He is not due back for an hour at the earliest. I ask the
voice to give him a message. That John Locke urgently
needs to see him. At three sharp this afternoon. At the
Biarritz bar on the beach at Anse Vata. And tell him he
needn't dress too formally. I'll be wearing trunks and the
jacket of a wet suit. In case he still can't recognize me, I'll
be carrying a dive bag with a leather porpoise on it.

I hang up, return to the sailboard. Once more I attach
the dive bag to the mast.

I wave good-bye to the officer, zip away, creaming out
of the marina, out into the Baie des Pêcheurs.

If I'm being watched, it is a matter of little concern to
me.

A procedure I have in mind should, I hope, confuse and frustrate whoever has the job of tracking me with binos.

Meanwhile, I give myself to the seething of the board and the benevolent palm of the wind out of a sapphire afternoon.

Such moments are worth all the rest of it.

When I'm holding the Club Med a kilometer ahead and the Biarritz Beach Club half a click off my port beam, I catch sight of what I've been hoping for, a cluster of neophyte windsurfers going through the learning agonies. A group of a dozen or so are in various stages of floundering, letting go their masts or struggling back onto boards off which they've just tumbled.

I scoot in among them, let my mast go. As the board stops, I slip off and underwater. When I come back up, I've already pulled off my red trunks and the jacket of the wet suit. I unzip the dive bag, put jacket and trunks into it, bring out a pair of black trunks and a flagrantly yellow tank shirt. Once more I submerge and while underwater tug myself into shirt and trunks. I pop back up and onto the board, looking to anyone watching from shore like a totally different windsurfer than the character in red trunks and black rubber torso who plunged in seconds earlier. Few people doing surveillance are trained enough to concentrate on the permanent characteristics of those they follow. Instead, they tend to fix on the superficial, and watch hats, trenchcoats, and other such integuments.

Using the sails of two other windsurfers on shoreward tacks as my screen, I jockey myself between them, keeping one to either side, and drive straight onto the beach directly in front of the Biarritz. Then, keeping my back to the highway, I slip the dive bag free, hurry onto the shelter of the club's beachfront veranda.

# ═══CHAPTER═══

# 11

The lunch crowd has already dispersed. All the outside tables are unoccupied. I select a corner table at which I can be seen only by someone approaching directly along the beach or from inside the bar.

It is five minutes to three. The rustling lagoon has lulled me, despite the good-natured stink of beachfront pizzerias and tanning oil laved by the acres of sunbathers. I sit contented and at peace in a wicker chair and never mind that some fatass has broken through part of the seat. I'm feeling so relaxed I don't even trouble to switch chairs. Time, I think, for a shot of self-congratulation, Locke, cunning old sea dog, you. You've lived through the first forty hours of the worst they could throw at you. They've got to be biting their nails, whoever they are, because they know—oh, yes, they know—that so far you haven't even started to bring it to them. You've just been doing your standard reflex counterpunching while establishing a beachhead. But what else could they have expected from a man machined over the years to do everything right automatically, without even thinking? When you've been taught by caring professionals, surviving is like breathing, just something you do until you're stopped by factors beyond your control.

I remember when I entered Ranger School wondering if I could ever cut it in competition with the heavyweights in my class. To qualify for an operating recon platoon you have to earn a minimum of two hundred and fifty points out of a max of three hundred on the physical-fitness test, not to mention being a first-class swimmer and passing both jump and scuba schools. I looked around at all the big jocks in our group and thought, no way am I going to pull it off over these godzillas. Even though I'm a hair taller than six feet, I've always preferred lean to bulky and sinewy to massive. Lucky genes, a careful diet, and a passion for staying on the prowl have kept me right on the one-hundred-and-fifty-pound marker since I turned sixteen. In this group of linebackers I looked like a junior-high quarterback. Yet I found as we dug into the three qualifying events that I could outscore the big guys. First, you do the pull-up. If you do twenty, you get the max of one hundred points. Pulling twenty was easy for me. Anybody who grows up in the surf at San Diego has no problem with this one. Then came the sit-ups. To max this you have to do eighty sit-ups in two minutes. That means you have to come up and get back down each time within less than one and a quarter seconds, so the trick here, if you've got the stomach muscles to match your count, is to get up and back down on every one-second count until you've counted past eighty. The final event was the three-mile run. You have to deliver this one in eighteen minutes for your one hundred points. This allows you a comfortable six minutes per mile. I breezed through that one.

Afterward, the instructor brought me up in front of the group and yelled out, Okay, you dudes, look at this man! Got the max and didn't even work up a sweat. Remember him when you're humping through the Mekong or getting your brains french-fried on some fucking gook hill. I'm here to tell you only the lean ones make it, the one-hundred-and-fifty pounders, like Locke here. So starting today, I want to see everybody slim down and none of this shit about you can't lose weight because you're all muscle and no fat. Fuck that! I don't give a goddamn if you have to take off muscle! Get thin! Get hard! Get to be one-fifty! Maybe then you'll come home in one piece!

"Been waiting long?"

Of course I'd seen Maurice coming. But I wanted to

finish playing back the memory of that Ranger School afternoon so many years ago, and here it all was, back in prime-time rerun today in Nouméa. Sometimes you wonder how any container as small as the human skull can compress all the memories. Must be we've got silicon chips in there. Must be.

I grin at Maurice. "Been sitting here remembering how it was to be nineteen."

He sits down.

"I gave up long ago trying to remember that far back," he sighs.

I gesture to the waiter.

"May I borrow a pencil and a piece of paper?" I ask him.

He produces both. He too is in an up mood. It's the contagion of the beach and the windsurfers out there in the water, cutting trails of dandelion flecks through the sun-pressed lagoon.

"What I'm writing down here," I tell him, "is a guide for your bartender, since what I'm ordering is a drink he will not be familiar with."

"He prides himself on knowing every drink there is," the young man says affably. "Would you care to test him? He's not above a small wager."

"Fair enough," I say, handing him back his pencil and paper. "If he can build *this* drink, tell him I'll give him a five-thousand-franc note. If he can't, he will follow my instructions and make my guest and me the drink as a courtesy of the house."

"I accept on his behalf," the waiter says.

"We call this one a Goombay Smash," I tell him. "But let's give the man a sporting chance. Tell him it's a drink popular among boating people in the Caribbean, particularly around the Grenadines, which is where I first got onto it."

Smiling, the waiter hurries out, as though he knows something I don't.

Maurice has been watching me and shaking his head. "Yesterday an ambush, which the police tell me almost took your life. And today you sit here in a bathing suit and order a Goombay Smash!"

"The occasion warrants it. I seldom allow myself a drink, especially not in the afternoon. But today is an exception."

"Do you *know* what's happening?" he insists.

"What's happening is that I'm about to win a bet with a bartender who never heard of a Goombay Smash."

"Paris is more alarmed over the local situation than I have known them to be since the general strike," he says in a remonstrative tone. "We have just come from a most critical briefing at the governor's office. The Deuxième Régiment Étranger des Parachutistes is being flown in from Corsica before the weekend. And a missile cruiser will arrive next week. For public consumption we are asked to publish the news that this is a gesture to New Caledonia, the homeland's participation in helping us celebrate Bastille Day. But in actuality the soldiers and the warship are being rushed in to reinforce our local military and the gendarmerie. The governor is now convinced of what Marcel Gallante has been predicting all along, that there will be an increase in terrorist activity culminating with some major revolutionary activity on Bastille Day."

"Very prudent of the governor," I agree.

The waiter returns, beaming, two drinks on his tray, both in tall glasses, both filled with cracked ice. At least they *look* like Goombay Smashes.

With evident pride he places one in front of me, the other in front of Maurice.

"Two Goombay Smashes," he announces.

I lift the glass and taste. It's the most superb Goombay Smash I have ever experienced.

"Where did he come up with the Demarara Rum?" I ask, still not able to believe that this unmistakable rum of Guyana could have found its circuitous way here.

"Not to mention," the waiter says, enjoying his little triumph, "the coconut rum! Of course, the pineapple juice, the triple sec, the lemon juice, and a dash of syrup were no problem."

A tall black man with gleaming white teeth suddenly appears in the doorway from the bar. He's wiping the pink palms of gigantic hands on his apron.

"I brought it with me from Guyana," he laughs. "A man can't live without a case of Demarara stashed under his bunk, can he, Skipper?"

I take out one of Rosine's five-thousand-franc notes.

"Thank you," I tell him, "not only for the best Goombay Smash I've ever tasted, but because you've just reminded me a smart ass is a dead ass."

I give him the money. He and the waiter bear it off together like Olympic gold.

"How do I regard you?" Maurice asks. "As an old friend or as a front-page story?"

"Old friend. I don't have the story yet. Okay?"

"I agreed to wait. It's okay."

He reaches into his jacket for an envelope.

"Here's what you asked for—every New Caledonian political party from far right to extreme left—and the names of their leaders. I threw in the approximate number of members in each group—and the phone numbers of the three or four figures who command some degree of influence. May I ask, John, what use you plan to put this to?"

"I'm thinking about going in and rapping with a few of the biggies. Just taking some soundings, getting a feel of the situation and opening myself up to different points of view, that's all."

"I'd start with Jules Sabourin of the Fédération Calédonienne."

"Why?"

"He's the closest to the Melanesians. And the most extreme of the French groups. And a devout communist."

"All *right!*"

"Who will you claim to be?"

"Myself."

"Will you tell them Marcel Gallante's paying you?"

"Don't you think they already know that? You just let slip that *you* know it—and I didn't mention it to you yesterday. Who told you, Maurice?"

"My contact in police headquarters."

"He's a busy little body, isn't he?"

"He doesn't do it only for the money, but because he truly believes that an informed press protects a helpless public from their government."

"Who protects the public from an informed press?" I ask him.

"You realize we were asked not to print the news that you were involved in the ambush?"

"Why were you asked to suppress *that* part?"

"We were asked—we complied. To a free press!"

He raises his glass to mine. We drink. He coughs in spasms from the first impact of the Goombay Smash, tears from the eye of the Caribbean hurricane.

"Mon Dieu!" he cries when he is able to breathe again. "Is this a drink or the neutron bomb?"

"You have to let the rum settle, and work your way down in stages, like a scuba diver going for a hundred and fifty feet."

I let him recover for another minute or so, then I ask him, "Any luck finding that go-between?"

"There is someone, half-French, half-Melanesian—the only person I'd trust with this. Unfortunately, she's still in Papeete. She works for UTA. They expect her back later this week. If *any*one can counsel you about the Melanesians, Kaméa can—*if* she'll agree. She's most unpredictable. A foot in one world, a foot in another. You are never sure just where she is standing at any given moment."

"What do you mean?"

"Her father was a Marist priest, her mother the daughter of a Kanaka chief. The mind boggles at the implications—*and* the complications of such a liaison. Let alone its offspring. If she comes back in time and consents to meet you, we shall see, no?"

"Maurice, I have to get up north. I have to get up there soon. I need an expert to steer me. I can't just leave it hanging in limbo! Who else is there?"

"Very well," he agrees, after a pause. "I will call Kaméa in Papeete. I've done favors for her in the past. I shall insist!"

"Thank you."

"Yesterday when we met," he says, more relaxed as the rum tingles his fingertips, "you said it was the Hienghène tribe you're interested in. Why that particular tribe?"

"Some of the indigs who attacked me at sea the other night were wearing masks from that tribe. At least, that's what Inspector Bazin says."

Maurice looks directly at me.

"You neglected to tell me about *that* attack! Was that *before* yesterday's ambush?"

"Their kick-off play."

"How did they know you were out there? Or that you were coming in?"

"That's got a very high priority on my list of unanswered questions."

"They didn't see you from shore?"

"No way! Not out where I was."

"Who knew you were coming?"

"Anybody who has access to telexes, marine-phone operations, memos on peoples' desks, or relatively sharp cars. You could spend weeks on that one and not know where the leakage really came down."

"Does Bazin know you plan to go north?"

"See, Bazin and I have this deal. I tell him very little. He tells me less. Frankly, I can't remember whether I specifically mentioned my immediate travel plans."

"Do you have any idea how dangerous it can be?"

"Come on, Maurice!" I grin. "More dangerous than beautiful downtown Nouméa?"

"Here you're in *your* world. Here you're a skilled and

formidable urban guerrilla, the best I've known. But up there—in *their* country . . ." He shakes his head. "This is not Vietnam. There are many things beyond our realities, things all around us, even in this city with all its façades of our imposed culture. But up there, up in the north . . ."

"I know," I say. "Blue bottles and sea snakes."

He doesn't appear to find any need to have this one fleshed out, so we just let it float there between us as we work on the bottom rung of the Goombay Smashes, down deep where the heavy good stuff lurks.

"Has he told you that he sent an officer?" Maurice asks suddenly.

"Sent an officer up north? When?"

"My contact at police headquarters," Maurice replies, "informed me this morning that Bazin's best Melanesian undercover agent left last night to check into certain matters relating to the Hienghène tribe."

"Well," I smile, "Bazin admitted he was full of feints. Still, how can I dislike a man whose wife bakes me pains chocolats?"

"John, his wife is dead."

"Dead?"

"Yes."

I hear compassion in his voice.

"When?" I ask.

I recall the slope of Bazin's shoulders as he'd left *Steel Tiger* just an hour ago. That cloud of loneliness. Of course his wife is dead! It explains so much.

"Almost two years ago."

"But why would he talk about her as though she's still alive?"

"It is something he does with everyone. No one has the heart to challenge the deception. We inquire after her health, we ask when we might next be invited to dinner. This past Christmas I even sent her a Hermès scarf. It seems to help him, so we do it, against the day he will come around and tell us he is all right again and that we needn't pretend any longer."

He smiles vaguely.
"Foolish, no?"
"No," I say.
I wish I could send Doan Thi a Hermès scarf.

# ═══CHAPTER═══

# 12

**I** carry the windsurfer up the beach to the Club Med boathouse.

"Another hour I'd have sent out a search boat," the Aussie beachboy tells me with more asperity than concern.

"All's well that ends well," I smile.

"You have some problems out there or something?"

He's waiting for me to admit I can't handle a speed board.

"Sea snakes," I reply.

He looks challenged and disbelieving, as though I've impugned all of New Caledonia.

"Where?"

"You'd never believe it if I told you."

I leave him properly dangling.

The acridity of vinegar bites at the lining of my nostrils as I approach our hotel room. I enter to discover Ken daubing the stuff on his crimsoned buttocks. One of the Club Med's prides is their open-door policy. In their natural state all rooms stay unlocked—the front desk doesn't even issue you a key—although there is a latch on the inside of your door if you're sullen enough to want to shut yourself in and deny yourself the possibility of convivial strangers joining you at any moment.

"How'd you ever manage that?" I ask Ken.

"Goddamn missionary position," he moans.

I put the dive bag on my bed, go back out to the ice machine down the corridor, come back with a plastic bucket of cubes, take the vinegar from him, and start eas-

141

ing his pain by gliding the cubes lightly over the burned area.

"Don't ever say you don't have friends."

He grins. "Reminds me of that old story about the guy who gets bit in the pecker by a cobra. Only way to save him is for somebody to suck out the poison. Remember the punch line?"

We chant it together: "That's when you find out who your real friends are."

"I have an ulterior motive," I tell him. "I need you to slide over to the marina, pick up a car for me. But if you can't sit, you can't drive."

Painfully, he eases his jockey shorts back on.

"I'll skate right on out," he says. "Harry flew me up here to help, not to have you pat my precious arse with ice cubes."

"Which one was it?" I ask. "Queenie or Marla?"

"That's the bloody surprise!" he says. "You'd think it would have been Queenie, but all she did was talk about Ronnie this and Ronnie that and when is Ronnie coming back from town? You bowled her over, Johnny boy. She'll be looking for you tonight, count on it! But this little mouse that hates all Aussie studs isn't on Amédée more than ten minutes—doesn't even *look* at the fucking light-house—when she signals me over behind a rock and the next thing I know she's pulled my trunks down around my knees—thank God I still kept my T-shirt on, or my shoulders would have been burned raw too—and we get this bash going. She keeps hanging on and panting in my ear like a Tonga war cry, 'Goddamn all men!' and jouncing up and down. Lucky all I burned was my arse, I'll tell you! Where exactly is this car, Johnny? What's she look like?"

"Green Renault 5-TX. Parking lot, Club Nautique. Keys taped under the front axle. You can take a cab over, okay?"

"Sure thing."

"Got any CFPs to pay the driver?"

"Harry gave me a bundle."

"Bring the car straight back. I'll be waiting at the gate. I

142

have to be in town before six or the guy'll be gone for the day, and I'm trying to make every day here count. Can you make it?"

He looks at his wristwatch.

"I'll make it."

He slips into his trousers as though tiptoeing into boiling water.

"You working tonight?" he asks.

"After this face-off in town," I tell him, "I'm on down-time til eleven hundred hours tomorrow. What do you have in mind?"

"Well, as I see it, the more Club Med types you have around you, the better your screen, right?"

"That's the hope, anyway."

"I was thinking maybe we can all have dinner together."

"All?"

"You, me, Queenie, and Marla. Maybe after dinner we could make the dance scene and the casino. Could be one of those Hall of Fame nights. What do you think?"

"Might just work out," I agree. I've been curious all day, ever since Bazin mumbled about the need to investigate the people aboard that Benetti power yacht tied up in front of *Steel Tiger*. There also still remains Kim's offer of fifty grand a month. Even if it's pie-in-the-sky, a man doesn't get one of those coming his way every day. Maybe I should meet my neighbors at the Marina. With Ken along and Queenie and Marla, I can whip in and out.

Ken gives me a V-for-victory left over from a war before our time that still hasn't ended and rushes out.

I step onto the balcony, watch another day fall away in slow-mo.

Am I getting anywhere? My conscious says, Hell, no. Okay, let's ask the unconscious.

I stare directly at the sun. When the images go black, I drop my lids, trapping the inky motes, let them pirouette while I try to slip the gears of my mind. This little self-hypnotic routine seems to help me team up the arcane messages of my dreams with my waking life. I'm still trying to perfect the flipside of that, to integrate my waking life into my dreams, but I haven't quite found the zipper for that one yet. When I'm awake, I can confront and conquer danger, but until I can conquer all the dangers in my dreams, will I not remain vulnerable?

I call now on tonight's dreams to gather up, please, the pieces of the puzzle, all the discrepant events and random images that have hammered at me since I stood offshore of New Caledonia only two nights ago, to gather up these scattered elements, the related and the unrelated, and assemble them into a mosaic I can recognize.

This programming done, I return to the bedroom and dress in reliable, unpressed, faded khakis, next to cammies the most inconspicuous costume for a man skip-dancing through hostile territory. Deliberately I haven't had this particular set cleaned in months, inasmuch as I'm mindful of the history of khaki. Among a native troop of Guides who skirmished at Peshawar, the survivors were not those wearing regulation white English drills, lustrous targets for enemy snipers, but only those soldiers shrewd enough before combat to dye their uniforms with tea or smear them with river mud. The lesson swiftly passed from regiment to regiment, so that when the 74th Foot, fighting the Kaffir War in South Africa, moved into battle in 1851, every man jack was wearing coverass khaki as uniform of the day.

I slap my tunic, note with satisfaction the tiny puff of dust, remind myself the word *khaki* comes from the Persian word *khak*, meaning dust.

I heft my dive bag with its heavy contents and go out to the Club Med gatehouse.

Ken arrives from the main highway within minutes.

I ask him to unlock the trunk. I place the dive bag under cover, then get up front with him, letting him drive and directing him toward Rue Jules Ferry. I feel momentarily safe, just another faceless passenger encased by a green Renault.

Late-afternoon traffic delays us, but we still arrive well

before the six o'clock deadline I'd been given when I'd telephoned earlier that afternoon from the Biarritz. Maurice had urged me to see the new secretary-general of the Fédération Calédonienne before I spoke to any other politicians. I'm still not sure why, but when I asked him, he simply shrugged, told me to go see Sabourin, then I would begin to have a better comprehension of the complexity of the situation I'd bought into, and possibly—this was more unsaid than said—come to the conclusion that the best thing I could do for myself and for New Caledonia was to get back aboard *Steel Tiger* and sail out, back whatever way I'd come.

"Park over there," I tell Ken.

"This the right address?" he asks doubtfully, scanning a number on the nearest building.

"No. But I don't want the people I'm visiting to make this car—or'connect me up with it."

I reach around to the fitted small-of-the-back holster, slip the Browning free, chamber a round, snap the hammer back and thumb the safety on, Ken watching with morbid fascination.

"That's a real big-guy gun, isn't it?" he asks.

"They come bigger."

"Some meeting you're going to!"

"This isn't for the meeting," I tell him. "The meeting is in the nature of intelligence-gathering. This is just for insurance, in case somebody sees me who shouldn't—on the way to or from the meeting—and tries to touch me off."

I reholster, get out of the car, evaluate the terrain. Purely industrial. Warehouses and garages. Fourteen separate driveways and recessed entrances between here and the corner. Someone waiting could be in any one of them. At least the rooflines look clear. No parapets for a man to lie behind.

"Place I'm going to is around that far corner," I tell Ken. "When you see me coming back, pull out right away, swing a U, drive back the way we came—away from me, and take that next intersection. I'll keep walking until I get

to the intersection. Then I'll turn in and you'll be parked in
there, facing my way. The minute you see me, start the
car, roll toward me, swing the door open and I'll hop in.
Okay?"

"You really *like* this kind of work, Johnny?"

"It's a growth industry."

I leave him.

A brisk walk, my eyes ranging everywhere, and I feel the
abrupt let-down of relief as I come to the warehouse I'm
looking for.

I enter, ascend the stairs Maurice had told me to expect.
On the first level up, I find a waiting room in which three
brawny roofing-and-siding types are each pretending to be
reading newspapers while feeding on me with octopus eyes.

"M. Sabourin?" I ask.

One of them cocks a finger at another door. I open it,
step through.

Sabourin rises from behind his bureau plat.

"Are you surprised I agreed to see you?" he asks.

"I'm surprised by just about everything in New Caledonia."

He is not what I had expected, nor does his office reflect
prevailing notions about what a communist headquarters
should look like. Nowhere do I see bold posters of tractors,
nowhere photos of sturdy young people joyously holding
up scythes in fields of waving grain. Instead, some Parisian
decorator transiting his mauve period has created a raw-
silk lavender environment for the secretary-general of the
Fédération Calédonienne.

I particularly admire an art-nouveau glass vase, a vortex
of purple and crimson.

"Galle," I comment, more than ask.

He doesn't trouble to nod. Obviously it's an early Galle,
worth thousands.

Sabourin himself is even more antipodal. In place of the
expected blue jeans and leather jacket, or in all decent
conformity at least a flattened nose or a squashed ear,
something to affirm he's paid his dues on the ascent from
the docks, I see a young man not yet thirty, a pink scarf

blossoming at the trachea, a polka-dot shirt unbuttoned to his solar plexus, and over his shoulders a black Italian-made jacket draped casually. Pale olive ski-glasses occlude his eyes. His delicate smile smokes like dry ice as he gestures me to a place on a sectional sofa.

I recognize that he has not yet learned to modulate his performance. He needs a stern choreographer and a lot more time in power. Nonetheless, I decide to take him seriously. The Fédération Calédonienne enlists a thousand voting members, many in key positions on the waterfront, and if they've chosen this laddie as their capo, they must know something about him I do not.

He leaves his desk to arrange himself across from me on the curved couch. His shoes, I see, are so new they still retain the maker's original gloss.

"Most impressive," I say.

"*What* is impressive, monsieur?"

"This layout. You'll have to admit it's not your standard revolutionary basement with a broken mimeo machine."

"Why should one abrogate taste simply because he's committed to a demanding political ideology?"

"Contradiction," I reply. "Esthetics demands the exercise of individual choice. Politics, especially your kind, necessarily preempts personal adventurism."

"Apparently you do not comprehend the unique nature of French communism."

"Apparently."

"How may I serve you?"

"By being as truthful with me as French communism permits."

"You'll find that of all political parties in New Caledonia we are the most forthright. If you accept honest protest as truth, then you will find us truthful."

I smile at him. Clearly I am not dealing here with Elmer Fudd from Moosecock, Kansas.

"What, if anything, have you heard about me?" I ask.

"That you've been imported by the international fascist Marcel Gallante."

"May I ask where you heard that?"

"Everyone in Nouméa talks about the American mercenary who was ambushed, then ambushed his ambushers."

"Do you regard me as a mercenary?"

"I do."

"Suppose I told you my perception of my job in New Caledonia is to work with the police, within the framework of your laws, though using certain special training I've had, to help the police try to put an end to the terrorism which is killing people on your streets?"

"I would reply that such a perception is yours, not mine."

"Why do you consider Gallante a fascist?"

"Why not? He uses crisis for his own purpose. He stands for forcible suppression of opposition. For a military solution. You are the guillotine of that policy, monsieur!"

"I'm sorry you feel that," I tell him genuinely. "I'd like you to know that one of the tasks I've set myself is to find out who killed the previous secretary-general of your Fédération. I feel there's a link in his killing with the rest of this—that it was not an isolated act, but part of a master timetable."

He blows out his lips, makes the sound of a bus door opening.

"Forgive me," he says. "I can't believe you mean that— or that Marcel Gallante would finance such an investigation."

"I am known," I tell him, "for my meddlesome behavior. I am not a likable person. No tenacious animal is. And to get the work done, I sometimes form all kinds of strange alliances—if necessary, even to the disadvantage of my employers. Right now, for example, I'm trying to find out if there's anything you and I might do for each other."

"I find the mere hypothesis ludicrous. We are committed enemies for more reasons than you know."

"Okay. I'll add you to my list. It seems to be getting longer by the hour."

"Why don't you leave our country while you still can?" he demands.

I elect to ignore this. "What I'm getting from you," I say, "is this nagging feeling that you support terrorism."

He makes the bus sound again. "At this very moment," he replies, "we are preparing a statement for the press. The position of the Fédération Calédonienne toward these barbaric acts is one of absolute condemnation. Two of our members and one of their children were injured in the bombing of the Treasury building yesterday. Such wanton acts, aside from their antihumanity, are politically counterproductive. I will add a personal comment. If you and the terrorists—whoever they are—care to go far out into the countryside, well away from civilized people, and mutually eradicate yourselves, I for one would applaud such noblesse oblige."

"You mustn't think you're getting to me with those little zingers," I smile. "You see, I come from a zip-code cluster in Southern California, the home of spreading franchise fungus. We are oblivious to all insults, even from those more skilled in invective than you. It is a natural immunity we develop early on from being raised in the womb of kitch and from being weaned on Big Macs."

He appears somewhat unnerved. "You *are* speaking English, are you not?"

"Let me ask you," I continue in the acentric manner which seems to suit me best, "what is the effective casualty radius of the Com-Bloc's RGD-5 grenade?"

"What would I know about Russian grenades?"

"Twenty meters," I inform him. "Our U.S. frags are good for only fifteen. But then we're a new country, still feeling our way around the real world."

"I fail to see your point," he says, and for the first time I observe that he has this compulsive mannerism with his lips. They nibble at each other between words, without his awareness, like two goldfish snatching at food pellets.

"There's no conceivable benefit for you in the program of your Fédération," I tell him, "at least in the program you announce publicly—*unless* the Soviet military moves in here after you've conned the Melanesians into supporting you. So I'd suggest you'd *better* start learning about Russian ordnance!"

He leans back in the couch, gazes at me for longer than I would have thought he could have faced my unremitting eyes.

"What do you know about the Melanesians?" he demands.

"Admittedly, not much. I've had trouble finding any I could talk to. Almost as much trouble as I'm having trying to figure out why elitist Frenchmen like you are so devoted to giving everything you've taken back to the Melanesians you took it from."

"Don't accuse me of the crimes of those in power! We are trying to redress what they've done. We demand that the people who were here before we came be given equality —socially, economically, and politically. Look around Nouméa, monsieur! You will see that the Melanesian has been shunted down the ladder. He has become at best the laborer for a white society and at worst a colorful exhibition for tourists at torchlight dances ordered up by the beach hotels. We say he must no longer be treated as a beggar without a culture, but as a free and equal man. But because we have stripped away from him everything that once made up his culture in order that the French state and the Marcel Gallantes of the world could enrich themselves, he's turned on the only person he dares to turn on—himself. And so he scorns himself and drowns himself in alcohol. If this goes on much longer, it can produce only one of two consequences—either his extinction . . . or his revolt. We propose an alternative—total independence from France—but on Kanak terms! And we will bring this about. It may take another year, even two or three—but we will make it happen! This is what our Fédération is committed to—nothing else!"

He rises from the couch, as though one cannot be permitted to deliver so rousing a statement from a seated position. He seems less foppish now. There is about him almost an air of magnificence, except that the smell of strong cologne and the hint of cappuccino-breath from his last coffee break tend to dissipate the nonworldly altruism he's posturing for.

I smile up at him. Good speech!

"We will not make the mistake you Americans made in Vietnam," he adds. "We *will* win hearts and minds!"

"Hooray for you!" I say, suddenly bored. I too rise. "Incidentally, there's an old Politburo proverb you should mount on the wall behind your desk. The Russians understand it better than anybody. It goes something like this: 'Grab 'em by the balls; their hearts and minds will follow!' Thank you for your time."

I move toward the door.

"Not yet!" he cries sharply, so sharply I turn back, fully prepared to discover he's turned into a pillar of salt. Definitely, the man needs a choreographer.

"You've been seeing Rosine!" he says accusingly.

"Rosine?" He's taken me by surprise.

"She and I have an understanding. A previous relationship. I insist you not see her again!"

"Sabourin," I tell him, "you're a bundle of paradoxes, do you know that? What possible understanding can *you* have with the daughter and niece of two such titans of fascism as Georges and Marcel Gallante?"

"I did not call Georges a fascist! Only Marcel!"

"Marcel works for Georges," I remind him. "I've seen the invisible whip Georges cracks. How do you reconcile that?"

"I have warned you! Just remember that! You have been warned!"

"This is what you meant when you said we're committed enemies?"

He nods.

"I'm sorry, M. Secretary-General, that it has to be this way. I came up here wide-eyed with goodwill and full of naïve hopes. I hoped that because your Fédération is close to the Melanesian fronts, you might deliver a message to anyone who has contact with the terrorists."

"Are you accusing *us* of having contact with them?"

"Just suggesting the word gets passed."

"What word is that, monsieur?"

"Tell them to wise up!"

"I'm not sure I understand what that means."

"Tell them they'll get a lot further if they stop giving everybody a rough way to go. If they don't, we're going to really foul them up. Already a battle cruiser and a detachment from the Foreign Legion are being rushed in here. So much for the big picture.

"Now, regarding your personal injunction that I stop seeing the lady, I quit taking orders a couple of years back. Only two things stop me from doing just about any damned thing I feel like doing: the codified law of whatever land I happen to be operating in, and superior force overwhelming me. If you can marshal such a force, you're when you do. If you can't, I'd suggest you puff out your free to send it against me—and risk whatever comes down lips one more time and make that sound of a bus door opening. It's the most fascinating thing you do."

I wait, giving him his chance to make whatever move he might feel obligated to make, but I don't trouble to shift weight or coil myself because it's apparent he's never taken fist or foot to another man.

I leave him ticking in fury.

As I go out past the three cephalopods in the waiting room and then down the stairs, I hear something smash against the wall of Sabourin's office.

I hope it is not the crimson-and-purple Galle.

It would have looked so right on a Louis XIV commode my mother positions between the two south windows of her apartment on the Left Bank.

# CHAPTER

## 13

**W**ith Ken still manfully at the wheel of the Renault, we drive from Nouméa back to Anse Vata alongside an apricot-streaked bay. I watch the sun melting and I feel my body awakening. Count Dracula and I, he out of his satin-lined coffin, I out of the jungle. You welcome the night because it cloaks you, even as the green metal sides of the anonymous Renault now cloak me from those hunting for me in Nouméa. If Dracula can loom up out of the shadows, so can you, baby.

It's just that simple a mind-set, but how inverse that most people feel safer in daylight when they can be more easily targeted. Must be the victim syndrome, yeah, must be. I observed this phobia in-country, when at the first sniff of darkness most troopers got spooked. They felt impelled to throw out all kinds of flank security and to dig in and wait for a new day, maybe even a better day, while in the forests around them, liberated by darkness from all our engines of war, the enemy took his country back. He was out there laughing and reciting ballads and maybe even staging puppet shows, acting as though he were on a Louisiana hayride, and it only drove our guys deeper into the ground.

Ken is chattering away, but I'm not receiving him. I'm engrossed with inner voices, mostly Rosine's. I can feel her waiting for me in that house up on the heights of Ouen Toro with the iron balconies on all four sides, and I'm drawn to her, God knows, for reasons I felt I'd managed to put aside, out of my life. But to go is to risk plunging right back into another firefight with all those gunsy bastards out there somewhere. I'm not yet ready to bring smoke in on them—whoever they are.

But I do catch something from Ken, something about our meeting Queenie and Marla at the lobby bar by seven —and something else about having to get down to the dining room before the mob hits.

My inner voices are finally drowned out by the noise level in the Club Med lobby. A contingent from Tokyo has just arrived and is being duly sworn in. The combined chatter of all the other guests congregating around the corner bar as they wait for the dinner call is roughly in the same decibel range as a battery of Big Mamas firing their steel hearts out.

Queenie and Marla manage to find us.

Marla appears as repressed as she had this morning at breakfast. If any part of her anatomy has been scorched, it's not showing. I observe that now her thumbs, not her pinkies, are folded into her fists and that she scarcely looks at Ken. So much for the immutability of intercourse.

Queenie comes flouncing up in a short skirt, revealing strong surfer's legs, and has herself imprisoned in something from the waist up I've heard the fashion people call a tube top.

We end up angled into each other, smiling and chatting away without a word getting through, but Queenie doesn't seem to mind. I have this sudden cartoon-image of someone in the crowd pressing her even more vigorously against me and of her popping like toothpaste right out of the tube.

Queenie's hand brushes my neck, then she hooks one of my ears with her index finger, pulls it close to her lips.

"Been thinking about you, hon, ever since breakfast."

Ken lumbers back in, collecting us. We flow with the others toward the staircase, then in a torrent of rumbling stomachs, a gigantic eating machine, we descend to the lower level where a chorus of affable GOs robustly sing us into the dining room.

"God, I love it! Don't you, Ronnie!" Queenie cries, clasping my hand. "People meeting people! What else *is* there?"

I look over at Queenie, at her bright, rapt, sincere little face—the face of a girl who needs ritual, who would wither up and blow away without soap and underarm deodorant and airline timetables, a girl who, when she marries, will certainly have dinner on the table ardently at seven each evening—and I wonder how, in all human decency, I am going to persuade her before this night has ended that I do not want to make her mine, that I want only her company and the smell of her lilac soap from a friendly distance and a chance to get quietly through all of it until Michael's message at eleven o'clock tomorrow morning.

We share the table for eight with two other couples, both Japanese, obviously newlyweds, the two young wives so Americanized they stare around with superficial indifference while chain-smoking their way through dinner, their husbands constantly attending them with dabs of flame from thin gold lighters.

The two wives ignore us. Their husbands politely try to speak a few obligatory phrases to us, but it's painful going until, by unspoken agreement, we simply divide the table into East and West and leave them to their exquisitely subjective language while they leave us to our logical and unequivocal English.

After dinner, I see them one more time at le Disco, but even more insulated now, through a haze of strobe-lit cigarette smoke. The Japanese girls in their Western clothes dance with studied detachment, looking everywhere about them and nowhere at the same moment, and watching them, seeing the loss, the metamorphosis from the willow-like suppleness of their pre-MacArthur grandmothers into these sticklike robots, I recall Sabourin's words from this afternoon about stripping a people's culture from them and what it does to any ethnic group to lose a war or a country or their very roots, and I wonder if I'm fighting for the right side here on New Caledonia. It is a fleeting thought, without great substance, but it is a thought that more and more often lately gives me a twinge of unease.

Nothing mechanistic about Queenie. In hyper-boost, traveling through black holes and the twilight zone, she bounds about me as we dance on the crowded floor, her shoulders and hips working, hands spearing up and down, sweat dribbling between her breasts, then in close to me, grinding like a stripper, then off again, a snap turn, a deep squat, up again with hands clapping to the music, then with a loud hoot kicking up one leg higher than her head, knee straight, toe pointed, the extension clearing space around us and exposing hard inner thighs, the men dancing about us peering zealously and storing the vision of that flash of secret thigh, the moist crease in her tight panties momentarily revealed, so that later, in the dark silence of their hotel rooms, in bed with their wives expecting a performance of vacation-triggered lust, these husbands will be able to stimulate their ardor by replaying the erotic memory, enhance what has long since become standard operating procedure by imagining it's Queenie who clasps them, that they are emptying into that unpossessed young vagina, and thus surprise and please their wives, deceiving them only to the extent that the adultery is fantasized, not realized.

Thinking to divert Queenie's resolute fix on me, I suggest we move the party to the casino, only a short walk, I'm told, across the hotel grounds.

The casino is a miniature of the gambling salon at Cannes with a Continental elegance alien to the South Pacific. For the most part the women are well dressed, the men in jackets and ties. Ken and I, in order to enter beyond the rotunda of slot machines, have had to put on the guest ties issued to us by a cloakroom attendant. Mine carries a faint odor of vomit.

The sounds are those you hear in casinos the world over, the muted, almost hushed medley of silent winners, even more silent losers, chips deftly swept off ill-chosen numbers, cards being shuffled by machine, rattle of roulette balls in spinning discs, clatter of dice in leather cups.

Queenie's eyes shine. I am relieved that her fever for gambling may even exceed her fever for sex. I bring her with me to the cashier's window where I buy chips with one of Rosine's five-thousand-franc notes, give Queenie a palmful, point her off to the nearest roulette table with Ken and Marla, while I cross to a blackjack table where Kim sits, so intent on the game she doesn't sense me coming up behind her.

I wait until a paunchy tourist, florid and muttering, pushes away from the table. I occupy his place, settle in next to Kim. Two thin straps support a form-fitting beaded gown that she's pulled up to the top of her thighs so she can sit on the stool.

She glances at me from the corners of her eyes, taking in the new boy next to her, discovers it's the neighbor from Club Nautique.

"Figured you'd show up," she says.

"You were right," I conceded. "I *could* use a new stem-head fitting. Even a beefier capstan."

The dealer is a Chinese girl. Her no-nonsense dark eyes signal me to place my bet or make room for someone who will.

I drop a thousand-franc chip in the indicated squares on the felt playing field.

"Which one's your boss?" I ask Kim.

"A thousand francs you can't guess—three shots at it."

"Okay."

I scan the casino. At least seventy men are clustered here and there or stalking the tables. No way I can't spot the owner of a five-million-dollar yacht out of seventy men, especially with three chances.

"Card?"

The Chinese girl has a feral look about her. I catalog her as emigrating from Shanghai, probably not more than a year ago. She exhibits all the rudeness of today's Shanghai young.

I look at my cards—two aces. I split them, doubling my bet, go back to studying the room. I eliminate twenty-two men with one glance—they're Japanese. Kim's boss is American. This eliminates another thirty non-American types. Now I'm down to twenty-eight Caucasians who could be Americans, Australians, New Zealanders, or English.

"Cards?" the Chinese girl asks again, more sharply this time.

I check out the cards she's dropped on each of my aces.

A king and a queen. I flip them over, go back to my quest as the girl pays me off at one and a half for each blackjack.

I begin to cherry-pick among the twenty-two by clothes style. I discard eight New Zealanders because of the broad seamy shoulders on their woolen jackets, seven Australians simply because I know them now by aura. This leaves me with thirteen candidates.

"Bets, please!"

"Oh," I say. "All of it, of course."

This dealer must be new here, because she now devotes herself to my defeat, deciding to ignore the other players until she's cleaned my plow. I award her my John Locke smile of amused compassion. No way is this little lady from Shanghai going to pull it off, not tonight. Tonight I am invincible.

As I had the first hand around, I again ignore my cards while I eliminate four other men because of the spastic way they throw craps. Card-carrying amateurs. Kim's boss didn't get his Benetti being a putz.

This time I look at my cards before the Chinese girl can scold me.

A ten and a four. I smile at her with the smugness of a man sitting pat with two face cards, turn away from the table once more and start to zero in on the Man.

The dealer exposes her cards. She's hoist on a fifteen. House rules require her to hit. She pulls a seven to go with her fifteen and breaks. She pushes another five thousand francs of chips across to me as though she's just cut off her hand and left it in front of me.

"He's the one playing baccarat," I say to Kim. "The one in the three-piece suit."

"You saw him on the boat!"

"You know better."

Kim tosses a one-thousand-franc chip onto the pile in front of me.

"Bets!" the Chinese girl demands, including Kim in her indictment.

I let the eleven thousand francs ride and the girl lays another blackjack on me, jumping me to twenty-seven thousand five and drawing an envious crowd.

A young man whose black hair appears to be glued onto a Sanforized skull slips into the dealer's slot, ousting the Chinese girl, who leaves without looking back at me. The young man's face is riddled with enormous pores, as though he's been evolved to breathe through his cheeks, not through his pinched nostrils. The whites of his eyes glow sallowly. He faces me with an almost inaudible sibilance, deals me two cards with a gesture that suggests both cards are saturated with bubonic-plague germs. Two magnificent buboes, the ace of spades, the ace of clubs. I split them, doubling up again. He appears to have stopped breathing, except through his pores. But he is incapable of interrupting my preordained winning streak. He rewards me with two simultaneous blackjacks and jerks back at their falling as though two fifty-caliber slugs have slammed into him.

I step away from the table with chips redeemable at just under a hundred thousand francs. His drill-like eyes follow me. I have seen more humanity in the speckled eyes of moray eels. I decide not to tip him.

I give Kim back her one thousand. I've got enough now to repay Rosine and still keep some thousands to play around with without having to tap into what few traveler's checks I'm squirreling in the safe aboard *Steel Tiger*.

Kim follows me to the cashier's cage.

"I still want to know how you picked him out of this whole casino."

"Process of elimination," I tell her. "It finally narrowed down to three. I went for the most unlikely."

"I've heard Otis called a lot of things, but never 'unlikely.' "

"Well, for starters, Otis itself is a fairly unlikely name for anybody who owns a Benetti yacht. Otis what?"

"Walden. Otis Walden. Why do you call him unlikely?"

"Why are you so interested?"

"Your thought process interests me."

"Okay, look at him, sitting over there in that three-piece suit. That kind of tailoring you can only buy in London for about fifteen hundred dollars and a month's time for fittings. That would suggest particularity on his part, right?"

"Right."

"Now, look at his hair. When was it cut last?"

"God knows. He won't let anybody touch it. He says cutting it would be like having his balls cut off."

"Exactly. The hair and the suit don't connect. That's what I mean by unlikely. And look at his eyes."

Kim studies him, her head cocked to one side as she reevaluates him. "He does have sort of off-the-wall eyes, doesn't he?"

"Driven," I correct.

"Who are you? *What* are you?" she asks, her tone so hushed I almost lean closer, for she's asking not out of curiosity but almost out of awe, or at least that's what I sense from her at this moment.

"It's the ex-cop in me," I say. "We never stop eyeballing."

"No wonder we don't get along," she says. "I hate cops! Fuck cops, I say! Fuck all cops and fuck all ex-cops!"

"It's been another enchanting get-together," I say. "We'll have to stop meeting like this."

I start toward the distant roulette table where Ken and the two Australian girls are still hanging in, but Kim blocks my way.

"Don't just walk away! Please," she says, "*deal* with me!"

"You're a yo-yo," I say, "wound too tight for my taste."

"Otis'll really be pissed if I don't deliver you. Please come over and meet him—just for a minute at least."

"Okay."

"You will? You'll take the job?"

"Not the job."

"You don't even know what it is!"

"I don't want to know. I can't afford to clutter up my mind."

"Then why bother to meet him?"

"He's got a helicopter. I like to know people with helicopters. Tell me about him."

"Well, it's hard to bottom-line Otis Walden. But you're right about his being driven. He's got good reason. A year ago the best doctors in the States gave him only six months to live."

"For somebody who's six months past due, he doesn't look as though he's got anything fatal. What's he supposed to be dying of?"

My question strikes me as vacuous the moment I ask it. All of us are dying of ticking clocks and coming events. Yet something about Otis Walden engages me.

"He had something they call terminal pulmonary vascular disease," Kim replies. "But he went into the hospital at Stanford for some kind of new, radical surgery—like giving him a heart and lung transplant from a donor who got zapped in a car crash, but whose lungs and heart were still undamaged at the time of death."

I have read only recently of this revival of heart-lung transplantation that had been performed more than a decade ago with no patient surviving more than three weeks after surgery. But with a new drug, cyclosporin A, combined with other immunosuppressive drugs which deceive the body's immune reaction against foreign organs, this decade's patients seem able to assimilate the new heart and lungs and to resume active lives.

I look again at the man at the baccarat table. What

draws me to him is the sense that both of us have already done our dying.

"Since this is his second time around, he's not missing anything," Kim says. "Okay, you're so all-seeing, what's *my* story?"

"Bring him over to the bar when he finishes his play," I say and start away again.

"I asked you a question!" she insists.

I turn back, see her standing there, willing to endow my answer, whatever it may be, with importance. For a girl who's clocked her mileage, she's remarkably open to slings and arrows.

"I think you came to the big city to see the elephant," I tell her, "and they broke it off up your ass."

She starts laughing, all the way from her knees, but that's one of the advantages of casinos, unlike libraries. You can laugh, you can even scream, and just so long as you don't interrupt the action at the tables, nobody's going to pay you too much attention. They all have their own engagements at the moment.

"Story of my life," she says. "In—let's see . . ." She repeats what I've said to her under her breath and counts the words. "In twenty words."

I cross to the bar.

I can feel Walden's approach on my shoulders. I rise from the bar stool, accept his handshake.

"This *is* a pleasure," he says, his eyes devouring me.

He settles in on one side of me, Kim on the other.

"Another of the usual," he tells the bartender. I note that the bartender is already taking out an iced magnum of Dom Perignon.

"Kim tells me you don't want the job," he says. "Frankly, I thought you'd jump at it."

"I'm working."

"Didn't she make that part clear? This would be when you've finished here."

"Do you know what I'm doing here?"

"Putting the fear of God into a bunch of assholes, from what I've heard."

"They've been managing to give me some gray hairs too. Anyway, I have something else to do if I finish here."

"*If?*"

"If!"

"I'm still willing to wait. Just tell me when you can give me a month——maybe we can do the job in even less time. But it does have to be before the end of this year. I've got a deadline to meet."

"I don't plan that far ahead anymore."

"How about seventy-five thousand?"

"It's not the money," I say. "It's just that I stopped laying out schedules. I hang loose."

"I can accept that," he says. "Okay, let me put it this way. If you can come to Borneo anytime from September to December of this year and give me thirty days, I'll pay you seventy-five thousand dollars, twenty-five of it tonight in any currency of your choosing as a deposit."

I'm intrigued. Borneo lies out there somewhere along my zigzag itinerary, and September's as good or as bad as any other month, especially since those are the shores of the Land Below the Wind, ten saving degrees below the typhoon belt straddling the seas from Japan to Luzon. I find myself touching the rims of their tulip-shaped glasses with the rim of mine, and we drink. Possibly it's the '75 champagne. Possibly it's that I respond to Otis' dynamism.

"Seventy-five thousand dollars is a lot of money for thirty days of honest labor," I say, stressing the word *honest.*

"Ah-hah!" he grins. "You hit the key word—*honest!* That is and always has been the cornerstone of my corporate and my personal life—absolute, unremitting, uncompromising, brutal honesty. It destroyed my marriage, cost me my kids, stripped me of friends, but I've clung to it anyway. Surprise you?"

"Greatly," I admit.

"You thought I scored it in narcotics, didn't you?"

"That thought did cross my mind."

"Don't misunderstand. I pack my nose from time to time. I prefer a good joint to a martini. I've done speed.

I've even tried hardballing, but that shit'll drop you in your tracks. But I've always been a customer, never a dealer."

"I misjudged you. I happen to know what a boat like yours goes for. It's hard to come up with five million dollars after taxes today, *unless* you're illegal."

"I made mine in Silicon Valley," he says. "Built a computer company from a garage operation into an electronics conglomerate, then sold it to the Pac-Man of conglomerates and walked away with forty-eight million big ones after taxes on the afternoon of my thirty-eighth birthday. On my thirty-ninth, having just lost my loving wife and two great kids in a divorce action which cut that forty-eight back to twenty-four—one of the penalties of living in a community-property state like California with its goddamned Gold-Miner-of-Forty-Niner philosophy—I was getting pissed at a party commemorating my misery when some doctor friends of mine who've never been wrong confided to me I'd be dead in six months."

"I told him about your surgery," Kim says.

"I was lucky," he says. "A year earlier I'd have died right on schedule. But with new drugs and some surgeons who must have learned from God Almighty Himself, I was resurrected. You any idea what that's like?"

"A little," I say.

"So I asked myself what I intended to do now that I'd been given another shot at it. Would you believe, Mr. Locke, that in all those thirty-nine years of existence I'd only made love to one woman?—the first girl I met in college, the same girl I married, the woman I lived with all those years, had my kids with. I said to myself, Otis, you uptight, rich bastard, what you need is a boat that'll take you anywhere in the world you want to go and a mistress of ceremonies who will help you find all the women you ever hungered for. I bought the Benetti and I hired Kim here away from the girlie magazine she was working for. I offered her a salary she couldn't pass up and now she stage-manages the parties we have aboard and helps me with my research. What research? you're wondering. Human sexual-

164

ity, Mr. Locke, in all its forms, traditions, deviations, perversions, and inhibitions. I am fornicating my way into the center of things. I have discovered, thank God before it's too late, that sexual behavior is the source of life itself. I have become obsessed with it, with understanding it, seeing it, doing it. So I go to different countries, different cultures, and I dig into the local sex scene. I turn over rocks, if necessary. But I get to the inner truth of a place. All the rest—their form of government, their economy, their GNP, their customs, their cuisine—that's all bullshit. What you really have to find out is how they fuck or don't fuck. I invite them aboard. We serve the finest cuisine in the world. I stole my head chef from Marius & Janette in Paris. I make people happy. I encourage them to make love aboard. To themselves, to each other—to me, if they elect to. And I interview them, tape their innermost feelings and their hidden thoughts and fantasies. I videotape them too, if they let me. Do I disgust you or fascinate you?"

"Few things disgust me, Mr. Walden," I say. "Certainly not the celebration of life. I totally approve."

"Good, very good." He grins at Kim, then concentrates on me again. "How better can I learn who and what *I* am than through direct relationships with men and women of different colors, beliefs, and cultures? And what relationship reveals more about another person than sexual bonding, letting down your mutual defenses?"

"None," I agree.

"What I did," he continues, "before I left the States, was to make a deal through the conglomerate that bought me out. One of their subsidiaries is a major hard-cover publisher with a paperback affiliate. I negotiated one of the largest advances ever paid by a publishing house, for a nonfiction book I'm writing documenting sexual habits, customs, and preferences in the various countries and societies I'm visiting. Would you believe I got a two-million-dollar advance?"

"I've heard," I reply, "that sex outsells Ming teapots by a country mile."

"You bet your sweet boopie it does! Okay, so here I am with a two-million-dollar advance to fornicate my way around the world. To a highly principled man that's downright immoral. So I marched straight over to Stanford University and set them up a two-million-dollar trust to be used by the surgeons who gave me my second chance to live. With the interest this trust now earns, they can perform five such operations each year into the infinite future without ever touching the principal. For your information, this kind of surgery goes for about seventy-five thousand dollars a pop. But what *is* a life worth?"

"Depends on who's taking it," I reply. "In Vietnam it cost us four hundred thousand dollars for every enemy body."

"Christ," he says, "that *was* a lousy investment, wasn't it?"

"One of the piss-poorest," I agree.

"Anyway, think of the purity of *this* arrangement. I'm experiencing sexual ecstasy, the highest achievement of existence, and through my efforts five human beings each year will be given new hearts and lungs. It's as though I'm personally conceiving them. The mere thought of it is in itself an incredible aphrodisiac!"

The bartender refills our glasses.

"Now—that gets us to Borneo," he continues, "where piracy has been an honored way of life along the coastline of the Malaysian state of Sabah for several hundred years. I intend to take my boat into the Sulu Sea, right into the heartland of these Muslim killers, either to the island of Tawitawi or to Jolo, and while the pirates are out doing *their* thing, I intend to go ashore and do *my* thing. Can you imagine the chapter I can pull out of *that* lash-up? Sex with the daughters and wives of Muslim sea-killers! Pillage where pillage is due!"

I hear a strange sound echoing from inside my throat and I discover I'm laughing. Such a splendid madness this man is seized with!

"At least two things are wrong with it," I say. "You

shouldn't go to the Sulu Sea to pull this off. You should go to the Gulf of Thailand and do it to the Thai pirates who rape Indochinese women trying to escape from Vietnam and Cambodia. That lot *deserves* it! But your *main* problem is you'll never survive—Sulu Sea *or* Gulf of Thailand."

"That's where *you* come in! I have top connections in Borneo. I've got my finger on a reliable guide who knows the area inside and out and whose native language is Tausug. I want you—when you're ready—to turn my yacht into a self-contained warship. I want you to hire a squad of top combat men, the best mercs money can buy, to defend us when and if we're attacked. I'm not asking for any offensive operation here, Mr. Locke, just honest-to-God-we-don't-shoot-back until the bastards start shooting at us. I have access to any kind of ordnance you call for—and I don't mean just heavy MGs. I mean long-range missiles, the latest and most sophisticated stuff on the international market. And don't forget I've got that chopper for reconnaissance. We can arm her too, if you think that's advisable, and blow them out of the water from above."

"Fascinating," I say. "Truly fascinating. But for me it's the wrong place and the wrong people. If you'd told me the Gulf of Thailand, I might have gone along. But I have nothing against the pirates in the Sulu Sea. As a matter of fact, I have almost warm feelings toward them, based, I confess, on a very flimsy sentimental and definitely out-of-date premise—my memory of Joseph Conrad's *An Outcast of the Islands* and his dashing pirate leaders with their opium and curry and rice and uncounted wives. And, believe me, I'm aware that these days they use fast Volvo-Penta speedboats, carry fifty-caliber machine guns, and cut your throat for a carton of cigarettes. But my heart wouldn't be in it. I'm sorry."

"Will you at least *think* about it?"

"I just did," I say. "You'll find a lot of other men who'll jump at the chance."

"I wanted the best!"

"Thank you." I get up. "And for the champagne. Please

excuse me. I'm here with friends. Looks to me as though they've just run out of money."

Ken is leading Queenie and Marla toward me. Their hands are empty.

Kim too is watching them approach.

"Why don't you bring them along?" she suggests.

"Along?"

"We're having a little bash aboard. You afraid?"

"Of what?"

"A cluster-fuck."

"I don't know. I've never been to a cluster-fuck."

"Well, then, come on, come on!" Otis urges. "If it turns you off, no problem, just drink and relax. If it doesn't, take off your shoes and stay awhile."

He's already measuring Queenie.

I introduce Ken, Queenie, and Marla.

"We've been invited to a party aboard Mr. Walden's yacht," I say. "You all too tired or are you game?"

Queenie drapes herself all over me.

"I haven't even got started yet," she murmurs into my ear.

"We'll meet you there," I say to Kim. "I'll take my car—in case I have to leave early."

"I'll go with *you*," Kim announces, wresting my arm away from Queenie. Queenie starts to flex her biceps, but Kim smiles at her. "Wouldn't you rather fly over in Mr. Walden's helicopter?"

I lose Queenie, Marla, and Ken.

But not Kim.

# ══CHAPTER══

## 14

**K**im reappraises me as I drive the green Renault toward the Club Nautique.

"Want to hear the payoff?" she asks.

I nod.

"He's never laid a hand on me."

"Is that good or bad?"

"You really are a contrary sonofabitch!"

"I was simply asking if you're disappointed."

"Yeah, I'm disappointed. I'm always disappointed when a fella doesn't want me. I may not want him—I usually don't want anybody. But at least I want a man to take his best shot. Which brings me to you. You don't intend to hit on me, do you?"

"I really haven't thought about it."

"Oh, come on, angel pants! You've seen my bare box. We both know damn well you've wondered what it would be like."

"How much honesty can you handle?" I ask her.

"How much you got?"

"I met a girl yesterday. We made love in a pasture. She's waiting for me. I'm trying to decide whether or not I should see her tonight. There are certain risks involved in the exposure. But that's the least of it. Truth is I'm still in love with a dead woman. What would you want from a man in that situation?"

She stares straight ahead at the lights of Nouméa's hillside apartments for a full minute.

"That *was* honest, wasn't it?" she says finally.

But I'm not really listening to her. I'm hearing another voice. Is it mine? Or is it the captain I was then, watching me sullenly from inside my eyelids, clinging inside there like pasties on a stripper's tit.

"Dead?" he's screaming. "How do you *know* she's dead?"

"I heard," I whisper.

"HEARD? Who the fuck from?"

"Just—heard."

"When? WHEN?"

"When did I *hear*?"

"When did she *die*?"

"I didn't hear that. No date. Just—that she died of pneumonia in a reeducation camp at Gia Rai Z30."

"Then why didn't your ribs snap?" he shouts at me. "If you loved her so fucking much, man, and she died, why didn't your ribs just cave in at the exact moment she stopped breathing? Why didn't your skull burst? WHY?"

"Because I'd already died," I tell him.

"Bullshit!"

"I died in late April, 1975. It's a well-known fact, known to me alone, that when she turned away from me and went bicycling out to meet General Tran Van Tra of the Liberation Army, poised in nearby Bien-hoa with four NVA divisions to enter the falling capital, I died right then and there. Now get off my case!"

He's gone again, his cammies blending with the night, but this time I don't trouble to chase after him, for I'm caught up in remembering the early months of 1975. Doan Thi had come in from the countryside and taken a flat in Saigon on Tran hung Dao Boulevard so she could complete the last verses of an epic poem about women at war.

Partly to be in-country when the shitstorm hit, mostly to be near Doan Thi, I had managed to wangle duty as a member of the joint military team of the U.S. Defense Attaché Office. After the Paris Accords, DAO became the successor to MACV and we inherited their Pentagon East facilities at Ton Son Nhut airport.

That last morning with Doan Thi, I had stepped sopping wet out of her shower to discover her dressed in ao baba, the black pajamas of the peasant, her hair bound up in the style of the north, worn rubber sandals on her feet, carrying a crude basket containing her personal possessions.

"Last night, while you slept," she told me, "I finished the last verse. I went out and gave it to someone I trust. He will see that it's published when the time comes."

"Why are you dressed like that?" I asked her.

"At Loc Ninh," she said, "they prepare new uniforms for their march into Saigon. The bo doi are too proud to enter the city in jungle clothes. I shall take my bicycle and go out to their command post. General Tran Van Tra was my history teacher."

I grabbed her by the shoulders and shook her until her hair broke free of the ties that held it up and tumbled to her waist. She hung limp before my rage until I finally stopped and began screaming at her.

"They'll cut off your hair!" I cried. "They'll shave you bald and parade you through the streets! Just another whore to the American!"

"We are not European," she told me. "We are Asian. We do not exhibit our women in public. These are not invaders. They are Vietnamese. It is not some faceless enemy out there, but brothers and fathers and sons and cousins. In a few more days, when you have gone, children will be playing on the bo doi's tanks. Adieu, my beloved. Chào anh."

"Goddamn it! I haven't even got my pants on yet! I just got out of the shower, and here you are planning to bicycle into more goddamned artillery and rockets than the Russians lugged to Berlin!"

Once more I grabbed her and once more she went limp and smiled up at me submissively. Fucking bamboo women! You can bend them, notch them, even kill them, but they just won't break!

"Listen to me!" I cried. "Even the ambassador's poodle is leaving! You dumber than a poodle?"

I ran over, trying to throw my clothes on as I attempted to drill some sense into her, and turned on the radio so she could hear the proof for herself—Bing Crosby singing "I'm Dreaming of a White Christmas." In April!

"That's the fucking signal," I told her. "That's the balloon going up, the code for all Americans to get the hell out, you understand? *All* Americans! And their Vietnamese friends! And *lovers*! Jesus Christ, lady, even the *hookers* are leaving! Even some poor bastard of a clerk who maybe one time made a Xerox copy for some passing grunt at a photocopy kiosk, even the *clerk* is blowing town because he's been tainted by the contact. Now if I have to carry you out, you're coming with me!"

She reached up, began to button my shirt.

"I will wait until you're dressed," she said softly.

How soon that was, how soon!

On the street I wanted to scream again. I knew I could not convince her.

The scent of jasmine was layered in the air.

How dare there be jasmine!

But then the wind began to blow briskly.

A cyclopousse driver labored by, his cargo a Vietnamese family, the father clutching a roll of straw mattresses.

The sound of mortars and cannonfire echoed everywhere, and above us an ominous sky muffled the continuous roar of jets loaded with fleeing Americans.

Yet somehow at that last moment we were absolutely alone on one block in a city of millions. Doan Thi stood there holding her bicycle, a tiny figure in black, the wind buffeting the legs of her trousers, her thin, delicate ankles appearing absurd within the broad flapping cuffs, her toenails without polish, ivory against the scuffed black of her rubber sandals, her second toe, as is common among Indochinese women, longer than her big toe, giving her such dexterity with her feet that we had had nights together when she caressed me so deftly with her toes I became confused about the geography of our relative positions in bed. I saw her standing there, silently entreating my permission to leave, and far down the block, from an open window on an upper floor, the two arms of a white curtain began to wave out into the street as though reaching for help. Black figure of the woman I love. Beyond her, white curtains beseeching.

"Too many have died," she said. "I stand on the top of a mountain of bones. From there, at least, let me look at the future with my own eyes. Let me see the revolution. Don't take that from me."

"This city'll be a lake of fire," I insisted. "I love you, Doan Thi! I can't let you die!"

"If you live," she said, "and if it all turns out the way I believe it will, you will return some day. I will stay here. Something of me will remain, I promise you. I will always be yours."

We stood, not touching, not kissing. For us that was over now.

She got onto her bicycle and pedaled off toward the Newport Bridge on the highway to Bien-hoa.

I stood there for a long, long while on Tran hung Dao Boulevard after she'd gone. I stood watching the desperate white curtains down the block and listening to incoming from Nhon Trach, southeast of the city. I wished one of the rounds would land on me.

But of course they never do when you want them to.

I hear the voice of another woman.

Kim, of course.

I discover I've turned onto the road to the Club Nautique in Nouméa.

"Look," she's saying, "you're not going to dig tonight's scene. Six local French girls, three motorcycle studs, probably got pimples on their asses, a couple of panting tourist couples from Sydney dying to play switchy, plus your three friends. If I know Otis he'll wrap up Queenie in no time, offer her a crisp, uncirculated one-thousand-dollar bill to go down on him while he's playing drums. He's got this fantastic system—an honest-to-God-top-of-the-line Ludwig, their Set-Up model with a modular design giving him unlimited flexibility in tom-tom placement. He loves to get off just as he reaches the crescendo on the toms. It's an act I do not rank among the Seven Wonders of the World. So we don't really need you for tonight's soirée, because if there's anything we're not short of it's people who want to get it on. We'll probably do a little taping, some girl-girl fucking out on deck under the stars, and maybe some anals while we're at it—we've got these great new ni-cad batteries that give you an hour-and-a-half shooting time before you have to recharge. It'll just be another shitty night in paradise. Another boring night, I have to tell you, Locke. May I call you John or Johnny or anything except Locke?"

I park the car at the foot of the gangway. The Benetti coruscates with lights. Rock music fires from her portholes. The helicopter has already landed and the crew is lashing her down for the night.

"John is fine," I say to Kim.

"I *did* come to the big city to see the elephant," she says. "And they broke it off, all right. I wanted to be a lead singer with my own band. I thought I could really make it big in the rock world. But I only got as far as the sequins-and-polyester circuit in a few motel lounges. So I started some high-priced hooking—out of boredom, mostly, at first, but then for the money. And I made it pay. I ended up with a really classy operation in Atlantic City—but I didn't buy in the right people, so I got bounced out of Jersey. I started writing a monthly sex column for one of the better glossy jerk-off monthlies. Then along came Otis Walden. How do you like it so far?"

"It's a killer," I say.

"Sure," she says.

She slips closer, reaches her palms up to my face. They feel softer than I would have expected. She holds my face a moment, then kisses me, looking for nothing in return.

She opens the door on her side, steps out.

"Go see your girl," she says. "The one who's still living."

I watch her clatter up the gangway, past the guard on

deck, then she's lost to my sight against the glare of the main salon lights.

I back the Renault a few yards, draw abreast of a watchful young police officer standing the night shift alongside my ketch.

I slide my window down.

"Do you know me?" I ask.

"I have your photo, monsieur. The inspector has issued it to the force on patrol."

"Will you please get a message to the inspector?"

"Certainly, monsieur."

"Tell him not to allow any bread to be delivered into police headquarters until further notice. No outside vendors to be permitted either. No supplies to be brought in—coffee, bottled water, cigarettes or candy for the vending machines—nothing is to be permitted onto the grounds. You have that?"

"But no bread? We always bring our baguettes. It is the custom."

"A custom that can get you killed! Please give him the message. Right away! And tell him I'll be in touch shortly after eleven hundred hours tomorrow."

"Very well, monsieur."

I look from him to *Steel Tiger*. Her bow line rasps in protest as she strains in dark seclusion against the tide. My need to be aboard her takes me swiftly, like a rising fever—to be aboard her and away from here, for I can feel things everywhere about me I do not comprehend, and I know, as I've known since I built her, that she is my ultimate refuge. How little different I am, no matter how often I reassure myself that I am different, from those troopers who dug in at night in Nam and listened fearfully or angrily to the casual mockery of the enemy about them. I am hearing the taunting cries of Melanesian chieftains on the New Caledonian wind and I wonder if their sorcery has not cut a niche in me, a wound I haven't yet been able to isolate or staunch.

"Good night," I say to the young officer. "And thank you for watching her."

"Bonne nuit, monsieur," he replies.

I pull the Renault out, go looking for the heights of Ouen Toro and a house guarded by a toothless dog, a house sheltering a fat grandmother and a French girl from a fascist family.

# CHAPTER

## 15

Next to the Maison du Tourisme in Anse Vata I find an all-hours snack bar. I buy six cheeseburgers to go.

I wind the Renault up a spiraling road to the summit of Mont Ouen Toro and stop at a blockhouse where a long naval rifle from World War II is emplaced within a concrete basin, its lane of fire commanding the passage at Woodin Canal thirty-five thousand meters to the southeast. Not more than half a click down the slope I observe a colonial estate on its own promontory and I know that must be where Rosine can be found.

I turn off the headlights, sit for a while listening to the wind-dance of roadside pines and letting my eyes adjust to the night.

When I feel properly plugged in, I get out, lock the car, debate with myself whether to leave the dive bag and all its goodies or to bring it along. From up here on the peak of Ouen Toro I can see clearly the coralline tin roofing on the Gallantes' townhouse, as tranquil in the moonlight as a saint's face on a medieval tapestry. I decide to bring all my marbles with me.

I take the dive bag from the trunk, then, keeping to the shadowlines and reducing the noise of my breathing, I move in segmented advances from one dark pool to another.

There aren't many other homes in the area, and what few there are show no lights at this late hour. Two hundred meters from the wrought-iron fence that surrounds the estate I ease down behind a tree and unzip the dive bag.

177

My fingers find the Starlight scope among the other items in my inventory for survival. I use the scope now in a meticulous survey of the world around me, first back the way I've come, then along both flanks. When I'm satisfied I'm alone on the backside, I put the scope on the house and grounds ahead of me.

Rosine's Ferrari is nested under the portico, its sloping back window running dew.

A mastiff slumps on the high porch near the front door, his head on his gigantic front paws. Who else but Monstro? As I watch him through the scope, I see that his ears, despite their drooping nature, are already alerted to the possibility of an intruder, his pendulous nostrils quivering, massive head starting to lift. He can't have picked up my scent. I've deliberately come in on the downwind side of him until I could look him over. He must have heard the faint parting of the stainless-steel zipper. Good dog!

I train the Starlight on every palm tree, following each column from its roots to its crown. I search the fronds for anything bulkier than coconuts, find nothing of concern. Then I peer into every shadow, every flowering plant, every bush. No one lurking in the shrubbery. Now I dissect the house, its arches, its angles, its windows, its porch, its roof. Nothing. I sweep the street outside the grounds. No parked cars. No human or animal movement. Visually satisfied, I switch all my voltage into the olfactory mode. As I open myself up to the smells of this place, I remember Harry Marston, a Spec 5 they sent me. I warned him about his giveaway scent, even ordered him to change his diet or to fast before every recon mission. I could sniff him out from twenty yards away, fifty yards on a windy night. It wasn't that he was wearing after-shave lotion or cologne or was using hair tonic. I never let any of my men use anything that would produce residual scents on their cammies or bodies. We even made our own soap from copra. Unscented soap, believe me. And I never tolerated smokers or dopers or tobacco chewers on my teams. They all smell too, especially after dark. Harry's problem was biochemical. He was so terrified within the dead-center of himself that the fear did things to his juices. First you'd hear his stomach churning. Then this musty odor would begin to rise from his pores. I feel good, remembering Harry Marston, because I got him transferred to clerical duty away from the killing zones before the enemy ever got a chance to smell him coming. Harry stays in the plus column of my mind.

I smell nothing hostile in the night around me, only the dominant waves from blossoms of eglantine.

Finally, I give my attention to the sounds around me. Aside from the scrape of Monstro's worn claws scrambling on the porch, I hear nothing in the immediate area that registers in as threatening.

I decide I will enter the grounds on the spreading branches of a banyan tree near the back of the property.

I am up, over and across, ready to drop into the yard when Monstro finally concludes he's been had.

His chugging roar as he gallops toward the banyan would unnerve the staunchest of men.

I toss him the first of the six cheeseburgers. He gulps it down, then continues barking. I toss him the second. This time his bark is less hostile. By the third cheeseburger he's mine. I slip down, holding the fourth in my hand and extend it to him. He takes it with toothless gratitude and munches on it less wolfishly than he had the first three. I move to the house, carrying the dive bag and the two remaining cheeseburgers. Below what I have fixed in my mind as Rosine's bedroom, I feed Monstro his fifth, and while he's busy with it I lob pebbles from the garden against the shutters on the second floor. Rosine opens them just as I am assuaging Monstro with the last cheeseburger.

She bends out of a coalescence of shadows above me, her welcoming smile a gleam of white teeth in the darkness. I hear her muffled gasp of pleasure, then the diminishing rush of her bare feet on wooden floors. I hurry to the porch, up the steps to the front door even as she opens it and comes out to me like a gust of wind.

She is naked except for a silk bandeau around her hair, and her sinewy nakedness envelops me. She pulls me inside. I push the door shut with my foot and surrender myself.

It is the first time in my life I have had sex without first uttering or hearing a few obligatory words. Something. Anything. Not that we're silent. Far from that. As we urgently attempt to occupy each other's space, there's a lot of burbling and babbling. While I carry her upstairs, she is ripping off my shirt to the accompaniment of panting little cries. By the time we've arrived at her bedroom, she has my belt undone, my zipper down, all to a medley of muted sobs and moans. Then with a cry which might have been mine she pulls me onto her bed and almost frantically husks off whatever else it is I may have had still covering my flesh at that moment. She permits me no overture of tenderness or gentility. She positions herself above me, cupping my hands over her breasts, forcing me to reach up and to grasp them hard, cruelly, and her legs widen across me, her hips driving down onto me, her whole being quivering to be taken as savagely, as thoughtlessly as I have it in my nature to be, while she freely does the same on top of me. Something in me locked away since I lost Doan Thi bursts free. The blessedness of escaping from myself. A homecoming to that incandescent place where there are no killers and no time except the never-ending present. I see Rosine's eyes glowing unappeasably above me. The circle of her mouth closes over my lips like a branding iron and I know I am no longer invulnerable. I am breached, and uncaring that I am.

When, later, we are lying side by side, her head on my shoulder, she whispers, "You are my wish. I knew you'd come to me. And so I haven't left this room at night, nor this house during the day, since I dropped you at Tontouta. I want to stay in your arms forever. When you close your eyes, I shall close mine. When you rise, I shall rise. When you laugh, I shall laugh. And if you die, I shall kill myself on that very day."

I turn my face to hers, observe that her eyes remain wild and untempered.

"I won't let you think that way," I tell her. "I am not a risk-aversive person. I have this behavioral mechanism that tells itself never to back down from anyone. You mustn't link your future to that."

"I already have."

For a moment I am tempted to accept the commitment. The telephone rings.

"That will be your friend," she says.

I stop her from picking up the receiver.

"What friend?"

"He said he's a newspaper editor. He called earlier."

I take the phone.

"Ai do?" I ask in Vietnamese.

Maurice's voice reveals his admiration.

"You *are* a careful one, aren't you?" he laughs in English. "Ai do yourself! This is Maurice, of course."

"How'd you know I'd be here?" I ask him.

"You forget, my police informant."

"How did *he* know?"

"I told him earlier this evening I was anxious to reach you and that if he heard anything at police headquarters to let me know. He called an hour ago to tell me you'd parked on the summit of Mont Ouen Toro. I asked myself, why would you park up there? But, of course, the Gallante townhouse is only a short distance down the hill. He is having a late meeting with Marcel. I call. Marcel does not answer. His niece answers. Then I understand."

"*I* don't!" I say, with concern. "How did your informant know I was parked up there? I'm positive nobody followed me."

"Bazin placed a transmitting device in the car he gave you. He's been tracking your movements."

"That sonofabitch!" I say, but not without respect.

"So," Maurice continues, "at that house, with company as exhilarating as Rosine Gallante's, you must not be detained by business. I shall come straight to the reason for my calling. It is good news. Kaméa has agreed to meet you. She will be back in Nouméa the day after tomorrow. She has asked you to meet her in the museum around two or so on Friday."

"Thank you, Maurice," I say. "I will be there."

Rosine is running her lips down my spine, as though counting the vertebrae with the tip of her tongue.

"You will *not* be there!" she announces. "Wherever 'there' is. Not until I release you. You are my prisoner. *I* will say when you may leave my bed."

I reach around, pull her across my chest.

"And when does that bleak moment come?" I ask.

"When I can look at myself in the mirror and see a distant and detached and slightly dazed look of total satisfaction. And when my smile is even more enigmatic than the Mona Lisa's."

I consider her burning eyes with their tinders of insatiability.

"I think we still have some way to go," I say.

Her lips lower to mine.

"We haven't scratched the surface," she murmurs.

I forget Maurice.

I forget Kaméa.

I forget Bazin.

But I cannot forget Doan Thi.

So many times after I'd lost her forever I would play back the memory of the time and place I met her.

January, it was, 1970. She'd gone up to recite poetry to one of the most decorated battalions in the South Vietnamese Army, the Black Panther Ranger Battalion. I was with a Hatchet Team. Actually, it was a combination of Hatchet Teams, what we called Brightlights, a combination of twenty-three-man platoons formed up in the FOB, then inserted whenever a Spike Team was getting names taken.

At the time I was operating out of Command and Control North, where CCN teams were named for snakes, mine being RT-Black Mamba. On this particular morning I was acting as One-Zero, the skipper of a caper we'd code-named "Steel Tiger." It was one of those hairy firefights where it's all direct-line-of-sight stuff, you and a resolute enemy down each other's front sights and the winner whoever's left standing when the cordite settles. There weren't a lot of us still standing when I hear my One-Two shouting something about John Wayne to the rescue, and here come these Black Panthers, these South Vietnamese Rangers wearing cocky red berets and moving up behind an advancing wall of steel and fire. We were in RON position, a remain-overnight, so that night after we'd extracted the dead and the splattered, we hung in and got tight with these legs from down south who'd saved our butts. They invited us to a poetry recital. Doan Thi's recital.

We sat around on the ground together, with good perimeter defense, two encirclements of claymores with trip wires, just to make sure nobody came in without asking. The Panthers were amused by all the precautions. They even put away their Mattels. They told us if there still happened to be any live NVA in the vicinity they'd behave because they loved Doan Thi's poetry as much as the southerners did. If we were to invite them they'd even come in out of the night and sit with us and listen to her speak of the human condition through verses that captured all the beauty and the tragedy of being born Vietnamese. I had only recently begun to learn the language and that night, watching this woman, listening to her magical voice, I heard what a supple instrument for poetry Vietnamese could be. Although it is predominantly a monosyllabic language, described by buddies of mine as sounding like ducks fucking, it has two separate tone categories which can be set against each other by an expert to create musical tonalities. It is also blessed with economical syntaxes that don't call for merely functional or connective words, of which we have so many in English, and can therefore leach an image down to its skeleton and give the listener a chance to add flesh from his own mind, if he chooses.

I tried to meet Doan Thi that night, but there was no way I could break through the throng of Vietnamese

Rangers who surrounded her like adoring children and kept her up past dawn chattering of things I did not understand. But I heard the laughter in this place of death and I saw the flashing smiles and I knew at that time that if I spent my life in the effort I would make this woman my woman and I would give her whatever of me she wanted, without stint, for as long as she wanted it.

I managed to get close enough to her just as she was leaving to mumble out my name and how much her poetry had meant to me, then to add that it was an effort for me to have approached her to tell her this and especially was it difficult for me to look her directly in the eyes, much as I wanted to and beautiful as she was.

"Why are you not able to look me in the eyes?" she asked.

"Because I'm killing your people. That's what I do. I kill Vietnamese."

"Is that your only purpose here?" she asked. "Only that?"

"God, no!" I cried.

"Then what *is* your purpose? Why *are* you here?"

I was still too immature in the early months of that year to be able to answer her. I'm not sure I could answer even now.

"When you *do* know," she said, "come tell me."

"Where do I find you?" I asked.

"Wherever you can find friends. Or enemies. I am in both places."

Later, when I did find her in Danang and our love affair began, I questioned myself night after night. Was I, by loving her, trying to expiate any guilt I might be feeling about the Vietnamese I was killing? Had I become addicted to that age-old narcotic common to all invaders—kill their men, rape their women, and sleep like a winner?

# CHAPTER

# 16

"**W**hat do you think now of the girl who lives in my mirror?"

I look over at Rosine brushing her hair and studying herself in the mirror above her dressing table.

"Distant," I reply. "Detached. Slightly dazed. As though she's in converse with the angels."

"How about the Mona Lisa smile?"

"Hers was a snarl compared to yours," I assure her.

"My father came to see me," she announces. "He warned me to stay away from you."

"He tell you why?"

"He said you're dangerous."

"To whom?"

"He loves me very much."

"I know."

"An incredible man, my father. So—complex . . . so unpredictable. He's always been that way. You think you've finally come to know him. And you find you don't. Not at all. I accused him of duplicity. How dare he cook for you, welcome you into his home, ask you to help him against his enemies, then come to me and speak against you! He said all that was quite possible. That he admired you. That he and Marcel desperately need your help. And that you're one of the most fascinating men he's ever met —a pure professional, he calls you, the new warrior, the man we need today, if there is ever to be a tomorrow. But for me, he says, you are not only wrong, but possibly even . . . fatal."

185

"He can be right about that, Rosine. We both know *how* right."

"He believes that what I need is a lover who has the time and the patience and the sensitivity to let me grow. He said you have the sensitivity, but not the time. You put him in mind of Napoleon Bonaparte. He told me Napoleon used to tell his generals, 'I will give you anything but time.'"

"What is your relationship with Sabourin?" I ask her as abruptly as she has brought up the matter of her father.

"Sabourin?" she asks, her reflection in the mirror catching at my eyes. "*Jules* Sabourin?"

"Yes."

"Why do you ask?"

"I met him this afternoon. He told me to stay away from you too. Like your father."

She whirls on the dressing-table stool to face me.

"How dare he!"

"I assumed as much."

"He is nothing to me! Nothing!"

She crosses to me, kneels on the floor beside the bed, takes one of my hands.

"I swear before God I have had no other men but that wretched doctor, my poor husband—and you. *Jules Sabourin*! He would be the very last man on earth!"

"Why would he make such a definitive statement?"

"I have no idea," she says, bobbing her head wildly from side to side a moment, as though trying to shake a reason loose. "Unless it comes from out of the past."

"He did say it was long-standing."

"Such a fool! He is referring to the relationship of our two families. When I was growing up here, before I moved to Paris, his father was a friend of my father's. Their fathers too had been friends—and their fathers' fathers. I can remember when I was six or seven some dinner-table talk about Jules and me, some aimless chit-chat to the effect that when we grew up we might finally marry and so bring the two families together. But it was never more than

186

that, never went beyond that. I haven't seen him since I was a child. Wait until I tell *this* to my father!"

"Something here puzzles me," I say. "Sabourin is highly radicalized. His politics are mainstream Marxist. How could he come from three generations that have been close to your family and end up opposing everything the Gallantes represent?"

"What *do* we represent?" she asks, with no trace of hostility.

"Sabourin calls your uncle an international fascist."

"My uncle is a mirthless and arrogant bully. You should see his apartment in Paris. So silent, so arid, I can't endure being in it. And his office is a shrine to the muted deference of a thousand employees. He is obsessed with work. But he wouldn't know what a fascist is if one came up and bit him. Now, to settle this once and for all in your mind, this matter of Jules Sabourin having any claim on me— you have to understand that my great-grandfather was one of the leaders of the Paris Commune. Do you know about that period of French history?"

"A little," I tell her. "My mother once took me on a walking tour of Paris to show me where the insurrectionists had burned buildings and monuments when they fought to hold the city against the French Army of Versailles. If I remember what she told me, that wasn't much more than a hundred years ago."

"From March through May, 1871," Rosine says as she rises from her knees. The skin across her kneecaps is pink from their contact with the hardwood floor, but not as pink as her small virginal nipples. She has the same tiny nipples Doan Thi had, unsuckled by greedy infants, except that Doan Thi's were more the color of cinnamon.

"My great-grandfather," Rosine says, "was one of the commanders of the insurgents, a colonel in the National Guard, a man of great energy and deep convictions."

I watch the subtle change in her body language as she puts herself back in time. Somehow her chin seems higher,

her posture more erect, as though she is hearing distant drummers.

"He embraced with all his being the cause of the Commune. He fought for the Republic. Against monopoly, militarism and special privilege."

She glances over at me almost guiltily. "All the things his grandson, my father, believes in." She moves in stately nudity, somehow more regal than if there had been an ermine cape around her shoulders, to the bureau on which aging photographs are displayed. I can't see their detail from the bed, but I can at least make out that they are family portraits in antique frames of tortoiseshell.

"He was landed on the Île des Pins, south of here, on October 4, 1872," she continues, her eyes looking at the likenesses of the strangers whose blood she bears, "after a year in prison in France and four months at sea. There were three thousand exiled convicts in that first shipment, at least a hundred of them leaders and intellectuals like my great-grandfather. Most of the others were simple artisans who believed in the Commune. The rest were the dregs of France, vicious criminals, considered beyond redemption."

She returns to me, settles on the bed alongside me, but sitting proudly. "In time, my great-grandfather achieved the coveted status of 'libéré.' He was given a farm and five years to make a success of it. If he chose to stay ten years, the property would be deeded to him and he could do whatever he wished with it. He chose to stay, even while most of the other 'libérés' were pardoned and repatriated to France. He married a young woman who was a 'forçat,' sentenced to eight years at hard labor for killing another woman with her bare hands in a streetfight in Montmartre. My grandfather, who was born to that union somewhere around 1874, married much later in life. By the turn of the century the family had prospered, raised cattle, bought the farm and little town you visited Monday. And when the first nickel was mined, the Gallantes ended up controlling a good part of it. My father was the first Gallante to return to France in three generations. As you know, he created an international cartel, the company he recently turned over to Marcel, and he has now returned to New Caledonia to live out the rest of his days. So you see I come from revolutionary stock sprinkled here and there with condemned and exiled criminals. Jules Sabourin descends from similar lineage, except that in his case his father and grandfather became merchants and suffered losses that bankrupted them. It would be easy for Jules to become as revolutionary as his great-grandfather. He has nothing to lose."

"So much for Sabourin," I say. "Consider that book closed. Now, next question. Your mother. Was she as beautiful as you?"

"I don't remember," Rosine says with a soft shudder. She slips into bed and curls into my arms like a kitten seeking warmth. "I don't want to talk about that. I want to know about *your* mother."

I decide not to push this mystery. There are others who will tell me in time.

"My mother's quite famous, actually," I tell her.

"Oh? Would I know her?"

"She paints in France under the signature of Amée."

Rosine whirls in my arms to face me.

"Amée is *your* mother?"

"You know of her?"

"I have one of her paintings in my apartment in Paris! My very best painting! I have it displayed directly over the fireplace. Papa bought it for me only last year. So incredibly expensive! Could we have saved anything if we'd bought it through you?"

"My mother would have painted something for you out of sheer pleasure, Rosine, at the good fortune of merely seeing you."

"Oh, I wish I could have had a mother like Amée!" she cries. "To think of being with such a person and calling her 'Mama'!"

"When I was a kid," I tell her, "I spent half my time with my mother either in Paris or in Auvers-sur-Oise, where she does most of her work, and the other half out sailing with my father around San Diego and Mexico."

"Why did they divorce?"

"They didn't. They never intend to give each other up, although they spend only Decembers together, always in some neutral part of the world. They won't let me be with them in December—not till Christmas. Then we're always together, if I can make it. But I understand from little bits and pieces that they devote those first three weeks of December to making love to each other substantially enough to last them through the year, storing it up like bears for hibernation. Then they go their own ways again on January first and give the following eleven months to their separate crafts."

"What does your father do?"

"Designs sailing boats. He designed my ketch."

"Such a sad story! But so beautiful! Why can't they be together all the time?"

"Apparently they've seen too many married people chip away at each other with what my mother calls 'ordinariness.' They feel their marriage deserves better. Then too, my old man's one of those apple-pie Americans. And my mother is particularly French. He doesn't care for France. She can't endure San Diego. But they do care for each other. So it's been this way since I can remember. I consider myself lucky to have a foot in two such different worlds. I learned about the sea from my father and the earth from my mother. Have you been to Auvers-sur-Oise?"

"Can you believe I haven't? And only an hour out of Paris! I'm not sure which way though."

"On Route N-328," I tell her.

I think of being with Rosine under the poplar trees that line the streets of the little town. I see myself strolling with her through the park just to the left of the railroad station, having apéritifs at the inn facing the town hall, where Van Gogh spent his last days.

"Did you know," I ask her, "that in his whole professional lifetime Van Gogh sold only one painting?"

"How could that be?"

"There's a painting of his in the Van Gogh Museum in Amsterdam," I tell her, "that he finished just two days before he died. He was up in one of the fields above town and was painting those menacing-looking ravens swooping down through the cornstalks when suddenly he took a pistol from his pocket and fired a bullet into his stomach."

"How terrible!" she whispers.

"He managed to get himself back to the inn, where he died two days later. He's buried in the cemetery in Auvers, just behind the church he'd painted a month earlier. Cézanne often went to Auvers to paint. And Daubigny. Now my mother. I can see us there, Rosine, the two of us, driving in some day, surprising her."

She kisses me sweetly, presses herself against me, even bending her toes straight out so that our ankles can match up flat.

"You're not really like Napoleon Bonaparte, are you, John?"

"I have more hair," I smile.

"What if we were to get dressed right now, go down to your boat, and sail away forever?"

She is ready, I observe, to do exactly that, with even the least encouragement from me, to put herself in my hands and devote her energies to our affair. Again, she baffles me.

"A beautiful fantasy."

"Would it make any difference here in Nouméa?"

"It might."

"But they're sending in a detachment of Legionnaires. And a warship. What more can you do?"

"I don't know. But I've taken the job."

"My father says you'll die."

"He's right." I kiss the tip of her nose. "The question is—*When?*"

"I've put my life with yours," she says. "Please remember that. Let it stay foremost in your thoughts. If they kill you, they kill me. The day you die, I join you. Before the sun sets. You do believe me, don't you, John?"

"I wish I didn't," I say after a while. "There's nothing out there after this, Rosine. Nothing. I *know*!"

"You're so wrong," she says. "The best of everything is out there. And when the time comes, I'll share it with you! That is my promise to you."

"What is this obsession with dying?" I demand. I've seen it on her face, behind her face. It envelops her. Now here it is again in everything she says. God knows I'm obsessed with it too, but for reasons I can justify, if I need to. And I am obsessed with it only for the purpose of trying to live one more day, then another one after that, if I can.

"You asked about my mother," she says. "She killed herself in this house . . . in the bathroom right through that door. She placed herself in a tub of hot water and slashed both her wrists. I found her sitting in there, dead, her eyes still open, the water running over the rim of the tub, across the floor and out here into this room, like a slow red tide."

I know nothing I can say to her.

She has told me this in an almost impersonal tone, like a bad recitation of a Shakespeare sonnet, as though the words are known, but not their meaning.

Light is painting the shutters, the almost-light of Thursday. My mother would go to it, let it wash over her toes. Only when she felt it rise to her heart would she mix her paints and pick up her brush and catch it for all time.

I dress and I feel my mother's presence in the room with Rosine and me. I feel Doan Thi come in and stand in the ribbing of new light, transparent, yet still corporeal, and she is smiling at me with approval that I have found someone who might ease the torture of my loss.

"When will you make love to me again?" Rosine whispers. "Tonight? Shall I wait here for you tonight?"

"I'll be going north," I tell her. "Probably the day after tomorrow. Between then and now I don't know. But, yes, wait."

I remember that I owe her money. I lay a stack of five-thousand-franc notes on her dresser.

"Was I really worth so much?" she asks playfully, suddenly pretending to be whorish.

"They will never print enough Pacific francs," I say, "to come even close, mademoiselle, to the true value of your favors."

I carry her grateful kiss with me.

Monstro slobbers over my shoes when I go down the porch steps. I run my fingers through the great scruff of flesh on his head.

I discover a sedan parked on the roadway.

Five men wait for me. One of them is Sabourin.

# ═CHAPTER═

## 17

**I** shift the dive bag to my left hand, unbutton my jacket, so that I can reach the Browning in a hurry if I need it.

I swing the gate open, walk out toward them.

"I have been waiting for you, monsieur," Sabourin declares, moving boldly toward me.

The four men with him appear as chunky as butcher blocks.

"You must be a light sleeper to be out this early," I say. "Or an early riser. Which is it?"

"I warned you, monsieur! Now we shall settle accounts!"

"How do we do that?" I ask. "Are you going to hit me?"

"We intend to send you to hospital, monsieur."

I don't want to fight with him. I no longer know how to fight without crippling or killing.

A dusky image flickers in my mind. I replay the memory of my last streetfight. I recall myself as a shadowy stranger with a police star staked out as a bum in the Mission District of San Francisco. Some dude had been slashing the throats of winos for a year or so and had piled up such a monumental score the mayor finally demanded the PD stop counting its blessings and looking the other way and do something before Mission District winos became an endangered species. So I was out trolling myself as live bait two blocks south of Market Street in this coffinlike alley, my partner hidden on the roof above me, when I heard him shout, "Behind you!"

Apparently Mac the Knife had materialized out of a

194

doorway and got himself so close to me my partner couldn't risk firing his pump-gun for fear of including me in its lethal pattern.

I didn't waste time turning. You can die trying to eyeball what's coming your way.

I pitched myself forward, head tucked into my chest, and I coiled onto my back, in the process looking up at the shadow lurching toward me, knife plunging down, and I rolled over, evading the clumsy stab, then up, all in one continuous movement, and snap-kicked his wrist, knocking the knife out of his hand. Then I knee-dropped him just under the short ribs. I could feel my knee driving in and I sensed that the blow had instantaneously separated the main arteries where they join the liver. He slumped to his knees, his eyes already starting to glaze as his brain shot out B-endorphin to narcotize him. Blood began to well from his mouth, but he stayed there on his knees in startled obeisance for at least one hundred and twenty seconds, performing his sacrament at this asphalt altar with garbage cans his choirboys and staring up in dull surprise at me, a high priest in rags.

By then my partner had scampered down the fire escape and come to join me. Both of us watched the man's shocked transition from assailant to victim, from life to death, and we made no move to help him, for there was nothing to be done after that precisely homed-in knee-drop. I remember hearing the neighborhood noises with exaggerated clarity, the spacy sound-tracks from a nearby video-game parlor, a woman's mocking laughter from somewhere above us, and a persistent car horn. We watched the Knifer edge onto one side, a collapsing balloon, growing smaller and smaller, shrinking into the street.

"What the fuck did you do to him?" my partner finally asked, his voice husky with whispered awe. "It was just a reflex," I may have said, but the memory is irising out, like those fadeouts at the end of old Felix the Cat cartoons and I'm back to Sabourin in fastidious and insistent Technicolor.

Sabourin has to prove something in front of his taran-
tulas. At least he has to start it, so they can finish it. He
continues to move on me. I back away.

"That's far enough!" I warn him.

He spits on my cheek, then appears surprised when I
don't even bother to wipe off the spittle.

He steps closer, draws back his right fist. I could read
*War and Peace* during all the time he's giving me. I wait
until he throws his vacuous, looping right, simply lift one
hand, flick the blow away. Mosquitoes are more annoying.
This infuriates him. He kicks at me. I evade his childish
kick. He kicks again and this time I grasp his ankle. I
could, if I chose to, kill him at that second. You do not,
ever, place your right ankle in the grasp of a man who
knows how to savage you. Instead, I simply dump him
backward. He falls awkwardly, but scrambles back up,
screaming now, frenzied and out of control, having to vali-
date himself, and rushes at me, both arms out to grapple
me down.

I've been trying to particularize some single blow I can
deal him which will not damage him permanently. For a
split second I even consider slapping him across one ear,
but here again I doubt that I could strike him without the
muscle-memory of ten thousand practice blows causing me
to put too much torque and sizzle into the slap, and why
should I be the cause of this man's having to wear a
hearing-aid for the rest of his life?

Instead, I let him come to me, grasp him with his own
forward momentum, bend away slightly and hip-throw
him, directing his force toward the bushes and away from
the harsh steel fence surrounding Rosine's property.

He tries to recover, but I can see he's had enough.

From the ground, he shouts up to his four apaches to
deal with me. I catch the glint of brass knuckles, see a
blackjack being tugged from a back pocket, a palm-sap
slipped into a gloved hand, a whole inventory of foolishness.

I reach for the Browning, level it at the nearest assailant, and thumb off the safety with operatic theatricality.

"You'd better be good at giving up," I tell them in French. "As a matter of fact, you'd all better rush out right now to a training school and take lessons in giving up!"

They are not without the intelligence to perceive that behind my florid French is a steady and undeviating trigger finger. Each man becomes transformed into a willing statue, arms hooked rigidly into the sky, saps, clubs, and brass knuckles clunking to the sidewalk.

"You have not seen me for the last time!" Sabourin cries from his couch of pain. But he carefully remains motionless, hands up, palms toward me.

"Sabourin," I tell him, "you are not a man able to refrain from beating a dead horse. Don't bother me anymore, or next time they'll have to hose you off the landscape!"

"Without your gun," he sneers, "you would be nothing!"

"You're so right," I agree. "Without my gun I would be garbage."

I pick up the dive bag, hasten back uphill while all five of them still remain under the spell of my Browning.

Dawn is only minutes east. I can already smell its moist rot as everything around me, even the air I'm breathing, turns another second older. The incident with Sabourin has separated me again from the living and angered me more than I usually permit such moments to do. What is this lemmings' stampede of the human species to pursue so avidly its own destruction? Sabourin's pitiful encounter with me, after knowing what had happened to a group of armed ambushers, simply doesn't make sense. There has to be a hidden reason he waited out there for me. How long *had* he waited, I suddenly wonder, how long had he stared in torment at Rosine's dark bedroom windows, knowing I was in there with her? Long enough certainly to have called in the terrorists to lie in wait for me when I left. But I feel no eyes watching me, I sense no warning friction along my nerve endings, and I know I will reach the

Renault unobserved. So that must mean he is not allied with them. Fascinating! And he has never possessed Rosine, if I am to believe her. Why then is his jealousy so intense? Or is that a pretense to cover up something else? And who told him I was there? More questions to be answered.

I come to the Renault, lock the dive bag into the trunk, drive off, away from where I left Sabourin.

I am still troubled by his remark that without my gun I am nothing, troubled not by the truth of his accusation or by the sincerity of my concurrence, but by the jagged memories of all the dead who did have guns and became nothing. They flutter toward me now, like bats at sunset, the dead in Indochina, the dead in San Francisco. It is not alone their dying that haunts me, but the ugliness of what they left behind. In death, the human body lacks grace. It is every bit as profane as a dead lizard, stiff as leather, or a dead bird, matted beyond recognition, or a dead seal washed onto a beach like another pile of rotting kelp. Only the jungle tiger retains any semblance of nobility after the flattening blow of death.

Nowhere will you see this gracelessness more graphically than in a morgue when you're the police officer assigned to an autopsy where the cause of death is going to be determined through a postmortem. Even the setting is numbing. White-tile room, stainless-steel tables with drains built into them, anchored into the floor like barber's chairs. Around these tables are arrayed the tools of the trade, the cutters, grinders, clippers, and saws. And always a dripping of water. Always bright lights. Always the odors of decaying bodies, of formaldehyde. You become immersed in a cosmos of light, formaldehyde, and dripping water the moment you enter the chamber. The only color other than white is gray. Gray is the color of the autopsy surgeon and of his assistants. They all look as though they've been stamped out of putty by a cookie-cutter—gray-rimmed eyes, gray-tallowed skin. They sit around in their ready room, contemplating centerfolds, drinking gray coffee and eating gray tuna sandwiches, with little fetuses wrapped in gray newspapers on their chairs and bodies still to be processed parked outside on gurneys.

Once the surgeon starts his autopsy, you get a lot of preliminary chalk-scratching on a blackboard, a certain amount of electronic whine as he makes sure his tape recorder's fired up and ready to go, then he starts on the body, looking at the hands, at the hair, at the feet, checking fingernails, toenails, the elbows, the back of the neck, the ears, taking his time with all of it, dictating into the machine as he goes. I remember the first time I saw this examination, I thought to myself what a fucking pity that the poor bastard on the table, one of those Mission District winos with his throat slashed, had never in his whole lifetime had anybody look him over with such care, touching, probing, making notes. He had to get his head sliced half off to merit all this time and attention.

Then the surgeon steps back to permit one of his assistants to move in with a scalpel and make the first cut. This is usually from behind one ear, up across the top of the head and down to the other ear, then back to complete the circle. Whether you happen to be listening or not, at that point you will hear the slight sound of something ripping, like Velcro on a mosquito screen across the hatch of your boat, as the assistant jerks the scalp, the forehead, everything inside out and down over the face—well, not entirely covering the face, usually just about down to the axis of the eyes. Then he peels it off and pulls it down so that it lies like a handy flap in back.

Then he picks up one of those quarter-inch drills with a disc saw attached and he grins over at you and says, "Be careful there, officer. Would you stand back, please? I may lose some of this." And you step back as he goes buzz-buzz, taking a circular path around the head and then he goes pop and pulls off the lid of the skull more easily than if he were capping a coconut.

Once they're into the skull they look for evidence of trauma or blood-clotting on the crest of the brain, then, taking it very gently, they scoop out the brain itself. The spinal cord usually comes dancing out with it, a shock if you don't expect to see it, as they end up with this gray mass and the spinal cord dangling like some obscene, mutant tail.

The good surgeons tend to concentrate on the brain, giving it a thorough going-over, and when they're satisfied they've unraveled every clue it can yield, they draw their hands down the wet spinal cord to check that out for telltale injury or severing, while you stand there, forgetting there has been a morning to this particular day or that there may ever again come an evening, and all you can see is a gray form on a stainless-steel table with the top of its head gone, its brain out, its spinal column out, skullcap back, face turned inside-out. While you're trying to adjust to that, the assistant cuts the torso from the point of the shoulder down to the diaphragm, then across, and finally makes an open slash in the groin. He picks up a clippers like an English gardener about to shear a hedgerow and snips the rib cage off clean, all the way up to the clavicle area on each side, then the surgical team lifts the cage, the ribs, and sternum, and exposes the lungs and heart. Out comes the heart, then the liver. The surgeon usually cups the liver in his rubber-gloved hand and examines it for color, studies its knobs, checks the man arteries that attach. The liver having told its story, now to the heart. This muscle is carved up in progressive servings as the surgeon pursues the little white vein he's chasing.

I learned, all in good time, that the only way I could get through one of these sessions was to dissociate in my mind the thing on the table from the living being it once had been. I learned how to force myself to concentrate on the investigation, to concentrate on isolating the cause of death to this particular organism and how to get in close to the job, not step back from it and view it from a distance, not to see the body as a former person, but to get in really close and to use tunnel vision and to try to determine where the killer's bullet had lodged and what havoc it had wrought getting there and where the murderer's knife had severed veins and arteries or blunt instrument committed its violation. I learned the trick of watching the doctor's gloved hands working, and so I fooled them all. They thought down there in the San Francisco morgue that I really had my shit together, and whenever I came in on an assigned case they'd always kid with me and tell me what a great guy I was and what a strong stomach I had and how I could handle it better than the rest of the asshole rookies, and they guessed that was because I'd been in Vietnam and had got used to it. I never did tell them that in fact it gets worse every time, that the weight of it accumulates within you, like slow mercury poisoning, that it becomes more of a nightmare every time, more unbearable. I have never heard any police officer say that being assigned to an autopsy was anything except a bad, a very bad scene. Every one of us always felt the same thing, both during and after. It came crashing home to us without exception that what we were seeing was the end of everything and that someday, possibly even this very afternoon, we too would be wheeled in there and slopped down on one of those stainless-steel drainboards, and that's why—that specific, visual knowledge—so many police officers end up as alcoholics or drift off to Oregon or simply take out their S&Ws and pull a round off into their yawning mouths. Because the mystery is gone. The not-knowing is gone. They positively know where they'll end up and how they'll look when *they* get touched off.

It's hard to walk in there and try to do your job and watch those gray guys in the white aprons destroy a body that a lot of people were taught in Sunday school or in church to regard as the temple of God. Seeing those saws and clippers at work attacks every principle that might have been built into you by thoughtless caring persons. At least I have been more fortunate, blessed with a father raised on the sea, where normal is being eaten by something larger, a father who taught me that once you're eaten, you're eaten, baby—fini—over and out. It's only a life, he always tells me. So enjoy it—while you can.

Seeing the body turned into garbage by a landmine or a mortar burst is one thing, I suppose, but seeing it hacked up like that by men whistling while they work is something else again. Then, of course, the part that really used to depress me was the tidying up, the gussying and primping afterward. All the sliced-up parts are gathered together and the liver is dumped in where the lungs used to be and the lungs maybe where the genitals were and then they sew it all up with heavy cord and turn the face rightside-out again and they even comb the hair and force the lips into an enigmatic smile and daub on the makeup and wheel out one more Barbie doll in full repose to the viewing room for mourning parents or husbands or wives brought in for the identification rites.

Yes, Sabourin, without my gun I am garbage.

Give me a world sans cannibals, I will throw away my gun.

I will pitch it into the deepest chasm in the sea.

But only then!

# ═CHAPTER═

## 18

**M**orning comes wet from a corrugated sky, splattering the Renault's windscreen like broken fruit.

It's been one scarecrow week, I'll have to say, and here I am only now about to punch Thursday's time clock.

Along the avenues the bordering palms grunt lazily against the rising wind.

Stop bitching, I say to them.

Be grateful to the wind for shocking you out of your foreverness.

Look at poor me, Emperor of the Transients, Lord of the Temporaries, passing through without a trace, except through the courtesy of a loan-out car wired for sound.

Always on mornings like this, mornings between dog and wolf, I sense that somebody's taken in all the safety nets. I get antsier than usual. Right now, for example, I can feel the insects of speculation crawling within me.

I decide I will not put off my confrontation with Inspector Bazin. I had passed the word I'd be along to see him sometime after eleven hundred hours this morning or as soon as I've collected my hoped-for telex from Michael. It's just now edging past six. Do it now. Now!

I drive to the gendarmerie, not far off the Baie de la Moselle, and am reassured to observe that Bazin has had the entrance to the courtyard sandbagged. Two officers armed with Fusil Automatique 5.56 mike-mikes are stationed vigilantly just inside the driveway.

I park outside, open the car door with high-profile visibility of hands, stand relaxed and nonthreatening, and smile at them.

In French I say, "Good morning, gentlemen. I am John Locke. Hopefully, you recognize me."

The taller of the two peers at me from behind the barricade. I sweep the hair from my forehead, for the wind is lashing scalp and clothes now, distorting the clear look at me he requires at this moment.

"It *is* M. Locke," he tells his colleague.

"I need your permission to drive into the courtyard," I say. "Then I need the operator-on-watch to call Inspector Bazin at home. Ask him if he will be kind enough to come at once. It is, I assure you, quite urgent."

The tall one says, "He is already here, monsieur."

They permit me to pass.

I park the Renault next to Bazin's car and hurry into the main building.

A full complement of officers, both men and women, are already on duty. I sense a siege mentality in the air. And something else—something I don't yet comprehend.

Bazin's door is open. He is sitting at his desk. He does not look up at me, even when I knock lightly on the doorframe.

As I enter, I see in front of him a basket. He has just cut the sisal which had bound up its leafy covering. He sits stonelike, his pocketknife graved in his hand.

His eyes lift to mine. His agony reaches out to me.

I inch closer to the basket. It cradles a human head, the head of a young man, a Melanesian, planted like a guttered candle on a cake of clotted blood. Where eyes once had been, only torn cavities remain.

My scrotum tightens. For a moment I lose my breath.

Bazin is whispering to me.

At first I'm not sure I'm hearing him.

"How can I even close his eyes?" he is asking.

Three times he asks, each time in more torment.

"We thought it might be a bomb," he says. "It was left just an hour ago outside the complaint window. The bomb squad was alerted. And I was called. As you see, it was not a bomb after all."

I know without being told that I am looking at what remains of the young Melanesian undercover agent Bazin had sent north only yesterday.

I hold out my right hand.

"Take it!" I command.

He takes it without question. Gently, but with a sudden surge of strength which wells in me against all the world's decapitators, I pull him from his chair and to his feet.

"Come with me!"

Nor does he question this.

Together we leave his office, leave the basket where it sits, leave the building.

I put him up front with me in the Renault and we smoke out of the parking lot.

I drive to the marina.

A new officer stands watch alongside *Steel Tiger*.

He salutes the inspector.

"We'll be going out for a while," I tell the young officer. "Please remain right here."

I unflap the boom covers, attach sheets, hoist the main, unslip the dock lines, slide *Steel Tiger* away from the dock in record time.

Ten minutes later I lay us forty degrees off the wind with everything up, strapped in hard, and I sail her, toe rail sizzling.

Bazin perches to windward, saying nothing. I let the wind pull the rusty rivets out of him. The spray could sting colder, I wish, but it will do for now.

"Like to drive her?" I ask.

He takes the helm.

At once, I see, he senses the boat. He lets the force of her come up through her hull, through his soles, and into his body, and he goes with her, letting her sail herself, letting the thrash and drive of her become his.

We purge ourselves into the wind until I observe the climb of a cadaverous sun on our quarter. I take the helm from Bazin, tack off, then jibe, bringing us around on a reverse course. We cross over from blistering run to that deceptive calm that sings astern of you when you have the wind on the nape of your neck.

On this reach a man can settle sociably into the cockpit without cocking one bracing leg and can even speak in less than a shout and be heard.

Bazin is gazing at me through half-lowered lids.

"Merci," he says.

"It's okay," I reply.

"You are wondering perhaps who the dead man was."

"I was told he was your best undercover native officer. You sent him north yesterday."

He lights a Gauloise, succeeding with the first match, clearly a man used to spending time outdoors.

"Told by whom?"

"It came to me in a roundabout way," I reply. "But it came courtesy of an informant within your department who believes staunchly in the freedom of the press. Who, I don't know."

He looks toward Nouméa off our bow. The sky out there has plunged straight down onto the city and appears now to be trying to lift the buildings off the hills with long gray talons.

"On my instructions he flew to Touho yesterday. I know he got that far because he called me from the Relais Alison in the late afternoon. He was scheduled to take a bus from Touho to Hienghène, a matter of only forty-five kilometers. At the moment, I have no other information."

"What law enforcement do you have up there?"

"Good men."

"What have they to report?"

"I have not yet told them."

"Oh?"

"I do not wish to place them in the same jeopardy."

"Then how do you intend to find out what's happening?"

"I am in the midst of deciding that."

"Is it so remote up there you can't just kick ass by phone and get a full report?"

"It is not necessary in New Caledonia, monsieur, to

'kick ass' to obtain the information one needs. I know everything that is happening in Hienghène. That is, everything that anyone else who is white might know. What I do not know—and what our detachment of officers on duty in that area also do not know—is what the Hienghène tribesmen and Kangara himself do not choose to *let* us know."

"Kangara?"

"The great chieftain of the Hienghène. Of all the Melanesian leaders who have retained any semblance of tradition or power, he is certainly the peer. I'm quite convinced it was he who issued the order to attack you at sea."

"He sure as hell doesn't have a telex up there, does he?" I ask.

"But of course not! He prides himself on resisting the encroachments of our technology."

"So he's got to have some paleface honchos in Nouméa," I say, "who are part of whatever he's into. *They're* the ones to zero in on! Let's start with Jules Sabourin."

Bazin flips his smoked-out cigarette into our wake.

"You have been busy," he comments.

"Why have there been no arrests in the murder of his predecessor?"

"Simple enough, monsieur. We have no evidence on which to base an arrest."

"Suspicions, though?"

"One always has those."

"Tell me about this God-to-the-Right group."

"It is indiscreet of you to ask."

"Why?"

"I could be a member."

"I don't think so. Do they, in fact, have a functioning death squad?"

"One hears rumors. But nothing more. And who knows? Was he, in fact, killed by the far right? Or by a disgruntled mistress? It developed post-mortem that he had three. Unknown to each other—or to his wife."

"Sabourin warned me to stay away from Rosine."

"Another indiscretion!"

"Mine or his?"

"I reserve comment, monsieur."

"Her father gave her the identical warning. That troubles me. The timing and the coincidence."

"How so?"

"For some reason, I sense a link-up between Jules Sabourin and Georges Gallante, paradoxical as that may seem. It's just a feeling, but it keeps hanging in there."

"There is, of course, a basis for it. Georges has always been fond of young Sabourin, le Dieu alone knows why, since I consider Jules a pompous little fool with less substance than a pomme soufflé. But I do happen to know that Georges paid for his schooling when Jules's parents lost their business. I suppose you could say it was a simple case of charity, with no other significance, but Jules remains quite devoted to Georges."

"Well," I admit, "that might simplify things. It could be nothing more than a concerned father asking a lackey to stand guard outside his daughter's door."

"Do I miss something?"

"When I left Rosine at Ouen Toro this morning, Jules and four buddy-boys were waiting outside for me. Jules announced his intention of putting me into the hospital."

Bazin looks concerned.

"You are not about to make a confession, I hope."

I assure him that nobody has been injured. He appears greatly relieved.

"I have three other items on my agenda," I tell him. "Since you appear to be in a more talkative mood than usual, may I run them by?"

"I am your guest," he says.

"I take that to mean yes."

He throws back his head, breathes deeply of the wind.

"About that Benetti moored in front of me at Club Nautique," I say. "I suggest you concentrate your available manpower on more important issues. That yacht is nothing worse than a floating cathouse. Nobody who comes aboard is kidnapped or coerced."

"Shortly after I spoke to you about Immigration's concern," he says, "I had a call from an important justice of one of our courts. You will forgive me for not being more explicit. He told me he would not countenance any harassment of so important an American financier while he was a guest in our territory. I called Immigration to report this judicial point of view. They hotly denied they had ever asked me to investigate. I wash my hands."

"Second item: You're hiding electronic gear in the Renault."

He looks back down at me. Apparently he's inhaled enough fresh air.

"Who told you that?"

"The same source who told me about your sending an agent up north."

"It is for your own protection."

"I would have preferred you discuss it with me first, at least give *me* the option of deciding which was more important—your version of what protects me, or mine. To me the only true protection is becoming invisible. You violated that for me."

"It was duplicitous of me," he admits. "But I am by nature a deceptive person. It is the single thing in police work which most fascinates me. Last year we apprehended a suspect who had raped a victim and bitten her savagely about the breasts. He had a perfect alibi. Three reputable witnesses. But I had something better. An electron microscope."

"An EMS?" I say. "*Here*? In Nouméa?"

"We may be on the far side of the world, monsieur," he says, "but we are not without our resources. In any event, by using the electron beams of the EMS and making three-dimensional comparisons of the tooth-mark patterns left on the breasts of his victim, we were able to establish twenty-one irrefutable points of identification. The man confessed."

"There is a confusion here," I point out. "A confusion of analogy. The EMS was *not* duplicitous. Its clear-sighted perception was the cause of the man's conviction."

"Ah, no!" Bazin smiles. "The EMS merely established in my mind his indisputable guilt. But it was the personal deception I employed with the suspect that induced him to confess. If police work were nothing more than looking down the barrel of a microscope or of a gun, what a dreary profession!"

"You're getting away from my point," I insist. "I want that bug out of the Renault. Or else I want another car. A *clean* car!"

"You may remove it yourself, if you wish. It's concealed inside the steering shaft and is activated by the ignition switch."

"How do I know you don't have two or even three more bugs in the car? You give me back one of them, but you still have me on your scanner with the ones you haven't given me."

"You have my word, monsieur. One bug to a car is enough, even for me. You said there were *three* items on your agenda. The third?"

"A local girl named Kaméa. She works for UTA."

"What about her?"

"Can I trust her?"

"With what?"

"My life."

He closes his eyes. He turns his head back into the wind. I discover something new about the structure of his face, something my mother would have noted instantly. The hollows under the cheekbones are deeper than I had thought. They would require darkening if you were to paint him.

"I cannot imagine *you*, monsieur, trusting anyone with something you protect with such zeal."

He is looking at me as he says it, watching me.

"I'm meeting her tomorrow. If she agrees to do it, she'll brief me for my going north this weekend."

"North being . . . ?"

"Hienghène."

"Suppose I told you there is no shortage of baskets in Hienghène?"

"They have to catch me first."

"The young man I sent thought the same way. And he had several advantages over you. He came from a nearby tribe. He spoke the language. And so far as I knew, nobody else was aware he was a secret police officer. There is no possible explanation for what happened to him, except, of course, that somebody else *did* know. Someone betrayed him. Now, we come to you. What can you possibly hope to learn by going up there?"

"I intend to run what we used to call in Nam a SLAM— a seek, locate, annihilate, and monitor mission. Then see what shakes."

"And how do you do this in a country not at war? Will you go in openly? By car, by bus, by foot? Do you announce to Kangara, Behold, here I stand, the man your warriors could not kill. Do you expect Kangara to conduct you on a tour? Or will you go in covertly? At night, with paint on your face? M. Locke, I can assure you, your going up there is not only ridiculous, it will be the end of you. I can tell you that in all of New Caledonia at this moment, there is no single human being who is more widely known about by the Melanesians than John Locke. They are singing songs of death about you. You are living inside a jungle drum, monsieur. Every heartbeat of yours is being listened to by every tribesman in this land. I marvel that you have survived these past two days. I truly marvel at that. They want you dead. Very dead!"

"Very stimulating," I say, in a tone as dry as I can muster up under the circumstances, "but it doesn't face up to my question about Kaméa."

"Kaméa is half-Melanesian. She cannot betray her own blood cells."

"You're saying I can't trust her."

"Only to a point. She is quite a remarkable young woman. If she decides to help you, that decision itself is worth a good deal. But what I am saying goes deeper. In a choice between you and some Hienghène tribesman, she is capable of reverting to her own. Do you understand?"

"I do."

"And you will still take the risk, of course?"

"I will."

"Where shall I send your things? What shall we do with this boat?"

"Just call my father in San Diego. Tell him it was a hell of a life. But only a life." ·

The marina lies dead ahead.

"You can ready that spring line," I tell Bazin.

And I bring *Steel Tiger* into her slip behind the stern of *Reckless Living*.

Bazin watches me putting the ketch to bed.

"She is made of fiberglass, no?" he asks.

"Heavily laid up," I tell him. "Especially her bow. She's a real bluewater boat."

"But if she's made of fiberglass, why did you name her *Steel* Tiger?"

" 'Steel Tiger' was a military operation," I say. "One I think of when I've got nothing better to do. And steel comes in all kinds of forms—like tigers."

I drive Bazin to police headquarters, neither of us speaking for the five or six minutes it takes.

Only when I have driven into the courtyard and parked and he has climbed out, I remaining behind the wheel, does he say anything more.

He comes around to my side of the Renault, rests his hands on the door. I see the mosaic of liver spots on the back of his hands.

"As you must be aware from the heavy security I have imposed here at headquarters, I have taken your premonition about a possible bombing quite seriously. So you must know by now I do not underestimate you. I simply ask you to think carefully about what I have said before you make a final decision to go north. I believe you can accomplish far more here. For example, this Saturday we are expecting a regiment of Foreign Legion paratroopers to arrive from Corsica. It is my understanding their commanding officer is a harsh martinet who detests all gendarmes. So I know he and I will clash. I would find it helpful if you were to act as military liaison between my department and this officer. He would be less inclined to bully another fighting man, such as yourself, than he would me."

"Thank you, Inspector," I tell him, for I know it's not easy for him to speak with such candor. "I will at least think it all out very carefully and give you my decision after I meet Kaméa tomorrow."

He continues to look into my eyes for another moment, and for an instant I have the feeling his eyes are the lenses of the electronic scanner. Then he turns away. He walks two steps, turns, comes back.

"I am having trouble enforcing your suggestion that personnel not bring their baguettes into headquarters. May I ask why you insisted on that precaution?"

"When I was attached to DAO in Saigon," I tell him, "I saw a young Vietnamese on a Honda, his girl sitting behind him holding a long loaf of French bread, stop alongside the car just ahead of my jeep. At a traffic light. As the signal went green, the girl broke the loaf in half, lobbed it into the back seat of the car. The half she threw held a charge of plastique. The car, of course, disintegrated in front of me, killing the Vietnamese general and his wife who had been sitting in the back seat. Ever since I've been wary of French baguettes."

He nods thoughtfully, steps off toward his office.

I back the Renault around, drive to the marina.

It is almost eleven and time for Michael, dear Michael.

I tidy up *Steel Tiger*, stow the sheets and flake out the sails, cover the booms, go below, and turn on the telex.

Promptly at eleven hundred hours I pick up a verification signal, then within seconds the words start clacking through, sixty to the minute had the message run a full minute. I tear the message from the carriage. Only thirty words—half a minute, no more. But everything I'd hoped for: INFO YOU REQUIRE COMING BY COURIER. BE IN STALL THREE, PUBLIC JOHN, PLACE DES COCOTIERS, FIFTEEN HUNDRED HOURS NOUMEA TIME TOMORROW, FRIDAY. PASSWORD MENU ERNIE'S DINNER. LOVE, MICHAEL.

I close down the telex.

Tomorrow seems to be shaping up.

Kaméa at two P.M.—give or take.

Courier at three with what I need to know about the Gallantes. And maybe a way to go.

That gives me the rest of today, tonight, and tomorrow morning to continue probing Nouméa til my slicks hit town.

I climb into the Renault and drive downtown with nothing definite yet in mind, across Rue Général Mangin, then around the lower leg of the quadrangle of Place des Cocotiers.

Something disquieting about the park this afternoon troubles me enough to make me pull over to the curb outside the cement-block building that houses the produce market. From this vantage point, surveying the Place des Cocotiers, I discover what it is that's caught my attention.

There is not a Melanesian to be seen in the entire park. Not one. Before this I've noted the customary gardeners and the lazing old habitués with their hachured faces and white, crinkly hair gossiping the mornings away on broken park benches. There have always been before the elephantine native women in their tentlike cottons, stentorious in reds and blues, dazzling the park with their vigorous chromatics, their thin-legged children scampering among them. But now on this Wednesday afternoon there are no mothers, no children, no old men, no gardeners. Only white faces, European cabbies waiting behind their newspapers at the steering wheels of their taxis for tourists to wander onto Rue Anatole France.

I ask Bazin about this moments later when I've obtained clearance to reenter the closely guarded courtyard of police headquarters.

"Is there something that happens on Wednesday afternoons that draws Melanesians out of downtown Nouméa?"

He offers me coffee. The same policewoman who had served us my first morning in Nouméa brings it to us now. This time she smiles at me openly, Bazin noting her freeness through veiled eyes, but saying nothing.

"I'm not aware of what it could be," he says when she's left us alone and we're savoring our coffee.

He opens a folder in front of him, hands it to me across the desk.

I read the heading: ABSENTEEISM AMONG NATIVE EMPLOYEES, SUMMARY OF CORPORATE REPORTS.

I scan the figures.

"Forty-six-percent absenteeism this past week?"

"And growing each day," he comments.

"Why?" I ask.

"I'm not yet sure. At first I thought some of the absenteeism might be attributable to Kangara's upcoming birthday. The natives have this rather laudatory obsession about taking off whenever there's a birth or a wedding or a death or any important life-event and bringing to it the gift of their personal presence. Sometimes they've been known to leave as early as a month before the event itself to make certain they have become an integral part of it. But important as Kangara is, these statistics of Melanesians drifting out of Nouméa are, I admit, not only inexplicable, but alarming."

"Why would you have had this report made in the first place?" I ask.

"Intuition," he says, after taking the last taste of coffee in his demitasse. "The same intuition that caused you to ask me to keep baguettes out of these offices. How much longer, incidentally, does that particular foreboding of yours extend?"

"It's stronger than ever," I say quite seriously. "Whenever I close my eyes I see automatic-weapons fire raking this building from one end of the block to the other."

He sighs. "I have met many men more gladdening to be around than you, monsieur."

"What would cause such a high rate of absenteeism?" I ask. "Unless something's coming down they know about that we don't?"

"Precisely," he agrees. It is evident he intends to give me no more than this.

I rise to go.

"You are meeting Kaméa tomorrow afternoon?" he asks.

"Yes. At the museum."

"You'll let me know your decision? About going to Hienghène?"

"Right away."

"If you should go—Saturday, was it?"

"Yes, Saturday. Around midnight, I think."

"If you should go Saturday, Madame and I would like very much to have you come to our home for dinner at eight o'clock—before you leave. Unquestionably, your last supper."

I try not to stare at him. He has spoken casually, but seriously. The man has actually invited me to come to dinner. And in the name of his dead wife. With a perfectly straight face.

Mine is equally straight.

"I'm honored," I reply. "Does Madame like music?"

"Very much."

"Has she a favorite artist?"

"She has always been partial to Aznavour. And more lately to Françoise Hardy."

"Good," I say.

I drive back downtown, wondering what macabre game Bazin is playing with me, yet I park outside a record-and-tape store. Inside, I buy the three latest Aznavour LPs, together with three of Françoise Hardy's, and ask the girl at the cash desk to giftwrap them for me.

I take my package, return to the Renault, determined to puzzle out Bazin's motives. It occurs to me I haven't eaten for hours. I find a stand just a few meters down the block, buy a casse-croûte, a loaf of French bread, fruit, and wine.

I sit in the car to one side of the wheel, rip into the bread ravenously, and watch the French girls passing, selecting those I would earnestly ravish, given the chance, and those that I would not, that fanciful roulette so many men play to the last days of their lives, still wondering with their dying thought what it would be like to nail the nurse who is pulling the sheet over their glazing eyes. I question if I would be as erotogenic if all the passing girls were stark naked. I have read that among certain tribes of primitive Indians where sex is as natural as defecation, the men never masturbate and never have erections until they take their wives into their hammocks.

I spill wine on my crotch. Sampling the new Beaujolais, are you, Locke, old man? I start to laugh out loud.

It reminds me of one night in San Francisco when I was still a cop. I'm sitting in an unmarked car with my partner and we're watching this house. We're in your basic Hispanic neighborhood, so we'd each picked up a Manuel sandwich plus a six-pack of beer. We weren't supposed to drink on duty, but with these Manuels, beer is the only fluid this side of lye-water capable of dissolving the guck in the sandwich enough to let you swallow it. So we're slurping beer and watching this house and I hear my partner say, "Ah, shit!" I look over to see that the ass-end of his sandwich has just fallen out and it's all plopped into his crotch. Now these Manuels are peppers and tomatoes and greasy beef and hot sauce. He just sits there looking at his groin area with all this garbage heaped on it and he holds up his hands with grease running down into his cuffs and laughs, "No fucking wonder they call us pigs!"

When my crotch has dried, I drive to the city library.

The young librarian has to climb a ladder to reach the dusty volumes on New Caledonian history, rites, and customs, all in French. She glances down at me reprovingly as I stand too close to the base of the ladder, smiling up at her legs.

"Just making sure you don't fall," I say. She doesn't believe me.

When the library closes for the evening, I wander out to the Renault. The shapely lathing of girls' legs, the memories of police partners, even Nam have been swept clear of the forefront of my mind by the things I've read.

I speed out of the city. I drive to Mont-Dore and park on a promontory near the unfinished communications project the Gallantes are bringing to Nouméa.

I compose myself. I meditate. I remind myself how fortunate I am to be attached to the sheltering earth on this magnificent night of disarray, while my enemy remains unknown to me. I begin to feel less troubled. I become uplifted and sustained. I let affection for my enemy enter my consciousness. I beg him to come to me, or else to guide me to him. I thank him for this opportunity. I feel him somewhere out there in the night, offering himself.

Across dark hours I lose track of, I continue to reach out to what must be, to make all of it a part of me, accepting and welcoming it, as Doan Thi has taught me. By the time dawn has seeped up and painted the shadowed Renault bright green again, I have even forgiven my enemy for insisting on this needless sacrifice of himself and for making me the accomplice to his death. Now I have neither hate for him, nor fear, left anywhere within me, only a vast sorrow that none of it will have any meaning whatsoever, either for him or for me.

Certainly not for the inexorable universe about us.

# CHAPTER

# 19

**S**hortly after fourteen hundred hours I'm standing in the middle of the main exhibit chamber of the Nouméa Museum and examining the carved elements of a New Caledonian ceremonial hut. I observe a young woman in a light-blue business suit briskly entering the hall.

She appears more French than Melanesian, her figure trim, her skin color lighter than mine, but as she comes closer I catch that special luster in her eyes, that primitive fire lacking in French eyes. Her nose is somewhat broader than the noses of European girls, her lips fuller, although they turn up saucily at each crease, giving her a look of wounded amusement. It is apparent she depends more on her mind than on her body to get whatever it is she wants from living.

She greets me with refreshing directness.

"You must be John Locke. Maurice said you look as though you sleep in your clothes."

"I do. Thank you for flying back from Papeete."

She glances past me to the ceremonial hut.

"What does it mean to you, the art of my people? Anything?"

"It's not entirely new to me," I say. "I didn't just fly in here yesterday from another culture zone. I've been out here in the Pacific for a while. For example, take that roof shaft. It's a lot more than simply a decorative piece. It is, in fact, a portrait of the face of the owner of this hut. You can see, if you know how to read it, how the volumes of the face have been spread out on vertical planes, the temples and the ears flapped forward to become level with the face—and the chin flattened. I believe you call that a 'threshold head.' Am I right about that?"

"You're right and I'm impressed," she says. "Maurice told me I would be."

"Can I take you somewhere for lunch?" I ask.

"I never eat lunch," she says. "But thank you. We can talk here, if you don't mind."

She begins to stroll through the hall. I accompany her. She stops in front of Cases 8 and 9, rather pointedly, I observe, for both cases display weapons of war.

"Maurice also told me you've had some recent experience with our local weapons."

"They look better under glass," I say.

"There's an art to fighting with these," she says. "We call it war-club fencing. You'll notice the clubs are basically of three patterns, bill-headed, phallic, or star-shaped."

"I've noticed," I reply.

I discover her looking at me with an expression I might interpret as pleading.

"Maurice and I are lovers," she says. "We have been for five years. He tells me everything."

"I can see that."

"But what I'm about to say comes from me alone. Please, monsieur, leave New Caledonia. Leave today! Get back on your boat and sail away from this island!"

"I keep waiting for one person to say to me, John, ol' buddy, tell you what, baby, stick around. Spend the winter with us. You'll love it here. Kick off your shoes and stay a while. What is this obsessive party line that runs through everyone's advice to me about leaving?"

"Those who care for you will tell you to go. Those who tell you otherwise will make certain you die here."

No amusement touches the corners of her lips. If I ever saw the face of conviction, I see it now.

"Okay," I concede. "I've been warned. And I believe you. God knows I haven't had much chance to enjoy the scenery since I got here. But let's go on to the next step. If I stay, will you help me?"

"How?"

"Give me a crash course in Melanesian culture, attitudes, motivations. Anything that might prepare me to confront the chief of the Hienghène."

"Kangara?" she says, almost whispering the name.

"Kangara," I say. "I intend to insert a recky into his domain. Then I may want to meet him."

"Maurice said you were more than just a little insane. He didn't tell me how insane!"

"Kangara doesn't talk to the white man, is that what you're saying, Kaméa?"

"Why should he talk to you? If, as Maurice thinks, it was he who ordered you killed, why should he want to talk to you?"

"I don't believe he did order it."

"You told Maurice you were attacked by Melanesians, both at sea and here in Nouméa."

"That still doesn't convince me it was Kangara. He may run the most powerful tribe on the island, but he's not the only chieftain. Nor is his tribe the only tribe. Matter of fact, I think by now he'd be fascinated to meet me face to face."

"Just long enough to make you disappear forever!"

"I'm not so sure about that. The history of combat is filled with surprising confrontations. Totally unexpected behavior between enemies. Sometimes these face-downs even resulted in peace. One emperor once learned that several of his generals had united against him and taken most of his army. He rode alone across the battlefield and knelt defenseless before his former generals, now his sworn enemies. He begged them either to return with him or else to kill him on the spot. He told them he had no wish to live without their loyalty and their love."

"So they killed him!" she says. Some of Maurice's irony has rubbed off on her in the five years they've slept together.

"Not just then," I smile. "Actually he conned almost twelve more good years out of them before they cut off his head."

221

"Even if I could arrange for you to have an audience with Kangara—and I don't promise that I can; it would have to go through a dozen intermediaries—but even if I could, it would have to wait until after Bastille Day. Can you survive that much longer?"

"The fourteenth?" I ask. "Why not until after Bastille Day?"

"He was born on our National Holiday. And this is a particularly significant birthyear—his sixty-seventh. The number has mystic overtones to my people. Tribesmen from one end of the island to the other—and from all the outlying islands—have been gathering in the north for the past week to prepare to honor the event."

"Could that be the only reason there are fewer and fewer Melanesians in Nouméa?"

"By this time next week," she says, "the only natives left in this city will be those of mixed blood, people like me. Or the professional Melanesian dance troupe that performs every year during the holiday street festival in Nouméa."

But I do not hear her. My mind has been abruptly jammed with the recall of other words, Marcel Gallante's words spoken to me that first day I arrived in New Caledonia as we stood at the foot of the high front stairway leading onto the porch of la Ferme de St. Paul. He is telling me about that terrible night his brother Georges was born in the maelstrom of a tropical cyclone on July 14.

So Georges and Kangara share a common birthdate. Same day. Same year. I wonder how close they are to the same hour, same minute.

Now Marcel's words are supplanted by the memory of something Rosine said to me outside the dive shop. "The true people love my father. He was brought into existence by one of their own t'katas. We are descended from the blood of the stone. Their ancestors read our dreams and we in turn hear their words without listening."

I am seized with a sense of urgency to pick up that report on the Gallantes. I glance at my wristwatch. Two and a half hours before I'm to meet Michael's courier.

"I can't wait till next week," I say to Kaméa. "I plan to

go north this weekend. Actually, shortly after midnight Saturday night. I'm going to sail up the coast as far north as Voh, then cross overland to Hienghène, coming at it from inland."

"It's at least forty kilometers across there, over mountain ridges and through wilderness!"

"I didn't say I'd *walk* across."

"Then how *will* you cross? There's only a dirt track from Tiéta along the River Faténaoué inland. Then it's another ten awful kilometers with no road until you come to Caavatch. And from Caavatch—"

"I'll work all that out," I interrupt.

She looks around the exhibit hall to make sure we're not being watched. Then she slips something from her shoulder bag into my hand. I glance at it covertly, following her lead of secrecy, see that I'm holding a knotted balassor strip made of vegetable-fiber cloth.

"I found this today in my mailbox."

"What is it?" I ask.

"The knots in that piece of cloth are coded. In times before, my people passed messages this way, from hand to hand, from sender to recipient through many middle hands. The knots can mean a peace proposal, a declaration of war, a new tribal alliance—any number of things."

"What do these mean?"

"I don't know. I don't even know why it was left for me."

"Unless someone knew you were meeting me. And wanted me to have it."

"What's the point?" she asks. "If you can't interpret the code?"

"One more thing for me to try to find out."

She seems, all at once, to have run out of words.

"Kaméa," I say, "you didn't want to come back to New Caledonia, did you?"

"I live here! My job is here! Maurice is here!"

"But you wanted to stay off this island a while longer, didn't you? Stay in Tahiti, I mean. Until when, Kaméa?"

Our eyes touch. And hold.

"Until after Bastille Day," she whispers.

"Thank you," I say. "Will you teach me what I need to know?"

"Yes," she whispers. "When?"

"I'll let you know."

I leave her by a small podium surrounded by a fiber fence in the center of the exhibit hall. She remains curiously poised next to the sarcophagus of a dead native chieftain who squats like old leather in a half-sized, hand-carved coffin.

Is it my imagination or does she no longer look so French, but rather more Melanesian?

Standing there alone among the artifacts of her people, she appears to have turned into the daughter of a chieftain from an earlier century.

I hasten outside.

At the curb a busload of Australian tourists is unloading.

I throw off the shudders and gratefully reenter the twentieth century.

I reenter it by way of the public toilet, a yellow block house in Place des Cocotiers adjoining Rue Anatole France.

An attendant with the sagging jowls of a bloodhound hunches lugubriously behind a counter just inside the entrance. He is doodling on a pad of butcher paper even while he evaluates me. Am I a paying customer worthy of ten seconds of his time or simply another transient zipper in need of a urinal?

I scan the card of fixed prices on the wall behind him. The lithography is proud enough to have come straight from the bill of fare of a four-star restaurant in châteaux country.

Twenty Pacific francs to evacuate one's bowels. Release of bladder free. I've often wondered why this favoritism? I conjure up a vision of the city planning commission in session, heatedly discussing price levels, debating how much longer they can hold the line, avoid raising the price to, say, thirty Pacific francs to keep abreast of inflation.

I give him his twenty francs, and in return he hands me a skimpy fold of toilet tissue.

"Is one expected to use both sides?" I ask him in French.

"Monsieur may, if he has further need, buy a second allotment for another twenty francs."

"I'll make do," I reply. "The edges do look fairly thick."

I observe that what he is doodling is not, as I had at first assumed, an ascending array of V's, but is in fact a ladder of vulvas. Poor bastard's on the wrong side of the public toilets. He should be guardian of the women's domain, where all customers pay to sit, regardless of the call—another discrimination, I am sure.

I enter a tiled and suprisingly clean section. An old man muttering to himself is bent over the long gurgling trough into which he is patiently trying to urge drops from an aging and reluctant urethra.

I count the doors of the water closets.

Michael has telexed I am to wait until I can occupy booth number three.

I determine that number three is vacant, number two occupied. Good sign. I open the door to three, go in, lock the door after me. I lower the seat and with trousers intact settle down. I hear my inner voice chanting, "How now, brown cow?"

The Memosail delivers a digital fifteen hundred hours. Time for Michael's prearranged rendezvous.

"Ernie's," I say in overture, addressing the password to the left foot of the man occupying booth number two.

"Who's the father of Scrappy Do?" a voice comes back.

"Jesus, man," I protest. "That's not part of it!"

I hear his laughter. "Humor me," he suggests. "I like to improvise."

"The father of Scrappy Do happens to be Scooby Do," I say, "but only people under twelve know shit like that. What if I hadn't known?"

"Okay, let's get back to the code book. 'Ernie's,' right?"

"I can even spell it for you, if that'll speed this up any."

"What did Marty order for dinner?"

"You're a tricky mother," I compliment him. "My dinner was with Michael, not with Marty."

"Okay, what did Michael order?"

"Michael ordered the lobster thermidor. Now that I think about it, he ordered the same damned thing in San Diego, that second time he showed up."

"He's obsessed with lobster," the voice tells me. "What did you order?"

"Beef Wellington."

"What for openers?"

"Caesar salad for two with extra anchovies."

"That was going to be my next question."

"The extra anchovies?"

"Yep."

"Hey, baby," I say, "I think you're enjoying this."

"It's a welcome change for me. It gets boring driving a 747. If I see one more gorgeous sunset I'm going to flip out. How do the angels ever stand it up there?"

A thick envelope is suddenly nudging my foot as he makes his pass under the partition.

"Tell Michael I owe him one," I say. "You too. If I can know your name."

"Better I don't tell you," he laughs. "If they should catch you and torture it out of you, they'll be coming for me next, right?"

"Wrong," I say. "I carry this deadly little pill inside a gold Mexican fifty-peso coin I wear on this chain around my neck. All I have to do is swallow the fifty pesos and if I don't choke to death doing that, the pill finishes the job. I've timed it. I'm gone in a tenth of a second. So you're safe."

I get off the john, open the door. And so does he.

He's your type-casting airline pilot, eyes blue as a Normandy tablecloth.

"Eddie Markham," he says, shaking my hand firmly. "Good luck, fella."

"Thanks, Eddie," I say.

I go out, stopping a moment at the attendant's counter.

"Do you give refunds?" I ask, placing the unused toilet tissue in front of him.

He doesn't miss a stroke on the latest vulva he's sketching.

"C'est la vie, monsieur," he shrugs.

"May the next man be more fortunate," I say, and donate the sparse wad of paper I'd bought.

# CHAPTER

## 20

**W**ith my envelope from Michael I go out into the afternoon.

The heavy packet feels like a hot brick in my hand, such is my eagerness to rip it open and devour its contents. But I have to be somewhere I can spread out papers and make notes and if need be pace back and forth while I cerebrate without all my energies being focused on casual passersbys who might turn into instant assassins.

I race the Renault from the center of Nouméa out to the beach community of Anse Vata, park near the Club Med laundry room, heft the dive bag, which grows heavier with each succeeding day I spend in New Caledonia, and go chug-chugging up to my hotel room like an expectant bene-ficiary rushing to tear open the old man's last will and testament.

Ken is stretched out on one of the twin beds, his legs spread painfully wide, his neck craning as he peers into a hand-held mirror reflecting his genitals and rectum.

"Don't let me interrupt anything," I comment as I set the dive bag down.

"Jesus!" he cries, his normally ruddy cheeks blazing even more crimson. "You might have knocked!"

"Is this or is this not my room too?"

"I was beginning to wonder if I should call Harry in Perth and ask him what I should do. Not a bloody word from you since the other night!"

"I was tending to business," I say, more and more an-noyed that he has to be here in the room right at this moment and not out on the beach chasing dollies.

228

"Well," he says, "I was tending to business too. Which is why I'm lying here now checking out my balls and my bung hole."

"Something the matter with them?"

"You know anything about herpes simplex, Johnny boy?" he asks, his voice lowering as though he's just uttered the two most sinister words in the language, anybody's language.

"First, I never want it," I reply. "Second, there's a lot of media attention to it lately. Some of the publications my dad mails me from the States have been carrying major takeouts on it. They're even making jokes about it now. If you've got it from the neck down they call it herpes simplex. From the neck up, herpes complex. Both above *and* below, you got herpes duplex."

"Extremely amusing, I'm sure," Ken mutters.

"Why?" I ask. "You caught it?"

"How long does it take after you've been exposed before you *know* you got it?" he asks uneasily.

"You worried about Marla or Queenie?"

"Not Queenie. She's still waiting for you. Although I have to tell you she was something else on that boat the other night. Boffed everything aboard except me. Said she couldn't do me because that would be cheating on you."

"She has a highly principled mind, that Queenie," I say.

"But that Marla!" he says. "She's a goddamned sex machine! She really hates men! Her way of killing them is to fuck them to death!"

"Well, don't blame her for giving you herpes," I advise him. "It doesn't show up that quickly."

"Yeah? Well, I never had this tingling sensation before. It's up the inside of my thigh. And I itch all over my privates."

"What were you doing a week, ten days ago in Perth?"

"The usual. But not with anybody new."

"You might as well put the mirror away and get your pants back on."

Hopefully, he gets up off the bed. "You mean I don't have it?"

"If you do, you won't need that mirror to tell you. Give yourself another couple of days. If you've really got it, you'll develop blisters filled with fluid, big enough to see with the naked eye."

He winces. "Oh, my God!" he wails.

"This may sound heartless," I say, my patience with him thinning, "but I really need to be alone now. Why don't you get out on the beach and work on your tan?"

"I don't think the sun's supposed to be good for herpes," he says. "Anyway, I'm feeling a little feverish."

"Then go down to the bar and order something tall and frosty. I need to least an hour up here by myself to work some things out."

Obediently, he starts to dress.

"Johnny boy, I feel like a shithead. I flew in here to help out. The five days are up Saturday. But you haven't made much use of me. Can't I beat up some guys for you or something before I leave? It would sure make me feel better about the whole trip."

"Nobody to beat up right now, Ken," I assure him. "And you mustn't feel any sense of failure. Because of you I was able to buy the time I needed. Everything's on track, moving right along. Matter of fact, I'm pulling out tomorrow night, just after midnight."

"Leaving New Caledonia?" he asks with surprise.

"This part of it, anyway. So I won't be seeing you for a while. Tell Harry I'll be in touch. Tell him I really appreciate his sending you up here."

Dressed now, he starts to hold out his hand to me, but, thinking better of it, moves quickly to the bathroom. I hear him washing away and scrubbing in there, then he comes out, wiping his hands vigorously on a towel.

Finally he holds out his hand to me.

"Germ-free," he grins.

I shake his hand.

"Take care, Ken."

"You too, Johnny boy."

He leaves me alone in the room.

I open Michael's packet.

I begin to read.

Michael doesn't know what I'm looking for, and since I don't either he's sent me a grab bag of secret facts and rumors and statistics about the Gallantes known only to the intelligence-gathering services he can access. He's sent all this unrelated data along to me printed out on computer sheets in what clearly has been an all-night, rush-rush session, picking it up from one source or another as he went along, like a shoplifter stuffing his overcoat with no particular regard to the merchandise's true value.

But as I read on about the Gallantes' international cartel, their Société Financière pour Coopération Pacifique, their complex, interlocking ownerships of banks and airlines and plantations and communications systems and mines, as I read about the private lives of both Georges and Marcel, I begin to tremble with a sense of discovery. I find more and more pieces of isolated information that begin to suggest a pattern. I become so excited I have to force myself to continue to turn the pages and not just leap to a conclusion already crowding my mind. I am impelled to move out right now, confront Marcel Gallante, dare him to try to explain and to justify what I'm now stumbling across in Michael's field report.

I get so stoked I have to force myself to cool down. Some of the things I'm reading exacerbate my long-standing fury toward the human abuse of authority, the callousness that comes with power.

I feel at this moment the way I remember feeling one night in an AC-47 gunship overflying Saigon on the way back north.

We were passing above the surrealistic glow of the Hotel Caravelle's roof garden.

An hour away men I had cared for still lay like cordwood in body bags awaiting shipment home.

Yet below me I saw American officers and Category 4

carpetbaggers, the civilians who follow war for the commerce in it, the people who sell beer and liquor and ice cream and building scaffolds and you name what else, dancing with Vietnamese girls or what few American women they could find.

In spite of the clatter of our rotors we could hear the lofting of the music. This particular night they were playing Cole Porter's "I Didn't Know What Time It Was" as we flew over.

I imagined I could even hear the rattle of ice cubes in their highball glasses.

I noticed that the gunner was glooming down the stub of his door-mounted 7.62mm General Electric Minigun, its four barrels pointing straight down at the dancers, four accusatory fingers, it struck me, pointing down at this pastel pattern of thoughtlessness, at all those frivolous foxtrotters profaning one more mindless night.

I saw the gunner's finger rub gently back and forth on the trigger, but only caressing, not stiffening, his eyes as empty as Orphan Annie's.

But I knew what he was thinking. I was thinking the same thing, fighting back the same urge.

I hunger to pick up the phone this very second and challenge Marcel Gallante. But this is not possible from a Club Med bedroom. The management prides itself on not providing guests with room phones. The entire concept of a Club Med vacation is to take away from you such exhausting links with the outside world. Good for sun-seekers, bad for me, at this moment.

I go down to the lobby and give Marcel Gallante's number to a girl at a reception table. She's pasted into a bikini with an indifferently placed bra strap and she's playing backgammon with a male guest who is concentrating more on the gravity factor of her bra than on his game. He's got a chest riotous with gray hair, yet he wears the most incongruous-looking jet-black toupee on his head. The sweat runs from under the false hairline and I wonder if the toupee might slip off and nest on the backgammon board before the GO's bra slides south. They are well suited to each other, I decide while the girl reluctantly dials my number, then dismisses me toward one of the phones in an open cross-hatch of stalls.

I pick up the ringing instrument and ask for Marcel Gallante.

A man's voice informs me that Gallante is not available.

"Tell him it's John Locke," I say in French.

"A moment, please, sir. I will call the captain."

Another voice reaches through to me almost immediately, this one alert and commanding.

"M. Locke, Captain Vandegans. M. Gallante is anxious to speak with you. He left instructions that if you were to call, I should let him know where and when he might meet you."

"The sooner the better," I say. "As a matter of fact, even sooner than that. Is he somewhere I can drive to?"

"No, monsieur. I am sorry. He is at the mine in Tiébaghi. He is staying up there overnight. In the town of Koumac."

"Where is that? How far from Nouméa?"

"Almost at the northern end of the island. Two hours by helicopter," he replies.

"Have you anything available to fly me up there?"

"Yes, monsieur. I can have a machine pick you up within fifteen minutes. The pilot will be Lieutenant Gallimard."

I look at my watch. If they can lift me off in fifteen minutes, that will make it sixteen hundred hours and twenty-seven minutes. Add two hours flying time, I'll still be able to confront Gallante before sunset.

"I'll wait on the highway," I tell the Captain, "just outside the guard's gate at the entrance to the Club Med. I'll be the fella holding a blue dive bag."

"Very well, sir. Would you like additional manpower along?"

"Not for this one, thank you."

"Au revoir, monsieur."

Thank God for can-do captains. They've always been my favorite people.

Not quite fourteen minutes later I hear a sound which of all sounds is to me the most soothing, yet the most evocative, that reassuring thwump-thwump-thwump coming at me from over the tree line.

The captain has sent a military chopper to extract me, not one of SFPCP's corporate aircraft, but now that I've read Michael's report this doesn't confuse me. After all, SFPCP owns an international arms department and one of their subcontractors is involved in working on the French Mirage fighter.

I heave my dive bag into a back seat, then strap myself up front next to Lieutenant Gallimard, a young officer who gives me the feeling that I'm in competent hands from the first minute he's lifted us off and skimmed over the red-clay tennis courts.

I suggest to him that he shouldn't feel hesitant on my behalf about climbing as high as he wants to. Speaking as the poor bastard who's been a running target all week, the higher the better, the sooner the better.

In spite of my desire to scout the terrain from the air, since I'll be sailing north along this coastline not too many hours from now, I plunge asleep within the first five minutes of our flight. This is another habit that clings to me from Nam. When I was in-country, the few times I ever felt comparatively safe was whenever I flew at high altitude in an armored gunship. Invariably I'd fall into a deep sleep once we got up there and I'd stay asleep until we began to descend. Once we came back within range of groundfire, I'd snap out of the dream-box like the birdie in a cuckoo clock, ease my helmet protectively under my rump, and fasten my flak jacket tight in front.

I awaken now as the lieutenant begins to lower over Tiébaghi.

I stare down at what he tells me is the largest and richest chrome mine in the world.

Dôme de Tiébaghi reaches almost as high as our skids. I feel as though were I to lean out I could touch its bristling guava trees. Mounds of silvered chrome glint in the sunset against the russet of the mine's overburden.

Gallimard tells me that more than a million tons of high-grade ore have been taken from the two small tunnels we're now overflying. He also confides with a measure of ill-concealed distaste that the mine is owned by the British, as though it is beyond his comprehension how the English could have managed to pull that one off. I decide not to tell him what I've read in Michael's report, that French mining law states that any foreign company operating in New Caledonia must have a majority of French directors on their board of directors, and that one of them is Marcel Gallante.

I trace the half-circle of a level-grade railway from the mineshafts around the side of the mountain to what appears to be the processing plant. Here the ore is being emptied into half-ton tip-trucks, which shift it down into a hopper.

The pilot points out the process. From hopper it travels to a revolving sieve. The fine ore is then passed through to machines which wash it, while the lump ore is rejected and dumped onto an endless belt. The high-grade ore, he tells me, is then shuttled into trucks and transported to Baie de Néhoué, where it is loaded into the freighters I can see now lined along the wharves like plundering pirate ships.

We pick up a radio transmission. Marcel Gallante's voice crackles through the cabin. He's asking to talk to me.

Gallimard's eyes indicate the second radio set hooked up in my seat position. I slip it on.

"Good evening, M. Locke." I sense no reproach in Marcel's voice, only relief that he has finally succeeded in reaching me.

"Good evening, sir," I reply.

"I hope you will take dinner with me," he says. "It won't be as good as our lunch, but I can guarantee you a

splendid sunset. We have a company lodge on a cliff overlooking the Coral Sea. What will you take as an apéritif?"

"Gin on the rocks, please, with a lime twist," I say.

"It will be chilling in the glass," he promises.

He ends the transmission.

I discover Gallimard looking at me.

"I've heard a lot of stories about you this week, Captain,"
he says. "I wish it were I having dinner with you. There is
so much I would like to ask. Especially about your shooting your way out of that ambush. I can tell you that was
a magnificent tonic to our paratroopers. They are all eager
to see action, envious that it seems to be coming only your
way, not theirs."

"They should get out a little more," I say. "Mix with the
population. They're not going to see any action cooped up
there on that farm."

"They know that, sir. Unfortunately, they do not have
your freedom."

"Please excuse me for falling asleep on the flight up
here," I say. "Maybe we can kick this around some more
when you fly me back to Nouméa."

"Thank you, sir. I would like that."

He sets the chopper down on the grounds of a lodge
built on the lip of a bluff overlooking the sea. The water
lies taut below us, restrained by the distant reefline. The
sun looks to me like a giant marigold about to be arranged
in a vast bowl of tinted water.

Gallante waits in the entrance to the lodge. He poses
there, silhouetted in the sunset, tall as a bronze heron in a
Japanese garden. To either side of him paratroopers with
automatic weapons stand guard.

The main room of the lodge opens onto a deck canti-
levered out over the cliff. Gallante leads me onto this deck,
awards me my icy gin and the always awesome show of the
descending sun, all this without a word, as though he hesi-
tates to initiate the conversation for fear he might guide it
along paths he prefers me to select.

I raise my glass to him, even though he is conspicuously

not drinking. He has, I observe for the first time, foraging eyes. No question, he's one of the true predators.

"I left you Tuesday after lunch," I say. "It's now Friday evening. You must be curious about what I've been doing between then and now."

"Not so much what you've been doing, monsieur, as why."

"Aha," I say. "It *is* a small town, isn't it?"

"I must be candid with you," he says, making an effort to be careful with me, not to go too far, yet not to let me think he is without his own resources. "I had thought you were as relentless as a heat-seeking missile. I misjudged you. You are, after all, like the rest of us, quite human."

"You are referring, please, to what?" I ask.

"My niece. You have begun a relationship with her."

"Through which," I add, "I have learned a number of relevant things."

"Are you saying, monsieur, your interest in Rosine is purely in behalf of research?"

"Do you disapprove of my seeing her?"

"She is Georges's daughter, not mine. I expect one thing only from you, a final result. If, by diverting time from your main task here, you fail in that, then, yes, by all means, I clearly disapprove!"

"Let's review a few basics," I suggest. "May we do that?"

"Certainly."

"Why did you send for me? To put an end to the terrorism which was interrupting your installation of a satellite-com system on Mont-Dore. Right?"

"Correct."

"Then it develops that was only the tip of the iceberg. Next the Treasury Building in downtown Nouméa is bombed. Obviously what you have here is something a lot more significant than what you led me to believe when you got me to come in here. Is that also not correct?"

"It is."

"Okay. For this reason I've put myself inside the jungle

drum, if I may borrow a figure of speech from someone who recently told me that's where I'm at—inside the drum. When you're in that situation, you start listening to things on all sides of you and all around you. If you don't, you'll never break out of the drum. Am I being too figurative?"

He shakes his head, keeps his eyes intently upon me.

"To all appearances, it would seem there's an incipient native uprising. But that defies common sense and all historical evidence. True, there was one last abortive tribal uprising less than seventy years ago. And recently there've been some scattered bombings in behalf of home rule, resulting in nothing more than property damage. Until this past week. When things heated up. I've been resisting accepting the theory that this is being run by the Melanesians. Granted, they were cannibals not too long ago. Granted, they have always been among the world's fiercest warriors. Granted, the guys who tried to touch me off were all Melanesian. But by and large these people have had their asses virtually kicked off New Caledonia. Either they had to belly up and become black Frenchmen, or they're out in the boondocks catching sea turtles and growing yams. Hardly a trained cadre of insurrectionists out there ready to assault Nouméa. So I've been looking for something else. I started with the unthinkable, with the illogical, and I've ended up with a conviction that you're not going to like even one little bit. As a matter of fact, you're going to wonder why you *did* hire me. *I* certainly wonder!"

He still waits, still says nothing.

"During World War II New Caledonia rose up and rejected the Vichy government. People in Nouméa seized control here and went over to De Gaulle and the Free French. That was just a little more than forty years ago. Prior to that, your people were among those who took over Paris and led an armed uprising against the French government in Versailles. All true?"

He nods.

"So the precedent for what I think may be the scenario

around here is pretty well laid in. Now," I ask, "what would happen if men with enough power, enough money, enough courage—and just enough recklessness—were to seize this island right now, take it away from the new socialist government in Paris, which has already got its own problems at home, and declare New Caledonia an independent country? Men with such inside connections that they already had control of the colonel commanding the French Foreign Legion regiment they'd persuaded Paris to send in to help put down the threat of a native uprising? Men who had already subverted the officers of a French missile cruiser due to arrive in Nouméa this weekend, once more ostensibly to participate in the Bastille Day fete? But really here for a much deadlier purpose."

"You are mad!" Gallante whispers.

"Possibly," I admit. "But I have questions to ask you based on information I've been given. Where have you concealed the ten thousand Fusil Automatique submachine guns shipped to SFPCP in New Caledonia these last three months from your factory in the Central African Republic? Where have you parked and hidden the fifty brand-new Panhard AMLs, each with guns effective at twelve hundred yards, each with a top speed of ninety kilometers an hour, with killing crews of three to each armored car? And finally, what is the present whereabouts of the more than twelve hundred young Melanesians you have trained in advanced weaponry over this past year in a secret base on the one-million-acre 'hunting lodge' you and your brother lease from the Central African Republic?"

Gallante withers in front of me. Yet he manages to cross to the bar. He uncorks a bottle of brandy and with shaking hand pours himself a two-inch slug which he swallows in a single gulp.

Finally he looks at me from behind the bar, where he seems to be bracing himself.

"You can prove what you've just told me?" he asks. "You have copies of invoices? Of weighbills?"

"Given a few days I could get copies," I say. "But I have no reason to doubt the authenticity of this information. My source is totally reliable."

He wipes his forehead.

"You won't believe me, I know," he says. "But until this second I was not aware of anything you've told me."

Now it is my turn to be startled.

I'm seldom deceived by another human being. Marcel Gallante, speaking to me out of pure shock, appears to be telling the truth.

"If you were to shoot me this very second," he says, "I would swear with my dying breath I know of no guns, no armored cars, no Melanesians we have trained."

"I have additional information, sir," I say. "This past year you personally contributed one million francs to an account in the Bank of Indochina in Hong Kong. These funds were subsequently transferred to Nouméa and paid out to an obscure local charity which is, in fact, a front for the God-to-the-Right group in New Caledonia. Do you also deny that?"

"No," he whispers. "That much is true."

He seems to be studying me now, making some kind of critical decision. He regains his full voice. "I am the founder of that group. I consider it necessary to maintain a paramilitary presence in a colony where so many things boil just below the surface. But we are a group of only thirty aging Frenchmen. None of us could march more than two kilometers before we'd have to sit down and have our feet massaged. Our weapons are the normal weapons of free men. Not submachine guns! Not armored cars!"

"Did your group kill that union leader?"

"I swear to God we did not!"

I believe him.

I am even more confused now than I was before.

If not Marcel Gallante, then who?

Marcel has straightened himself, got his shoulders back once more and his head up. He comes from behind the bar.

240

"I think, monsieur, we should leave at once. And fly straight to the farm. The questions you asked me, together you and I will ask my brother Georges!"

I see growing outrage in his eyes. I feel a chill across my shoulders.

My God, yes! If not Marcel, then Georges!

# ═CHAPTER═

# 21

**O**rdinarily Marcel Gallante is not a man who compels sympathy, yet as our chopper comes thwopping in toward la Ferme de St. Paul I feel a subtle quiver of pity toward him. He has hardly spoken in the more than two hours it has taken us to fly south from Koumac.

We pass above the Norman church and the cross canting from the top of the steeple. I envision the dark encroachment of this long-enduring family tragedy, the broken figure of Georges Gallante's father crumpled sixty-seven years ago on the cobblestones at the foot of the church.

Paratroopers have ringed the helipad in the courtyard of la Ferme de St. Paul with pot-lights. Lieutenant Gallimard brings us down softly, cuts the rotors. I discover that Marcel, usually impatient, makes no move to hasten from his seat.

"I wish to be alone with M. Locke," he tells the pilot and the paratrooper sergeant who's flown shotgun with us.

They both salute, climb out, leaving Marcel and me the sole occupants.

"Before we go in and face my brother," he says solemnly, "there are a few other things we must acknowledge between us. One of the matters that has disturbed me from the first is the inexplicable leak in our security. Only someone close to me, someone who knew my every move, would have known where and how to attack you, where to set an ambush when you were on the way here for lunch. Is it conceivable my own brother was responsible? But why have *you* killed? He knew you were here only to protect a communications project he himself had conceived, to be his pride and joy for New Caledonia. He enthusiastically supported my bringing you in to look for the murderers of our engineers. None of it reconciles! None of it!"

Marcel is a man overwhelmed by the incongruous. He is dealing here with paradoxes he cannot accept simultaneously.

"Inspector Bazin has suggested I might have become the symbol of resistance to whatever it is that's planned," I point out, "and that my death would encourage others still on the sidelines to join the terrorists. At least, that's Bazin's explanation for the hostility I seem to generate around here."

"But why would Georges deliberately seek to destroy everything he's been trying to build? And why should he have singled *you* out for attack? At that point in time, anyway? How could he have known you would uncover what you did?"

"True. *I* didn't even know any of it until this afternoon."

"In any event," Marcel says, too perplexed to continue this line of speculation, "not only do I understand why you felt it imperative to break off contact with us as you did, but I compliment you on the foresight that made you do it. I have the greatest respect for your expertise, monsieur, as well as for your discretion. I call upon that discretion now, for there are things which I must now share with you."

He almost trembles at the need to release himself of thoughts he's been pushing deep into the closets of his mind.

"My brother's been acting strangely over the past few years," he begins. "The truth is he did not willingly surrender control of our companies. He was forced to do so by our partners and a committee of our major stockholders. You might say his retirement to New Caledonia is a form of imposed exile, much like that our grandfather suffered."

"Acting strangely—how?" I ask.

"He was—how shall I say this? He was manipulating too many apparently unrelated and minor affairs. I would get an operations sheet documenting a chartered flight which had never officially been scheduled—from Nouméa to Central Africa. Or one of our airlines would report a cargo plane inexplicably diverted from its original routing. Invoices that I could not understand would be issued from unpredictable points of origin and through new companies created without my knowledge. I began to check on these irregularities. In each case I found they could be traced all the way up to Georges. When I tried to ask him about it, he refused to discuss the issues. He ordered me to keep out of it. Obviously, I couldn't. I went over his head to the stockholders. Yet, strangely enough, when we prepared to challenge him, he calmly announced his retirement—and came here, as though nothing had happened. We never did receive an explanation for any of it."

"You're saying," I ask, "that he is definitely the one to have had the weapons shipped into New Caledonia?"

"Who else?"

"And the one who organized the secret military training of Melanesians at your hunting grounds in Africa?"

"If, in fact," Marcel concedes unwillingly, "such a program did take place."

"My source claims it did."

"Then there is the final matter," Marcel says, "the most perplexing of them all. Just yesterday he told me he's left all his fortune to an institution he calls Te Kanake."

"What is that?"

"A bank he intends to establish. He told me he's set aside eight hundred million dollars U.S. to fund it. Here, in New Caledonia."

"In Hienghène?" I ask.

He looks surprised. "How did you know?"

"Old Melanesian proverb," I say, smiling thinly. "In New Caledonia all roads lead to Hienghène."

"Apparently over the last few years Georges has quite

cleverly succeeded in transferring most of his money out from under French control—that is, out of francs and into dollars, a ploy which, with the deterioration of the franc, has made him even wealthier. Nobody but he and his bankers know where his funds are concealed—I suspect between Singapore and Hong Kong in certificates of deposit and other short-term instruments. But I do believe him when he says they will be repatriated here at what he calls 'the appropriate time'—whatever that may mean. He took particular pleasure in telling me that Te Kanake will have not so much as a single French official on its board, not even himself, but that it will be run solely by and for the Melanesian people. With the exception of a trust he left to Rosine, a penthouse he deeded her in Paris, and the family château in Normandy, which she already owns, the rest of his estate and all his royalties into perpetuity have been assigned to this still nonexistent bank."

By now Marcel has my sustained attention.

"You must have some theory about what this means," I say.

"Until you came to me with your startling accusation, convinced I was about to seize the country, any personal theory I might have been entertaining was too tenuous, too fragile—and far too frightening—for me to take seriously."

"What theory is that?"

"I would prefer not to articulate it until we have faced my brother and can evaluate his response."

He starts to climb from the helicopter, but stops in the hatchway, turns back to me.

"Oh, yes, something else before we go in. I want to assure you that neither Georges nor anyone else could ever succeed in subverting the Deuxième Régiment Étranger des Parachutistes. They are an elite unit of the Eleventh French Parachute Division, whose commander is my dearest friend. Had Georges so much as approached one of their officers and suggested any treasonous adventure, I would have heard of it instantly. Besides, one must remember that in the Legion, service to France is incidental.

The real loyalty of the Legion is to the Legion itself, to a tradition one hundred and fifty years old, forged in blood across Asia and Africa. No Legionnaire would betray that!"

"Yet some did in Algeria," I remind him.

"This is not Algeria!" he says mordantly. "One last thing. I will stake my life on the loyalty of the officers and crew of the *Rochemont*, the guided-missile battle cruiser I'm expecting in Nouméa this weekend. Her captain served with me in World War II. Together as junior officers we succeeded in sailing part of the French fleet out of Toulon."

I know now without any remaining doubt that every word Marcel has let escape from his suppressed anguish is true. One of the footnotes in Michael's rundown on the Gallantes was a comment on the gallantry and the skill exhibited by Marcel as a young naval officer under attack at Toulon from German dive bombers.

Marcel climbs stiffly from the helicopter.

I follow him with my dive bag. The longer I stay in New Caledonia, the more this carry-all seems to have become a necessary appendage, almost my life-support system. And yet today's turn of events makes me question the future validity of the AK-47 against this still-faceless enemy. Tuesday's terrorists had been armed with Soviet ordnance, in the light of developments obviously a deception on the part of the people doing the orchestrating. But with ten thousand Fusil Automatiques floating around this island, tomorrow's attack teams may be firing at me with bull-pups capable of fielding nine hundred rounds per minute. The combat chatter of the AK-47 will no longer blend with this new symphony of firepower, but could isolate and pinpoint me.

A captain of the troopers meets us at the top of the steps, salutes Marcel.

"M. Gallante has instructed me, sir, to tell you he is waiting for you and Captain Locke in the study."

Instantly I link up this captain with the voice I'd heard on the telephone when I'd called Marcel from the Club Med this afternoon.

"Thank you, Captain Vandegans, for arranging that lift-off so promptly," I tell him. "I appreciate it."

"Yes, sir," he replies. He's lean as a long-distance runner. His nose has been smashed and he's chosen to leave it that way. It gives him the look of a man with nothing left to break.

Marcel's left eyebrow still remains arched in response to the captain's announcement.

"Just that? No other reaction?"

"No, sir."

"When you told him, as I asked you to, that I'd radioed you I was flying back tonight with M. Locke to discuss with him a shipment of Panhard armored cars, he had no visible reaction?"

"None, sir."

"Thank you, Captain."

Marcel leads me into the house.

We pass a paratrooper standing watch in the foyer. We approach a pair of hand-carved Melanesian doors.

Marcel opens them, strides into the library, taking a deep, preparatory breath as he enters.

I'm right behind him.

Georges Gallante is nowhere to be seen.

Marcel glances at me, steps back to the door, calls to the sentry.

"Did you see my brother leave?"

"No, sir. He's in the study."

"Not here!" Marcel snaps. "Did you see him actually enter this room?"

"Yes, sir."

"At what time?"

"Twenty hundred hours, sir, plus fifteen minutes."

"Thank you."

Marcel closes the door, looks at me with dismay.

"Over an hour ago!"

He rushes past me to an inner door at the back of the study. I run after him.

We pass through a pantry and come out into a kitchen

larger than those of most restaurants, copper pans gleaming on overhead racks.

"Tachéa!" Marcel calls. He continues to pull doors open and to call her name more insistently with each banging door. I assume she must be the Melanesian woman who served us lunch.

Marcel disappears down a corridor. In a moment he reappears from what I judge must be the woman's bedroom.

"Her things are gone. Everything. Gone!"

He flings open the kitchen door to the main corridor. He calls to the sentry to bring Captain Vandegans on the double.

While Marcel waits, he flips through the pages of a shopping list on the kitchen counter.

"Here's the inventory of what Georges requested us to buy for his birthday dinner next week. Everything so normal, and yet . . ."

The captain presents himself.

"Where is Tachéa?" Marcel demands.

"She left an hour ago, sir. We cleared her through the front gate at twenty hundred hours and thirty minutes."

"She can't have walked too far," Marcel says to me, self-reassurance in his voice.

"She left by car, sir."

"Car? What car? Who gave her a car?"

"Her son came for her, sir."

Marcel stiffens. "Thank you, Captain."

The officer leaves us.

"He went with them!" Marcel decides desolately. "Hidden in the trunk, probably. My brother, crouched like an animal in the trunk of a Melanesian's car!"

I suspect that he finds this more reprehensible than the matter of the ten thousand bull-pup guns.

Something else hits me.

"I have to call Rosine," I announce.

"Of course," Marcel agrees. He picks up the kitchen phone, dials for me.

He speaks to her first, telling her I'm with him at the farm, then he hands me the phone.

"Beloved," she cries. "I can't stand this another night! What's happened to me? I live only for your call. I think I'll give this just one more week, then I'll have to put you out of my thoughts forever. There's just too much pain attached to loving you!"

"How can you forget me so casually?" I ask. "You promised to die the same day I do. Or have you already forgotten?"

"That's only if I'm *with* you! If I can't be with you, then it's a stupid promise, n'est-ce pas?"

"Rosine, listen to me. I'll be with you as fast as I can get there. I mean tonight! But until I arrive, you have to promise me something. And this is a *real* promise!"

"You don't believe my promise to kill myself is real? Just wait right there till I get the little gun in my drawer. You will hear the final shot! I shall fall dead on the same floor where my mother's blood ran."

"Stop it!" I demand. "God damn it, *stop it*!"

I hear her crying.

"Rosine," I say to the background of muffled sobs, "I want you to promise not to leave the house. No matter what, no matter who asks you. Including your father. Do you understand what I'm telling you?"

"Papa? Is papa coming here?"

"I don't know. But I'm asking you, if he does, *not* to leave with him! No matter how persuasive or insistent he is!"

"Why should I leave with him if *you're* coming? *Are* you, John?"

"I promise. Now *you* promise!"

"I promise. Do you love me?"

"One more thing, Rosine. I'm going to hang up, then I'm going to call Inspector Bazin. I'm going to ask him to send some men, some armed officers, to stand guard outside your house—just to make sure nobody bothers you."

"John, what *is* happening?"

"I don't know yet. Is Koué still there?"

"Koué? Why do you ask about Koué? Do you desire a fat old grandmother? Do you want her in place of me?"

"Call her! I need to know if she's still there."

"Very well."

I wait. Marcel has been watching me, evaluating my words, my attitude toward his niece. I feel that he trusts me now—all the way. I feel that toward him. Right or wrong, I finally have the conviction I'm firmly on the side of the man who hired me.

"John . . ."

Her voice comes through with a strange little wavering, nothing playful or teasing in it now.

"Koué is gone! But she can't be! She's never gone. She never leaves this house. She never leaves me."

"You sure she's not there?"

"She left me this note. She says she'll be away a few days. And that's all. Nothing more. No explanation. No apology. Oh, she added a postscript. She said I should not fail to wear the knotted signal strip she left with the note. She writes here that I'm to pin it over my heart and wear it day and night until she comes back."

I start to get the shudders again. I take from my pocket the knotted strip Kaméa gave me in the museum. I look it over carefully.

"Does your strip have three small knots at the top, two large knots in the middle, then four very small knots at the bottom?"

"Yes," she exclaims. "How did you know that?"

"Somebody gave me one just like yours," I reply. "I'll be there as fast as I can get there."

I hang up. "Can one of your officers fly me right over to Ouen Toro?" I ask Marcel.

"I will arrange it at once."

While he does, I call Bazin at police headquarters in Nouméa and bring him up to date.

The inspector finds what I tell him so alarming he assures me he will not only have an armed patrol on Ouen Toro in a matter of minutes, he will be waiting there for me himself.

The young lieutenant who'd flown me north draws the assignment to whisk me back over the hills to Nouméa.

He's picked up the scent of action.

"May I know anything at all, sir, about what's shaping up?" he asks, once we're airborne.

"Sorry," I say. "None of us knows. Only that some kind of shit seems centering in on Bastille Day. Do you always fly without a flak jacket?" I add.

"Around here, sir, they're not called for."

"Requisition one, Lieutenant, whether they're called for or not. And wear it from now on, as long as you continue to fly this machine or any other over New Caledonia."

"Yes, sir," he says. By then we're already lowering toward Rosine's house.

She has every window streaming light. Bazin's men direct their citron headlamps along the street to brighten our way in.

We slide down in a gentle whirlpool of air and settle on the pavement outside Rosine's front gate, Monstro too bewildered to contest or even to bark at the gigantic insect that has pounced on his turf. I see Rosine in the doorway in a satin nightgown, shamelessly silhouetting herself against the illuminated living room, the air from our rotors flattening the gown against her tensed body.

I climb out with the dive bag in tow. I wave Rosine back into the house with five fingers held aloft to ask for only five more minutes. The slam of the front door cracks louder than the chopper's racket. I return the pilot's salute and he whisks back up into the night and away, Bazin and I fluttering like small-craft-warning flags in his down-draft.

Bazin has brought me a gift of the weapons he confiscated at our first meeting, my High-Standard .22 with silencer and my HK-91.

"From what you tell me," he says, "you may not find the AK-47 of much use against ten thousand Fusil submachine guns.

"Exactly what I've been thinking," I agree. "Thank you."

"I'm still in shock," he confesses. "What you have told me invites nightmares I've never permitted myself to entertain. I still cannot accept even the possibility that Georges

Gallante is implicated. I have known him all my life. But if he *is* involved, there can be only one explanation. His mind has snapped. He's lost his reason, become hopelessly insane!"

"You don't really believe that, do you?"

"At the moment, what else can I believe? Who else but Georges Gallante had the power or the means to deceive our Immigration and Customs people? Transporting young natives in and out of the country, shipping in guns and armored cars. How else could it have been done except aboard the ore boats owned by his company or by his airline?"

"Tell me: What usually happens in Nouméa on Bastille Day?" I ask him.

"During the day, parties, parades, street festivals. And at night the fireworks display from the deck of a navy frigate sent in from Tahiti for the occasion."

"This year it's a major ship of the line, the *Rochemont*."

"For which the Good Lord be thanked!" he says, crossing himself with a flick of fingers so incidental I almost fail to see the gesture.

"Something bumps me here," I say.

"Oh?"

"I was present when Marcel and Georges discussed this, this matter of the navy ship coming in for Bastille Day. If I remember the way it went, Marcel suggested bringing in a heavier ship of the line, a cruiser instead of a frigate. And Georges said something like 'Good idea, Marcel. Contact Paris today!' Why would he have agreed if he's involved with a native rebellion? Why invite that kind of opposition? All the sub-machine guns in the world aren't a match for a missile-cruiser."

"You're sure of that conversation?" Bazin asks, as though drawing hope from it, hope that Georges will prove to be exonerated of whatever it is we suspect him of.

"Yes," I say.

"Well, I can assure you," he says, "I find the scheduled arrival of the *Rochemont* most comforting. I spoke to the governor the moment after your call from la Ferme de St. Paul. I gave him the full range of facts, shocking as they are. He asks me to extend his deepest appreciation to you for what you've contributed. You have, in effect, monsieur, achieved official status in New Caledonia."

"Will that get me some special equipment if I need it?"

He sighs. "You are not a man who can simply accept the status quo. You always find it necessary to add a condition. What type of special equipment?"

"I'll let you know in the morning. As you must be aware, we're keeping the lady of the house waiting. She has an extremely low threshold of boredom."

"You did not call me after your meeting with Kaméa, as you said you would," he reminds me, ignoring my need to get into the house.

"I'm still waiting to learn if she'll brief me. But with or without, I'm casting off tomorrow at midnight. That is, after my dinner with you and Madame. That *is* still on?"

"Very much so!" he affirms, slightly ruffled I should ask him.

I wonder, Who is the madman now? Georges Gallante or this oddly tragic figure of an inspector holding so desperately to a memory? Then it strikes me I'm a dues-paying member of this trio. I too hold stubbornly to the memory of Doan Thi and of Vietnam.

"May I suggest," I hear Bazin's voice continuing, "that if you insist on going north, you go as part of a military detachment, properly armed. The governor has agreed with me that the time has come for us to get into Hienghène with a show of force and take a direct look at the situation up there."

"Worst thing you could do," I say. "If push comes to shove, you can still do that, fly the Legion in by chopper and blow the place off the map. But then you'll never get to the roots of all this, will you? It's better I go in first, alone, unnoticed—or at least keeping out of contact—and do what I do best, reconnaissance. Will you give me that chance before you decide to send troops up there?"

"I will consider it," he concedes.

"Goodnight, Inspector."

"Bonne nuit," he says, so softly I'm not sure he's said anything.

I lug my dive bag and the two guns he's returned to me toward the house.

Most suitors come with flowers or candy. I come with firepower.

Monstro greets me in confusion, half of his effort given to barking, the other half to licking my hand.

He too is a prisoner of memory, his of cheeseburgers, mine of empty glory and lost love.

# CHAPTER

# 22

To ease Rosine's distress, I tell her as little as I feel she needs to know about her father. I take care to point out that the intelligence report I have is preliminary and superficial. Until her uncle and I have had a chance to review Georges's side of the affair, all of us will have to withhold judgment.

"I don't want to hear any more tonight," she states abruptly. "Please take off your clothes!"

She holds out her arms for my khakis. I undress, wondering what could possibly justify her deliberately placid reaction to my revelations about her father. Her intense calm at the disclosure is so unnatural it alarms me more than a little.

Nevertheless, I undress, hand her my clothes. When she has them bundled in her arms, she heaves them across the room and points to the bed.

"I don't want you to move," she commands. "Nor to touch me. I want you to pretend you're dead. Then I shall resurrect you with my hands. If you move or touch me, I won't let you make love to me ever again!"

She lathers her hands with coconut oil, cups my genitals in her palms, and begins to caress me ceremoniously as she starts to whisper incantations in a language I suspect is Patyi, the dominant Melanesian tongue of New Caledonia. I stare up at her masklike face, alabaster in the moonlight through the bedroom shutters. I watch her hungering lips form alien words, and as she increases the rhythm of her stroking so does she raise the volume of her chanting until with masterful timing she emits a piercing scream precisely as she pulls from me a scalding birth which flies like knives. Her scream turns triumphant and ends in an animal moan as she circles her face into the cutting heat, her lips and cheeks catching all the spendings of my eruption.

I start to say something. She places a finger on my lips, forbidding me.

Lightly she slips from bed. I hear water running in the bathroom. She returns with a warm scented towel. She cleanses me, but not herself, then stretches out beside me.

"Sleep," she whispers.

I dream of forest spiders shimmering toward me down endless webs. As I recoil from the advance of their angular black legs, the legs mutate into Rosine's supple thighs, the gaping fangs become Rosine's lips, the remorseless spider stare softens into Rosine's eyes.

I'm awakened by a crackling sound.

Rosine sits naked at the foot of the bed, her legs folded under her, a bag of coffee berries about the size of small damsons within the fold of her legs. She is popping a handful of these berries into her mouth, then with incredible dexterity, spitting to one side two kernels from each berry and to another the wrinkled jellylike rejected skin. I observe that she's already chewed out a potful of kernels.

"This is the time-honored method of hulling coffee berries," she tells me. "My great-grandmother learned this from the popinees. I will roast these for you, then grind them and serve you coffee you will remember."

I reach out one hand, touch her cheek.

"Will I ever understand you?" I ask.

"Never," she replies. "For that reason you'll never tire of me."

"What *happened* last night?" I ask. "What *was* that?"

"I never want any night of ours to be the same," she says. "If we begin to do the same things over and over, we'll be like everyone else. And then you won't want me anymore."

She leaps up, her coffee beans all spat out.

"Shower and dress," she announces. "Breakfast in thirty minutes!"

She leaves me alone. I look at my wristwatch—just past oh seven hundred.

Half an hour later, refreshed as though I'd slept for two days, I find her in the kitchen, still naked except for an apron made saucier by the natural sway of her hips as she hurries to finish the preparations for breakfast. She hands me a cup of steaming coffee so delicious I know Bazin would scuttle his Turkish grounds if he could only taste this.

She serves us omelettes and croissants in a breakfast nook overlooking a tropical garden of ferns and flowers dominated by red toothbrush plants.

"I'm going with you!" she announces.

"Going where?"

"North. At midnight tonight. On your boat."

"How do you know about that?"

"The same newspaper friend of yours who called you here the other night phoned you again while you were in the shower. He said he'd have to leave the message with me, since he'll be out most of the day, something about covering the arrival of a regiment of parachutists. But he wants you to know that he and Kaméa will be giving you your briefing. You're to meet her at his home promptly at noon. Who is Kaméa?"

"His old lady. Did he give you an address?"

She hands me the slip of paper on which she's written a number and a street name.

"You know something?" I say. "I'm going to surprise you. I'm going to say okay."

"You are?"

"Know why?"

"Because I'm sexually arousing."

"That's not why."

"Then why?"

"Because I intend to get some mileage out of you."

257

"Oh, I like that!"

"I'm going to use you as a buffer—as a DMZ."

"What's a DMZ?"

"A line they maybe won't cross. You're the daughter of the man who may be their patron saint. If so, they'll think twice before they kill me. It's smart. It's cowardly. It's beautiful. I learned it from the VC."

"Is that the only reason you're taking me?"

"There *is* another."

"What?"

"That language you were speaking last night."

"What about it?"

"I'd like to learn a little of it. I'm convinced you've come up with the perfect way to teach it."

She slides onto my lap, begins to kiss me entreatingly.

"Here in the chair?" I ask.

"On the table," she whispers.

Afterward I discover she's sobbing. She cries with such despair I wonder if she will ever stop.

"Poor Papa," she sobs. "Poor, poor Papa!"

I keep her close, let her cry it through. She's held back for all these hours, so now it wracks her. I find myself tempted to cry along with her as I consider how I would feel if somebody I believed in had told me the father I trust and adore is quite possibly a man beyond reason or redemption. A living miracle, this Rosine, an emotional chameleon. As suddenly as she's begun her hysteria, she ends it.

"You must have much to do if we're to leave tonight!" she announces. "I'll get dressed, take you wherever you wish to go."

"Thanks, but I can call a taxi. I only need to run down to the Club Med."

"What's at the Club Med?" she asks suspiciously. "Do you know somebody there?"

"I left my car there."

She won't hear of my calling a cab. She's off upstairs, leaving me with my fourth cup of coffee, then she's back, ready to rush out the door before I've finished.

I notice she's wearing the Melanesian knotted strip over her heart.

"Put yours on too, please," she urges.

I fumble in my pocket for the tiny wad of fiber cloth. She compares it to hers. The two strips are identical.

She finds a safety pin in a kitchen drawer, fastens the strip over the breast pocket of my rumpled, stained khaki jacket.

"You look so beautifully disheveled," she says, "so grimly preoccupied. Handsome-with-problems appeals to me every time! I truly believe, John, I'm becoming fonder and fonder of you!"

"You are not without a certain charm yourself," I concede. Laughing together, one of my hands in hers, the other gripping the dive bag, and both of us sharing a simultaneous feeling that the only way to get through this particular day is to theatricalize every second of it, to ignore objective reality, we dance out the door to the red Ferrari. When you're wearing a knotted-badge of God-knows-what significance above your hearts and your Papa's missing and is regarded in high circles as maybe the country's number-one baddie of the hour, what else can a girl and her guy do but show their smiles and tap-dance their way out?

I wish I were free to stay with her, I truly do, for I can see she's still on slippery ground. But I can't. It takes time alone, thinking time, when you're getting ready to saddle up and ride out to meet the nasties, and I have little time left.

"It's all tricks anyway," I suggest as I prepare to leave her at the Club Med gate. "Remember that all the world's a sound stage and we're all somebody's software. Think of this as just one more media event. Or better yet, pretend today they're doing a photographic essay on you for French television: 'Afternoon in Nouméa with Pretty Girl in Pink Dress.' "

"Oh, not *French* telly!" she moans. "It used to be the most boring in all of Europe. But now with the socialists deciding we have to be educated instead of entertained, it's become the most boring in the *world!* Who cares about the childhood of Paul Gauguin or the preteen crisis of Madame Curie? Can't we pretend it's for an *American* network?"

"You want mind candy, not culture, right?"

"Right!"

"Okay. Let's make it for ABC. Now, the remote truck is right over there—see it?"

"I see it."

"And right there in front of you is the camera."

She exhibits her teeth in a winning grin, favoring the imaginary camera in front of the Ferrari.

"Now," I instruct her, "be a star! Keep smiling. Give it energy. Give it decisiveness. Reaffirm yourself as you go along. And get your act down to the Club Nautique dock at eleven-thirty tonight—sharp!"

"À tout à l'heure, mon réalisateur," she calls, blows me a kiss, and punches the Ferrari into hyper-boost.

"You just ran over the camera crew!" I shout after her.

I settle up the little F owe the Club Med for one phone call and a round of drinks, leave a "have a good flight home" note for Ken, load everything into the Renault, and clatter off toward Nouméa and my appointment with Kaméa.

At the intersection of Rue du Docteur and Rue Frédéric Surleau, traffic is delayed by the march of the 2e Régiment Étranger des Parachutistes of the French Foreign Legion, obviously just arrived and now parading past the building of the Gendarmérie Nationale in what appears to be a line of march designed to take them across town to Place des Cocotiers.

They advance with deliberate slowness to the beat of somber music, eighty-eight steps to the minute, a column of fit men in red and green, all singing their little song, "Death, we have seen you from Algeria to Tonkin. When shall we see you again?"

On Bastille Day, on this tropical paradise in the Coral Sea, I am now convinced.

# CHAPTER

## 23

**T**he address I've been given for my meeting with Kaméa will take me to Île Nou, Rosine has told me. Île Nou is connected by causeway to Nouméa. I drive from the center of town in eight minutes to a Tahitian-style hut thatched out on stout pylons over the lagoon on the beach near Pte. Lacombe.

Kaméa waits for me on the deck, silk halter around her breasts, white gym shorts by Adidas scalloped deeply up the thighs. Maurice, I see, has something to come home to—and only eight minutes from the office.

Cold lobster and chilled wine wait for me in a living area open to the water. Kaméa has prepared nothing for herself. I remember her telling me she never eats lunch.

"You can eat while I talk," she says.

Fair enough.

"How to begin?" she muses. "Can you give me any sense of what you think you will need?"

"I need it all," I tell her. "The past, present, and future of your mother's people. The good, the bad, everything you've never said before to any white man—Maurice included."

"You ask a lot."

"I risk a lot."

"Okay," she agrees. "Let's take a run at it."

She brings me shreds of jackfruit on ice. "Everything the Melanesian does or feels or believes must be understood as a trinity of reactions. Incidentally, that's jackfruit—when you're ready for dessert."

"I know jackfruit when I see it," I say.

"That's right. I keep forgetting you didn't just get here. Well, where were we?"

"Trinity of reactions."

She looks toward Presqu'ile Maa across the lagoon from us, cresting out of the northwest in bright admonition. "The Melanesian," she tells me over her shoulder, her face to the north, "lives in a world of three coexisting dimensions—of space, of time, and most importantly of myth. And each of these words suffers in the translation, for time has a different meaning to us than it does to you."

Attentively now, coming back to where I sit, she refills my wine glass. "Space has a different meaning. Myth, well, what myth do *you* really believe in?"

"I was brought up by a pagan father and a Catholic mother," I tell her.

"All right, then," she says. "Let us take the myth of Christianity. Ineffective, is it not? Do your Ten Commandments stop you from killing each other or from stealing your neighbor's wife?"

"That is Mosaic law," I correct. "But I'm not going to be able to make much of an argument about the effectiveness of Christianity in terms of human mercy."

"Well, *our* taboos are inviolable! We seldom break them. But if we do, we *know* the penalties will be swift and certain. This is to protect the tribe against the individual. To us everything is born out of the tribe. The tribe is the center of the stone. It is the Word—and the Womb."

All through the hours that follow as Kaméa talks to me, her voice as soft as the offshore afternoon wind, I sense the land reaching north and its unseen people slowly invading my persona. Kaméa talks of earlier times, but not that long past, not even a hundred years ago, when the great chiefs had absolute power of life and death and when war was the rule, peace the exception. Even the women went to battle in those days. When they saw an enemy fall, they were expected to rush forward, pull the body free, and prepare it for the oven. The dead warrior's hands were awarded to the priests, who also went to battle. These holy men sat hunched off on the flanks, wailing for victory and fasting until the hands of the fallen could be savored at leisure. These were times when the people's appetite for human flesh was insatiable. If a friendly European challenged the practice, the natives would cry out in rebuttal, "Would you forbid us the fish of the sea? These fallen enemies are our fish!"

"Isn't it ironic," Kaméa asks, "that your society—which has developed nuclear weapons and practiced genocide, the bombing of helpless civilians, defoliation, gas and chemical warfare and the dropping of napalm—should consider cannibalism so shocking?"

How do I refute this?

"If you understand the myth," she explains, "*and* the symbolism, you will have to approve of cannibalism. What it provides is a feeling of solidarity within the tribe and dramatic evidence of a united opposition against intruders and aliens. In effect, it is a holy, bonding sacrament."

By sixteen hundred hours, my mind reeling, I am almost relieved to discover Maurice hurrying in.

"Well?" he asks, "are you beginning to grasp the complexities?"

Kaméa answers for me. She reaches for my hand, with Maurice's open approval, and warms it between hers as she comments to him in Patyi, "E nîmîrî kivéti." "He is wise, this one," she tells me is the meaning of what she's just said. I thank her, wishing I were indeed wise, not just clever. "You see how wise?" She points out to Maurice that I'm wearing the cloth strip she'd given to me in the museum at our first meeting.

I tell her that Rosine Gallante was also given one, the same as mine, and that she insisted we wear them. I question Kaméa once more about their significance.

"I have asked around," she says. "When I gave it to you, I wasn't sure, so I hesitated to tell you. But now I am sure. It is a safe-conduct symbol, worn by clanspeople permitted to pass without harm through the territory of other clans. What I'm not so sure about is which tribe might have issued it. It might be the Lindéralique, Lecoulnoué, Pindache, or Ganen. It might even be Poindjap or Lewarap."

"How many tribes are there?" I ask.

"Several hundred."

I have other pressing matters to attend to. I ask her to forgive me for the apparent arrogance that I can presume, all within the span of a long lunchhour, to comprehend the heart of another race. I assure Kaméa it is not arrogance on my part, simply a compression of time and a dearth of options, but what she has taught me today might—just might—help me be less stumble-footed when I go north.

"Are you really leaving tonight?" Maurice asks.

"That is a secret," I reply, "which is known only to the two of you, to Rosine and Marcel Gallante, and to Inspector Bazin. If anyone else even suspects, then the next time you see me I might be minus a head."

Somehow, when I've left, I feel buoyed by my time with them. I realize it is Kaméa who has made me feel this way, not Maurice. At the museum she was trying to hide an undercurrent of fear. Today she has been open and guileless. I have drawn from her the sense of a powerful life force, a perceived ethic which has renewed me. I'm so uplifted by her strength and her sureness that it doesn't occur to me until much later, when it's too late, that Maurice's lighthearted attitude this afternoon has been an impoverished masquerade, and that under his fixed smile there lurked a raw terror I completely overlooked.

I spend the rest of the day preparing to go north.

Most of the time with Bazin.

He promises to provide me with what I'll need, two of the best sailors from the local Marine Nationale to sail *Steel Tiger* back to Nouméa when I leave her off the headlands of Voh, a military—and I repeat this to him—a military, not a police, helicopter, to handle insertions by STABO rig, jungle fatigues and boots, rations for forty-eight hours for two people, radio transmitter, first-aid kit, a four-wheel-drive truck fully fueled and airlifted into grid points four clicks south of Caavatch precisely thirty minutes before I'm to be set down, and finally two Fusil MAS bull-pups with enough 5.56-mike-mike ammo in twenty-five-round mags to hold off whatever I might stumble into.

I insist, although Bazin does not dispute the need, on test-firing both weapons. He takes me to a police firing range where in the long shadows at afternoon's end I lay in effective patterns with both guns out to three hundred meters, firing from either shoulder, one of the features unique to this weapon because of its two extractor positions on the bolt face.

Between magazines, I stress to Bazin the life-or-death need to maintain absolute secrecy about my mission. I remind him of the leak in his police headquarters, a leak which led to the death of the agent he sent north. I can't risk his telling anyone at headquarters about my trip or let any requisition for the materials I need be processed through his office. Everything *must* be obtained from Marcel Gallante's military detachment.

Solemnly, he concurs.

Then a final conference by phone with Marcel Gallante —no word of brother Georges from any of the places he might ordinarily have gotten to, none of the mines or refineries or obscure little hotels along either coast. It is as though Georges has consigned himself to one of his own mysterious charter flights. He could be anywhere by this time, Marcel fears. In Chad, in the Central African Republic, in Singapore, in Hong Kong, in Bali, or even in Beverly Hills. Marcel swears that if I have not returned to Nouméa in time to be his guest for dinner on Georges's birthday—with or without Georges—he will personally lead the small detachment of paratroopers assigned to guard la Ferme de St. Paul up to Hienghène to bring me safely back. I assure him that Inspector Bazin has already indicated a similar disposition and that I'm going north only to scout, not to sling with mundos who mail back heads in baskets.

Between the high Kaméa has induced in me and my excitement about finally being set to raise some sand in Hienghène, my state of mind is almost euphoric when I head the Renault out Rue du Capitaine Desmier to Bazin's home for my still-astonishing eight o'clock dinner invitation. I find the house perched along the spine of Pointe Chaleix overlooking the Baie des Citrons on one side and the Baie des Pêcheurs on the other. I park the car in a yard bordered by ironwood and gum trees. From this height I can see all the way to the northwest the Club Nautique's marina and the massive hull of *Reckless Living*, blocking my view of *Steel Tiger* except for the ketch's tall masts. I lock the dive bag in the trunk, bring along only the gift-wrapped LP albums. Then, charged with wonder about my imminent confrontation with Bazin and a wife buried two years ago, yet nonetheless about to be my hostess, I knock on his front door.

From inside I hear a woman's voice speaking in French and asking Bazin to please attend to the door—our guest is here.

I am so startled by the unanticipated sound of a woman's voice that when Bazin opens the door to admit me my mouth is still slack.

"Are you well, monsieur?" he asks with concern.

"Yes, thank you," I manage.

He ushers me into a small sitting room, made more spacious than it really is by the judicious placement of wicker furniture. There is only one really comfortable-looking chair in view, obviously his, a worn lounge in maroon leather with a battered footstool. Beyond the sitting area I see the dining room and its mirrorlike mahogany table gleaming in candlelight, bone china and heavy sterling service set for three, crystal wineglasses in front of each placemat.

From the kitchen I hear the woman's voice.

"Would you please see what our guest will have as an apéritif, my love?" she calls to Bazin in French. Then to me, "I am so honored you could be with us tonight, monsieur."

"Thank you so much for inviting me," I call back toward the kitchen.

"What will you have to drink?" Bazin asks.

"Something strong, I believe," I hear myself saying, trying to make sense of the moment. Have I misunderstood Maurice when he told me that Bazin's wife had died two years ago, that the man pretends she is still alive and that all his friends play this macabre game, asking after her health and sending her gifts?

"Gin, if you have it," I add. "Gin over ice with a twist of lime."

He has a small back-bar in the dining room, where he prepares my drink. As he does, he glances out at me.

"Everything you requested—has it arrived to your satisfaction?"

"All there," I say. "Thank you."

"I'm still at a loss as to why you're *sailing* north, not flying."

"That way I'm harder to pinpoint. Under darkness I can leave the boat and come ashore where nobody expects me."

He brings me my drink.

"Forgive me for not joining you," he says. "I'll have my one glass of red wine with my wife at dinner."

"Well, cheers!" I drink to him and the lady in the kitchen. "Oh," I say, remembering, "I brought this for Madame."

I hand him the gift I'd almost forgotten I was holding. He looks touched.

"Very kind of you, monsieur. Excuse me for a moment, please."

He carries the gift off to the kitchen. I can hear his voice, but not his words, then he comes out, closing the door after him. But I can still hear his wife's voice calling to me, "Thank you, monsieur. I shall open it the moment we sit down for dinner."

He waves me into the leather chair. It rises up around me like swamp mud.

He perches himself on a wicker stool across from me. He seems hesitant to speak, yet impelled to.

"You are our first guest in a long while," he says at last.

"Thank you."

"I discussed the wisdom of this—of inviting you—with Yvette. She has not been well."

"I'm sorry," I say, feeling I'm on the edge of a cliff without bottom.

"I told her that in my considered opinion, much as I hated to involve her in office matters, you were an extraordinary man who for reasons I shall never comprehend chooses to become his own executioner. I have watched you, monsieur, observed you and studied you and speculated about you from the first moment I boarded your boat. I have come to have an honest affection toward you. You operate only by rules you have personally created, yet you yourself have not been able to figure out what those rules are. And so you are a living mystery. To let you sail off to certain death has been a problem of conscience for me. I could, I suppose, find some official way to keep you from going. But to have done that would have been to tamper with the mystery. I have no right to interfere with a destiny you have so arduously designed for yourself. And so I thought it would be fitting tonight, our last night together, to match the honesty of your willingness to die with an equal honesty of my own, one which I hope, by making me live the rest of my life with no more deception, will in some small way balance and compensate for the possible loss of your life. Will you please sit right there, monsieur, and do nothing, say nothing, until I bring my wife to the dining-room table?"

I feel gripped by the terrier teeth of some dreadful feeling I sense, but can't yet delineate.

I nod.

Bazin goes back to the kitchen and in a moment reappears with a portable tape recorder, which he plugs into a wall socket in the dining room. He places the machine next to one of the table settings and punches the PLAY button.

"Dinner is served, monsieur," I hear Madame's voice saying. "Will you please take your place across the table from me?"

I see Bazin gesturing for me to come, come take my place at the table across from the machine.

"My love, will you please sit as well?"

"You first," he says, and actually pretends he is seating someone, pushing the chair in after her.

I ghost-walk in to join him and the tape machine, take my place and watch him sit at the head of the table and pour burgundy into Madame's glass, then into mine, and finally into his.

"I hope you'll like this little wine," the machine says in Madame's voice. "We have it from my family in France. Most red wines travel so poorly all that distance, but this particular burgundy seems to hold up rather well. I hope it won't disappoint you."

I see Bazin nodding at me, his glass raised, and I raise mine, and with him we drink to the empty chair.

"Ah," the voice says. "It *is* a nice wine, isn't it?"

I look to Bazin for permission to speak.

He nods.

"Indeed it is," I say. "It puts me in mind of one of Gerard Pontel's burgundies from la Côte de Beaune."

Bazin reaches across, punches the stop button.

"When Yvette fell ill, we had sufficient time to discuss how she could look after me when she was gone. As you can hear from that tape, she has an especially beautiful speaking voice, calm and soothing . . . It occurred to us that if we could make a number of tapes of her voice I would have them here to help maintain a sense of continuity. And so, over the course of her final weeks, we thought of every possible situation to which she might have responded. A guest for dinner, an exchange between her and

269

me when morning comes, a good-night conversation—actually many of those, because that's the most difficult time for me, going to sleep without her—conversations to cover our driving to the produce market, conversations about what happened during the day, about the weather, our families in France, letters from home. We covered everything, I believe, and then I taped only her side of these conversations, leaving space in between her questions or comments, so that later I would be able to improvise and try to think of new things to tell her, yet still link them up with what I have heard her say on those tapes hundreds of times since she died."

He looks across at me. "You are the first person I have permitted myself to speak those words to: *'Since she died.'* Yes, I will admit now, finally, she is dead. I will admit it to you here and now and I will admit it to all the good friends I have in Nouméa who have had the humanity to let me play out this charade without calling me foolish or even demented. I am supported and sustained by their affection. Now I will prove to them I can accept Yvette's passing."

I feel my eyes swell and blur. I cannot prevent the spill of tears down my face. I make no move to wipe them off.

Bazin rises suddenly.

"I had better take the roast out," he says.

He goes to the kitchen, leaving me with the silent tape machine.

His phone rings.

Something ominous strikes me by the third ring and brings me out of my tearfulness.

I start to reach for the phone.

But Bazin returns with the roast, places it on the table, moves with an apologetic gesture to the phone.

"Bazin here," he says.

I watch his forehead crease, his color change.

"Coming," he says, letting the receiver find its own way back into the cradle of the telephone.

I'm already out the door, scrambling for the dive bag in

the trunk of the Renault. I have the AK-47 out before Bazin can run out to join me.

"One of my officers disobeyed," he says tightly. "He brought in his baguette. He's dead now, of course, and two others with him. At the precise moment it exploded, the terrorists attacked the station. They have it under fire now, from one end of the block to the other."

I slip out of my khaki jacket.

"Put this on!" I order.

"Why?"

"I'm hoping that for a few seconds, anyway, they'll think you're me."

I hand him my Browning.

"You're going to drive the Renault. Straight to the station. As we approach the fire zone, keep the car in gear, but jump out behind cover. Begin firing the Browning at any terrorist you can see."

"Where will you be?"

"Wherever I can hurt them the most."

I double-tape AK-47 mags as he races the Renault downtown.

Within three minutes we're hearing gunshots. I am reassured to recognize the heavy pounding of other AK-47's dueling with the more subdued, cleaner rapid-fire of French weapons. Intermittently I hear the plump burst of rocket rounds.

"Theirs?" I ask Bazin.

Unhappily, he nods, his eyes straight ahead as he drives. "We have nothing that heavy in our armory."

Just ahead I see smoke laced with fire rising beyond the rooftop of the post-office building which backs up to the adjoining police station.

"I get out here," I say.

Bazin stops the car.

"Stay frosty," I tell him.

I jump out with the AK-47 and begin running toward the firefight.

Bazin speeds the Renault away.

I'm halfway to where I'm going when I watch him make the turn onto the street fronting his headquarters. I have no way of seeing from here whether he's out and clear, but by the time I reach the intersection, keeping myself down at curb level, I discover the Renault burning down the block where it has crashed into a truck, apparently one the terrorists have placed in the middle of the street to block any traffic. Flames wrap both truck and car.

I work myself beyond the station and past the line of fire until I am well behind the gun flashes of the attacking force. Incredibly enough, they're spread out along the avenue facing the police station and are firing wildly at the walls and windows, their shelter minimal, their flanks and rear totally unprotected.

Why are they so openly inviting their deaths?

I have little to do but skirt one flank, climb onto the roof of the library building behind them, and position myself above them. They are in such immediate range and so vulnerable to attack from the rear I have no need even to use the night scope. I find it difficult even to raise my adrenaline level.

I simply point the AK-47 and time my first burst to synchronize with the almost continuous barrage they are directing across the street at police headquarters.

I finger three rounds from the AK-47 into the man furthest from me. Nobody around him appears to question his silent collapse or to look around to see what it might be that has taken him off.

The rest of it becomes as mechanical as a target sequence on a firing range. As the apparitions below me drop, one after the other, I am not thinking of how effortless a turkey shoot this has turned out to be, but rather what a superb killing instrument the AK-47 remains. It virtually coos in your hand, lying there like a sleeping infant as you squeeze off the rounds.

I didn't mark the time of my first burst, but an inner clock tells me when I'm done that it has taken less than seventy-five seconds to silence the full complement of attackers. None of them exists any longer except as an inert figure on a smoking avenue. How ironic that if some of these men had not tried to ambush me a few days ago and left this AK-47 behind, they might still be alive!

What can it be? One hundred and fifty years of existence shared among these seven dead enemies? All their aspirations and energies, all the time and effort expended from birth to young manhood, all torn away, made meaningless within seventy-five seconds of ritualistic stupidity.

I remain unmoving upon my executioner's platform until I observe Bazin appear from behind a palm tree. He walks, as though dazed, toward the nearest dead Melanesian, the Renault still burning beyond him like a sunburst. Within seconds he is joined by other officers, who emerge mutely from the shattered headquarters building.

He looks up toward the roofline behind the pockets of slumped-over terrorists, for it has not taken him long to observe that each man has been struck down from behind, the tiny entry-point at the intersection of spine and shoulders, the exit at the front of the chest raw and massive.

"John Locke!" he calls.

I remain prostrate on the roof as I call back.

"Up here! Tell your men not to fire when I stand!"

He shouts to his oncoming officers, ordering them not to shoot under any condition.

I get to my knees, then to my feet.

I look down at Bazin, directly below me on the street.

"You killed them all?" he asks quietly, but his voice carries up to me. "You couldn't have saved even one for us to question?"

"They wouldn't have surrendered," I call back.

"What makes you say that?"

"They were programmed to die."

"How do you know?"

"Leaving themselves open the way they did. No doubt in my mind. What I don't know, though, is *why*."

Later, as the bodies are searched, Bazin still hopeful my shots might not all have been terminal, he comes across a document clutched much too conspicuously in the hand of a terr.

Bazin reads it to me in the light of the burning Renault.

"We are the last of a group of Melanesians chosen to die for the liberty of our people. We die so that our deaths may weigh upon the consciences of all decent citizens of France. We beg you, free our people! Do not let us die in vain!"

"Arrant bullshit!" I tell him. "I guarantee you, a tape of that has already been delivered to the radio station and Xerox copies to all three newspapers. Georges Gallante *wants* us to think the heat's off, that these men are the final spasm of a spontaneous patriotic outburst. Now everyone is expected to feel guilty and supposed to try to forget it by celebrating Bastille Day!"

Bazin nods in agreement. "We must let him think he's succeeded. I will plan a memorial service for these patriots and announce that New Caledonia remains united and that a committee will be appointed by the mayor to study ways of improving the living standards of all Melanesians."

He looks directly at me.

"You have my full support in going north, monsieur. While I calm public opinion here in Nouméa, *go* to Hienghène. Learn everything we need to know. Then hurry back!"

His hand is extended toward me.

For the first time since Bazin has entered my life, he is not demanding that I turn something of mine over to him.

I take his hand. Our eyes meet and hold.

This time he does not close them on me.

# CHAPTER

## 24

**A**t midnight I slip my stern line once my bow has cleared the high transom of *Reckless Living* tied directly forward. As we swing out I can hear the echo of Otis Walden's tom-toms pounding from his stateroom.

*Steel Tiger*'s mainsail luffs for a moment until I harden its trim and slide us seaward on a close reach. Rosine stands with me at the wheel, the two loan-out sailors still concealed belowdecks. The sea and sky combine to create a tunnel effect so dark I have the feeling I'm steering us down the barrel of a cannon. But I'm grateful for so black a midnight. Harder for inquisitive eyes to track us.

Rosine presses herself against the small of my back, places her hands over mine on the wheel.

"I want to feel what you feel," she whispers.

I put her hands on the wheel, cover them with mine, let her sense the water pulsing past the rudder.

"When did you start sailing?" she asks.

"I was about nine," I tell her, remembering my first lessons in a Sabot in San Diego Bay, my father alongside in a motorboat, calling instructions to me through an old-fashioned megaphone he still insists was given to him by a long-ago crooner named Rudy Vallee.

Twenty-four years ago! And all the times away from the water somehow less honest. And infinitely more dangerous. To me, the land is the cruelest sea of all. Too diffused. Too complex. Out here on the waters you seem better able to focus in on some kind of ordered universal reason. There are times you almost think you have it, that you understand it, but of course you haven't and don't. It's simply that the sea sharpens your perceptions and deceives you into thinking you've finally got a handle on the architecture of the universe. You're hyped by the texture of the sky, by the shifting might of the oceans. You feel the fat dribbling off your muddled brain and you get this hard-core remnant in focus and there's nothing else you'll ever need.

I try to say some of this to Rosine, but it's not an easy thing to communicate to anyone who has not lived offshore under both the best and the worst of conditions.

Later I give her the helm and go below to instruct the two young sailors. I show them on a French marine chart how we'll continue along the present reach toward the southwest and out through the fringing reef at Passe de Dumbéa and into the Coral Sea.

I've laid out a course calculated to deceive anyone trying to spot us with field glasses from the New Caledonian headlands, even to baffle the more sophisticated who might be tracking us with radar. To all appearances Rosine and I have departed Grande Terre and set sail for New Guinea. Once we've passed outward of the one-thousand-fathom line, I plan to turn northwest and continue parallel to New Caledonia, but far beyond the vision of anyone ashore. Then at Passe du Duroc I will point us northeast again and come back in through the reef, placing us once more within the New Caledonian lagoon, but far to the north of Nouméa and along an unsettled coastline. We'll maintain this reach until we're in the bay outside Voh.

I set the watches, assigning each of the sailors a successive three-hour tour. I get the forepeak bunks squared away for the crew to use off-watch, turn over the helm to the first of the two, then lead Rosine into my bunk in the aft cabin.

Until tonight I have never brought a woman into this cabin. I have never until now found one with whom I wanted to share this last place of refuge.

Rosine is in an almost mystic mood as she crawls into the bunk and fits herself into all my nooks and crannies.

For the first time, we make love gently and for a while, without harm to either of us, I let myself imagine what it might be like to have a lifetime of such intimacy. To have that opportunity, all I need to do is to go topside at this moment, turn *Steel Tiger* back toward Nouméa and abort my Hienghène mission.

Now that I know Rosine, can I still dismiss the possibility of my imminent death as simply one more pharmacologic incident among billions, no more significant over the long course of human history than the swatting of a fly?

I am tempted to start unbuckling the armor I've layered around my feelings. My teachers have warned me that by loving selflessly I would endanger my own survival. There is no more crashing vulnerability than to let yourself enter into the lives of others and care to the point of self-extinction what becomes of them.

I think of Rosine and how unpredictable the moments would be, how joyful. With each surge of these images I feel myself becoming weaker.

But another suddenly thrusting memory helps me resist the temptation. I remember hearing about one particular Vietnamese family in Hué during the executions that followed the Tet offensive of 1968. A Liberation Front officer and his men dragged a boy to a house and demanded of the mother and her other children that she identify as her son this child who had been found shooting at the VC. The mother, knowing that if she identified him her other children would also be executed, said she had never seen the boy before. To call her bluff, the VC officer shot the boy through the head as the mother watched. She never blinked an eye. Her other children also stood without speaking or showing any emotion. The officer waited around for hours to see if the family would try to reclaim the body he'd left on their front porch. But the woman escaped from the back of the house and evacuated her remaining children among a stream of refugees and never looked back at the son she'd had to leave behind, a son she'd sacrificed to save her other children.

I fall asleep, thinking of the awesome strength of that woman, drawing from her and resolving never to turn back.

By dawn I've untangled myself from Rosine, dressed without sound, left her sleeping and gone topside to play catch-up. We're cruising well off the reef and still in the Coral Sea, but the ride is easy. We're cutting through flat, dove-gray water on a steady reach, fourteen knots of warming wind just where they should be.

I duck down into the salon to get the latest weather and a Sat-Nav readout.

I punch in the Sat-Nav, get the Weather-Fax humming, and turn on the SSB, dialing in Sydney first to make sure none of their muscular stuff from the Tasman Sea is booming our way. Reassured of picnic weather for the next few hours anyway, I return topside.

I congratulate the helmsman for having kept so steady a course, send him below to sleep. I fine-tune the set of the sails, then settle in behind the wheel.

All Sunday we continue northwest, keeping well offshore under hazy sky, Rosine teaching me the Patyi language as it was taught to her in her childhood by Koué. I try to concentrate on those words and phrases I feel might be of value.

We take dinner in the salon in candlelight, the curtains drawn to preserve the integrity of our dark passage, sailing toward Voh without running lights.

After my watch late Sunday night, I find Rosine waiting for me expectantly in the aft cabin bunk.

"Tonight," she challenges, "you will see if it's possible to bring me to climax without entering me or kissing my breasts or my neck or my ears."

"You *are* quite the complete mistress of ceremonies, aren't you?" I exclaim and proceed to help her discover her other tingly zones, the boundaries around the kneecaps, the small of the back, the inside of the thighs. I joyously cannibalize her until she's sobbing for me to take her and she keeps trying to tug me over on top of her, but I resist and force her to experience the rush of getting off on a nuzzled left knee, a feeling she describes later as having eliminated any further dependence upon the clitoris. She insists that she adores me beyond all reason, for I have liberated her from clitoral serfdom.

Monday breaks gusty, with squall lines racing up on our stern quarter, causing me to reef the main and run up the storm jib. Even then we're still overpowered, but I have to reach the rendezvous point by midnight Monday, so I keep us driving. Surprisingly enough, no one gets seasick. My last lesson in the Patyi language is given to me by Rosine as I keep the wheel during a rainburst, both of us drenched, but both exhilarated. For a while anyway, until I see her pouting.

"What is it?" I ask, knowing it's not the rain.

"You've never once used the word 'love' with me—not once!"

"A tough word."

"*Do* you love me?"

"I could," I admit. "Given time."

"What time *have* we left?" she asks.

"Not any! Or maybe, if this works out, more than we'd ever need or want."

"I love you," she says.

I help her dress for the lift-off—jungle boots, STABO rings, and finally the safe-passage totem on her tunic.

"Going to dust you up first, baby. Then I'll come. Nothing to it. Just relax, okay?"

"And then what?"

"We go for it!"

Two minutes past midnight, as Tuesday snaps into place, the prearranged chopper approaches from the south. I have already doused sails. *Steel Tiger* drifts into lake-flat water well offshore of Voh, its scattered inland lights barely discernible from here. I have turned the ketch over to the two sailors with final instructions about their passage south to Nouméa.

Now, with all our equipment, Rosine and I squat in my Avon tender. I have the dinghy's painter looped onto a longer line connecting us to the ketch so the sailors can haul her back once we've left her. I paddle us out a good hundred feet into the lee of *Steel Tiger* to keep the approaching chopper clear of the masts. I flash the signal upward.

The rotors' down-draft spins the Avon, but I still succeed on the first pass in grabbing the lowered lifting hooks and in linking Rosine's STABO rig to them. Her mouth forms an astonished open loop as she is swept up. Within another two minutes I've been cranked into the chopper with her.

I confer with the pilot. He peels east and we're over New Caledonia, passing Voh, cutting inland. In a matter of minutes we're above the spot I've marked on my map. We reverse the process now, being lowered to earth instead of lifted off. I go down first, my French bull-pup ready to fire.

I touch down in a small clearing bordered with Cook pines. I release the lifting hooks, wait for Rosine to be powered down next to me, then finally the rest of my equipment. The chopper vectors south and in a moment Rosine and I stand in silence not more than twelve kilometers inland from Hienghène.

Getting cross-bearings and using my hand compass, I pace off a measured number of steps toward an abandoned mine and the faint trail of old tire tracks. Some four hundred meters along this axis I find the truck, exactly where I have asked Bazin to have it lowered. It is shrouded with a cammie net. I uncover it, disarm the bomb I had insisted he have his men install in the ignition for the edification of any hostiles who might have tried to steal the truck before I got to it. I climb behind the wheel, start the engine. I drive the truck into the clearing, then to the treeline, where I have hidden Rosine.

I bring her into the cab with me.

"You're chief lookout," I tell her. "Okay?"

She smiles. Enjoying every second of it. And gripping

the French sub-machine gun in the way I've just taught her.

"All right," I say to her, "if you were Kangara, where would you park fifty armored cars and ten thousand sub-machine guns with all their ammo?"

"In the limestone caves at Tilougne," she says without hesitation.

I bring out a map, open it on the dash in front of her.

"Show me."

She points out the location.

"Where *else* could they be?" I ask.

"There's a valley here," she indicates, "with a huge stand of araucaria pines. You could hide all the cars in Nouméa under those trees."

"Tell me more about the caves at Tilougne," I say.

"Well, one of them's almost two miles long. They're really sort of eerie. Filled with stalactites and stalagmites. But the caves are taboo. They're a sacred burial ground. They're always guarded by warriors sworn to kill all intruders."

I study the map. It appears I can drive to within two kilometers of the coastline where the caves front the Pacific.

I use the truck's traction to carry us over rough back country where no vehicle has gone before and down to Tilougne. As I approach the coastline Rosine begins to look more and more agitated.

Suddenly she reaches over, turns the ignition key.

The truck grinds to a stop.

"No closer!" she whispers. "These people have hearing keener than a dog's."

I climb out. Rosine starts to jump down from the cab.

"Stay here," I tell her. "Move away from the truck, over there behind those rocks. I'll be back before daylight."

I see her eyes pleading with me not to go.

"What's there to worry about?" I ask. "Didn't you say you feel safer in New Caledonia than you do in Paris? And let's not forget we're both wearing these safe-conduct badges." I wink at her reassuringly and trot off.

Less than half a click in I cool it. I have observed a sharp cut of tire tracks leading across the sand toward a wave-beaten cliff thrusting out into the surf.

The tracks have been made by new tires, the tires of Panhard armored cars, as far as I can determine in the darkness.

I sling the MAS over one shoulder and tape it to my left arm. Then I slip the High-Standard .22 free with its long dull-finished silencer, chamber a round, keep the safety off, and move forward, more carefully now, from pooled shadow to pooled shadow. As I take my next step a blackness detaches itself from a tree directly ahead and hurls itself at me. I see the loom of the descending club. I roll to one side, firing as I fall, taking the blackness in dead center with a tiny spurt from the muffled gun, no louder than a soft tap of a hand on a tablecloth. I leap back to my feet, look around for other blacknesses, but this one appears to be it for the immediate area. I bend over him. A mark like a Hindu woman's wedding spot oozes from his forehead directly above his eyes. Nevertheless I check him for pulse. Sometimes these head shots enter on an angle and the corpse recovers in time to blow you apart from the back. Not this baby. Gone downriver forever.

I lose track of time. I am propelled into that special sphere where I fly, not walk, where I become immortal for a while, where all my senses are godlike. I slither along now like the Black Mamba I used to be.

The tide is high, sweeping across the opening into the cave in the cliffside. What they did, obviously, was to drive the Panhards in here when the tide was out and the beach exposed.

I bring out the Starscope and study the rocks above me. If there's anybody up there he's not showing himself. I decide to wade into the cave.

I slosh through thigh-deep surf until I've arrived at one side of the cave. I reholster the .22, unlimber the submachine gun.

I walk in behind twenty-five rounds ready to go, but surprisingly not a war mask jumps out to challenge me. Nothing in here but a ledge of sand thirty feet wide ascending into a cave which opens into adjoining chambers angling endlessly back under the cliff, all laced with coral columns and limestone pillars as grotesque as the bones of dead chieftains propped up everywhere about me. They loiter in squatting positions against carved totems. I don't dare click on my flash in here. Instead, I kneel beside one skeleton still laden with his weapons of war and I get the scope out again, using what little light filters in.

I soon find what I'm searching for. Row after row of brand-new Panhard armored cars equipped with cannon and machine guns. At least thirty of them. The others must either be in another cave or already out being serviced for the punch-up.

I start to move closer to the depot of Panhards but freeze as I hear a metallic sound. Someone is moving behind me. I drop to the sand. I hear another swish of movement to my left, a foot shifting in sand. Another brushing to the right. Then I hear a sound I haven't heard since I left Nam—the absence of sound. Men all around me are either holding their breath or breathing as softly as they can.

Before I can decide what move I'll have to make, the cave blazes with light. Spots in a circle around me crash on, enveloping me in blinding beams.

"Please, John, don't move!"

I couldn't if I tried, after I hear that voice. Maurice!

I squint through the radiance, isolate him as a dark, pulsing shape against the curtain of whiteness, his submachine gun leveled at my stomach.

"Drop your gun, John! Let it fall!"

I do what he tells me.

"Now the Browning."

The sonofabitch!

I pull it from the back holster and put it down carefully on a flat rock. The mere thought of sand inside its glistening bore is more dreadful than being shot.

"*And* the .22!"

This is what comes of friendship! Your friends know your entire arsenal. I place the .22 next to the Browning.

My eyes are beginning to adjust to the piercing lights.

I imagine I'm seeing Kaméa behind Maurice.

"Kaméa, is that you?" I ask.

"Yes, John."

"You set me up, didn't you?"

"At your insistence."

"How did you know where to find me?"

"Simply by coming to what you were looking for. We tried to warn you," he says, and to his credit, I will have to concede, I do hear genuine regret in his tone. "I told you to get out of New Caledonia. From the first day. But you refused to listen."

"I too tried to tell you," Kaméa says.

"Hey," I ask, "what about this safe-conduct badge I'm wearing? Not worth a shit, huh?"

"It would have saved your life if certain tribespeople had seen you before we could get here."

"Well, thanks for that. Where's Rosine?"

"She's being taken to her father."

"Where?"

"In Kangara's main encampment."

"Maurice?"

"Yes, John?"

"I'm going to ask you something. For all those guys we knew in Nam who died ahead of us, tell me the truth, okay? Did Rosine know?"

"No, John," he says. "She fired a full clip at us before we could move in. She went screaming, her hands and feet tied, calling me things I hope never to be called again."

"What happens now?"

"They're going to take you away."

Past him I see a closing circle of Melanesian warriors.

But these tayos are not wearing flowered loincloths. They're outfitted in combat cammies and boots, armed with sub-machine guns and grenades. They look about as trim as I've seen troopers look anywhere, anytime.

Two of them come alongside me. Each takes me by an arm and urges me forcefully toward the mouth of the cave.

I go without resisting.

By the time my captors and I are rattling in a jeep through pine groves, I can hear roosters crowing from tribal encampments perceived only dimly through the smoke of dawn campfires.

The situation is not too stable, but I don't feel entirely surplused yet, for I know that Georges Gallante, being French, will insist on his moment with me before they feed my hands to hungry priests.

We enter what Kaméa has told me her people call a sunpoint. Here, in a beehive community opening out from a central clearing, construction gangs are already up and at work building additional conical huts to shelter Kangara's guests coming from everywhere on the island to honor his birthday.

At one end of a clearing larger than a Roman stadium I observe something which in any other village would be considered by Melanesians to be without precedent—two gigantic conical houses, larger than all others, but identical in size, built side by side, each with its own symbolic encircling fence signifying that each is a sanctuary of the high chief, in this case, *two* high chiefs—Kangara and who else but his white twin, born on the same night of typhoon —Georges Gallante?

In the center of the clearing a Y-shaped tree stump has been placed. Kaméa has told me that speakers addressing the tribe climb into the Y, brace their feet within the joint of the branches, then exhort the people from this lofty perch.

The jeep drives straight for headquarters. For a moment I debate with myself whether I should kill the driver, grab his gun, then jump from the jeep and shoot the two men in the back as the jeep piles up. No one has bothered to body-search me. I'm still carrying my Randall fighting knife inside my jacket. Apparently Maurice had failed to notice it under my outer garment. Either that or they don't consider a mere knife important enough to trouble anybody that much. Suppose I did kill three or four of them. Hundreds of others would shoot me down. Take the case of that sentry they posted outside the caves last night. Was he sacrificed simply to make me more determined to fall into their trap? Probably. I recall a story Kaméa had told me about the old days when a chieftain plucked the eye out of his nearest warrior and presented it as a tidbit to another visiting chieftain and the blinded warrior dropped gratefully to his knees in front of both chieftains to thank them for paying him such great honor. I marvel at it; what I could have done with a thousand such warriors north of the DMZ!

I decide what the hell, what's the point in killing this driver? He doesn't look more than twenty. He even smiled at me as we drove into the village. I'm not entirely sure what he was smiling about, but a smile's a smile, so I forget about his subclavian artery and the fact he came within five seconds of death. I let him drive me up to the twin conical huts.

One of the men behind me pokes the muzzle of his sub-machine gun into my back and tells me in French to get out. I get out. They conduct me to the gate of the hut on the right. Before they can knock or call out to anyone inside, the gate swings open.

Georges Gallante smiles out at me.

"I hope you're famished," he says. "I've prepared a marvelous breakfast for us."

# CHAPTER

## 25

The interior of Georges Gallante's conical house is more spacious than I had estimated from outside.

It has been Westernized for him to the extent that there is a cot with a crown of mosquito netting, a desk and chair, cushions around a large, ornately decorated ground mat, and to one side of the hut a dining table and chairs. The table is set for two. The Melanesian woman Tachéa, who had spirited him out of la Ferme de St. Paul, is already pouring coffee as Georges leads me to the table and gestures me into one of the two chairs.

"Oeufs en croustades à la béarnaise," he announces as the steaming pastry shells nestling poached eggs covered with mushrooms and béarnaise sauce are placed on the table.

"The condemned man ate a hearty breakfast," I say.

"I was up long before dawn," he says, "preparing a breakfast dessert. Here on the island we call it 'confiture de papayes.' Frankly, I'm somewhat disappointed in it. It should have been refrigerated at least another hour. But we have only the one cooling unit up here, with a rather obstinate generator."

"How is Rosine taking this?" I ask. I taste the eggs. "Superb," I say. "My compliments to the chef."

"Do you really like them?"

"Immensely."

"She's being quite emotional," he says. "Between her fears for you and her disillusionment with me, she's having a bad morning."

"I've had better myself," I confess, "although the breakfast alone is worth the trip."

He watches me with undisguised interest.

"Are you really unafraid? Or have you learned that well to conceal your true feelings?"

"I conceal nothing," I tell him, "except my anatomy when people start shooting at me. Am I afraid? Of what? Being killed? Tortured? Not afraid, no. Resistant? Yes! I mean, I won't slide down without protest."

"I'm hoping you won't have to 'slide down.' I much prefer that you stay."

He speaks to Tachéa in Melanesian. She refills my empty coffeecup.

"What do you know about the Battle of Hastings?" he asks.

"Not a great deal," I reply, "except that it took place in 1066, a date that for some reason or other they pounded into us at school. And I seem to remember that the Saxon king was struck in the eye by a Norman arrow and that the Normans succeeded in doing what neither the Romans nor the Vikings before them ever quite succeeded in doing, conquering Britain."

"I've studied the Battle of Hastings in great detail," Georges says. "Along with other decisive battles over the last thousand years or so. They all have, for the most part, one remarkable element in common—the actual fighting force is invariably much smaller than one would have thought. But then that was true in your fight in Indochina, wasn't it?"

"Somebody in the War College once told me we had eight men behind the lines for every man on patrol," I say.

"At Hastings," he says, "the English fielded four to five thousand foot soldiers armed with Danish axes and Saxon shields. That was their entire defensive force! William of Normandy landed a Franco-Norman army of cavalry, wearing light armor, and a force of archers and pikemen— all together no more than six or seven thousand men. In short, a contest among a mere twelve thousand men decided in a single afternoon and evening the fate of an entire society and changed forever the course of Anglo-Saxon history.

"Another thing I find noteworthy among these decisive battles of history is that they all had a focused turning point, one particular zone on which everything failed or succeeded. At Hastings the entire battlefront was only one thousand, three hundred and ten yards across. Can you conceive of the fact that history was made within a crucible only three-quarters of a mile wide?"

He sees that I've finished my eggs.

"May I serve you more?"

"No, thank you."

He gestures to Tachéa. She slips out of the hut.

"It came to me over a long period of study," he says, "that the secret of victory lay in finding a focal point, then directing one's maximum force, no matter how small that force might be, against an unprepared enemy otherwise occupied with problems of his own—political, social, economic . . ."

Tachéa returns with the candied papayas. The combination of this confection with the strong local coffee creates a delight on the palate. Georges watches to see if I'm enjoying the sensation.

"Wonderful," I comment.

You'd think the two of us were somewhere in France tasting wines, not sitting here outside of Hienghène with my longevity in question.

"What do you know about the French Navy?" he asks next.

"Virtually nothing," I respond.

"It has had a lamentable history in comparison to the glory of our land forces," he says. "During the Napoleonic Wars, while the French Army basked in popular acclaim, the French Navy remained bottled up in port. When they did venture out they were crushed by the British at Aboukir and Trafalgar. Why else do you imagine Na-

poleon had to sell Louisiana to the United States? He knew
he had no fleet capable of resisting the British and could
therefore never hold a colony that far away by force of
arms. Historically, except for brief flurries, this sorry state
has been the destiny of the French Navy. I suppose a
typical example of the official attitude toward it is best
exemplified by a remark of Louis XV. He joked that the
only navy left to France was the ships represented on the
canvases of the painter Joseph Vernet."

He observes that I have finished the meal.

He rises. I too rise, wondering when what comes next
will come. And in what form.

Georges settles on a cushion at one end of the floor mat,
waves me to another cushion. I sit on my haunches in the
fashion I learned from Doan Thi, as though I'm scaling
fish. Unlike most Caucasians, I can sit this way for hours.

"Now," he continues, "we come to a third point. French
colonialism."

"I know a lot more about that," I say, "than I do about
the Battle of Hastings."

"Few nations," he says, "have ever gone to war to fight
for the freedom of a lesser nation, and please, John, don't
tell me that was the motivation of your American government in Vietnam. You were not fighting for the Vietnamese. You were fighting against a hostile political system
assuming control over a part of the world where American
interests might be threatened by Soviet ambitions. Like-
wise, the French and the Dutch and the English and the
Spanish and the Portuguese and all the other powers of
earlier centuries carved up the world for profits, raw materials, markets, bases, and national prestige. Yet, as a
Frenchman, I have to add in all fairness to Paris, that the
taproot of French imperialism, at least in the Far East, was
national pride more than markets. Under Louis Philippe
our priests were regenerated with religious zeal and our
military charged up with supreme confidence in the superiority of French culture. The main driving force of
French colonial policy in Asia was to enhance national

prestige and to vindicate French cultural superiority to the point where it was inconceivable in Paris that any black or brown-skinned native wouldn't be ecstatic at the prospect of being elevated to the highest state any human being could possibly achieve—becoming a full-fledged French citizen. But in fact, the *actual* history of French conquest in Indochina and in the South Pacific, despite these lofty pretensions, was one of ruthless force and oppression. The modus operandi was boringly repetitive. Catholic missionaries paved the way. Then they were either executed or eaten by natives who wanted no part of their teachings. Subsequently, the Church protested to Paris. And Paris sent in its gunboats. At least, if we couldn't face the English in honest sea battle and win, we could certainly savage the savages. And so we did. Admiral Dupetit-Thouars, fresh from annexing the Marquesas, sailed to Tahiti and declared the island group a French protectorate, in spite of the protest of the Tahitian Queen, who openly declared her preference for a British presence. The admiral thereupon landed several hundred French troops, deposed the queen, and arrested Reverend George Pritchard, the British missionary who'd been serving as her adviser. New Caledonia too fell to French gunboats. So, now that I've covered the Battle of Hastings and the inglorious history of the French Navy and touched on the splendors of French colonial policy, you sit there wondering what all this means to you!"

"On the contrary," I reply. "I'm fascinated by what clearly appears to be a strong anti-French attitude from *you!*"

"Don't deceive yourself. I am first, last, and always a Frenchman. If I were to permit my head to be severed from my body, I would still remain French, though dead. It is impossible for me to be *anti*-French. But it is *not* possible for me to continue to support a policy which is exterminating one more culture in a world where the extermination of cultures means nothing to ruling governments unless the preservation of some alien culture happens to coincide with national policy, which it seldom if ever does. Now, we come to the fourth matter. In France we have a word you may not know. 'Alternance.' Have you heard it?"

"Not in the sense I suspect you're about to use it," I reply.

"It is a word which means that every society, every government, every family, should be subject from time to time to change, to *radical* change. We French have had many uprisings and revolutions because we sense the need within the human spirit for such shakeups. This is the moral basis I use as the guideline for what I have planned. This, and an even more pressing need—to stop the world from becoming one massive technological digital readout, to stop, if you will, the implacable march of science, and at least in one part of the earth, here on New Caledonia, to create a sanctuary, even as sanctuaries have been created to save endangered species in Africa. The Melanesian is no less endangered than the whooping crane or the white rhinoceros. What did this Melanesian man have before we brought him all our benefits? You might well ask me this. By *our* standards he had very little. By *his* standards he had everything. And if you use time as a yardstick, he was doing far better than we're doing. This Melanesian culture existed for twenty thousand years until we came here. In a little more than a hundred years we have reduced it to a sideshow for tourists."

"That's more or less what Sabourin said to me."

"I'm sure. I taught him."

"He's part of this too, isn't he?" I ask. "Like Maurice and Kaméa. How many other Frenchmen?"

"We have strong support in Nouméa where it counts. Would you care for more coffee?"

"No, thank you."

"So—I was saying that the culture here had lasted for twenty thousand years until we came. Tell me, monsieur, do you honestly believe that American society or French society as we know it today will survive for twenty thousand years?"

"There," I agree, "I'm in absolute sync with you. No *way*. I'd settle right now for *twenty* more years. Just to get to the year two thousand will be a monumental achievement!"

"So you agree that the inevitability of disaster is not in question?"

"Only the timetable," I say.

"And yet, look at the irony here," he says. "We are imposing upon primitive man the very values which you and I have lost faith in. Why, then, do you risk your life defending a system of values that is doomed, and oppose a system which, left alone again, can't possibly do worse than we're doing?"

His earnest eyes implore me to answer this. I can't. To try to deal with it I would have to rip myself apart and go back to a time I was twenty-four months old. Then I would have to find different parents, different teachers, a different society. Too late, too late.

"Do you know what Captain James Cook wrote in his log on the last of his trips to the South Pacific?" he asks. " 'It would have been far better for these poor people never to have known our superiority in the arts that make life comfortable. It may be too late to go back to their old, less perfect contrivances. For by the time they learn our way, they will have lost the knowledge of their own ways.' I, Georges Gallante, cannot accept the fact it is too late! And for this reason—and as an atonement for all the ill France has done—I plan to seize control of New Caledonia on July 14, Bastille Day. I intend to free the Melanesians from our society and restore to them their lawful land and their God-given right to their own ancient way of life!"

I say nothing for at least a full minute while he evaluates my reaction. "I went off course one hundred and eighty degrees," I finally say. "When I learned about the guns and the armored cars and the Melanesians who'd been given secret military training, I put it all down to a right-wing coup led by your brother Marcel. When all along it was you. Did you have Sabourin's previous boss killed?"

"It was necessary to confuse the authorities," he says painfully. "A sacrifice had to be exacted from the left."

"Why did you try to have me killed after you told Marcel you approved of his hiring me?"

"It was critically important to create the impression that terrorism was rocking the country. Killing you in broad daylight would have resulted in worldwide media coverage. After all, John, you are an American. Yet I must tell you that secretly I kept hoping your abilities would bring you through. If they did, as they have, I resolved to make sure you were delivered to me here—alive—so I could propose that you join me."

"I was one helluva screen test!" I say. "That attack against police headquarters. That was planned deliberately to fail, wasn't it? To make us believe the terrorists were finished?"

"Most perceptive of you. Once I *knew* the Rochemont was only hours away and the Legion paratroopers on the way, I needed to defuse the tension, encourage a holiday spirit."

"Why?"

"So *you* can lead the attack against the Rochemont. Then, after we have taken Nouméa, you can command our armed forces and supervise the training of the defensive army we'll need to hold this island against the inevitable French counterattack."

"Attack a missile cruiser?" I shake my head. "Why did you encourage Marcel to beef up the visiting naval power? That was really suicidal!"

"Not at all," he says excitedly. "It is the cornerstone of our strategy. While the city of Nouméa is celebrating Bastille Day and the night is brilliant with fireworks, you and a team of our best young warriors will slip aboard the Rochemont, overpower the crew, and take control of the vessel. Only one-third of the ship's company will be aboard, the others on shore leave. And no one aboard except the duty watch—three men and one officer—will be armed. You will secure the *Rochemont*, then signal us with a prearranged fireworks display of our own. At that point the rest of our units will seize the barracks, the hospital, the banks, the government buildings, and all communications facilities."

I shake my head in awe. "It's almost perfect! Where were you when Napoleon was at Waterloo?"

There is no sense of triumph about him. If anything, he appears almost depressed.

"I have much on my conscience to live with," he says. "Having old friends murdered at the Mont-Dore project is something I will never be able to forgive myself. But there was no other way to alarm Marcel enough to get him to persuade Paris to send in the *Rochemont*."

"Why did you give yourself the added problem of the Foreign Legion parachute regiment?" I ask.

"I will need them later in Nouméa to help keep order," he replies.

"You don't believe *they'll* cooperate with you, do you?"

"They will have no choice. You see, I don't intend that we continue to occupy Nouméa. I will turn all the rest of New Caledonia back to the Melanesians. But Nouméa must necessarily remain French—and white. It will become to this island as Hong Kong is to China, a window on the outside world. Unfortunately, one must have such a window in order to obtain hard-currency credits. But no Frenchman will be permitted to go beyond the city limits. And no Melanesian will be permitted to enter Nouméa. If the Germans can build a wall through Berlin, we can build a wall around Nouméa. But there's an even more important reason. The missile systems aboard the *Rochemont* will be removed at once from the cruiser and moved inland. They will be trained on Nouméa. If the French try to take back this island, I shall order the missiles fired against Nouméa. I doubt that Paris will dare to sacrifice fifty thousand French men, women, and children in the name of their nickel mines."

"You won't last more than two months," I tell him, "if

that long! I could land guerrillas almost anywhere on your coastline, find out where your missiles are, knock them out, then radio the fleet standing offshore to attack you. However inglorious its history, at least it's a fleet. You have no ships. You have no airpower. They could also seize any one of the offshore islands and set up bomber strips in less than ten days and pound you into surrender. Georges—I'm going to call you that, if you don't mind—you're a man I could, under different circumstances, join with all my heart. Almost everything you've said touches me where I live. Aside from the killings you've caused, I can forgive everything you've done and understand what you're trying to accomplish. But you couldn't hold this island, even against *me* and one good division. And I'm only a ground-pounder. They've got people out there in the real world, Doomsday specialists and crisis managers who deal in terms like 'megaforce' and who sit in electronic offices in Washington and in a lot of other centers in Europe and Asia whose sole fulltime business it is to know how to crush concepts like yours and dreamers like you. They'd never believe you'd fire your missiles at fellow Frenchmen. They'd string you along while they put a package together to call your bluff."

"Then we'd perish," he says. "And with us all hope for the oppressed of the world would perish too."

"May I see Rosine now?" I ask.

"Certainly. Discuss this with her. She may listen to you. Tell her I have not lost my senses, but have finally gained them. We've all been accomplices of genocide. Tell her my action is a revulsion against having been an accomplice. A revulsion—and a redemption. I must atone while I still have time—and the will."

"I'll try," I say.

We both rise.

"How long do I have to make up my mind?" I ask.

"Not later than breakfast tomorrow. I wish I could be more generous, but the timetable is unforgiving."

"I'll need to check out certain things. Men, equipment. Without knowing your strength, I can't commit myself."

"For both our sakes, I truly hope you are not simply playing for time. Please, monsieur, reassure me on that point."

"My problem here is not a moral decision," I say. "It's purely a tactical decision. Yes, I think you *could* take over the cruiser, the way you've planned it. And I think you could probably knock out your targeted objectives in Nouméa. The element of surprise alone might neutralize the effectiveness of the parachute regiment. But from the first second the news hits the world press and TV, you go on borrowed time, even though you have got some things working for you. Pure distance, for one. What limited sea-power France has would be spread pretty thin, trying to stay on site both in the Atlantic and in the Med to protect France herself. But, believe me, they'd strip themselves down to a few home-patrol torpedo boats if they had to and send everything else they've got halfway around the world to concentrate on your case. Exactly as the British did in the Falklands. That'll take at least four weeks. Then *look out!*"

"Time for us to appeal to world opinion."

"World opinion?" I ask. "Who do you think *controls* it? The Melanesians? Or those fellows who are in the business of controlling things? If anytime between now and tomorrow morning I can't convince myself you can make this work, if I keep on feeling that all the killing won't achieve the ideals you intend to fight for, I'll let you know."

"Merci, John Locke," he says. "I can't ask for more."

He calls Tachéa. She takes me to Rosine.

Rosine is being comforted by a fat, elderly Melanesian woman.

Not until Rosine has run to me and climbed into my pockets does she finally introduce me.

"Koué, this is my lover."

I try out my limited new Melanesian vocabulary. Koué flashes her gold teeth, then leaves us alone.

I tell Rosine everything that's been said between me and her father. She's desolated. I try to point out to her those parts of his concept that contain inherent nobility. I even defend the underlying use of force to achieve a political and cultural end. Without rebellion, my American forebears would still be English. Without rebellion and violence, there would be no state of Israel. Can it be that if it's you doing the killing, you call yourself a patriot? If it's the other fella, that's a terrorist. She keeps shaking her head and insisting she has no interest in the outside world, only in herself and the immediate world around her, and this choice of focus is not a matter of blindness nor of selfishness nor of immaturity but pure and simple self-defense. She weeps for herself that she was cursed at birth, born of a mother who opened her veins in a tub of running water, sparked into life by a father so hopelessly mad he murders old friends and betrays France. What hope is there for her? What possible future? How can she bear my child if we ever decide we want a child? What kind of frightful monster would we be loosing upon the world?

As her hysteria mounts, it serves to clear my own reasoning powers, to keep me off the reckless siren's path that so many times beckons to me. I know that I must do whatever I can to stop Georges Gallante, even though much of what he believes in I too believe in, and even though the things about the world and its leaders he detests I too detest.

"I'm going to try something, Rosine. The chances of pulling it off are minimal. But there's nothing else I can try. If you start to hear a lot of shouting and fighting out in the clearing, I want you to leave this hut—get out of here fast, but try not to let your father see you. There's a spot over there . . ." I take her to the opening in the hut and point to a place a few yards beyond the fence surrounding Kangara's conical hut. "I want you to station yourself there —looking as inconspicuous as you can—and wait til I make my move."

"When?"

"I don't know yet. I have to pick the right time. Probably after dark. Just watch and listen. All you have to do when you start to see things happening out there is to slip out, get yourself over to that spot. Can you do that?"

"See *what* things happening?"

"Probably something messy—and noisy. I'll be at the center of it. That's all I know at this point. From where you'll be it's only a hundred yards to where I saw three armored cars. If we can get to one of them, I might be able to shoot our way out. But first I have to start enough of a ruckus to cover our getting over there."

I hold her until I sense she's going to be up to it. Then I go out to where two young men with sub-machine guns wait to march me back to Georges Gallante.

# CHAPTER

# 26

As Georges, walking briskly, leads me out of the encampment toward a nearby hill, six armed Melanesians spread out behind us, he becomes less the visionary, more the realist.

France, he informs me, possesses a meager carrier force, only two attack carriers and one helicopter transport. Although the attack carriers can, given sufficient time, serve as advance airbases anywhere in the world for their new Super Étendard fighter-bombers, which have tactical nuclear capability, these aircraft, in his opinion, would be of no use whatsoever in a people's war.

The *Rochemont* itself, he says, rattling on like the engineer who might have designed her weapons systems, is armed with both ship-to-shore missiles and antiship weapons, all capable of fast combat reaction and the ability to accept multiple types of rockets. She also carries an arsenal of Exocet missiles, each capable of sinking an aircraft carrier.

Georges has devised concentric fire centers circling out from Hienghène, to be the new capital of the country. Each center will be capable of covering twenty thousand square kilometers once his men have disassembled the systems from the *Rochemont* and brought them ashore, installed them in the hardened cites of these defense points.

He leads me straight to one of these sites, an abandoned mineshaft being reinforced with steel and cement, half-naked Melanesians working at the task with more enthusiasm than their previous French employers would have thought possible.

To one side of this site, a massive wall of cement fifty yards in length rises a sheer thirty feet out of the forest. A platoon of soldiers are scampering up nets secured to the top of the wall.

"When they began this training," Georges says proudly, "not a man could climb that net in less than fifty-five seconds. Now they're doing it in twenty-five! And by Thursday night, when you lead them up the side of the *Rochemont*, I expect them to climb from their dugouts onto the deck within fifteen seconds."

"You see, Georges," I say patiently, "right there is an example of how these things break down."

He frowns at me.

"This is the heart of our strategy," he says. "It must *not* break down! What do you mean?"

"Those men you've selected. Are they only *soldiers*?"

"I do not understand your question—*only* soldiers?"

"Have any of them ever handled dugouts? Do they know what it's like to start climbing from a shaky boat, then to try to make it up the freeboard of a cruiser in fifteen seconds?"

"I begin to understand," he says. "But this is precisely why I can use you."

"Or there's *another* way to look at it," I continue. "Maybe the trick here is not to set a world's record scrambling on board. Maybe the trick here is to find the smallest men, those who are less visible than some of the ones I see climbing the net over there. Or maybe you should pick them for still another reason. Some men have better natural noise discipline than others. You wouldn't want somebody allergic to ship's paint who suddenly sneezes."

"I simply called for our best men," he says. "The ones you see *are* the best."

"At what?" I ask.

"At fighting."

"There's fighting and there's fighting. I don't like the looks of at least half of them."

"Don't let *them* hear you say that!" He has lowered his voice and now glances behind us to be sure the six who are guarding me haven't understood my English. He looks at me more carefully. "Is this a trick?"

"Trick? What trick? I said I had to look for myself. Okay, I'm looking. I'd rather cut that boarding party down to six of the absolutely right men than go crashing and thumping and sneezing and snorting on board with fifty assholes like some of those!"

Georges is no longer amused. He motions me to follow him. Once more we troop off, the six gunners behind me virtually in lockstep.

"Who trained those men?" I ask.

"A French colonel."

"That was another mistake!"

"Why?"

"Once an officer makes it past the rank of major, he turns cautious. Not the best choice to train fighting soldiers. I think you've got yourself some real problems here, Georges."

He is becoming visibly annoyed with me.

"In what sense?"

"Well, most natives, whether they're Melanesian or the indigs I slung with in Nam, are just plain natural-born fighters and trackers. Maybe *because* they're unspoiled and natural. They're like animals. They've still got all their instincts. They can rush through heavy bush without disturbing it. Their heads pivot like space saucers, picking up sound waves, their nostrils wide as a dog's, following the scent. All you really have to do is teach them how to shoot, then point at the guys you wanted greased, and you've got it. I get the feeling, looking at these lobos of yours, that some book-colonel started laying on the spit-and-polish bullshit and in the process he may have taken away your troops' natural talent. That's just a first reaction, Georges, but you said you wanted my honest opinion as we went along."

I hear gunfire reverberating from nearby. Georges's lips have tightened. He says nothing more until he's led me closer to the firing. Two dozen Melanesians are in prone positions shooting at fixed targets in the bank of a natural cul-de-sac. I watch them for a while, then shake my head disapprovingly.

"Wasting too much ammo," I comment. "Who was *their* instructor?"

"We left all the instructors back in Africa," he says.

"You should have brought them along till these men finished their courses. They wouldn't last ten seconds in a firefight with anybody who's ever been in combat."

He begins to change before my eyes, the way a cobra changes when it puffs out its mantle and gives you that beady stare.

"Your answer is no," he states flatly.

"You've got a beautiful plan and something worth fighting for. But you're stuck with some piss-poor troops, from what I've seen so far. They're going to blow it for you."

"Come with me!" he demands.

He sets a fast pace back to the central encampment.

When we get there, more people—men, women, and children—are arriving. They pour in along a trail, some of them singing, most of them laughing, all looking for relatives and friends.

But Georges's mind is not on these people. He leads me past Kangara's compound to an area a hundred yards beyond, to where I'd already made my mental notes about these Panhard armored cars and their crews parked and ready to go.

"Well?" Georges demands.

These drivers and gun crews look good. Damned good. I tell Georges so.

"Different instructor, I'll bet."

He nods, waiting to see if this will change anything.

"Do you need more time?" he asks.

"Not really," I say. "I've made up my mind. I can't go with you."

"I regret that," he says.

"That makes two of us," I say.

In French he tells the senior officer of the guard to place me in a secure place until further advice.

They lead me off. Behind me I can almost imagine I'm

hearing another notch being cut into Georges's lacerated conscience. He'll sigh, of course, when he has me killed, but then he'll consider tomorrow's cuisine and manage to carry on.

They shove me into a small hut and close the door, posting a guard directly outside.

No floor mat or cushions in here. Only hard-packed earth. The Memosail tells me it's just past the meridian. I have little appetite. I need an empty stomach for what I have to do. And I need sleep. I settle onto my back on the warming earth and let myself sink into it.

I'm awakened by the snorting of conch shells. For a split-second I wonder where I am, wondering if while I slept they'd pitched me into a deep well, for the darkness is enveloping, then I realize it's already night.

I hear the conch shells being augmented by other sounds I can't identify. They might even be coming from a flurry of pigeons, but with the flurry I hear a deep, harmonious thump-thump-thump and a constant squeaking, then over all these a muffled whistling as though a hundred men are whispering a song.

I slip my knife free, cut a vertical opening in the straw side of the hut.

The central clearing has become banked with Melanesians, the women in mission dresses, the men in loincloths, some of them naked except for their penis sheaths. The women form a massive encirclement around the dancing men. Now I am able to determine what's making the sounds I hear. The thumping comes from what Kaméa has told me are called djo, long sections of bamboo of varying lengths being pounded vertically on the ground. I observe the djepa, which create the beating sound, and the touu, the conch shells with their mournful echos of the sea, and around the legs of the dancers coconut shoots squeaking with every stomp of the dancers' feet. The pigeon sound too comes from the dancers, their lips puffing in and out as they move with more and more intensity.

Then I see the kings of Big Rock-Candy Mountain. The

dancers turn to honor Kangara and Georges as together each steps from his towering cone-shaped hut and proceeds regally through the gateways in their fences. They are greeted by three hundred naked tayos waving spears and clubs and shouting their loyalty.

Together Kangara and Georges share the carrying of the clan's ceremonial axe. As they advance toward the center of the clearing and the Y of the tree stump, the crowds around them whistle and cry out, "Hoo! Hoo! Hoo!"

The pilou ceremony is building to its climax, binding the members of the clan, calling upon past roots, forging new ones.

Time, Locke!

I remove my clothes and my shoes. Naked and barefoot, I squat and with my knife dig up the earthen floor. I spit into a handful of dirt, smear it over my cheeks, across my bare chest in an ancient pattern Kaméa had described, then in a circle over my abdomen, with streaks of lightning down the front of my legs. I fashion a crude bagayou with straw I cut from the inside of the hut, blending it with cloth from my shorts to make a penis sheath.

I stand now in darkness, composing myself, letting my thoughts order themselves. When I am ready and can no longer hear the pandemonium outside except as a rhythm to move to, I shout to the guard.

He swings open the door, but stands back, gun pointed at me.

Yet as I advance upon him, his eyes widen at the strangeness of my appearance, and he falls back.

In French I tell him I speak out of the spirit of the great aliki Baouarat, the founder of his clan, and that under the ancient laws I am invoking the right of mortal combat to avenge a fallen clansman. I demand to be taken to Kangara.

The sentry leads me past the dancers.

Now I have achieved such control of my concentration that I can no longer hear the tayos shouting or the dancers cooing. The silence presses upon my eardrums.

I blot out all peripheral vision, cutting away from my sight whatever reactions might be out there in the eyes of the others.

Only four eyes make up the universe I enter—the eyes of Kangara and the eyes of Georges Gallante. Kangara's massive face is to me only the substance that supports his immense eyes. I see them as sockets awash with surprise, like tidal pools filled with darting movement.

Keeping my eyes focused on theirs, I climb into the Y of the tree stump before which the two high chiefs have halted.

"The tribes," I shout in French, "will accept a madman as an honored guest. The tribes will destroy a dhianoua. I am not a madman. I am not an evil spirit. I ask not to be accepted as an honored guest. I ask not to be slain as a sorcerer. I am, like the tayos here, a warrior. I have abstained these past hours from alcohol, from food, from women to prepare myself to speak the sacred words. Now let my words awaken the sleepers and the timid ones. Let them fly like spears in the morning air. Like stones from slings."

My concentration on Kangara and Georges is replaced by something infinitely more powerful. I feel a spirit welling toward me from the hundreds of people around me. I dare now to let true sound and natural sight return to my consciousness and so I hear the unbroken night, the waiting ears of the people.

"The firstborn of this clan," I call out to the assembly everywhere about me, "the link with the invisible world, the one who walks ahead, the great aliki who was born from the wapki pine, gave to each warrior the right to avenge the death of a brother, the right to challenge those responsible. My clansman was killed as he drove me across the city by men who came with guns. Others were the killers, but it is *these* chiefs who ordered it done."

I point my knife at Kangara and at Georges.

"By the ancient law of the tribe, they must both face me in hand-to-hand combat—or, since they are no longer as young as I, they may appoint champions in their places. I will fight the champions. But I will be fighting not only for my dead clansman. I will be fighting to save the lives of all of you. These chiefs are not satisfied with those they have already killed. They now plan to risk a war with an enemy who has more power than they do, an enemy who will bring death to all of you unless you stop your sons and fathers from marching against the French. The coward has neither food nor respect, so I do not speak these words out of fear, for I will fight their champions and I will pray to the gods that I may see the spears as they fly toward me. I tell you not to listen to their counsel of war. Let them lead you in peace, not in death. If they will agree to that, I will withdraw my challenge and accept the sorrow of losing my clansman."

I hear the crowd divided, arguing.

A squad of soldiers gathers around Georges.

He whispers to them.

Their guns lift toward me. I stand higher than anyone else in the clearing, a clear, elevated target.

Kangara roars at them. They lower their weapons.

In Patyi I'm unable to follow, he orders a young man forward. And then a second.

Both are in superb condition, their muscles delineated and rippling, neither more than twenty-five.

Half-naked like me, they are handed spears and clubs.

Kangara orders that I be given spear and club.

I wave off the weapons.

I'll stay with my fighting knife.

I leap down from the tree as the dancers fall back, making more room for us.

Past the guttering torches that light the clearing, I think I see Rosine doing what I had hoped she would, easing away from her hut toward the place I told her to go.

I face my opponents. Like me, they are as calm as the core of a hurricane. No distractions here. These two are pure. So be it.

I rush the man nearest me, correctly anticipating he will

thrust with the spear in his left hand. I pass outside his thrust and he turns to strike me with his club, but he's not my true target. As I pass him I roll onto my shoulders and come up in a crouch just in front of the second warrior. In the fragment of time it takes him to realize he, not the other warrior, is the object of my primary attack, I have whipped up the razor-sharp Randall in a backhand slash that opens his jugular so wide my hand is splashed with his blood.

I hear a terrible moan from the crowd.

Club upraised, the first warrior charges me from behind.

I wheel and throw the Randall straight into his chest from less than ten feet. Even though it splits his heart and lungs, he keeps coming at me, the great club smashing downward, but falling short of me by less than a foot. He drops to his knees, tugs the knife out, prepares to throw it at me with his dying effort. I kick it out of his hand. He falls next to the other tayo and I pick up my knife and face Kangara and Georges. Kangara seems to be rocking to some rhythm of his own, like a beached whale. I notice for the first time the pale bones thrust into the steely crown of his hair reddened by lime juice.

"Kill him!" Georges says softly to his soldiers.

But Kangara himself moves in front of me, his imperious eyes withering the gunmen.

"He spoke the words of the great aliki. He fought alone against two, one of them my son. He is free to go!"

"He knows too much!" Georges cries out.

This aspect troubles Kangara, for all his code of honor.

Rosine appears from nowhere, pushing past her father and running to me, putting her arms out to either side of me.

"Kill us both!"

I see Georges's torment, his rage at being confronted with so impossible a dilemma. Kangara has lost a son. Can he not contribute a daughter? But the loving years destroy his resolve, his softening memory of this girl growing from child to woman. He is thinking no longer of New Caledonia, but of Paris and Normandy, of Rosine on his lap calling him Papa, of horses he's bought her, of Ferraris and her unfaithful young husband and her mother with slashed wrists. I see his hand wave the machine guns away. I see him die in front of me, as certainly as if I'd taken the Randall and passed it across his throat.

Here it comes again, as torturing as ever, my sudden pity for an enemy who might have been my brother. How much simpler to hate than to love! Georges's agony becomes mine. I watch the abdication of his spirit, the death of his dream, and I know that I've killed something very precious, that all the remaining days of my life I will ask myself what might have happened—yes, what really might have happened had I gone with him to Nouméa on Bastille Night and fought to give a people back what had been pillaged from them a century ago, by others like me who came in boats, bearing guns.

Without a word, Georges walks back into the hut where only this morning he had prepared for me oeufs en croustades and confiture de papayes.

The gunshot is singularly soft.

I know without running in with the others that Georges Gallante has muffled the shot with his mouth.

I reach for Rosine.

She neither cries nor moves in my arms.

# EPILOGUE

**I** could have waited until after Bastille Day, I suppose, before I left New Caledonia.

Bazin begged me to stay.

Marcel Gallante insisted.

They both guaranteed that the fireworks this year would be the most spectacular since the end of World War II.

But when I drove Rosine to Tontouta International Airport, loaded her red Ferrari onto a cargo plane flown in for that purpose, then saw her off for Paris, I knew that for me Nouméa had lost its charm.

I would never again go up to the house on Ouen Toro.

I would never see Monstro again.

Rosine and I promised each other we'd meet this fall in Deauville. Possibly we shall.

I reminded Marcel Gallante about the matter of the boat in memory of André. He showed me a cable just received from a cousin of the dead driver, thanking all of us on behalf of the village for so unanticipated and so welcome a gift. Marcel had tended to it the day André was shot. He simply hadn't told me until now.

I accompanied Marcel to the Banque de l'Indochine on Rue de la République, and with his help had the fee he paid me for my services in New Caledonia transferred to Singapore for my account at the Oversea-Chinese Banking Corporation.

I visited Maurice in the cell where he was held with others Bazin rounded up after the Legion brought in all the Panhard armored cars and most of the sub-machine guns. Kaméa was in another section with the women, but I did see Sabourin with other young Frenchmen—as many as thirty, all part of the conspiracy, apparently.

Maurice tried to explain that he had only wanted to become the historian of the event. I understood completely, because I came close to being its field commander. At least, close to being tempted. He said he would never forgive himself for betraying me, but he had had enough belief in my intelligence and my idealism to have convinced himself that once he got me safely into Kangara's encampment, I would willingly become a part of the movement. He wasn't far from wrong.

I walked through the Place des Cocotiers. I imagined how it must look in the New Caledonia summer, crimsoned with flamboyants. I discovered that the Melanesians were back. The grass cutters were cutting, the children were scampering, the mothers were gossiping, and the old men slumped on their benches. They had left for a while, but nothing had changed. And now they were back, accepting their destiny.

I took a taxi out to la Ferme de St. Paul and walked through the pasture where Rosine and I had first made love. Already the grass had sprung back up in the places we had pressed upon. I asked the driver to stop a moment at the Gallante church. He asked me if I knew the story about the family curse and the bent cross, and I told him, yes, I'd heard that story, but I didn't really believe it was true.

I did the shopping I needed to do to restock *Steel Tiger* for our crossing into the Coral Sea. I was going out there next on that sentimental journey to honor my grandfather and his bones of coral.

After that, I'd see. I'd see.

Kim brought Otis Walden aboard just before I left.

He raised his offer to one hundred thousand dollars.

I told him if he'd give up his fixation about the Sulu Sea and go on over to the Gulf of Thailand, I'd help him cuckold every Thai pirate in those desperate waters, and for free. He said he'd think about it and get in touch. I gave him my sel-call and radio numbers. We wished each other luck and Kim asked if I'd mind if she kissed me. Nothing personal, but it had been so long since she'd kissed an American she was getting homesick.

And so we kissed and left the matter of the Sulu Sea versus the Gulf of Thailand unresolved.

Bazin came last, of course. I think he waited deliberately until I had done all my business and put everything else behind me.

He brought me my dive bag, my High-Standard .22 and my Browning, which Maurice had returned to him, my passport and exit papers, and six pains chocolats, which he told me he'd just now bought from this superb little bakeshop only three blocks down the street from his house.

He told me he would miss me.

I said, Me too.

He was troubled by one thing only, something I'd told him when Rosine and I had come back from Hienghène. He'd lost sleep over the fact that I had actually been tempted to throw in with someone as patently insane as Georges Gallante, that I had seriously considered joining the insurrectionists. He had thought about this for hours, and it defied all reason, all his former conclusions about me. Did I truly mean what I'd said?

I wasn't sure anymore. Could I have done it? I don't know. I really don't. I do know that I was deeply moved by the beliefs and convictions of Georges Gallante and that I shared most of them.

"How *could* you?" Bazin demanded, standing there on the finger pier with me at the Club Nautique, *Steel Tiger* straining at the spring line, which still kept her prisoner in Nouméa. "Georges Gallante was the most hopelessly insane man in the history of New Caledonia!"

"On the contrary," I had to say. "Of all the men I've ever known, he was the sanest."

I slipped my spring line and took *Steel Tiger* to sea.

Bazin remained on the dock looking after me until I was well past the dip of Îlot Brun and could no longer see him.

## About the Author

Stirling Silliphant was born in Detroit on January 16, 1918. Working as a reporter and rewrite man for local southern California newspapers during high school, Silliphant then graduated from the University of Southern California. Afterward, he began his first motion-picture work for the Walt Disney Studio. Over the years he has been responsible for many successful television series and screenplays, among them *Route 66*, *Alfred Hitchcock Presents*, and more recently, *Salem's Lot* and *Fly Away Home*. Screenplays include the Oscar Award winner *In the Heat of the Night*, *Charly*, and *The Poseidon Adventure*.

STEEL TIGER marks his fourth novel. Silliphant lives with his family in Mill Valley, California.

# The
# Best Modern Fiction
## from
# BALLANTINE